STEPHEN COULD NOT RESIST

Megan looked so sweet and innocent, he dipped his head and gave her a long, tender kiss. The melding of their mouths became hot and deep and exciting.

He thought he heard the sound of the door opening. The wind must have caught it. Well, it could bloody well wait! Then a strange male voice boomed, "V...... Meg?"

Stephen instantly r..... up at the intruder. ...... shadows behind th...... Stephen's gaze did not linger on him, though. The first man captured his full attention.

He was the one with the flintlock musket pointed at Stephen's heart.

Praise for Marlene Suson's
MIDNIGHT BRIDE

Other **AVON ROMANCES**

Coming Soon

And Don't Miss These
ROMANTIC TREASURES
from Avon Books

MIDNIGHT LORD

MARLENE SUSON

AVON BOOKS ◆ NEW YORK

**To Charlotte Lobb and Mindy Neff,
the midwives of the Midnight Lord**

MIDNIGHT LORD is an original publication of Avon Books. This work has never before appeared in book form. This work is a novel. Any similarity to actual persons or events is purely coincidental.

AVON BOOKS
A division of
The Hearst Corporation
1350 Avenue of the Americas
New York, New York 10019

Copyright © 1995 by Joan Sweeney
Inside back cover author photograph by Debbi De Mont
Published by arrangement with the author
Library of Congress Catalog Card Number: 95-94308
ISBN: 0-380-77852-1

First Avon Books Printing: November 1995

AVON TRADEMARK REG. U.S. PAT. OFF. AND IN OTHER COUNTRIES, MARCA REGISTRADA, HECHO EN U.S.A.

Printed in the U.S.A.

RA   10 9 8 7 6 5 4 3 2 1

Chapter 1

Virginia, 1741

Run. Damn you, run! he ordered his blistered, recalcitrant feet, which felt as though they had been plunged into boiling pitch. He had to keep going.

He had to escape his pursuers. He would not be taken alive.

He would not be sent back to that living hell. No man should suffer what he had, torn from everything he held dear and treated as though he were something less than human, some brute breast born only to toil for a cruel master.

He did not deserve such a fate. No man did, especially one who was guilty of no wrong.

And as God was his witness, his conscience was clear.

He plunged on, picking his way through the dark forest. The night was bright, but not here among the dense trees and brush in this godforsaken American wilderness. The canopy of foliage overhead—thick as a newly thatched English roof—blocked the moonlight.

In the darkness, he had lost the narrow path he had been following through the woods, and he could not find it again. Pushing dizzily ahead,

1

he made his own route through the undergrowth, stumbling over protruding roots and debris. He wore only ragged breeches torn off above his knees and a homespun shirt with the sleeves missing. The thorny brush tore at his bare legs, arms, and face.

His head whirled like a dervish. He was so hot with fever that he felt it was consuming him. His every muscle and joint ached agonizingly. His back tormented him as though it was one raw wound.

Perhaps it was.

He vowed woozily to himself that not only would he escape his pursuers, but some day he would find a way to return to England. He would ferret out who had done this to him, and he would make the bastard pay.

No matter who he was.

The sweet promise of vengeance kept him moving, but he soon reached the limits of his endurance. He stumbled and nearly fell before he managed to catch and steady himself on the thin trunk of a sapling.

How tempting it was to let himself sink to the earth. His fevered brain urged him to do so. He was too weak and sick to go on. Why not let his tortured body lie down and die and end his suffering?

Raucous sound like the bark of muskets suddenly pounded at his head. Or was it the bark of dogs? The noise came from behind him.

Close behind him.

He thought he had lost those vicious, howling, man-chewing hounds out of hell two days ago, but apparently he had been wrong. They must still be on his trail.

That possibility gave his sick, exhausted body a

final spurt of energy. Those snarling beasts were not going to rip his flesh from his bones.

Something was wrong. That was Meg Drake's first thought as she awoke in the darkness. Apprehension swept away the sluggish haze of sleepiness from her mind as a driving rain washes the air.

She was not timid or easily frightened. Were she either, she would not be living in this frontier cabin surrounded by wilderness with only her fifteen-year-old brother for company and her own wits for protection.

Meg listened intently to the sounds of the night, analyzing what had triggered her subconscious alarm. It came to her quickly. The neighing of the horse, the hoot of the barn owl, and the howl of the wolves had taken on an unusual urgency.

Someone or something alien was out there.

"Meg?" The voice of her young brother, Josh, drifted to her from his narrow bed. It was no more than a frightened whisper. "I—I fear we have a caller."

"Yes," his sister agreed. She knew she had not been asleep very long, and she guessed it was about midnight. No visitor who meant them well would be skulking outside their cabin at this hour.

Choking down her fear, Meg got out of bed, her voluminous white night shift billowing around her, and grabbed one of the muskets that she kept loaded and ready.

She went to the window by the door and moved a corner of the greased paper covering it so she could peer out.

Brilliant moonlight illuminated the clearing in front of the cabin. She searched it and the trees beyond but could detect no sign of life.

The eerie howls of the wolves were very close now. They had never come so near to the clearing before. The hair on the back of Meg's neck rose.

Then a movement near a large oak tree caught her eye. She clutched the musket and went to the door.

He could go no farther. His tortured, abused body no longer obeyed his brain. If only he could fall down and die and get it over with.

But his pursuers would find him, and they would keep him alive.

Not out of kindness, though. No one had been kind to him in the endless months since he had been abducted from his luxurious, pampered former life and consigned to perdition on earth. No, they would keep him alive because he was more valuable to them alive than dead.

At that moment he stumbled out of the forest into a clearing. A small cabin stood in the center like a welcoming beacon. He wondered dizzily whether it was a mirage in the moonlight.

Real or not, he staggered toward the cabin, but he could not make it. His legs buckled beneath him and he collapsed on his knees three feet from the door.

It opened and an ethereal figure in a flowing white gown appeared there. An angel! His fevered mind, on the edge of delirium, decided he must already be dead. The angel before him had come to lead him to the gates of paradise.

Then he saw the ugly musket in her hands, pointed at his chest.

An angel of retribution!

He looked into the barrel of the musket without fear. Better to die cleanly from a ball through the heart than to suffer more agony.

"Kill me," he croaked defiantly. "Kill me and be done with it. Put me out of my misery!"

Then blackness claimed him, and he keeled over face first on the hard ground.

Chapter 2

Meg stared down in shock at the man lying unconscious before her in the dirt.

His bleak words echoed in her mind: *Kill me and be done with it. Put me out of my misery!* Dear God, what had driven him to her door—and to such despair?

Josh stepped beside her and peered at the fallen man. "What happened? You didn't shoot him."

"Apparently he fainted."

"What a lily-liver to faint at the sight of a musket," her brother said contemptuously.

The wolves began to howl again, closer now. They must be hovering among the trees at the edge of the clearing.

The sound sent shivers through Meg. "Quick, we must get him inside before the wolves attack him."

She put the musket aside, leaning it against the wall, and ran to the stranger.

"You take his feet," she instructed Josh as she bent down and grabbed the man by the shoulders. She could feel the heat of his body through the rough cloth of his shirt. He was burning up with fever.

6

Josh hesitated, looking first at the man, then up at her. She could see her brother's apprehensive frown in the moonlight.

"Perhaps we should not," he said timidly. "He looks dangerous, and we know nothing about him."

"Nonsense. Are we to leave him here for the wolves to eat?"

Josh's thin young face remained dubious and troubled, but he voiced no more protest. He was used to doing as Meg said. Nine years his senior, she had been more mother than sister to him, nurturing him since he was an infant and giving him the love their mama could give no one but herself.

Between them, with much tugging and grunting, they managed to half carry, half drag the stranger on his stomach into the cabin.

Meg lit one of her precious candles. With it in hand, she knelt beside him as he lay facedown on the floor. She was dismayed at how filthy he was.

His disheveled black hair hung in greasy tangles. Yet as her eyes ran down his body, she felt an involuntary tingle of appreciation. He was tall and well-formed, with broad shoulders and slim hips beneath the rags he wore, which were coated with dirt and dried mud.

He wore no shoes or stockings. Instead his feet were wrapped in dirty rags stained with blood. She wondered how far he had come on them.

Meg seized his chin and turned his head in order to see his face better. He appeared to be relatively young—thirty at most. His broad forehead was marred by an ugly red scar that ran diagonally across his left temple above a thick, slashing black brow. His closed eyes were wide set. Meg suspected he was handsome, but she could not tell, for the rest of his face was hidden beneath a thicket of wild, unkempt black whiskers.

She lay her hand on his forehead and flinched. He was hotter than a blazing fire. Unless she could bring down his fever quickly, he would surely die. No wonder he had collapsed.

But first he must be washed. He was too filthy to put into a bed.

Meg rose and gathered cloths, a coarse blanket, and soap. Then she filled a basin of warm water from the kettle hanging over the embers in the fireplace.

As she spread the blanket beside him, she instructed her brother, "Help me get him on this."

Working together, they rolled him from his stomach to his side on the blanket, then over on his back. His agonized moans as he settled on his back tore at Meg's heart. She wondered if he had a wound there or perhaps a broken rib.

Only two buttons remained on his shirt. She hastily undid them and pushed the cloth aside. His chest was richly tanned, indicating a man who had been in the sun for long hours without a covering. His broad shoulders were muscular, but he was too thin. Each rib stood out starkly.

"I want to check his back first," Meg told Josh. "I think he is hurt. Help me roll him on his side again."

As they moved him, she pulled his shirt down. Horrified gasps escaped both Meg and Josh at the stomach-wrenching sight of the vivid, angry welts and festering cuts that crisscrossed the stranger's back. No wonder he had groaned so piteously when they had rolled him on his back.

"He's been whipped something fierce!" Josh exclaimed. "What do you think he did to deserve such a beating?"

"I don't know," Meg said, but in her heart she was afraid she did. This midnight stranger must have committed some terrible misdeed to have been whipped so brutally.

A little tremor of fear rocked her. Dear God, was she aiding and sheltering a dangerous escaped convict?

For a moment her courage failed her. She had Josh's safety as well as her own to consider. Help in the form of their nearest neighbor was a half mile away. This stranger had to be a desperate creature, and she was a fool to allow him in her home.

Yet she could not turn an unconscious man out of the cabin to become fodder for the waiting wolves that still howled among the trees at the edge of the clearing. Even if the beasts had not been there, she could not turn her back on a man as dangerously ill as he clearly was.

In his present condition, he was no threat to anyone. Indeed he would be lucky if he lived at all. Her pity vanquished her alarm. She must help him.

Her mind made up, she pushed him onto his stomach again, pulled away his shirt, and gently cleaned the horribly torn flesh on his back, removing as much of the dirt and dried blood and oozing pus as she could. Although she worked carefully and he was still unconscious, he whimpered like a beaten puppy when she touched a particularly tortured spot.

She was thankful that she had just made a new—and large—batch of healing salve from her treasured collection of herbal recipes. Meg suspected she would need all of it.

Before she applied it, however, she wanted to

wash the rest of him. Rather than subject him to the torture of rolling him on his back again, she told Josh, "Help me turn him on his left side."

When they had done that, she instructed, "Hold him while I wash his front."

He complied, and she began to clean the stranger's chest. His hot, supple flesh, rising and falling raggedly beneath her hands as he drew raspy breaths, kindled a strange warmth deep in her own body.

His breeches had slipped down an inch or so to reveal skin below the waist that was startlingly white in contrast to the sun-darkened expanse above it. Meg would not have thought him so fair.

Then she noticed the ring of chafed skin around his wrist. She glanced at his other wrist and frowned. The same pattern was repeated there. Meg could think of only one thing that would have made such marks.

Shackles.

The thought strengthened her fear that he was a fugitive convict, but she said nothing about her suspicion to Josh.

As she washed the stranger's hand, long and well formed but thickly callused, it tightened around her own. A little quiver of excitement raced through Meg, and for a moment she was paralyzed, unable to make the effort to withdraw her hand.

When she belatedly pulled away, he muttered a hoarse, wordless protest. His arm came up as though searching for her hand, and his hand closed over her breast, squeezing it as he had her hand a moment earlier.

No man had ever touched her body so intimately, and Meg was stunned by the lightning flash of reaction it touched off within her—acute pleasure and an even more acute yearning that she did not understand at all.

She pushed his hand and it fell away. He murmured incoherently.

Hastily she turned her attention to his legs. Although deep, red scratches crisscrossed them, she could not help admiring how shapely they were, uncommonly so for a man. How fine they would look in silk stockings beneath a pair of dress breeches.

Meg's heart was beating faster. What was wrong with her? she wondered impatiently. No man had ever had this effect on her before. Certainly none of her handsome, fickle suitors back in the Tidewater had.

Her hands clenched in determination. She would not permit herself to act like one of those silly, contemptible girls who turned to mush over a virile man. She was too practical and sensible for such nonsense.

She noted the same circles of chafed skin around the man's ankles as she had found on his wrists. It added to her certainty that the stranger was a fugitive. Yet her fear was tempered by a softer, more puzzling emotion toward him.

Meg unwound the crude cloth wrappings from his blistered, bleeding feet and discovered he had used his shirtsleeves and his stockings to make them.

"Considering the sorry condition of his feet, I am astonished that he could have managed to walk at all," she observed to Josh, marveling at the stranger's grit and determination.

Meg unknotted the rope that held up what was left of his filthy breeches, but she hesitated at the

buttons that fastened them. She had never undressed an adult man before, never even seen one
who was not clothed below the waist. But this
was no time for maidenly modesty. The man was
in terrible condition.

As Josh helped her slide off the stranger's
pants, she could not help looking inquisitively at
that part of his lower anatomy that was so different from her own. Since she had come to the
frontier, she had heard much vulgar talk and
bawdy jokes about a man's rod and its size, and
she was curious.

When she saw it nestling flaccidly between his
legs, she could not help but be disappointed at
the sight. Why, it was such a puny little thing.

What was all the tittering and excitement
about?

Then she remembered hearing that some men
were considerably smaller than others in this de-
partment. She had once overheard her older
brother Quentin and a male friend boasting about
the size of their "endowments" and remarking
how sadly lacking another friend was. Clearly
this man was one of those whom nature had
cheated.

Meg glanced toward the trio of beds that occupied one end of the cabin. The middle—and larg-
est—of the three had been used by her stepfather,
Charles Galloway, until his death. "Josh, we must
get him into Charles's bed. We will slide the
blanket he is on over to the bed so we do not
have to carry him. Then we can lift him into it."

After much effort, they managed to deposit the
stranger facedown on the bed. Meg winced at the
sight of his filthy hair, dingy and greasy, against
the snowy whiteness of the clean sheet. Heaven
only knew what dreadful vermin were crawling

about in it. Some could be gotten rid of only by burning the bedclothes and the mattress. Rather than chance such an infestation, she poured clean water into the basin, pushed his head off the edge of the bed, and washed his hair.

Then she pulled over a three-legged stool and sat down beside him. "Go back to bed, Josh."

Her yawning brother happily complied. Within a minute of his head touching the pillow, he was again asleep.

As the night waned, the stranger's fever waxed, and Meg got no more sleep. She sponged him, trying in vain to bring down his temperature.

Delirium set in, and he raved and hallucinated. Twice he shouted in terror, "The dogs! Can't let the dogs get me!"

She took his hand in her own, held it, and murmured comfortingly to him that he was safe. Her voice seemed to penetrate his fevered brain, for he quieted a little. His hand tightened around hers, and he clung to it.

Several times during the long night, he cried in a cracked, feverish voice. "I am Arlington. You must believe me! I tell you, I am Earl . . . Arlington."

Other times he called out pleadingly for Rachel, and Meg wondered with an odd pang whether the woman was his wife or his sweetheart.

As the new day dawned, Meg was certain the midnight stranger would not live to see another one. She felt the hot sting of compassionate tears for him. He was dying far from anyone he knew and loved, far from the Rachel for whom he called repeatedly, far from anyone who would visit and tend his grave.

Once again, he cried out in agonized tones,

"Why won't you believe me? I swear to you, I am Earl . . . Arlington."

Sadly Meg took careful note of his identity. When she and Josh buried him, she would be able to put a cross marked with his name over his grave.

Chapter 3

◦◦◦◦

As Stephen emerged slowly from the depths of unconsciousness, he heard that wonderful voice again, low and sensual and soothing, the voice of an angel speaking comfortingly to him.

He had heard it often during his tormented, tortured journey through pain and darkness. He had felt the gentle touch of the hand that went with the voice—the soft, soothing hand that tugged him from the terrible nightmares and fevered hallucinations that had engulfed him.

Perhaps, he thought woozily, the woman with the sublime voice and sweet touch was his guardian angel.

With some difficulty, Stephen forced his gritty, burning eyes open. It was a moment before he could make them focus properly on the woman who stood over him.

When he succeeded, disappointment snaked through him. She did not look like an angel.

Not at all. Her anxious face was thin and plain with a nose that was too small and gray eyes that were too large. Nor did her mouth please him. Her upper lip was too thin and her lower too full.

She also looked exhausted. Her eyes were dulled by fatigue and underlined with dark half circles.

Stephen guessed her to be about four-and-twenty, but her hair was tucked beneath an ugly cap that reminded him of one his grandmother used to wear. So well did the cap hide this woman's hair, he could not even guess its color, although from the shade of her eyebrows he surmised it must be a nondescript brown.

She was short, and her drab olive gown, worn and shapeless, gave little clue to the body beneath. He suspected it was as thin as her face.

She lay her hand gently on his forehead. He was amazed at how calming and reassuring her touch was, and he stifled a protest when she removed her hand.

"I am still alive," Stephen croaked in a voice that sounded as though it had not been used in a hundred years.

Her sudden smile was brilliant, transforming her face and her eyes with a radiant warmth that seemed to penetrate to his very soul. He knew then that she was his angel after all, knew it even before she spoke, and the low, rich timbre of her voice confirmed it.

"Yes, to my considerable surprise, you are still alive."

"Why . . . surprise?" he rasped. Every muscle in his body ached, and his parched mouth felt like dried leather.

His angel's face sobered. Her smile disappeared, and he felt as though the sun had just faded from the noon sky.

"There were several times when I did not think you would live another hour."

"Several times? How long have I been here?" Stephen asked in mingled confusion and fear. He had to keep running or they would find him.

"Four days."

That surprised him. Illness still clouded his mind. Stephen stared up at the rough-hewn timbers that supported the roof over his head. He had no idea where he was and only the haziest recollection of how he had come here. "Where am I?"

"At the Drake farm."

"Where is that?" His voice sounded like a saw rasping on metal.

"You do not know?" she asked in surprise. "On the Virginia frontier."

It began to come back to him in nauseating waves: his escape from that sadistic bastard Hiram Flynt, his desperate flight from the Tidewater across the Blue Ridge Mountains to the frontier, the vicious, man-sniffing dogs that had trailed him like the hounds of hell.

Stephen did not know how many days he had been running before he reached this temporary haven. Crossing the mountains had been pure torture. With his body racked by pain and fever and fear, it had seemed like eternity.

He had thought he had lost the dogs, but then he heard them howling again. It was the last thing he remembered before collapsing into a dark netherworld of hideous, fevered nightmares.

Stephen suspected that he owed his life to the petite, plain woman before him. "Did you nurse me through my crisis?"

She nodded, her expressive gray eyes—her best feature—mirroring the apprehension that his illness had caused her. She was the first person who had shown him kindness and concern since he had been cruelly ripped from the life of privilege and wealth that was his birthright.

His throat and mouth were as dry as the Sahara, and he muttered, "Thirsty."

She picked up a tankard from a table beside the

bed. Stephen tried to raise himself and found he was too weak. He felt as helpless as a newborn pup.

"Let me help you." She bent over and lifted his upper body.

He breathed deeply of her sweet, exciting fragrance, redolent of orange blossoms. Her breast, surprisingly full beneath her shapeless gown, brushed against his cheek.

No, he sure as hell wasn't dead yet, he thought wryly as his body reacted to her soft provocation. He found himself speculating ardently about the rest of her body hidden beneath that wretched dress.

Stephen was surprised by the strength of his response to her, for he would not have glanced twice at her in his former life across the sea. She was commonplace, with none of the flirtatious allure of those beauties who had eagerly vied for his attention.

Supporting him with one arm, she brought the tankard to his lips with her other hand. "Drink as much of this as you can."

"What is it?" he croaked.

"Barley water."

"My sister makes great quantities of it for the sick." The memory of his kind, lovely sister nearly brought tears to Stephen's eyes. Would he ever see her again? Would he ever escape from this hellhole called the American colonies?

"Where is your sister?"

"In England."

"I thought you must be from there when I heard your accent."

He looked around him. The bed he occupied was one of three, resting foot-out along one wall of a roughly constructed, one-room cabin. A stone fireplace dominated the opposite wall, and a long trestle table had been placed near the broad hearth. Beside it clapboard shelves formed a makeshift cupboard. In one corner stood a loom with a spinning wheel nearby. The rough walls were decorated only with clothes hanging from pegs.

Two years ago, Stephen would have been appalled to find himself in such a rude shelter. Now he was thankful for it—and for his benefactress.

She puzzled him though, for she had the refined voice of an educated woman, whom he would not have expected to see in such poor circumstances. Had she, like him, once enjoyed a far better life?

After he drank his fill of barley water, she lowered him to the pillow. Her sweet scent of orange blossoms receded and so did the tantalizing closeness of her breasts. He longed for an excuse to keep her holding him, but he could think of none. Instead he asked her name.

"Meg Drake."

He loved her throaty voice. "Is Meg short for Margaret?"

"No, for Megan."

Stephen liked Megan better, but he was not certain it fit this humble creature. "Do you live with your husband or your parents?"

"Neither. I am unmarried, and my parents are dead. I live here with my brother, Josh."

A spinster keeping house for her older bachelor brother, Stephen thought. Did Megan Drake bestow her marvelous smile on a suitor? he wondered with a peculiar melancholy that puzzled him.

"Who are you?"

Her question stopped him. He did not want to lie to her after her kindness to him, but how honest did he dare be?

If he told her the full truth she would never believe him. More than likely she would send for the authorities, convinced that he was either crazy or a dangerous transported convict who had escaped. If she did that, he would be returned to Hiram Flynt in shackles. Stephen would not, could not, chance that. Cautiously he said, "My name is Stephen Wingate."

To his surprise she stiffened and her eyes narrowed in cold disbelief. "Do not lie to me."

"I am not!" What the hell made her believe that he was lying? She was watching him warily, and he missed the warmth of her beautiful smile. "As God is my witness, I am not lying. Why do you think I am?"

"When you were unconscious, you kept muttering that you were Earl Arlington."

Stephen cursed himself silently for having given that away in his delirium. He had learned the hard way never to reveal that. It had invariably earned him worse beatings for "lying." Fortunately Meg had misunderstood the meaning of what he had said.

She would never believe him, dressed as he was in coarse rags, if he told her the truth. Like everyone else, she would think him a lunatic or a liar. Were he in her place, he would not have believed his story either.

He said in as firm a voice as he could muster, "Bring me your Bible. I will swear on it that I was born and baptized Stephen Wingate in Yorkshire, England. My sister lives there still, and I have a brother, George Wingate, who is a captain in the British army in New York."

Megan was watching him with troubled, uncertain eyes, clearly still skeptical of his claim. "Why did you come to America?"

"I had no choice," he said truthfully. "I was returning to England from a journey to the Continent when I was seized by ruffians at Dover and handed over to an impressment gang. I was impressed aboard a frigate, *The Sea Falcon*, for several months."

Meg's face puckered. "I have heard terrible tales about impressment. Is it as bad as they say?"

"Worse. Once a man is impressed, he is unlikely to go ashore again. Officers use their whips freely on impressed sailors to force them to work like beasts. What does it matter if they die? The press gangs will quickly provide replacements. I knew that if I did not escape I would die aboard that ship. So when we reached the coast of your colony, I jumped overboard and swam for shore."

All he had told her so far was the truth, and Stephen stopped his story there, letting her think he had reached land under his own power.

Unfortunately that was not true. He closed his eyes, remembering that terrible night.

Stephen had known that the ship was off the coast, but he had not realized how far off it was. Shortly before dawn broke he saw lights through the black mist. Thinking they beckoned from land, he dived into the water and swam frantically toward them. He was a strong swimmer and he was certain he could reach shore.

Only after he was in the water and dawn broke did he discover that he had mistaken a passing ship for the land that was still several miles away. The ship was coming toward him. Its crew spotted him bobbing in the water and fished him out.

As the sailors hauled him aboard, he thought that his rescue was a superb piece of good luck.

How wrong he was. He had believed that there could be no worse hell than impressment aboard

The Sea Falcon. But it had only been a purgatory compared to what came after.

Stephen dared not tell Meg the rest of his story. It was too fantastical to expect anyone to believe it, and she was already watching him with doubt and suspicion in those big gray eyes. He would not lie to her. He simply would not tell her about the accursed ship that had picked him up and what happened to him after that.

The ship was a merchant vessel loaded with English convicts being transported to Virginia for sale as indentured servants. Disease had run rampant among the chained, half-starved convicts during the voyage, and the evil, greedy captain had lost half his human cargo.

Eager to increase his profits, the captain seized Stephen and gave him the identity of one of the convicts who had died during the voyage, a notorious murderer and rapist named Billy Gunnell.

The captain picked Gunnell's identity for Stephen because the convict's heinous crimes had earned him transportation for fourteen years instead of the usual seven. Buyers were willing to pay a higher price for a young, strong man who must labor for them for fourteen years.

It was Stephen's misfortune to be sold to Hiram Flynt, a plantation owner notorious throughout the Tidewater for his cruelty to his slaves and indentured servants. Stephen's dogs in England lived better than Flynt's people.

For Stephen, it had been escape or die. He had fled across the mountains to the frontier, hoping to make his way to New York and his brother George.

Meg asked, "Where were you going when you stumbled on us?"

"I told you I have a brother in New York. I was trying to reach him."

Her big gray eyes narrowed suspiciously. "This is not the way to New York."

"I dared not travel along the coast for fear I would be recognized. I might have been forced back aboard an English warship." More likely he would have been seized by someone eager to collect the large reward Flynt had undoubtedly offered for his return. "I could not chance that. So I thought to make my way north along the frontier."

"Why were you whipped?"

"All the impressed seamen aboard *The Sea Falcon* were." That was true, but the whippings on the frigate had been nothing compared to what he later suffered at the hands of Flynt and his overseer.

It belatedly occurred to Stephen that he was lying on his back, something he had not been able to do for many days, thanks to the sadistic Flynt. "You must have done something for my back. It does not hurt as it did."

Meg visibly shuddered. "It was in terrible condition. I put a special salve on it to soothe it and draw the pus." She still seemed suspicious. "How long ago did you jump from the ship?"

"I am not certain. I lost track of time." This was true as far as it went, but he also knew he had left the ship months ago. He dared not tell her that, though, or he would have to explain where he had been in the interim.

Meg's mouth thinned. "Some of the wounds on your back were fresh."

"If you do not believe my story, what do you think I am?"

"A transported convict who escaped from his master."

Megan Drake might be plain, but she was no fool. "I swear to you that I am not a convict. I am an English gentleman who was wrongly impressed. I have never committed a crime in my life, nor have I ever been found guilty of one."

And that was the truth. Stephen might have been substituted and sold as a convicted murderer, but the crime had not been his. It had been against him.

She raised a skeptical eyebrow. "Shall I bring you the Bible so you can swear to that, too?"

His gaze met hers squarely. "Yes. What I say is the truth, and I will happily swear to it."

Despite his emphatic answer, Stephen could tell she still did not believe him. Miffed, he demanded, "Do I look like an escaped convict?"

"Yes," she said bluntly.

That was not the answer he expected. Her candor disconcerted Stephen. He was used to women who simpered and sighed and spoke in delicate euphemisms. Only his mother and sister had been different. After he had grown to manhood, he had discovered just how unusual they were.

"If you are not a convict, why do you have the mark of shackles on your arms and legs?"

"I was mistaken for one, a man named Billy Gunnell." Stephen tried to dissemble as little as possible to her. He had been deliberately substituted for Gunnell, not mistaken for him, but he feared Meg would never believe that. "I was seized and shackled, but I am not a convict."

"Why would they have seized *you?*"

Angels, it seemed, were damned hard to fool. "Perhaps I resemble him." Stephen was still trying to stay as close to the truth as he could. "Perhaps they were eager to collect a large reward that was offered. But I am not Billy Gunnell, I am Stephen Wingate of Yorkshire."

"Then why are you running?"

"Because I cannot prove who I am until I reach my brother. I escaped from the blackguards, but if they find me they will seize me again and force me into a life of slavery."

"But once the owner sees you, he will know you are not his runaway servant and will release you."

He regarded her with a mixture of irritation and admiration. She was too damned smart. Why could she not have been one of those hen-witted females who abounded in London drawing rooms? He tried sarcasm. "Do you think so? Or will he merely see a strong, young back to replace the one that he has lost? I cannot chance that." Stephen sought to disarm her with his smile, which had always won him quick female compliance.

But her unwavering gray eyes continued to regard him with silent skepticism.

Women had never been able to resist him when he set his mind to it, but Megan Drake seemed entirely unaffected. Chagrined, he said, "I have told you my story. Now you must tell me yours."

"I don't think so."

"What?"

"I do not believe you have told me your story, and I have too much work to do to tell you mine."

Stephen, much taken aback, longed to give this maddening creature the setdown she deserved. How he wished that he possessed the Duke of Westleigh's freezing hauteur. That would put her in her place. The duke had made Stephen feel like nothing—less than nothing. And Stephen had hated him for it.

"Your cordial hospitality overwhelms me," he said with biting sarcasm.

"As your gratitude for saving your life overwhelms *me*."

He deserved that. Her reminder of what he owed her made Stephen feel like an unappreciative bastard. He gave her his most irresistible smile. "I am most grateful to you, but I do not understand why you question my honesty."

"Perhaps you have not looked in the mirror lately."

That startled him, for most women considered him very handsome. Stung that she clearly was not one of them, he said, "I am surprised you took me in, thinking what you do about me."

"I could not leave you to die with the wolves hovering to feast on you."

Christ, was that the howling he had heard as he collapsed? He had thought it came from Flynt's dogs, that they had somehow picked up his scent again. Wolves! Stephen shuddered. He owed Megan Drake even more than he had realized.

He knew that Flynt would not abandon his search for him. The dogs might pick up his scent again. Even if they did not, it would only be a matter of time before one of Flynt's human bloodhounds turned up here looking for him.

Stephen's only hope of evading them was to keep running.

He would rather die than be recaptured. He had seen the way Flynt punished escaped servants and slaves, and it would be worse for Stephen. Flynt had a special hatred for him.

Meg had said that he had been here four days. That was too long, but he was so weak he feared it would be several more days before he would be strong enough to leave.

What if Flynt's men found him before that? Stephen could only pray that they would not, but the way his luck had been running, he was pessimistic about having his prayers answered.

Suddenly, without warning, the door to the

cabin crashed open. Stephen swiveled his head and saw the barrel of a musket poking through it.

Panic spread through him like the burning sting of bad brandy.

They had found him.

Chapter 4

❧〰〜∽⌒∽〜〰❧

The door, mounted on wide leather straps, hid the man carrying the musket from Stephen's view. He looked around wildly for a place to hide but saw none, not even a closet, in the crude structure.

Trapped! His hands clenched helplessly into fists.

The newcomer stepped beyond the door. To Stephen's surprise, he was not a man at all, but a skinny young boy of no more than fifteen with sandy, sun-streaked hair.

He wore a peculiar, overlarge shirt of coarse flax that hung almost to his knees. Belted around his waist, it covered all but the bottom two inches of his breeches. On his feet he wore deerskin moccasins that had flaps tied with thongs extending up the sides of his legs.

The musket he carried in his right hand was an aged flintlock. From his other hand dangled the carcass of a wild turkey, which he thrust at Meg.

She took it, giving the lad a luminous smile as she laid the bird on the trestle table. "Thank you, Josh. We will have it for dinner."

"This is *Josh!*" Stephen blurted. When Megan had said she was living with her brother, he had envisioned a big, strapping man at least as old as his own twenty-six years.

What in hell was she doing on this godforsaken frontier with no other protection than a boy not yet old enough to shave? What of the bears, wolves, wildcats, and panthers that prowled the wilderness? What of Indians? While he was in the Tidewater, Stephen had heard terrible tales about bloodthirsty savages.

Megan Drake was either a fool or the most courageous woman he had ever encountered.

Or both.

The boy turned to face Stephen. His gray eyes were much like his sister's, except that they were snapping with hostility. "So our *unwanted* guest has come 'round at last." Josh lifted his musket toward Stephen in a threatening gesture. "I warn you, I will shoot you if you try to rob us."

"*Rob you*," Stephen echoed, looking around the primitive, roughly furnished cabin in astonishment. Even if he were not beholden to Megan Drake for saving his life, he could not see a single thing worth stealing. His anger rose at having his honesty again challenged, and by a halfling at that.

He gestured at the crude cupboard by the fireplace. "Ah, yes, no doubt you have a fortune in silver plate in that fine cupboard." He looked down pointedly at the hard-packed dirt floor. "Or perhaps I would want to steal your priceless French carpet."

Meg flinched and a flood of color rose in her face. Damn his sarcastic tongue. Stephen had shamed her, and that was the last thing he wanted to do after her kindness to him.

Josh turned to his sister. "You have only to look at him, Meg, to see what a desperate character he is."

The boy was right about that. Stephen was desperate. He would fight to the death rather than be returned to Hiram Flynt.

"You should never have risked taking him in, Meg."

Josh's reproving tone set Stephen's teeth on edge. Hiding his anger, he flashed Meg his most ingratiating smile and said smoothly, "But I am eternally grateful to you, Mademoiselle Drake, for doing so."

Stephen would disarm her with the charm and politeness that had worked so well for him in his former life. "You need not worry that I will murder you in your beds. Nor will I repay your kindness to me by stealing anything from you. I give you my word."

Josh glared at him. "You can repay her kindness by leaving as quickly as possible. Meg has too much to do to nurse you. She's had scarcely any sleep these four nights past, what with trying to quiet you and keep your fever down."

Stephen gave Meg a startled look. So that was why she looked so exhausted.

"It is too much for her." Josh's fiercely protective tone, full of love and concern for his sister, touched Stephen, and his anger dissipated. Josh was a boy attempting to do a man's job.

It was hopeless, but Stephen respected the lad for trying. He said without rancor, "I intend to move on just as soon as I possibly can."

"That won't be soon enough for us," the boy muttered ungraciously.

Nor for Stephen.

He must flee deeper into the wilderness before Flynt's animals, either two-legged or four, tracked him down. Stephen was determined to escape the American colonies and get back to England. There he would identify the unknown enemy who had reduced him to this desperate plight and exact his revenge. Stephen's thirst for vengeance had driven him onward when it would have been easier to lie down and die.

"Josh, he cannot help being ill," Meg interjected. "Now, please fetch me some water."

The boy set his musket down by the door, picked up an odd yokelike contraption similar to what might be used on a draft animal, and placed it around his neck and over his shoulders. He attached two large wooden pails to the hooks that hung from each end, then disappeared outside.

After the door shut behind him, Meg said, "I apologize for my brother. I do not know what got into him."

Stephen loved to hear her low, soothing voice. "He is trying to protect you. He looks to be a good lad, but . . ."

"But what?"

"This brutal frontier is no place for a woman and a halfling without a man to protect them."

"The last thing I need is a man!" Anger crackled in Meg's voice. She snatched up the turkey from the table. "Men are generally far more trouble than help." Her flashing eyes told him that he was one of those troublesome men. "So do not think you have found yourself a home here."

His own anger flared. As if he would want such a plain, scrawny female—he who had once had his pick of the most beautiful women in England! Hell, some of the most courted beauties in the land—the daughters of dukes and marquesses—had vied for his attention. And this colonial drab was telling him she wanted to be rid of him. Well, so she would! "Believe me," he snapped, "I will be gone from here as soon as I have the strength to move on.''

He prayed that would be very soon.

That night, while Josh was outside milking Bess, their only cow, Meg was alone with the stranger. He was sitting in bed propped up by pillows and eating the broth she had prepared for him from the turkey Josh had killed.

The man was so emphatic that Stephen Wingate was his real name, even ready to swear to it on the Bible, that Meg was inclined to believe him.

But if he was Stephen Wingate, who then was Earl Arlington?

And who was the Rachel for whom he had pleaded in his delirium?

When Mr. Wingate or Mr. Arlington or whatever his name was finished his soup, Meg took the empty wooden bowl from him.

''That was delicious,'' he told her. ''You are an excellent cook.''

She was surprised that his compliment should please her so. After all she was not certain she could believe anything this man said. She observed with skeptical amusement, ''I suspect you are so starved that boiled grease would taste good to you.''

He chuckled. ''Believe me, I know the difference.''

The look he gave her made her heart skip. He had the most remarkable eyes. They were a shade unlike any she had seen before: not quite blue, with a violet cast.

She dropped her gaze to his muscled chest, deeply tanned from the sun and decorated with swirls of midnight black hair. An overwhelming urge to run her fingers over his chest beset her. Was his hair there coarse—or silken to the touch?

Had she taken leave of her senses? How could she allow herself to be attracted to this stranger? His scars branded him as a transported convict who had escaped his master. And a liar to boot.

Meg, taking herself firmly in hand, asked coldly, "Do you want more soup?"

"Yes, please, ma'am."

He was treating her with faultless politeness. He might be a desperate character, but she had to concede that he had the manners of a born gentleman.

And the voice of one, too. His faultless diction revealed a well-bred, well educated man.

He looked at the bowl in her hand. "This time, could I please have more than just broth?"

"That might not be wise. It has been a long time since you have had solid food in your stomach, Earl." Meg slipped the name in to test his reaction.

His eyes narrowed. "I told you my name is not Earl. It is Stephen, Stephen Wingate. I offered to swear to it on the Bible. What else will it take to convince you?"

She looked down into his unusual eyes. "Perhaps if you would explain to me who Earl Arlington is."

He hesitated for an instant. "I cannot." He sounded as though he was picking his words carefully. "No man of my acquaintance has the given name of Earl, and I do not know of any family named Arlington."

"Will you swear on the Bible to that, too?"

"Aye, I will."

Frowning, Meg glanced down at the empty bowl in her hand, then back at him. "Why did you keep crying in your delirium that you were Earl Arlington?"

"A man is not responsible for what he says when he is out of his head with fever."

She stared dubiously at him. He was convincingly adamant that his name was not Earl Arlington. Yet she was certain that he was hiding something from her.

Stephen opened his eyes with a start. He had dozed off, still propped against the pillows. His eyes unconsciously searched the cabin for Megan Drake. When he saw her working at the trestle table, he drew a deep, relieved breath. He was disconcerted by how much the presence of this plain, dowdy woman in her shapeless dress comforted him.

Recalling the brush of her soft breast against his cheek as she had lifted him, he imagined what her body, hidden under that ugly olive cloth, would be like. His own body tightened in response to the picture his mind drew.

He had been too long without a woman. That must be why he was responding to her the way he was. In his other life, he would never even have noticed her.

But he sure as hell was noticing her now.

Despite her unprepossessing appearance and sorry dress, her manner was that of a gently born lady, not an ignorant frontier woman.

He wondered whether she had been plantation born. He knew from his servitude to Hiram Flynt that the families of plantation owners in Tidewater Virginia lived very well indeed. The mansion at Ashley Grove, which Flynt had acquired some months earlier, was as fine as many of the country houses in England.

"Mr. Wingate . . . Mr. Wingate?"

He belatedly realized she was speaking to him.

His name might be Stephen Wingate, but he had never been Mr. Wingate. He had been Viscount Hastings before he succeeded to his father's title.

Meg was regarding him suspiciously again, her mouth pinched. "You seem not to recognize your own name."

Damn. He had revived her doubts about him. "I fear I was woolgathering. Forgive me. What did you ask?"

"Whether you would like more barley water."

"Not now."

The linen sheet that covered Stephen had fallen down around his waist. It occurred to him that not only was his chest bare, but so was the rest of his body beneath the sheet. Surely this prim spinster could not have undressed him?

"Where are my clothes?" His voice was still hoarse.

"I burned them." Meg shuddered. "Nothing but filthy rags."

"They were all I had." Stephen was surprised at what it cost him to admit that to her.

"They were undoubtedly crawling with vermin."

The disdain and repugnance in Meg's tone humiliated him. In his other life, he had owned closets full of clothes finer than any this impoverished provincial could imagine.

He tried to conceal his shame behind angry sarcasm. "What the hell am I supposed to do now? I can hardly leave here naked. Or perhaps you wish me to stay after all."

She stiffened. "I want you to leave the instant you are able to do so. I will find you something to wear."

"When did you burn my clothes?"

"The night you arrived."

That meant he had been lying here naked for the past four days while she tended him. Had she ever seen a naked man before? If not, he wondered in amusement, what had her reaction been? Had she been embarrassed, startled, impressed? If she was like other women he'd known, it would be the last.

She went to the fireplace to ladle water into a basin from a kettle suspended over the glowing embers by a hook that hung from a lug pole extending across the width of the fireplace.

With the basin in hand, she came briskly toward his bed. "I must clean and redress your back."

Stephen protested, shuddering at the agony it would surely cause him.

"It must be done. Surely, you are not such a coward that you would flinch."

For some reason the possibility that Meg would think him a coward hurt worse than anything she could do to his back. With a resigned sigh, he slid down in the bed and turned over on his stomach.

She sat down beside him, and her sweet scent of orange blossoms drifted over him. She peeled away the cloth bandage with the greatest of care, causing only a minimum of discomfort to his tortured back.

Then she washed it carefully with soap and water from the basin. Her sure yet gentle hands filled him with a pleasure and well-being that he had not felt since that terrible night when he had been seized at Dover.

He remembered his fevered nightmares and how her comforting hands and her sensual voice had pulled him from them. He remembered the howling of the wolves that had preceded the nightmares and shuddered. God, he owed Megan Drake so much.

She applied a fragrant salve from a tin container

to his wounds. "Your back is healing nicely. I am very pleased with your progress."

He closed his eyes. Her smooth, smoky voice was so lovely that it sent male yearning snaking through him.

The salve was as soothing as her voice, and her touch filled him with such contentment that when she finished, he was loath to have her quit. As she started to rise from beside him, he grabbed her hand with his own and lightly caressed the back of it with his thumb.

"Please, do not stop," he pleaded in his most seductive tone, the one women had never been able to resist.

She stood up abruptly, jerking her hand away as though his touch repulsed her.

"Nay, Mr. Wingate, that is enough." The warmth had vanished from her voice. Without a backward glance, she went to the fireplace to retrieve a cloth that she had hung there to warm.

He stared after her. Had he lost, along with everything else, his ability to charm women?

Perhaps you have not looked in the mirror lately.

Unconsciously his hand came up to his face and found it buried beneath a rough thicket of whiskers.

He wondered uneasily what he looked like. It had been a long time since he had seen his reflection in a looking glass.

Meg returned with the cloth, placing it on his back. Its warmth seemed to melt the soothing salve into his wounds. He gave a smothered moan of pleasure. "That feels so good."

But not as good as her hands had felt, and he wondered what it would be like to have them touch him again in more private places. For a long time, he lay there facedown, his eyes closed . . . imagining.

Then he heard a strange creaking. Curious, he rolled on his side and raised himself on his elbow. The noise came from the odd chair in which Meg sat. It had curved wooden runners rather like a child's rocking horse and moved in the same manner. It was, he reflected, the first time he had seen her sit down except briefly to eat. But she was not idle. Her needle was flying as she mended a rip in a pair of breeches.

"Where did you get that peculiar chair?" Stephen asked as her brother came back into the cabin. Josh was weighed down by the two buckets hanging from the yokelike carrier on his shoulders.

"It is not peculiar," Josh contradicted. He set the buckets down near the fireplace. "It is very clever. Wilhelm made it for her." A note of awe crept into the lad's voice. "Wilhelm can do anything."

Stephen asked in a voice tinged with irony, "Who is this remarkable paragon?"

"Our nearest neighbor," Meg answered. "He lives about a half mile down the road."

Stephen's eyes narrowed. Was Wilhelm Meg's suitor as well as her neighbor? Her tone gave no clue to her feelings about him, but it was clear that he was a hero to her younger brother.

Josh headed outside again. At the door, he paused. "There is a halo around the sun. That means there will be a long, slow rain within eight hours."

Stephen thought the prediction nonsense. "Why would you think that?"

"Because Wilhelm says so. He's always right." Josh disappeared outside, shutting the door behind him.

"Does Wilhelm walk on water, too?" Stephen muttered.

If Meg heard him, she said nothing. She continued with her mending, paying him no heed.

Stephen was not used to having any woman, even a beautiful one, treat him with such disinterest. Pushing himself into a sitting position, he asked for the small, cracked looking glass hanging on the rough log wall near the bed in the corner to his right.

Meg rose and brought the mirror to him.

When he looked into it, he started at the unnerving image reflected there. He had an ugly red scar above his left brow. Wild, unkempt whiskers covered most of his face and neck. His disheveled hair fell in tangles below his shoulders. Christ, *he* did not even recognize himself.

Shame coursed through him. He thought of how he must look to Meg, a gaunt, wild-maned, wild-whiskered creature with the scars of the lash on his back and the mark of shackles on his arms and legs.

He could not blame her for not believing his story. His admiration for her courage soared. She had been brave indeed to give refuge to a man who looked as menacing as he did. He doubted any other woman would have done so.

Nor most men either.

Megan Drake was a remarkable woman.

Stephen had to show her he was not the dangerous, untrustworthy man that he looked to be. He had to make himself presentable.

Presentable, hell! He had to make himself look human.

"I need a brush and comb." He hesitated. Would the Drakes even have a razor? Young Josh did not need one yet. "Do you have a razor?"

"Aye, but this is what you need first." She picked up a wicked-looking knife from the trestle table and started toward him.

"What the hell is that?" he yelped in alarm.

"A scalping knife."

"*Scalping knife!* Are you mad?"

Her gray eyes sparkled with laughter. "Trust me. Have I hurt you yet?" She grabbed his beard with one hand. With the other, she made several slashes with that mean knife so close to his face that his breath caught. Bloody hell, the woman was dangerous!

Finally she stopped. "There," she said with satisfaction.

Stephen resumed breathing. He saw in the glass that Meg had dispatched most of his bushy growth with the same sure, quick competence she had demonstrated on the turkey carcass that she had turned into dinner.

She laid the knife aside and brought him a brush and a comb.

As he worked at the tangles in his hair, Meg went to the fireplace. She returned to his bed carrying a tin basin of water, a container of soap, a towel, and a razor. She placed them on the crude pine table beside his bed.

Stephen was startled that the razor was such a fine instrument, with its excellent blade and mother-of-pearl handle. Only a gentleman of some wealth could have afforded it.

She explained, "It was my father's. I am saving it for Josh."

It strengthened Stephen's conviction that Meg had been born to a far better life than this one.

He pulled his knees up, propped the looking glass against his thighs, and looked in frustration at his whiskers. In England, a valet had shaved him, just as other servants had attended to his every need.

Even if he'd had a razor on *The Sea Falcon*, Stephen would not have dared use it while the frigate pitched and heaved on the stormy seas. Indentured to Hiram Flynt, there had been no such luxury as a razor for a lowly field hand whom the master had hated.

Now Stephen was too embarrassed to admit to Meg that he had never shaved himself. He'd be damned if he would reinforce her contemptuous assessment of him: *Men are generally far more trouble than help.*

"I—I fear I am still so shaky that I do not trust myself to handle this razor without cutting myself. Could you help me?"

With an impatient sigh Meg began to lather his beard. When she wielded the razor, her sure, quick strokes told him this was not the first time she had shaved a man. Why did that disturb him? "You have done this before."

Her gaze met his without subterfuge. "Yes, for my father. He disliked shaving himself."

Was her father one of the men who had been more trouble than help to Meg?

Stephen stifled a sigh of pleasure as her sure, capable hands worked on his face, and he felt himself relaxing.

He studied her features, admiring the long, sensuous sweep of golden brown lashes that fringed her luminous, intelligent gray eyes. She was, he decided, much prettier than he had first thought. Her nose might not be of aristocratic shape and length, but something about its cute, upturned tip made him yearn to kiss it. Initially he had thought her upper lip too thin and her bottom too full, but now he had to fight the urge to run his tongue teasingly over her tempting lower lip.

His gaze dropped to her body. As she leaned forward into her work, her gown gaped a little at the neck, offering him a fine, tantalizing view of her soft, white bosom. He could not tear his gaze away, and desire shot through him with stunning force. He ached to cup her lovely breasts in his hands and stroke their coral tips into taut response.

Beads of sweat broke out on his forehead.

"You are perspiring. Has your fever returned?" Meg put her palm to his forehead.

Her gentle touch against his skin sent another bolt of desire through him. He was truly shocked by how much he wanted this woman.

She frowned, looking puzzled. "No, 'tis not a fever. You are quite cool."

Like hell he was. He was burning up with lust for her.

She resumed shaving him, utterly unaware of the effect she was having on him.

And, damn it, he seemed to be having none at all on her.

Gritting his teeth, he reminded himself that he was a gentleman. As soon as he regained his strength, he would be gone from here. And he would not repay this prim spinster's kindness to him by trying to seduce her. He owed her too much.

When she was done shaving him, she remarked coolly, "How altered you look."

Disappointed by her indifferent reaction, Stephen looked into the cracked mirror. His face had an unattractive gauntness to it. His cheeks were sunken. Removing the bushy growth only emphasized the nasty scar over his left brow, and his eyes had the look of a man who had suffered much.

His countenance reminded him of a description from Shakespeare, and he quoted self-mockingly:

> " 'A needy, hollow-eyed, sharp-looking wretch,
> A living-dead man.' "

He wondered why Meg gaped at him.

"Is that from *The Comedy of Errors?*"

"Yes." Stephen was surprised that a provincial colonial recognized the quotation's source. "You have read Shakespeare?"

"Aye." Her perplexed gray eyes studied him. "I am astonished that you could quote from him. I would not have thought you could read."

That stung, and he said sharply, "I can read very well—in several languages. I told you I was a gentleman until those villains seized me at Dover."

She clearly could not decide whether to believe him. Stephen looked down again at his altered visage in the cracked looking glass and understood why.

It was no longer a face to impress a woman, he thought bitterly, not even an on-the-shelf spinster like Meg Drake.

Stephen sank back against the pillows. He had been born with so much.

And not once had he appreciated what he had, until he lost it all.

He silently cursed himself for what a stupid, ungrateful fool he had been.

Meg carried the basin of shaving water to the trestle table, where she cleaned her father's razor while she considered the puzzle of Stephen Wingate. He quoted so easily and aptly from Shakespeare, yet he bore the marks of a dangerous convict. He did not sound like one, though, but rather like what he claimed to be—a gentleman wrongly seized and impressed.

And now that he was shaven and his hair brushed, he no longer looked like a desperate criminal either. She cast a surreptitious glance at him, and her heart skipped. It had been a mistake to shave him.

If she had had any idea how attractive he would be once he was shorn of that disreputable beard, she would not have. Now it was all she could do to keep from staring at the hard planes of his face, which attested to character distilled by adversity and suffering.

None of her former suitors' faces, handsome as they had been, had aroused the excitement and warmth in her that Stephen Wingate's did. An excitement and warmth that he could never feel for her in return. A plain, practical creature like herself did not inspire passion and undying love in men, especially not one as handsome and charming as Stephen Wingate.

She had accepted this failing in herself. She was not a woman who wasted time wailing over what could not be changed. She was far too practical for that. But she was also unwilling to settle for less than love and fidelity from the man she wed. That was why she would never marry.

Meg's gaze fell from Mr. Wingate's face to his tanned chest, thick with curling midnight black hair. Once again she was seized by the most ridiculous urge to run her fingers through it.

What was wrong with her? She jerked her gaze away. But a moment later, it crept admiringly back to his bare chest. She could not seem to keep her eyes off it. Furious at her own weakness, she went to one of the wall pegs and grabbed a long nightshirt that had belonged to her dead stepfather.

She tossed it to the stranger, snapping, "Put this on."

Her angry tone clearly surprised him, but he complied.

Meg recalled his plaintive cries for Rachel. Who was she? His wife perhaps? Meg shied away from asking him that directly. Instead she inquired, "Do you have children back in Yorkshire, Mr. Wingate?"

He grinned impishly. "Not to my knowledge."

"A wife?"

His grin broadened. "No."

"A betrothed?"

The grin faltered, and he paused a telltale instant too long. "No."

He was lying, Meg thought with an odd pain in her heart. Just as he was most likely lying about his background. She would not allow herself to be taken in as her mother had been by a handsome, untrustworthy man.

The price was too high.

Chapter 5

The big, ugly dogs were upon Stephen, snarling and snapping. Behind them, Hiram Flynt's malevolent face was alight with triumph. In his hands he carried a pothook, the terrible studded collar that he sealed around the necks of recaptured slaves and indentured servants.

One of the dogs leaped and seized Stephen's arm, its fangs ripping into his flesh.

He screamed in pain.

Suddenly the vicious dog was swept miraculously away by hands that soothed. A low, sensual voice called to him. "Wake up. 'Tis a nightmare."

Stephen opened his eyes and saw Meg's concerned face in the shadowy dimness of the candle that she had left burning. He gripped her hands hard in his own to banish the lingering terror of the nightmare. Strange how holding her hands made him feel safe.

But he knew that he was not. That evil bastard Flynt would never give up until he caught Stephen.

He heard a steady patter on the roof. "It sounds as though the rain Josh predicted has arrived."

"It has been falling for three or four hours. Do you think you will be able to sleep now?"

Stephen shrugged. The nightmare had reminded

him of how precarious his current freedom was. He prayed to the God he was certain had deserted him that Flynt would not find him here before he could leave. Stephen could almost feel the cold metal of the pothook closing around his neck.

It was still raining lightly a few hours later when Meg served a breakfast of hasty pudding and milk. She gave Mr. Wingate his breakfast in bed, then placed her brother's food before him on the trestle table.

Josh glanced at their guest. "See, I told you it would rain. Wilhelm's always right."

Meg was amused by her brother's faith in their neighbor. She would always be grateful to Wilhelm for his patience with Josh, answering his eager questions and taking the time to teach him so many things he needed to know about life in the wilderness.

When her brother finished his breakfast, he announced he was going out to feed the animals.

Meg glanced at the glowing embers in the fireplace. Even though these August days were hot, the fire must be kept going, for she had no way to restart it if it went out. "We are getting low on wood, Josh. You had better chop some today."

He pulled an unhappy face. Chopping wood was the chore that he hated above all others, and he would put it off as long as he possibly could.

After Josh went outside, Meg asked, "Are you done with your breakfast, Mr. Wingate?"

He nodded. As she reached for his bowl, his hand closed gently yet firmly around her wrist. Her heart skittered at his unexpected touch.

"Please." His voice was husky, cajoling. "Call me Stephen. I much prefer it."

Meg suspected he was quite used to persuading

females to do whatever he wished. "That would be improper." She was proud of how prim she sounded. He could have no notion that her breath quickened every time she looked at his handsome, shaven face. She would not let him guess how much he affected her. "I do not know you well enough."

He gave her a wicked grin that seemed to turn her bones to water. "After nursing me while I was unconscious for four days, I would say you that know me very well indeed."

She blushed at his reminder that nothing about his body had been hidden from her.

Amusement danced in his blue violet eyes. "It is I who should be blushing. After that, surely you can call me Stephen." His fingers slipped from her wrist to her hand and gave it an imploring little squeeze. "Please."

Meg tried to pull her hand from his, but his fingers tightened. His blue violet eyes were suddenly hard and penetrating. "Who was the bastard who soured you on men?"

"I beg your pardon!"

"You said the last thing you needed was a man. A woman does not feel that way unless some scoundrel has given her reason. What happened, Meg? Did he seduce you and then desert you?"

She could feel her face coloring. No man had ever spoken to her so bluntly before. She glared at him, but the sympathy in his remarkable eyes melted her anger at his impertinence.

"Did he?" he pressed. His coaxing voice invited confidences.

Because he thought only one man was responsible for her attitude, she would tell him about the worst of the lot. "He did neither, unless you call dying deserting me. In truth, I was relieved to be rid of him."

"Who was he?" Stephen still held her hand.

"My stepfather."

"Did he bring you and your brother to this god-forsaken wilderness?"

"He forced us to come," she blurted bitterly.

With his free hand, he put his bowl on the other side of the bed, then tugged her gently down beside him.

"Tell me about it." Stephen's warm, callused hands engulfed her smaller ones, holding them comfortingly, and she could not seem to summon the strength to pull away from him. "How did he force you?"

"As soon as my mother married Charles—that was my stepfather—he had himself appointed the guardian of both Josh and me."

"You are too old for a guardian."

"Tell that to Justice Nathan Baylis who signed the order." Bitterness welled up in her. "When Charles moved to the frontier, he insisted that Josh and I, as his wards, had to go with him. Not long after we got here, before we had even finished the spring planting, he was killed in a fight."

Stephen's hands tightened over hers. She should not let him hold her hands, yet she could not rebuff the silent solace he offered her. It had been a long time since anyone had given her that.

Meg looked down at their hands. Against the whiteness of her own, his were nut brown. They were slender and nicely shaped, with long, tapering fingers. Despite their calluses, they were the hands of a gentleman.

She looked up at his face. Was his story about being Stephen Wingate from Yorkshire true? She hoped it was, but it seemed too fantastical.

"Am I occupying Charles's bed?"

Meg nodded. She marveled at the change in his voice. Yesterday it had been hoarse and raspy, apparently from illness and lack of use, but today it was softer and more pleasing and sent a little shiver of appreciation through her.

"And since your stepfather died, you and Josh have been struggling to hang on."

"Believe me, it is less of a struggle with Charles gone." Meg made no attempt to disguise her disgust for her worthless stepfather. He had sat around doing nothing and treating his stepchildren as the slaves he could no longer afford while he played the gentleman of leisure.

"With him dead, why did you stay here?" Stephen looked around the crude cabin, his disdain for it plain. "Why not give up this sorry place and go back to where you came from?"

"Because there is nothing to go back to, thanks to Charles." Meg thought of her beloved Ashley Grove and its people, now in the hands of that evil Hiram Flynt, and she felt nauseated. "This farm is all that is left of my brothers' inheritance. I must make it viable for them."

"Them? You have more than one brother?"

She nodded. "My other brother Quentin is a year older than I."

"Where the hell is he now? Did he not come with you?"

"Aye, but he left before Charles was killed. Quentin has no interest in farming."

And even less in the hard work it required. But Meg kept that caustic thought to herself. Initially Quentin had wanted to come to the frontier, thinking it a grand adventure. But once her irresponsible, hot-tempered older brother had seen how much physical labor was involved in farming the wilderness, he had disappeared. "The note he left said he was going back to the Tidewater."

"*Note?* You mean the bastard did not even tell you to your face that he was leaving but wrote you a note instead?" Stephen sounded incensed. "After abandoning you like that, Quentin does not deserve an inheritance!"

"Perhaps not," Meg admitted, "but Josh does."

Stephen smiled at her. "Josh is very lucky to have you for a sister. Too bad his luck—and yours—ran out when it came to Quentin and your stepfather."

Meg felt compelled to defend her brother. No matter how much Quentin exasperated her, she loved him. "He did promise in his note that he would come back to help with the harvest."

"How generous of him." His thumbs drew lazy circles on the backs of Meg's hands.

Unnerved by his effect on her, she pulled away from him and stood up, saying coldly, "I have much work to do, Mr. Wingate." More than she could ever hope to get done in this lifetime.

He grabbed her wrists and held her. "Call me Stephen. I want to hear you say my name."

"If it is your name!"

Anger flashed in his eyes. "It is! Now, say it."

For a moment she mutely returned his glare. His hands tightened warningly around her wrists.

"Let me go—Stephen."

He instantly released her with a smile that made her heart turn over. She turned quickly away, afraid that her face might betray her disconcerting reaction to him.

Meg went to her bed, which occupied one corner of the cabin. She pushed back the heavy curtains that, when extended at night along the foot and left side of her bed, created her own tiny bedchamber.

Although two of this makeshift room's four walls were cloth, she still had nighttime privacy.

He said, "Those curtains are clever."

"Thank you." Meg looked up at the slender rods from which the curtains were suspended. One end of each rod had been inserted into a notch in the wall, and the other into a slender, upright pole buried in the dirt floor near the lower left corner of her bed.

"Were they your idea?"

Meg nodded. " 'Tis the only way I can have any privacy. Our neighbor Wilhelm hung the rods for me."

"You should have a room of your own."

Meg sighed wistfully. "I would give anything for my own room, but that is a rare luxury on the frontier."

When Meg's other chores were done that night, she began to work on a hunting shirt for Stephen.

Such a garment was simple enough to make because it was large and loose and required no fitting. She only had to cut it and stitch it together.

More difficult was what to use for cloth. The only material she had was deerskin, which she had intended to make into breeches, a hunting shirt, and moccasins for Josh. She disliked sacrificing it to a stranger, but it was all she had.

Initially she had intended to send him on his way wearing some of her stepfather's garments. But Charles's clothes were the elegant garments of a Tidewater gentleman and utterly impractical on the frontier.

Worse, a fugitive in such clothes—and Meg's common sense told her that Stephen Wingate must be one—would never be able to make his way quietly along the frontier to New York, if indeed that was where he was trying to go. He would attract attention like a peacock amid a flock of barnyard chickens.

And she did not want him caught and returned to the life from which he had escaped. She shuddered at the thought of his tortured back. No matter what he had done, he did not deserve the treatment that had been meted out to him.

She went to the chest that held her late stepfather's clothes and pulled out a lawn nightshirt.

Using it as a rough pattern, she quickly cut out the hunting shirt, making it narrower and longer to compensate for the difference in the two men's sizes.

Josh, busy cleaning his musket, paid her no heed. Stephen said nothing, but she felt his intent gaze on her. She recalled how warm and sympathetic he had been when she had told him about Charles. And how comfortable she had felt confiding in him. Not since her father had died had she had anyone with whom she had been able to talk so freely.

When Meg sat down in the rocking chair to stitch the pieces of deerskin together, Stephen asked, "What are you doing?"

"Making you a hunting shirt to wear when you leave."

The quick flash of gratitude in Stephen's eyes told Meg that he understood and appreciated her reason for sewing the garment.

As she worked, she felt his gaze lingering on her, and she looked up at him. At his request, she had cut his jet black hair that afternoon, and he had brushed it neatly back. He gave her a smile so devastating that it sent her heart thudding against her ribs. She felt as though she were melting beneath its brilliance like ice in the sun.

Then her mouth tightened in determination. She could not allow herself to fall victim to this man's charm. She had no doubt that many women had.

Had he loved any of them in return? Even for a fleeting moment?

She remembered his cries for Rachel in his delirium—and his hesitation at the question of whether he was betrothed. Rachel must be the betrothed he denied having. Meg felt a dull ache in her heart.

She recalled his other delirious cries, too: *Why won't you believe me? I swear to you I am Earl ... Arlington.*

The memory of how emphatic he had been about being Earl Arlington strengthened her resolve not to be deceived by him. This man who called himself Stephen Wingate had to be a liar—and perhaps a dangerous convict in the bargain.

Only a fool would allow such a man to worm his way into her heart.

And Megan Drake was not a fool.

Chapter 6

—⟨⟨○◯○⟩⟩—

Meg came into the cabin the following day carrying a large wooden bowl containing pea pods that she had picked from her vegetable garden. Josh had gone off hunting, and Stephen was sitting up in bed. The look of relief on his face as she came in surprised her.

"Where the hell have you been? I was worried about you."

For some reason, his concern pleased Meg. "Picking peas for dinner."

He patted the edge of his bed. "Come talk to me."

Meg wanted to accept his invitation. She remembered the caressing, comforting way he had held her hands the previous day and yearned to have him do so again.

Dear God, this man turned her will to mush. Irritated at her own weakness, she said far more brusquely than she intended, "I have too much to do."

That was all too true. Stephen had been right when he had said she and Josh needed a man—or at least a man's strength—to deal with the backbreaking labor of clearing more land. Until they could do that, the farm would produce barely enough to sustain them. The thought depressed even Meg's determined, optimistic spirit.

Running a great plantation like Ashley Grove, as she had done for years after her mother had taken to her invalid's bed, had been easy compared to eking out an existence on the frontier.

Stephen gave her that coaxing smile of his. "Please, just for a few minutes."

Determined not to succumb to his charm, she snapped, "I told you I have no time."

"Can I do anything to help?" It was the kind of polite question one asks when confident the reply would be negative.

With a mischievous gleam in her eye, Meg decided to surprise him. "Yes, you can." She deposited the bowl of peas on the bed where he had intended her to sit. "Help me shell these."

He looked as if Meg had just dumped a bowl of squiggling worms on the bed. She bit back a smile. That would teach him to make offers he did not think would be accepted.

She went to the clapboard shelves and took down a small iron pot. As she passed the trestle table, she snatched up a three-legged stool and sat down on it beside the bed.

Stephen had lifted one pea pod from the bowl and was staring at it as though it were some exotic botanical specimen that he had never before encountered.

He dropped the pod, unshelled, back into the bowl. "It is clear to me you were not born and raised in these rough circumstances. Your family must once have had a great deal more than this farm."

He sounded so sympathetic that Meg confided, "My father was a rich planter in the Tidewater, and we lived in a fine mansion." She picked up a pea pod from the bowl. In one quick motion, she snapped off the top of the pod and pulled the string down the side.

"What happened to the plantation?"

Meg popped the peas from the pod into the small pot. "Papa died of apoplexy two years ago." She and her jovial, energetic father had been so close that the memory of his death still tore at her heart, and she had to blink back tears.

As she reached for another pea pod, Stephen's hand caught hers and squeezed it comfortingly. "You clearly loved your father very much."

Stephen Wingate was proving to be a man of surprising perception. "Yes, I did. People said I was much like him, which I considered a great compliment. After Papa was stricken with his first seizure, my mother fell prey to the charms of Charles Galloway, a shiftless fortune hunter several years younger than she."

"And married him."

Meg nodded. "I am afraid my mother was a very foolish woman. She gave him control of everything. Within a year, through mismanagement and gambling, he had lost all my father's estate but this farm."

"Where is your mother now?"

"Dead. The shock of discovering everything was gone precipitated a fatal stroke."

"Leaving her children behind to pay the price for her mistakes." Stephen's hand tightened on Meg's. "Tell me about your father's plantation. Where was it?"

"On the James River." Meg swallowed hard at the memory of her former home, a great neoclassical mansion overlooking the water. "It had a beautiful house that my father filled with fine furnishings and art."

And now it was all lost, thanks to her mother. And Charles.

"What was your plantation's name?"

"Ashley Grove."

"*Ashley Grove!*" He dropped her hands. His stunned expression startled Meg into asking, "You know of it?"

"Was your father Anton Drake?"

"Yes. How did you know him?"

"I—I did not, but he was the preeminent planter in the Tidewater. Everyone has heard of him."

Meg's lower lip trembled as she thought of how her father's years of labor to build a great estate for his family had been for naught because her vain, self-absorbed mother had lost her head over a lying, smooth-talking scoundrel.

Her daughter had sworn that she would never make that same mistake. And, Meg warned herself sternly, that might be precisely what she was doing with Stephen Wingate, if that truly was his name. Even though her heart wanted to think better of him, the marks of lash and shackle upon him proclaimed that he could not be trusted any more than Charles Galloway.

Meg jumped up, nearly overturning the stool in her haste to get away from Stephen's potent charm. "You finish shelling the peas."

She hurried over to the trestle table and began to measure cornmeal for a batch of johnnycake.

Stephen asked, "If you had stayed in the Tidewater instead of coming here, what would you have done? Married?"

"No, I will never marry!"

Stephen's black brows rose in silent question. "Such vehemence. Did your stepfather and Quentin sour you on all men?"

"It was not just them," Meg confessed. "I had several suitors, handsome sons of neighboring planters, when it was thought I would inherit Ashley Grove."

Her mother's waspish voice echoed in her ears: *Poor Meg. A woman as plain as you can never inspire passion and faithfulness and undying love in a handsome, young husband. You are a fool not to accept old Nathan Baylis's offer. He will at least be faithful.*

She shuddered at the memory of that snake Baylis. He had exacted his revenge on her for rejecting him by appointing Galloway as her guardian.

Meg's papa must have been pessimistic about her marital prospects, too. That was why he had cautioned her about her suitors' motives, and they had proven him right. Papa had also warned her repeatedly to settle for nothing less than a man who loved her.

'Tis misery to be married to one who does not love you, Papa had said. He knew firsthand, for he had married a woman incapable of loving anyone but herself.

Then he had added that someday Meg would meet a man worthy of her. But she knew that her father did not truly believe this any more than she did.

And she preferred never to marry rather than wed a man who could not give her love and fidelity.

Her decision against marriage had not been so hard to make because she had not met a man who caused her own heart to palpitate as other young women's did with such frequency. She had thought herself deficient in romantic tendencies until Stephen Wingate invaded her life.

He asked softly, "What happened to those suitors?"

"Once Ashley Grove was gone, so were they." Although Meg had loved none of them, their behavior had hurt her deeply.

"All of them?" Stephen sounded surprised.

"All except the Reverend Peter Burnaby." And even he had not been motivated by love, but by his conviction that she would make a perfect minister's wife.

"Why did you reject Burnaby?"

"He did not love me." *And I did not love him.*

Stephen looked startled. "Is love in marriage that important to you?"

"Of course it is! I would require two things of a husband, his love and his fidelity. Not that it matters, since I shall never marry."

"How would you have supported yourself if you had stayed in the Tidewater?"

"As a music teacher."

"What instrument do you play?"

"The harpsichord is my favorite, but I also play the violin and the flute."

"Do you have an instrument here?"

She looked up from the johnnycake batter. "Only my flute."

When Meg had told Stephen her name, he had not connected her to the Drakes of Ashley Grove. He was still reeling from her revelation that Anton Drake's daughter had been reduced to such lowly circumstances.

Stephen contemplated telling Meg the truth about how he had been bought by Hiram Flynt, but he feared she would not believe he had been wrongly substituted for a convict.

Meg said, "If you do not get to work on those peas, we will be having them for breakfast tomorrow instead of dinner today."

Stephen stared helplessly at the bowl. He should

have watched Meg more closely while she was working on the peas. "You will have to show me how."

She looked incredulous, then exasperated. "Have you never seen a pea shelled before?"

Hell, he had never even been in a kitchen. English lords did not descend below stairs. "No," he grumbled, hating to appear so damned inept to her.

She came back to the bed, picked up a pod, and demonstrated how it was done. He watched her quick, competent hands in admiration. They were small, delicate, and beautifully formed but now roughened by work they should never have had to do.

"Now do you think you can shell them?" She sounded as though he were a hopeless idiot.

That stung him into replying with more pride than honesty, "Certainly."

"Good." She went back to the trestle table.

He tried breaking off the top of a pod and pulling the string as she had done, but it was not nearly as easy as Meg had made it look. Her fingers had fairly flown. His were slow and awkward. And the damned peas had a tendency to shoot in every direction except the pot.

As he worked, Stephen's thoughts turned to her father. He had heard much about Anton Drake, one of those rare men whom everyone had liked and admired.

Stephen had heard much, too, about Drake's only daughter. She had run the domestic affairs of Ashley Grove because his wife was an invalid. By all accounts Meg had done an excellent job. The daughter had been as well liked and respected as her father. The same could not be said for her mother.

Stephen frowned thoughtfully as his thumb slid

along the moist valley of an open pod. During the time he had labored for Flynt, he had heard rumors that his unscrupulous master had cheated Drake's heirs out of Ashley Grove. Knowing Flynt, Stephen readily believed the rumors were true.

He retrieved an errant pea that had escaped the pot and landed in the bedding. If he could figure out Flynt's swindle, would it be possible for Meg and Josh to reclaim the lost estate? The thought excited Stephen. It would be a way to help them and, at the same time, exact his own revenge on Flynt, for Ashley Grove was the bastard's most prized possession.

Meg went to the fireplace. She was wearing that awful, shapeless olive gown. Stephen dreamed of her dressed in a fine silk gown, the kind she would have worn at Ashley Grove. Remembering the tantalizing curves of her body, his wayward imagination began to *un*dress her, first the gown, then the petticoat, and finally her chemise.

His fingers worked at removing a string from a pod, but in his mind's eye they were busy undoing the fastenings of her chemise and letting it fall about her. A vivid image of her naked before him rose in his mind and had an instant effect on his own anatomy.

"What are you doing?"

Meg's angry question yanked Stephen back to the present. He discovered that while his mind had been imagining, his fingers had been popping open the pods with such vigor that the peas had flown well beyond the pot and landed on the floor.

"You will have to pick them up," Meg said.

As aroused as he was by his thoughts of her, he could not get out of bed to look for peas. He gave her a mulish look.

"You dropped them, you pick them up. Otherwise we will have mashed peas on the floor."

Smothering a curse, Stephen placed the bowl and the pot on the other side of him and climbed out of bed, thankful that Galloway's nightshirt was so long it fell to his knees. Glancing down to make certain he was well covered, he saw that his erection was making the damned garment stand out like a lopsided tent.

Hastily he grabbed the sheet and held it loosely around him as he bent over to pick up the peas from the dirt floor. He recovered them, only to discover that several more had rolled under the bed. He had to get down on his hands and knees to retrieve them.

As he did, his legs tangled in the sheet. Muttering a barnyard expletive, he yanked the sheet away and lowered his head so that he could spot the perverse peas under the bed. He was retrieving the final one when he heard Meg's shocked gasp. At the same instant, he felt the breeze on his behind. Bloody hell, his bare arse was sticking up in the air like a damned flag. He jumped up as though he'd just been prodded with a hot poker.

For God's sake, a lord of the British realm did not get caught with his backside hanging in the wind.

As he crawled back into bed, his face burning with embarrassment, Meg began to laugh. He might have known she would have an enchanting laugh, full-bodied and melodic.

"'Tis not that funny," he grumbled. But it had been worth his embarrassment to hear her laugh. He longed to hear her do so again.

He intended to find ways to make her laugh frequently.

After a moment, he stole a glance at her. She was

vigorously sweeping the hard-packed dirt floor of the cabin. Only the muffled giggles that escaped her betrayed that she was still thinking about the incident.

Stephen considered all she had lost. From mistress of Ashley Grove to this crude cabin—her story was as unhappy as his own. Yet instead of complaining about her lot, she did what had to be done. Her quiet strength and courage awed him.

Her damned brother Quentin ought to be shot for abandoning her and Josh in this dangerous and precarious situation.

Stephen felt badly that nursing him had added to her already heavy burden. He wished there was some way he could repay her kindness to him. If he escaped Flynt's tentacles and got back to England, he would send her a generous sum of money.

And he would see whether anything could be done to recover Ashley Grove for her and Josh.

Meg picked up a stick and began to draw something in the dirt. Stephen watched as an artistic display of flowers and leaves emerged on the floor. The design reminded him of a patterned carpet. "Why are you doing that?"

She gave him a sheepish smile. "'Tis foolish, I suppose, but it pleases me. It looks less like a dirt floor then."

Yes, it did. Perhaps Stephen would send her a carpet, too. She deserved one—and a hell of a lot more.

Meg looked up from the pattern she was making. "Where did you live in Yorkshire?"

"On my es—" He caught himself before he said estate. As suspicious as she was of him, she would probably think he was lying. "My, er, farm, Wingate Hall."

"Does your betrothed live in Yorkshire, too?"

Meg had picked up instantly on his hesitation when he had denied being betrothed. "I told you I am not betrothed."

Her expression called him a liar.

And perhaps he was lying, but he did not think so.

He had been betrothed before he had been seized and impressed at Dover, but he was certain that he no longer was.

He had been missing for two years and must be presumed dead. Knowing his beautiful betrothed, the ambitious, impatient Fanny Stoddard, Stephen could not imagine that she would still be waiting for him to reappear.

His mouth curled cynically. By now she would have found another man of sufficiently impressive title to marry.

The near certainty that Fanny had dropped him for another man ought to disturb him.

Instead it filled him with enormous relief.

He loved Fanny no more than she loved him. Men of his position did not marry for love. He had chosen her for her connections. Her father, Lord Stoddard, was one of the most powerful men in English politics.

The more Stephen had seen of Fanny after their betrothal, though, the more he had regretted his choice and secretly longed to escape. But a gentleman did not jilt his betrothed, and he had resigned himself, as so many men of his class did, to turning to his beautiful mistress, Lady Caroline Taber, for what he would not find in his marriage bed.

"Is your farm large?" Meg asked.

"Yes." He did not tell her how large. She would never believe him. Even now she was regarding him so skeptically that he was goaded into saying,

"I told you that I was a wealthy gentleman before I was wrongly impressed."

"You did not say you were wealthy." Her face told Stephen she thought he was spinning a tale. "I know enough of England to be quite certain that a wealthy man would not be impressed."

"True, but I was not seized by happenstance. My impressment was arranged by a very clever enemy."

Meg's eyes widened. "Who is he?"

"I wish to God I knew! Until I was seized I did not know I had any enemies."

Meg frowned. "Why do you think your impressment was deliberate?"

"Because I heard the two ruffians who grabbed me talking." Their rough voices still echoed in Stephen's memory: *'Twould be easier and safer to kill the cove and dump 'is body in the water than turn 'im o'er to the press gang.*

Nay, the cove what 'ired us wants 'im to die slow and hard, wants 'im to suffer aplenty afore 'e goes to 'is maker. If we wants our blunt, we does it 'is way.

Whoever Stephen's enemy was, he was diabolically shrewd. He had instructed the ruffians to tell the press gang that Stephen had been impersonating himself to obtain rich clothing and other items on credit from gullible merchants eager for an aristocrat's custom. Thus they explained away in one stroke the elegant garments Stephen wore and made certain no one would believe his declarations of his real identity.

But someday, somehow, Stephen would get back to England. Then he would unmask his enemy and exact his own retribution. He would make the bastard rue the day he had ever been born.

Chapter 7

⌒◯◯⌒

The next day, Stephen, clad in Galloway's long nightshirt, forced himself to get out of bed and move around the cabin despite Meg's objections that it was too soon.

His weakened body told him she was right, but he did not have the luxury of waiting. He must resume his flight through the wilderness as soon as he possibly could.

When the door to the cabin flew open, Stephen whirled toward it, his heart pounding in fear that it might be Flynt's hirelings. But it was only Josh.

"I've done my chores, Meg. Can I go over to Wilhelm's? I haven't ridden for days."

She nodded her assent. Josh let out a whoop of joy and ran out the door, clearly eager to be gone before she could change her mind.

Smiling, Meg turned to Stephen. "Josh loves to ride, and Wilhelm has two horses that he lets my brother exercise."

Stephen remembered the fine stable at Ashley Grove. "Your father raised racehorses, did he not?"

Meg's smile faded and her eyes became wistful. "Yes." She turned away hastily. "I must weed the vegetable garden."

67

Stephen followed her outside, cursing himself for reminding her of what she had lost.

Tree stumps were scattered around the clearing, which had two smaller structures besides the cabin. At the edge of the clearing, a path led through the trees toward the sound of rushing water.

While he watched Meg, Stephen sat on one of the tree stumps in the warm sunshine, listening to the chirp of robins and breathing deeply of the fresh, clean air scented with pine. He wished he was strong enough to help her. She was such an energetic and capable woman—and so talented. He and Josh had prevailed upon her to play her flute the previous night, and Stephen had been impressed by her ability.

When she finished working in the garden, she came over to him. "You have a faraway look in your eyes."

Stephen smiled. "Yes, I was thinking of Wingate Hall, my home in Yorkshire. When I was a boy, I loved walking through the woods there."

"How you must miss it."

"It is strange. When I lived in England, I preferred the excitement of London." Now when he thought of his native land, as he did so often, he did not yearn for the city but for the green valleys and heather-covered moors of Yorkshire. Would he ever see it again? he wondered dismally. He had had so much, and he had not appreciated it until he lost it. "Now what I miss most is my home, and I rarely think of London."

Meg started toward the shed that she called the barn, and Stephen tagged along. They passed the smallest of the three structures in the clearing. The clucking emanating from it told him it was a hen-house.

He put into words something that bothered him.

"You said you came here this spring, but the farm looks as though it was here longer than that."

"It was. Three years before my father died, he leased the land to a man named Matson, who settled it with his family. They cleared the land and raised the buildings. After Charles lost everything else, he tried to increase the rent on this land. The Matsons were barely eking out a living as it was. They abandoned the farm and moved on."

"So your stepfather decided to farm it himself? Did he have any experience at that?"

"The only experience Charles had was partying, gambling, and wooing rich widows," Meg said acidly.

"It makes no sense to me that a lazy wastrel like Galloway would have had any interest in trying to farm the frontier."

"I own I was surprised, too. After we arrived here I had the feeling that he did not expect to be here long. To tell you the truth, I thought it would be my stepfather, not Quentin, who would vanish." She shrugged. "Perhaps Charles would have, too, had he lived a little longer, but we were only here three weeks when he was killed."

The more Stephen heard about Galloway, the more suspicious he became of him. "You said he died in a fight?"

Meg nodded. "In a brawl with two strangers at the ordinary."

"What is an ordinary?"

"You would call it a tavern."

Meg and Stephen reached the barn. It held three animals: an ox, a milk cow, and an old swaybacked horse.

Stephen was dismayed. If that sorry horse was the only one the Drakes had, it was no wonder that

Josh was so eager to ride Wilhelm's mounts. "Is this all the livestock you own?"

Meg gestured toward the woods. "We have three pigs that we let root among the trees for food."

"What happened to the wagon and team that brought you here?"

"Charles sold it immediately after we arrived to a German family that was going back to Pennsylvania." Meg frowned. "I guess that contradicts my impression that he did not expect to be here long."

Or perhaps, Stephen thought, Charles did not intend to stay but wanted to ensure that his stepchildren could not leave with him.

Stephen and Meg walked back toward the cabin. He observed how crudely it was built. Its windows had no glass, only oiled paper and pine shutters that hung from leather hinges and could be lowered at night to seal the openings.

Stephen had pushed his weakened body as far as he dared, and when he reached the cabin, he retreated to bed. He was dozing off when he heard a shout outside the cabin.

Stephen jerked himself upright, instantly awake. *Flynt had found him!* He looked desperately at the window nearest his bed and wondered whether he could squeeze through it.

But he had no time to find out. A giant of a man, both in height and girth, ducked his head beneath the cabin's low door frame and shuffled inside.

He wore a deerskin hunting shirt similar to the one Meg was making for Stephen. He carried no gun, but his belt held a small, odd looking ax and a leather sheath containing a long knife.

Stephen could not help noticing the man's huge hands. They too could be lethal weapons. The giant's hair was the shade of sand. His round bovine face and flint-colored eyes gave Stephen the impression that his intelligence was as slow as his gait.

"Wilhelm! How good to see you." Meg's face lit up with a radiant, welcoming smile for her neighbor.

Stephen was startled by the sharp twist of jealousy he felt.

Meg asked, "What brings you here, Wilhelm?"

No doubt she was what had brought him, Stephen thought grimly.

Instead of answering, Wilhelm stared at Stephen with suspicion and distrust and unspoken male warning.

After a long silent minute, Meg pressed, "Why are you here? You are always in your fields at this time of day."

Wilhelm pointed at Stephen. "I come to see this man Josh told me of."

From the look Wilhelm gave Stephen, Josh's description of him had not been flattering.

When Meg introduced the two men, Wilhelm asked Stephen from where he hailed.

"Yorkshire, England."

There was another long pause, as though the answer required Wilhelm's careful consideration.

At last he asked, "Vhy you come?"

Stephen had given Meg part of the truth, but he had no desire to discuss what had brought him here with anyone else. "I am on my way to my brother's. He is a captain in the British army in New York."

Wilhelm continued to stare silently at Stephen for another minute, then said, "I vatch out for Fräulein Drake." There could be no mistaking the hard threat in those flinty eyes. "You understand?"

"She will come to no harm from me," Stephen said, a hard edge of anger to his voice. He was

getting damned tired of having his honor ques-
tioned. "Even if I were that kind of man, and I am
not, I would not repay her kindness with evil. *You*
understand?"

Apparently not immediately, for the man continued to scrutinize him suspiciously for another minute. Then he reached into a pocket in his long
deerskin shirt and pulled out a folded paper that
he handed to Meg. "I found this on my fence. Vill
you read it to me?"

So the ignorant fool was illiterate, Stephen
thought contemptuously. And this was the man
who Josh thought could do anything?

Meg unfolded the paper, studied it, then looked
up. "It offers a reward for the return of an indentured servant who escaped and is believed to have
come over the Blue Ridge Mountains in this direction."

A chill enveloped Stephen. Had Hiram Flynt already papered the frontier with a description of
him?

Meg said, "The runaway, a man named Tom
Grise, is described as being about five-foot-five and
balding with light brown hair."

Stephen stifled a sigh of relief that he was not
the subject of the notice.

Meg refolded the paper and handed it back to
Wilhelm. "I am surprised that it was put on your
fence. Usually these notices are posted at the ordinary where they will be seen by more people."

"Perhaps it vas posted there as well." Wilhelm
put the paper back in his pocket. "Do you need
anything done vhile I am here?"

"No," Megan said. "You have already done so
much for us. I wish I had some way to repay you."

Certain of the repayment Wilhelm would eventually seek from her, Stephen was astonished when

the giant replied, "You already repay me. You save both my vife and my little Villy."

Stephen's feelings for Wilhelm mellowed with startling rapidity upon learning he had a wife.

After he departed, Stephen asked Meg, "How did you save his wife and child?"

"Willy was a breech birth and for a time—" Meg shrugged. "But I managed to deliver him."

She said it so calmly, as though such a crisis were an everyday occurrence. What an indomitable woman she was. He was deeply impressed by her quiet strength and unfailing calm and cheerfulness in the face of challenges that would have reduced most women to hysteria.

He looked down admiringly at her small, slender hands. Such adept hands.

"I do not know what we would have done without Wilhelm. Despite all he has to do on his own farm, he does what he can to help us. He has taught us so much."

Stephen was incredulous. "That ignorant slow-wit taught you?"

Meg's gray eyes glittered with sudden fury. "He is not a slow-wit! He merely likes to ruminate a bit before he says something. More people ought to cultivate that trait. Nor is he ignorant. He has merely had a different education than yours."

Her passionate defense of Wilhelm goaded Stephen into saying contemptuously, "Why he cannot even read."

"Perhaps not, but when it comes to farming and how to live on the frontier, no one knows more than he does. Wilhelm is the *only* man I can think of who would be more help than hindrance around here."

Meg's pointed jab hit its mark, and Stephen said recklessly, "You have not seen what I can do."

"Nor will I! I want you gone as soon as you are able to move on."

"You will have your wish," he retorted stiffly, miffed that she thought so little of him. "I am as anxious to leave as you are to have me go."

That night, as Meg was finishing the hunting shirt for Stephen and her brother was cleaning his musket, Josh said, "Play your flute for us, Meg."

She wished that she could oblige him, but she had not the time. "I must finish this shirt so our guest can leave as soon as he is able."

"How anxious you are to be rid of me." Stephen, who was sitting up in bed propped against the pillows, asked mockingly, "Are you not afraid you will miss me?"

Meg feared that would indeed be the case, but she was not about to admit it to him. "Not likely," she said tartly. "But as Shakespeare said, 'Unbidden guests are often welcomest when they are gone.'"

Josh looked up again from cleaning his musket. "Speaking of Shakespeare, Meg, you promised you would read me *Macbeth*. I enjoy it so much more when you read it to me. You make a story come alive."

"Perhaps after I finish this shirt."

"Would you permit me to read it to you?" Stephen asked Meg. "It seems the least I can do in repayment for the shirt."

His offer pleased her. She put the shirt aside and went over to the small leather trunk that held her most precious possessions, including the half dozen books that were all her stepfather had allowed her to bring from her father's large library at Ashley Grove.

She pulled out the big volume of Shakespeare's

plays, with the bard's name stamped in gold on the leather cover, and gave it to Stephen.

He proved to be as good a reader as Meg had ever heard. And he clearly knew the play well. In the opening scene, he rendered the voices of the three witches shrill and cackling. In the second scene, Duncan spoke in the low and sonorous tones that befitted a king.

As the play progressed, Stephen employed a wide range of voices to distinguish the characters from each other.

Meg glanced up from her sewing and saw that Josh had become so engrossed in the play that he had stopped cleaning the musket.

When Stephen finished reading, Meg said, "You are a fine thespian." Although her compliment was sincere, his skill troubled her. Such a man could make any tale, including one of wrongful impressment and daring escape, sound believable. "Was acting perchance your profession in England?"

He grinned. "My theatrics there were confined to the amateur ones that my mother loved to put on at our home while I was growing up." His smile vanished, and his face turned grim as though the memory caused him pain.

"Why do you look so sad?" Meg inquired.

He stared at the book in his lap. "Like so many things I had, I did not appreciate either my parents or my home until I had lost them."

The sorrow and regret in his voice tugged at Meg's heart. She found herself wanting to take his hands in hers to comfort him as he had comforted her when she told him about her father.

She caught herself. What was wrong with her?

Meg knew what Stephen Wingate must be, yet she could not seem to resist him. She was shocked and unnerved at how quickly this man managed to demolish her wariness. What had happened to the strong-willed woman who had run Ashley Grove with a firm, intelligent hand, her emotions always in check?

The next morning, as Meg emerged from the henhouse with three eggs in her basket, Josh trudged off to weed the corn.

When she went into the cabin, Stephen, still dressed in Charles Galloway's overlarge nightshirt, was seated at the trestle table before the tin basin with her father's razor in his hand. He had removed the cracked looking glass from the wall and propped it against the basin.

He had tried to shave himself yesterday, too, and had nicked his handsome face so often and muttered so many curses that Meg had insisted on finishing the job.

Now she said, "Pray, let me do it. It will be easier on your face and my ears."

He laughed, that infectious laugh of his that sent excitement twisting through her, and held out the razor to her.

"My face will be eternally grateful."

When Meg finished shaving him, he examined his face in the looking glass. "An excellent job," he complimented her.

"Thank you." She had never paid much heed to compliments before, dismissing them as vain flattery, and she wondered why his should fill her with such pleasure. Especially when he was a man she dared not trust.

Meg went to the oak chest that contained her late stepfather's belongings and rummaged through the useless, elegant clothes that he had brought to wear on the frontier.

"What are you doing?" Stephen asked.

"You will need a pair of breeches to wear under the hunting shirt I made for you. Charles had a buckskin pair that you could have."

Near the bottom of the chest, below a packet of letters and documents tied with a purple ribbon, she found the garment she was seeking and handed it to Stephen. "Try it on."

"Only if you turn your back and promise not to look," he teased. "I am a modest man."

"I doubt that," Meg retorted. But from some of the conversations she had overheard among men, she guessed that a male of his puny "endowments" would be sensitive about them, and she did as he bade.

When he told her she could turn around, he had donned the breeches and taken off the nightshirt, exposing his tanned chest. Her eyes feasted on it. Nature might have cheated Stephen in his endowments below the waist, but it certainly had not been stingy above it.

He was looking dubiously at the breeches. Meg's stepfather had been much larger in the hips and waist.

Meg reached for her sewing basket. "I shall have to take them in."

As she pinned the side seams, Stephen grew strangely silent. His breathing seemed more labored.

When she turned her attention to the rear of the garment, she could not help staring admiringly at the curve of his trim, slim-hipped backside. A strange insidious heat curled within her.

Then she blushed furiously as she realized what she was studying. Surely no respectable woman noticed such a thing about a man, did she?

Forcing her mind back to the task at hand, Meg smoothed the buckskin down to see where she would need to take tucks. There was something very exciting about his firm body beneath her hands, and they lingered there a moment longer than necessary. He jerked convulsively beneath her hands, ruining her effort.

When she tried a second time to smooth the material down over his backside, she heard his sharp intake of breath. A muttered expletive escaped his lips.

She decided the back of the breeches would require two rather deep tucks from the waist down. She slipped her fingers beneath the buckskin, groping to form one of the darts. The feel of his skin, surprisingly soft and warm against her fingers, sent a tingling through her.

With her other hand she patted the material to make certain it lay properly. She lost her grip on the tuck. Her fingers moved between the cloth and his skin, working to fold it again.

Just as she poked the pin through the buckskin to mark the dart, he uttered a vicious curse. "What the hell are you trying to do to me?"

Thinking she had stuck him with the pin, she said contritely, "I am sorry."

Without removing her hand from his waist, she slid it along his skin—marveling again at how smooth and soft it was—to where she wanted to take the second dart.

"So you are sorry, are you?" he asked in a dangerous voice. "Why is it I do not believe that?"

Startled by both his tone and his question, she glanced questioningly up at him. He was looking down at her over his shoulder, his blue violet eyes glittering with an odd fire.

"Surely you cannot think that I meant to stick you with the pin."

He blinked at her. "Bloody hell, is that what you think I am talking about?"

"Well, yes," she answered in confusion. "What else could I have done to cause you discomfort?"

Amusement tugged at the corners of his mouth. "What else indeed?"

She pinned the second dart in place, then said briskly, "Now let me see what tucks need to be taken in the front."

She thought he would turn around for her, but to her astonishment he jerked away, keeping his back to her. "I think not."

"What?" she stammered.

"Believe me, at the moment the front of these breeches needs no tucks at all," he said in a strangled voice.

"Are you certain?" she asked dubiously.

"Very certain, my innocent."

"Why did you call me that?"

"Because you do not understand why I did."

"You are talking in riddles," Meg cried in exasperation.

"Sometimes it is best when conversing with innocents. Now you must excuse me. I have a pressing need to go outside."

He sounded as though he was truly in pain, and that worried her. "Why? A call of nature?"

He chuckled ruefully. "You could describe it as that."

To her amazement he sidled sideways toward the door, carefully keeping his back to Meg.

Men, she thought. Would she ever understand them?

Chapter 8

The following day, after Josh had milked the cow and fed the animals, he picked up his musket and announced he was going out to hunt a wild hare or turkey for dinner.

Meg looked up from making her bed and reminded her brother, "You have not chopped the wood yet. There is barely enough left to keep the fire going until tomorrow."

"Ah, Meg, I will do it as soon as I get back from hunting, I promise."

Josh loved to hunt, and she could see how eager he was to get into the woods. She hated to stop him. "Very well, if you promise you will do it as soon as you get back."

"I promise, honor of a Drake," Josh assured her as he rushed outside, musket in hand.

"You should not have let him go until he chopped the wood," Stephen said with a frown. He was standing by the fireplace, wearing the hunting shirt that Meg had made for him and the buckskin breeches that she had altered.

It had been five days now since he had regained consciousness, and he had put on some weight. His ribs were no longer so noticeable, and some of the gauntness had left his face, making him even more handsome.

His strength was returning rapidly now, his abused feet were nearly healed, and his back looked much better, although he would always bear the scars of the whip. Soon he would be able to move on. Meg should have been pleased to be rid of him, but instead the thought of his departure pained her.

"You have been asking Josh to cut wood for days now, Meg, and he has not done it."

"You think I was too easy on him, but I know how much he hates to chop wood." Meg finished making her bed and turned her attention to wiping the crumbs from the trestle table.

"He ignores other chores, too, and you end up doing them for him."

Stephen was right about that, Meg thought. Quentin, who charmed his way out of so much, had been a poor example for Josh. And Charles Galloway an even worse one, although Josh had not paid much attention to that sorry excuse of a man.

"You should insist Josh do his chores first."

Meg smiled pensively. "I know, but I have a difficult time being too hard on him. Poor Josh has lost so much."

Stephen turned to face her. "He has lost no more than you have."

Frowning, she said, "But he has. He has lost his future. My brother excels at every subject but Latin. Papa intended for him to go to college at William and Mary in Williamsburg or north to Harvard. Or perhaps even to England. But now Josh has no hope of that. I would give anything to be able to send him to college, but since I cannot,

I am determined to make this farm into something for him."

"And what of your future, Meg? You deserve better than this crude cabin in the wilderness."

She shrugged. "Life is full of surprises."

"Aye, it is."

The sudden bitterness of Stephen's tone reminded Meg that if his story was true, he had lost even more than she and her brother.

"You do Josh no favors by making excuses for him, Meg."

"No doubt you are right. But even though he does not do all he should, he does a good deal. Without Josh's help, I could not hope to make it here."

Stephen was watching her intently. "Your burden will be a little lighter tomorrow. I will be leaving at dawn."

Meg felt a sharp pain in the vicinity of her heart. She had not expected him to leave quite so soon. She forced herself to say emphatically, "Good!"

Something that could have been disappointment flashed in his eyes, then he said with an edge to his voice, "So you are delighted to be almost rid of me."

"Where will you go?" Meg was proud of how steady she managed to keep her voice.

"I will work my way west and north to New York to reach my brother. I pray that he is still in New York."

And Meg prayed that Stephen would get that far. Surviving on the frontier took skills that she feared he did not have. "When you leave, follow the path through the trees to the main road and head north on it. It will take you into Pennsylvania. That is where Wilhelm came from, and he can give you directions on what you should do when you get there. You will pass his place in about a half mile."

Meg's tone was so matter-of-fact that she was sure Stephen could have no inkling her emotions were in turmoil.

He sounded as though he truly did have a brother in New York. She wondered again whether he was a gentleman wrongly impressed as he claimed or the dangerous convict that the marks on his body indicated. Meg no longer knew what to think about her midnight stranger.

Except that she was going to miss him.

She busied herself making an extra large batch of johnnycake that he could take with him.

A little later, wanting solitude in which to sort out her roiling emotions about his departure, Meg slipped away from the cabin with a blanket and her comb, brush, towel, and a container of soap stuffed into a wooden bucket, intending to wash her hair.

Stephen called after her, "Where are you going?"

"To the watering place," she answered as she started down the path that led through myrtles and cedars and red flowering maples to the spot three dozen yards behind the cabin.

There pure, sweet water from a spring bubbled up from the earth, then danced down a miniature cascade into the stream that flowed through their land on its way to the Gerando River. They took their water from this spring.

Meg made her way below the cascade where the stream had left a small half-moon of sand along its bank. It was a peaceful spot, well hidden from the cabin by the drop in elevation and the thick growth of trees that scented the air.

She spread the blanket on the sand, warmed by the midday sun, unpacked the contents of the bucket, and filled it with water. Taking off her cap, she removed the pins from her long honey-colored hair, brushed it, then began to wash it.

Normally she performed this ritual in the cabin, but she could not bring herself to do it with Stephen there to watch her. It seemed far too intimate an act to perform in front of a man—though, oddly, she had often done it in Josh's presence. Was it only with Stephen Wingate that she felt such unease?

After rinsing the soap from her hair, Meg combed it out, then lay facedown on the blanket and spread her wet tresses around her so the midday sun overhead would dry them. She was so tired that she promptly fell asleep.

Stephen wished that Meg would come back to the cabin. He missed her when she was not here, missed her low sensual voice and the touch of her hand.

It wounded him that Meg did not seem to care he was leaving. As nearly as he could tell, she was utterly indifferent to his departure. He had hoped that she would want to spend the remainder of his brief time here with him, but instead she had disappeared.

Restlessly he moved to the cabin door and looked out, but he saw no sign of her.

Although he was still weak and far from his old self, he dared wait no longer before pushing on. He had been here too long already.

But he was not anxious to leave this cabin and the woman who lived in it. He told himself it was because she had been so kind to him, the first person who had been so since he had been torn from his other life. And it ate at his conscience to have to abandon her here on this rough, dangerous frontier.

He pondered his strange attraction to her. She was not beautiful as so many of the women who had thrown themselves at him in London had been, yet he was drawn to her as he had never been before. But they had been idle, vain, self-absorbed women, and Meg was none of those things. She was kind and selfless.

He cursed her damned brother Quentin for deserting her and Josh. The irresponsible cad ought to be whipped before the cart. Stephen's hands tightened into fists at the thought of what he would do to Quentin if he ever saw him. The bastard did not deserve a sister like Meg.

Stephen wondered what she could be doing. She had never been gone from the cabin so long—close to two hours, he estimated.

As more minutes crept by, he grew increasingly worried about her. She had said she was going to the watering place.

Bloody hell, what if she had fallen in?

The thought propelled him through the door at a run and down the path he had seen her taking through the trees. The faint sound of rushing water grew louder, telling him he was headed in the right direction.

Soon he reached a profusion of young willows in full leaf, then a spring that bubbled from the earth and tumbled down a small incline into the stream below.

There, near the bottom of the little cascade, he caught sight of a woman, her back to him, standing on a small crescent of sand. She was stretching sinuously, as though she had just awakened.

Stephen's breath caught as he saw her glorious hair, honey touched with gold, that fell to her waist and swirled around her in thick, silken waves. A twig cracked beneath his foot.

The woman turned, the shining curtain of her hair rippling provocatively around her, and he saw her face.

Megan Drake's face.

For a moment, he could not believe that the magnificent fall of hair could be hers.

He pushed through the willow screen toward her, unable to drag his eyes from her.

When Stephen reached her, he touched her burnished hair and found it as soft as the finest silk beneath his fingers. He ran his hands almost reverently down the long tresses. He could not help himself.

"My God, Megan, how could you hide such beauty beneath that dreadful cap?" Initially Stephen had thought Megan too pretty a name for her, but now he knew that it fit her perfectly.

She opened her mouth, but no sound came out. She stared up at him with big, startled gray eyes, fringed with a thick sweep of golden lashes. She reminded him of a frightened fawn. The scent of soap and orange blossoms mingled in a heady perfume, both sweet and sensual, that enveloped him.

"Megan, Megan," he murmured. He could not resist her lips any more than he could resist the shimmering waves of her hair that swirled around her like an erotic veil.

Meg, her heart pounding like an Indian drum, watched as Stephen Wingate's mouth descended toward hers. He was going to kiss her, and she should stop him. But she did not, conceding to herself that she wanted him to do so, wanted to see what his kiss would be like.

She had been kissed before, and she had not

liked it very much. Would Stephen's kiss be different?

His lips touched hers lightly, like the soft, tantalizing brush of swansdown, and then they were gone. It was so gentle and provocative that her own lips parted slightly in surprise. She was certain that her eyes must mirror her wonder.

A knowing smile curved his sensuous mouth. He brushed her lips again as subtly as a barely heard whisper. He smelled of cinnamon and sunshine. His blue violet eyes, so near her own, were watching her through midnight black lashes.

A third time his mouth dipped to caress hers with its enticing, all too brief touch. Their breaths mingled, warm and moist. Strange sensations blossomed within Meg, and a small moan escaped her lips.

His mouth met hers again. This time it lingered in a long, tender kiss that was unlike anything she had ever experienced. It made her ache for something that she had never suspected existed. His tongue took advantage of her surprise to tease her mouth with a lazy, tantalizing dance while his hands smoothed her hair in long, seductive strokes.

A heat that was both pleasure and hunger gripped Meg, and she trembled. Her response seemed to fire his own ardor. His kiss grew harder, more demanding, more exciting.

The heat within her flared into open flame, incinerating her doubts and the constraints of propriety. Mindless of what she was doing, she returned his kiss with unschooled passion and a hunger that matched his own.

She had never returned a man's kiss before. Until now she had been the passive recipient, but she could be passive no longer.

Yet she did not know what to do, so her tongue

mimicked his in the hope of returning a little of the pleasure he was giving her.

Apparently she succeeded, for she heard him groan.

His hand slipped from her hair to cup her breast in his hand, his thumb gently rubbing its tip. Her body seemed to turn to liquid fire beneath his touch. For a moment she was held in such thrall that she could comprehend nothing but the exquisite pleasure that was coursing through her.

After awhile, how long she had no idea, his hands moved to the buttons on her dress and began to undo them. That shocked her into jerking her mouth away from his with a gasp. She pushed his hands from her dress.

"How could you, Mr. Wingate?" Her voice was shaky and not nearly as indignant as it ought to have been.

He raised one of his thick, handsomely arched brows mockingly. "So we are back to Mr. Wingate, are we? And after what we just shared?"

"Because of what *you* just did!" she shot back.

He gave her an unrepentant smile. "The blame is not mine alone, Megan. You liked what we did. You wanted it. Do not deny that."

She did not try. He was right, and she was too honest to lie. Her face flamed in embarrassment. Without a word she turned and fled down the path toward the cabin.

Meg stumbled through the door, her cheeks still a hot red. She shivered at the memory of the desire and the excitement that Stephen had stoked in her body. The fact that he clearly knew the effect he had on her only added to her humiliation.

Oh, yes, he was a man who knew his own charm very well. In her agitation, she began braiding her hair with quick, jerky movements.

How could she have acted so . . . so wantonly with a stranger who would be leaving on the morrow, never to return again?

A stranger who bore the marks of a dangerous convict.

Why she was a bigger fool than her mother had been over Charles! Everyone knew that Galloway had been trying to marry a fortune for years. Yet Mama had fallen so easily for his flattering, obvious lies. Meg had been embarrassed by the spectacle Mama had made of herself, fluttering and cooing and batting her eyes whenever Charles came near her, acting like a silly sixteen-year-old instead of the mother of grown children.

Watching her mama, Meg had sworn that she would never be guilty of such foolish behavior over any man, and especially not a scoundrel like Charles Galloway.

Now her pride was shredded by her body's reaction to a man whom she feared was a liar and perhaps worse.

Much, much worse.

No matter how convincing the tale he told, no decent, honorable man bore the scars of whip and shackles that he did.

She was so mortified at her own weakness that she was not certain she could bear to face him again. Thank God, he would be leaving on the morrow.

But even as she told herself this, she felt a sharp pain in her heart that she would never see him again.

She wound her long braid around her head and fastened it. As she snatched a cap from the wall peg on which it hung, Stephen came through the door of the cabin, carrying the blanket and the wooden bucket she had left by the stream.

He handed the bucket to her, and she saw that it contained her towel, soap, comb, and brush. He must have gathered them up after she fled to the cabin.

"Thank you," she said, avoiding his eyes. She set the bucket down and began to put on the cap.

He plucked it from her hand and hid it behind his back. "Please do not wear that." His voice was husky. "Your hair is much too beautiful to hide."

"Next you will try to tell me that I am the most beautiful woman you have ever met," Meg said scornfully, trying to harden her heart against him.

And failing utterly.

"No, I will not tell you that." His eyes were grave, the color of a troubled sky at sunset. His fingertips brushed her cheek lightly. "I will not lie to you, Megan."

She feared that lying was all Stephen Wingate or Earl Arlington or Billy Gunnell or whatever his name was had been doing all along. Her eyes narrowed. "Who is the most beautiful woman you have ever seen?"

He shrugged. "It hardly matters."

"Who?" she persisted, remembering his delirious cries. "Rachel?"

For a moment he looked astonished, then he chuckled ruefully. "Well, yes. As a matter of fact, she is."

"Then it is she that you should be kissing as you just kissed me."

He grinned, a charmingly boyish, endearing smile that broke her heart. "No, I cannot kiss Rachel like that."

"Why? Because she is not here?" Another, more shocking thought occurred to Meg. "Or because she is married to someone else?"

His grin widened. "No, because she is my sister."

Meg's jaw went slack. She knew that she was gaping, but she could not help it. Rachel was his sister! Her heart, instantly mended, seemed to do a wild little dance in her chest.

"I told you I had a sister in England and a brother in New York."

"Yes." Meg was so flustered that she began to babble. "I must start dinner. I was at the stream far longer than I intended. I fell asleep. I must have slept for two hours."

Meg started toward the fireplace, only to stop abruptly at the belated realization that Josh had not returned from hunting.

He should have been back before now. Fear ripped through her at the possibility that something had happened to him. Every dreadful story she had ever heard assailed her mind: the bear that had attacked and killed the hunter who was trying to slay him, the panther that had jumped and mauled a traveler, a buck elk with magnificent antlers that had tried to gore a curious lad of fifteen.

"Bloody hell, Megan, what is it?" Stephen's alarmed voice penetrated her frightened mind.

"Josh! He has not come back from hunting. Something has happened to him. We've got to find him."

"Perhaps he did not find anything to kill and is still looking. Or perhaps he stopped at Wilhelm's."

"No! Josh knows that if he has not found anything by early afternoon, he must come back regardless. I tell you, something has happened to him."

To her relief, Stephen did not waste time arguing

with her. "Did you see in which direction Josh was headed when he left?"

Meg nodded, pointing to a path that led southeast through the woods.

As they hurried along it, they took turns calling Josh's name, but the only answer was the raucous screech of a mockingbird.

After they had followed the path for what seemed to Meg like several centuries, but was probably no more than ten minutes, they heard a faint cry of "Help, help," ahead of them and to the left. Stephen instantly veered off the path, pushing his way through the scratchy undergrowth directly toward the sound.

They found Josh propped up against the trunk of a maple tree, his musket and the carcass of a wild turkey beside him.

Meg fell to her knees beside him. "What is it?"

"My ankle. I caught my foot under a tree root, tripped, and fell. Now I cannot put my weight on it."

She did not need to ask Josh which one he had hurt. Above the soft moccasin his right ankle was swollen to more than twice its normal size.

When Meg finished examining it thoroughly, she said, "I do not think any bones are broken, although it is so swollen I cannot tell for certain. You will not be able to walk on it for a while."

Meg tried to hide her dismay. He would be laid up for days, perhaps longer. She swallowed hard. She already had more than she could handle, and she did not know how she would manage without his help. Meg fought against the wave of despair that threatened to flatten her.

With the yoke contraption on his shoulders, Stephen made his way from the stream to the Drake cabin. He was nearly staggering beneath the weight of two full buckets.

As he stepped into the cabin, Megan was still bent over Josh, tending to his injured ankle. Stephen smiled at the sight of her. Since he had seen that magnificent, shimmering veil of hair and had shared that shattering kiss with her, he could think of her only as Megan.

It fit her better. Meg did not do her justice.

Once she had realized that Josh was missing, she forgot all about putting her cap back on. Before they had gone in search of the boy, Stephen had unobtrusively hung it on a wall peg by the door.

Meg flashed him one of her luminous smiles and thanked him for bringing the water, then turned her attention back to her brother.

It had not been easy for her and Stephen to get the boy back to the cabin, but by supporting him between them they had managed. From the look of Josh's injury, he would not be able to walk for several days.

Stephen set the buckets down by the fireplace. Now that he had transported their weight himself, he was surprised that a thin halfling like Josh had managed them.

He contemplated all the work that had to be done around the farm, far too much for Megan to do alone. Even with Josh it was too much, but it sure as hell was without him. *If it were not for Josh's help, I could not hope to make it here.*

No, she could not. She already worked from dawn until long after dark. Stephen thought of how small and thin and fragile Megan looked, thought of her struggling with these heavy buckets of water that Josh carried into the cabin every day.

Seeing the fireplace reminded Stephen of Josh's promise to chop wood when he returned from hunting, a promise that he would now be unable to keep for days.

Stephen turned and went back outside. Megan might not be willing to admit it, but she had to have a man's help.

And Stephen could not leave at dawn as he had planned, abandoning her in her need. He would have to stay and help her until Josh was back on his feet.

He caught himself abruptly. What the hell was wrong with him that he could even think of staying here?

Had he lost his bloody mind?

He had to flee, and he had to do it now. If he did not, he would be caught and dragged back in chains to Flynt.

Stephen had seen what Flynt did to recaptured slaves and indentured servants, from the hideous pothook around their necks to the whippings and the other, more subtle forms of torture he enjoyed inflicting.

Any hope Stephen had of returning to his former life in England and of avenging himself on his unknown enemy would be gone forever.

Flynt was tenacious about finding the human properties that fled from him. The rewards he offered for their return were so generous that he liked to brag no one had escaped him permanently. They had all been found and dragged back to their horrific fate. No wonder no one even tried to escape from Flynt any more.

Except Stephen.

And no one had ever escaped from Flynt twice.

Stephen could not risk being recaptured. If he stayed here any longer, he surely would be. He could not remain, no matter how much he wanted to help Megan. He had to run.

But the thought of leaving her when she needed him so badly twisted his gut.

Chapter 9

Stephen sat on a bench near the door of the Drake cabin, listening to Megan's soothing, smoky voice as she talked to her injured brother.

She was not at all like the beautiful, helpless females who had caught his attention in his former life. Yet he felt a need to protect her that he had never felt for them. Not even for his exquisite mistress, Lady Caroline Taber, the most beautiful woman he had ever seen after his sister Rachel.

He had had many affairs, and he thought himself a sophisticated man of the world. But if the truth be known, he had been damned near as shaken by the kisses that he and Megan had shared today as she was. Those few moments with her by the cascade had been as sweet and as exciting as Stephen had ever known.

And Megan had been so kind to him, taking him in when no woman in her right mind should have done so. How could he repay her by deserting her now when she desperately needed help?

Once again he cursed Quentin for abandoning her and Josh like this. Stephen's mouth twisted in disgust. How could any man treat his sister with such callous unconcern, shoving on her shoulders the burden that belonged to him as the eldest son and head of the family?

How indeed? a nagging little voice within him asked. *What of Rachel?*

Stephen froze. Had he not burdened his own sister with the management of his estate so he could pursue his life of pleasure in London and on the Continent?

But that had been different, he told himself. He had left her in the safety and security of a large, prosperous estate, surrounded by servants and tenants who loved her. He had not abandoned her unprotected on a hostile and dangerous frontier.

But you left her to manage an estate that was your responsibility. Was it so very different?

Of course it was. Rachel loved running Wingate Hall. And she was so good at it. Stephen was very proud of his little sister's talent for management. Rachel was far better at it than he was, and he was the first to admit it.

Just as Megan is undoubtedly much more competent than Quentin was here on the frontier.

But that did not make Quentin's deserting her right, any more than Stephen's leaving Rachel to manage his inheritance while he pursued his heedless, irresponsible life had been right.

If only Stephen had listened to the Duke of Westleigh instead of following the hedonistic example of Anthony Denton, widely heralded as the most irresistible rake in London. A few years older than Stephen, Denton was the mentor and leader of an exclusive, much envied group of pleasure seeking young aristocrats.

Stephen was honored when he was asked to join that sophisticated, sought-after circle. Its members' lives were given over to the pursuit of pleasure, and they ridiculed those who embraced more sober and responsible existences.

Now Stephen wondered why he had not seen its members for what they really were.

Or his own behavior for what it was.

Westleigh had tried to tell him. The duke's contemptuous assessment echoed in his mind: *Your problem, Arlington, is you think of no one but yourself and your own selfish pleasures.*

Stephen had hated Westleigh for his criticism, but now he was forced to concede that the duke had been right.

What if Rachel was having problems at Wingate Hall? Who would help her? George was in America. The only other Wingate male, their Uncle Alfred, was an old fool who would be of no help at all to Rachel.

She was worth a dozen Alfreds. Only a few months before Stephen's departure, his uncle had proved yet again that he was an idiot by marrying Sir John Cresswell's ambitious, wanton widow. Stephen had tried in vain to talk Alfred out of the marriage. Everyone but his uncle, who was three decades older than his new bride, knew that she had married him only for his connection to the Wingate family.

No, Uncle Alfred would be of no help at all to Rachel if problems arose at Wingate Hall, Stephen thought with a worried sigh. He belatedly appreciated how wrong it had been for him to go haring off to the Continent, foisting his responsibility for Wingate Hall on his sister.

And it would be more wrong to desert Megan now when she needed help so desperately. Yes, he owed it to Megan to stay after all she had done for him. Even if he were not so indebted to her, he could not abandon her here.

Stephen would have to stay until Josh was back on his feet, no matter what the price might be to himself.

He fervently hoped that shaving the unkempt whiskers from his face, cutting his hair, and wearing frontier-style clothing had altered his appearance enough that the men tracking him to collect the reward Flynt offered would not recognize him.

But if he was caught! He shuddered, then pushed the thought from his mind. He would not allow himself to think about what would happen to him then.

Stephen rose from the bench to go into the cabin to tell Megan. He smiled in anticipation of her relief when he told her that he would stay to help her. She had tried to hide it, but he had seen her look of dismay bordering on despair when she had assessed the severity of Josh's injury.

Yes, Megan would be so grateful. His smile broadened as he thought of some of the ways that he would like her to express her gratitude.

When he came into the cabin, she was peeling potatoes for dinner. She looked up questioningly as he strode over to her.

"I will not be departing tomorrow. I cannot go off and leave you here with Josh laid up like this."

She looked at Stephen blankly as though she did not understand what he was saying, so he spelled it out. "I will stay here and help you until his ankle is better." He awaited her joyous response.

"Help me?" Megan sounded confounded by the idea, as though it was such a novel concept she could not grasp it. Then she blurted, "But you cannot even shave yourself."

So she had guessed the truth about that, had she? Stephen felt his face grow red with mortification as he realized what scorn this woman, who was so dauntingly competent, must feel for him.

"You intend to do Josh's chores?" Megan was regarding him with such skepticism that Stephen was chagrined.

Well, he would prove himself to her. By God, he would! He recalled that Josh milked the cow every morning and night. He would begin with that. He picked up the empty milk bucket by the cabin door.

"I am going to milk the cow."

Megan's gray eyes widened in surprise. "You know how?"

Actually he did not, but the incredulity in her voice raked Stephen's pride. He would milk that damn cow or die trying. How hard could it be? He remembered the pretty bevy of young milkmaids who were employed to perform the task on Wingate Hall's sizable dairy herd.

If they could do it with such seeming ease, surely he could, too. "I know how," he lied gruffly.

"You will also need to feed and water the animals and muck out the barn," Josh said.

Stephen stiffened, affronted at the thought of a lord of the realm mucking out a damned barn. He drew the line at that.

"I do it every night," Josh said.

"I see I have my work cut out for me," Stephen muttered in resignation.

Meg watched Stephen stride purposefully toward the barn, milk pail in hand. She called after him, "Be sure you wash the cow's udder and flanks well before you begin milking her."

She had never dreamed that he would offer to help her. Her past experience had shown her that men could not be depended upon. They had failed her when she had most needed them.

Yet this man, whom she had not dared to trust at all, had volunteered to stay.

And turned her thinking about him upside down.

Surely he could not be as bad as the scars on him indicated.

Meg had a good notion of how desperate Stephen was to continue his flight into the wilderness and what he risked by remaining here to help her. She had seen how he jumped at unexpected sounds, fearing his past had caught up with him.

She was deeply moved and grateful to him that he was staying, even though she feared he would prove as inept as Quentin. At least he was observant enough to have some idea of what needed to be done.

Somehow the terrible weight of responsibility that Meg had felt crushing her since Josh had injured himself seemed a little lighter now.

But Meg also knew that the burst of elation she felt at Stephen's announcement was more complicated than simple gratitude. She was too honest not to admit to herself that deep in her heart she had not wanted him to leave. Much of her joy that he was staying had nothing to do with his performing Josh's chores for her.

Meg was attracted to Stephen Wingate in a way she had never before been attracted to a man.

Her breath unconsciously quickened at the memory of how he had looked at her this afternoon when he had discovered her by the stream. The strange, exciting heat that had gripped her then now permeated her again. His startled, almost awed appreciation when he had first seen her hair had made her feel for the first time in her life as though she was attractive, maybe even beautiful.

Not that it was true. Meg Drake had been born

with many advantages, but beauty was not one of them.

Josh said, "I am glad Mr. Wingate is going to stay."

Meg looked up from the potato she was peeling. "I do not think that he is as bad as I first thought." Her brother's face was very serious. "If he were, he would not have offered to stay."

She prayed that Josh was right and that she was not as blind to Stephen Wingate's real character as her mother had been to Charles Galloway's.

When Stephen reached the barn, the black-and-white cow looked at him with one big, bored bovine eye, then ignored him.

The damned cow had about as much regard for him as Megan Drake did! He had expected her to be ecstatic that he had decided to stay. Instead she bloody well didn't want him around.

It surprised him how much Megan's lack of enthusiasm and appreciation for his offer to help her had wounded him. Ah, the irony of it. For the first time in his life, he had put someone else ahead of himself, and she did not even appreciate it.

Megan had no conception at all of what he risked by staying here. Not only his future and any hope of returning to England but his very life.

And for what? To muck out a barn!

Stephen realized to his dismay that he did not have the foggiest notion of how to do that. Everything about a barn, including milking a cow, was a mystery to him.

It would not have been to Stephen's father. He had loved his land as though it was one of his children. People had come from all over England to observe his farming methods. He had tried to introduce his son and heir to them, but everything pertaining to agriculture had bored Stephen.

So had life in the country, and he had wanted nothing to do with that prospect either. His little sister Rachel had been different. She had followed their father around as neither of his sons had.

Stephen placed the milk bucket beneath the cow's teats, picked up the three-legged stool, and moved it into position so he could sit beside the cow. Remembering what Megan had said, Stephen carefully washed off the animal's udder and flanks.

Now the moment of truth was at hand. He eyed the bovine tits with trepidation.

What the devil was he supposed to do?

The milkmaids at Wingate Hall had made it look so easy. He wished to hell that he had spent more time studying the maids' hands at work instead of concentrating his attention on their own mammaries and other feminine assets.

Now if this damned cow had been a human female, Stephen would have known exactly what to do.

After considering the problem for a moment, he wondered whether the same principles that worked so well for him in the bedchambers of assorted beauties could be applied to this cow as well.

Accordingly he gently massaged and pinched her teats, surprised by how soft and velvety they felt. As he worked, he tried to coax her into compliance with the soft, seductive voice that had never failed to win him exactly what he wanted from females of his own species.

Now, though, he did not have to worry about the content of what he was saying because the cow couldn't understand his words, only the tone. "Come on, you blasted bovine," he crooned in his most enticing voice, "give me what I want, and be damned quick about it."

The cow did not comply.

As the minutes ticked slowly away, it became increasingly clear that Stephen was not going to seduce this particular female into giving up her milk.

And if he did not succeed, he would have to go back to the cabin empty-handed. He would have to admit to Meg that he had failed, thereby strengthening her already scornful assessment of him.

His pride revolted at that mortifying thought. For some reason Megan Drake's opinion of him was very important to Stephen. He was determined to win her esteem.

His voice took on an angry edge as he talked to the animal. "What the hell's the matter with you, you contrary, ugly beast?"

The cow gave a sharp switch of her tail, swatting him hard across the face with it.

Stephen was nonplussed. This was the first female of any species that had ever slapped his face.

So much for kindness and coaxing. He'd show this damned cow who was master. No more being gentle with her.

He attacked the teats with vigor, pulling on them and squeezing them hard, determined to force the damned milk from them.

The cow retaliated with a sharp kick to his thigh, knocking him off his three-legged stool and sending him sprawling amid the straw and dirt.

He let out a yelp of pain. "Why you damned bitch," he cried, lifting his bruised leg to rub it. "You fight dirty."

Feminine laughter, rich and sensual, rang out from the door of the barn. Megan, a wide grin on her face, came over to him. He looked up at her as he lay ignominiously at her feet.

He had never felt so humiliated in his life. "Not much damned help, am I?"

Her big gray eyes danced with amusement. "Nay, but you are vastly entertaining."

Stephen felt his face turn hot with embarrassment, and he scrambled to his feet. He wondered how long Megan had been listening to him try to seduce that miserable cow into doing his bidding.

"It is safer to tie Bess's hind legs," Megan said as she did that. "She likes to kick."

Megan righted the overturned stool and sat down on it. She took one of the long teats in her hands, demonstrating with it as she talked. "You must begin at the very top and work the milk down it like this with firm but not rough strokes."

To Stephen's chagrin, a steady stream of milk began to flow almost immediately into the bucket. He silently cursed damned, contrary females of all species.

He was thankful that Megan did not further mortify him by reminding him that he had lied when he said he knew how to milk.

Stephen watched her hands, so small yet so skilled, as they coaxed the long teat into producing milk. He considered the part of his own anatomy that he wanted her to stroke like that, and the thought had a very pronounced effect on the part in question.

Then he contemplated where on her body he would like to reciprocate such attention.

With an effort he pulled his attention upward. Her glorious hair was again hidden beneath that dreadful cap.

Stephen did what he had been aching to do since

the first time he had seen her in it. He yanked it off her head.

The flowing waves of gold and brown were imprisoned in a single braid wound around her head. Now it tumbled down her shoulder.

Megan gasped in surprise and outrage. She tried to snatch the cap back, but Stephen held it beyond her reach with one hand while his other lifted the heavy braid.

"Why do you insist on hiding such beautiful hair beneath this sorry cap?"

Anger at his audacity sparked in her gray eyes and she yanked her braid from his hand. "Why did *you* decide to stay on? I cannot pay you, you know."

"I do not expect to be paid in coin."

She stiffened and suspicion darkened her face. "What kind of payment do you expect from me?"

He grinned. "A smile, a flute concert . . . "

Megan relaxed a little.

" . . . a harmless kiss."

She stiffened again. "While I appreciate your offer to stay here and help me until Josh recovers, it must be with the understanding that there will be no recurrence of what happened this afternoon by the stream."

"Why not?" He gave her an impudent grin, unable to resist teasing her. "We would both enjoy it."

Indeed they would. Stephen would make certain of that.

"No, Mr. Wingate." Her words were like chips of ice. "I would not enjoy it at all."

Like hell she wouldn't! Stephen thought.

"Now do I have your word you will behave yourself?"

He sighed. "Megan, your virtue is safe with me,

if that is what you want. You may not believe me, but I am a gentleman. I would never force—or even cajole—a lady, and especially not one to whom I owe so much, to do anything that she does not want.''

That was the truth, but Stephen already knew from Megan's response to his kiss that afternoon what she wanted.

She just did not realize it yet.

But he would see that she did.

Chapter 10

After dinner Meg gave Josh an herbal concoction that would lessen the pain in his ankle and help him rest. As Meg washed the dishes, Stephen cleaned her brother's flintlock.

She could not help chuckling at the recollection of Stephen trying to charm Bess into giving up her milk. He might not know what to do around a farm, but she had to give the man credit for trying. Even his ineptitude was endearing.

By the time she finished the dishes, Josh had fallen asleep. She picked up his torn hunting shirt to mend it. The evening was warm, and she carried the garment outside.

She seated herself on the rough pine bench near the door and was enjoying the soft breeze that carried the scent of the woods when Stephen joined her. He had brought a three-legged stool with him, and he sat on it, facing her. "Tell me what your father was like, Megan."

She looked up from her sewing. "He was so jovial and good-natured that people could not help liking him. He started with nothing but a small tract of land, and he built it into the great plantation Ashley Grove is today."

"I heard that your mother was once a great beauty."

Meg nodded. "She was the belle of the Tidewater when Papa married her. She had dozens of suitors, but she chose Papa." It was easy to see why her mother had picked her personable, energetic father from among her many beaus.

But he had rued the day that she had done so.

Mama had required admiration and attention the way a bud requires the rays of the sun to bloom. After her marriage she could not bear losing the affection of her adoring ring of suitors. Desperate to regain the attention she had lost, she sank into querulous, demanding invalidism to gain it.

Papa's love, blighted by Mama's incessant whining and her neglect of her two younger children, had faded to tolerance, then indifference, and finally disgust. He had turned his abundant energy to building Ashley Grove into the greatest plantation in Virginia.

Stephen asked, "Was she a good mother?"

Meg jabbed her needle into the hunting shirt. "Quentin was the only one of us that Mama paid any attention to. Perhaps it would have been better for him if she had ignored him as she did Josh and me, instead of coddling and spoiling him. Quentin quickly learned that he could get out of anything by appealing to her."

"I heard that you were the real mistress of Ashley Grove."

She nodded. "I took over running the household when I was fifteen. I was old for my years." And she had inherited her father's talent for management.

Stephen shifted on the stool. "I do not understand why your father left your mother in control of his estate."

"He didn't." Meg's needle stilled, and she let the hunting shirt drop into her lap. "Papa's will left Ashley Grove to me with the stipulation I take care of Mama during her lifetime and provide for my brothers."

"How in hell did your mother circumvent your father's will?"

"When it was clear Papa would not live long, Charles began to court Mama, and she married him the day after Papa's funeral."

Meg's hands involuntarily clenched the cloth of Josh's shirt. "Two days later she and Charles went to court to have him appointed our guardian."

"Bloody hell! And as your guardian, Galloway controlled your inheritance."

"Yes." Meg tried to swallow the lump as big as a duck's egg that swelled in her throat. "And he quickly lost it. I could see what was happening, but I was powerless to stop it. Galloway had my mother so charmed that she would listen to no one except him."

"God, Megan, I am so sorry."

Tears welled up in her eyes. "So am I. Papa would turn over in his grave if he could see what has happened to the plantation he spent his life building. It was bought by Hiram Flynt, whom Papa despised." Meg shuddered. "You cannot imagine what an evil man he is."

Stephen's face was strangely grim. "I can imagine." He jumped up from the stool and began to pace angrily. "How old were you when Galloway was named your guardian?"

"Twenty-three. It never would have happened if I had been a man. But I was a weak, unmarried woman who had inherited a great estate. In his ruling the justice said the estate and I had to be protected from my certain foolishness and incompetence."

"He did not know you well, did he?"

"Oh, he knew me very well. " Meg made no effort to disguise her anger. "But everyone knows a woman is far too feebleminded to grasp business and property matters and cannot be trusted with them. Never mind that I had been managing the household for eight years and acting as Papa's right hand in running the estate."

"Could you not challenge his ruling?"

"I tried, but the general court in Williamsburg refused to hear my appeal. The only avenue left open to me was an appeal to the king in council in London. I cannot imagine the outcome would have been any different than it was in Williamsburg."

Stephen was still pacing in front of her. "You should have married Reverend Burnaby, if only to break Galloway's guardianship of you."

"I would never have married any man for such a reason. Nor would it have done any good if I had. The justice who appointed Charles my guardian decided that my inheritance had to be protected from fortune hunters. If I had married without Charles's permission, he would have retained control of the estate. Ironic, is it not? In the guise of protecting my estate from fortune hunters, the justice handed it over to the worst of the lot."

Silence, broken only by the sweet song of a nightingale, reigned between them for a long moment.

"What did you mean, Meg, when you said the justice who issued the ruling knew you very well? Who the hell was he?"

"His name is Nathan Baylis. The guardianship was his revenge on me."

"For what?"

"When I was eighteen, he wanted to marry me."

Stephen's eyes narrowed dangerously. "How old was he then?"

"In his fifties. Mama urged me to accept, but fortunately Papa disliked him as much as I did and backed my refusal."

"And that was the end of Baylis's suit." Stephen ceased his pacing and sat down on the stool again.

"Not quite." Meg shuddered as she remembered the night that Baylis had caught her alone in her father's library. "He refused to take no for an answer, and I was forced to rebuff him in a very forceful manner."

Stephen grinned. "You slapped his face."

"No, I aimed my father's pistol at him and told him I would shoot him if he did not leave me alone."

Stephen looked so incredulous for an instant that Meg said defensively, "I would have done so, too."

"I am certain you would have." His voice was grave, but his eyes were alight. "Undoubtedly he left you alone after that."

She bit her lower lip unhappily. "You are laughing at me."

"No, I am applauding you." Stephen's smile sent odd yearnings ricocheting through her. "Too bad you did not carry out your threat and shoot him through the heart. I am certain the world would have been a better place if you had."

Stephen lay in bed that night, wondering whether he should have told Megan the truth about him and Flynt. After all, she knew what a bastard he was. But Stephen had feared she would not believe he had been substituted for a convict, and her fragile trust in him would be destroyed. He did not dare chance that.

He was certain that Flynt had used Galloway and Baylis as his instruments to gain control of Ashley Grove fraudulently. But how could Stephen prove it? He thought of the letters and documents tied with a purple ribbon that he had seen stored among the clothes in Galloway's chest. Perhaps Stephen might find something there.

A noise to his right drew his attention. It was time for his nightly torture.

He turned his head on the pillow and looked toward Megan's bed. She was chastely hidden from his view by the curtains drawn closed on the poles that Wilhelm had constructed for her.

Stephen wished the damned oaf had minded his own business.

The cloth walls might hide Megan from Stephen's sight, but they did nothing to dull the sounds that emanated from behind them as she undressed.

Listening to the provocative rustle of clothing being discarded, Stephen visualized what he would be seeing were it not for the flimsy barrier, and he grew more aroused by the moment.

First she would remove her stockings, disclosing a pretty calf, then her dress, revealing the shape that it only hinted at. Finally her shift would go, leaving her naked.

He pictured her unfastening her braid and freeing that glorious honey hair, letting it tumble down to her waist with the tips of her breasts peeking through the shimmering waves.

His manhood swelled. Bloody hell, he was driving himself mad. He had to think about something else.

He tried.

Tried desperately.

He failed.

When at last he heard her settle into bed, he ached to join her there. He thought he might die if he did not.

What was it about this particular woman that reduced him to a quivering ball of lust?

Before breakfast the next morning, Stephen, ax in hand, announced he was going out to chop wood.

Megan gave him a skeptical glance.

Damn it, did she think he was so totally useless that he could not even do something as simple as chop wood?

"I will show you where Josh does it." She led him outside the cabin to the woodpile. Or what had once been the woodpile. It had been depleted now to a few scraps of kindling.

Near it on the ground sat a portion of a crotched tree trunk, old and weathered. Beside it a downed elm had been chopped into long rounds, preparatory to splitting them. One of these had been placed upright between the two forks of the crotch.

"This holds the wood in place while you are chopping," Megan explained. "It works beautifully. We have clever Wilhelm to thank for it."

Stephen stiffened at the mention of the paragon. It infuriated him that Megan was so much more admiring and appreciative of that damned slow-wit than she was of him.

She turned back toward the cabin. "I will call you when breakfast is ready. Bring some wood in with you."

Stephen intended to make up for his abysmal failure at trying to milk Bess the previous night. He would prove to Megan Drake that he was not the bungling idiot she clearly thought him.

Why he'd have a month's supply of wood chopped in no time.

Not that he'd ever chopped wood before, but how difficult could it be? He had only to swing the ax.

And when he was done with the wood, he would take the musket into the woods and hunt game for dinner.

Stephen swung the ax over his head and brought it down squarely in the middle of the elm log held by the crotch, expecting it to split in half. The blade sank to the handle in the wood, but that was the only visible effect it had.

He tried to pull the ax out and could not. Spewing out a lurid stream of profanities, he struggled to reclaim the blade from the elm.

No wonder Josh hated chopping wood. His irritation at the boy turned to rueful sympathy. Finally he managed to extract the ax blade and tried again. With the same result.

No wonder Megan had not looked more appreciative when he had announced he would stay and help her. She must have had a good notion of what little help he would be, he thought with chagrin.

He could speak four languages fluently, could argue the latest scientific theories with the most learned members of the Royal Society, and could recite Shakespeare's love sonnets from memory, but he could not even do something so necessary to survival as chopping a goddamned piece of wood.

Help me? But you cannot even shave yourself.

Megan's words burned like a firebrand in his memory.

Which was about all that would be burning around here at the rate he was going.

Stephen's pride revolted at the thought of admitting to Megan that he had not managed to chop a single piece of wood.

Then he remembered seeing a pile of split wood stacked neatly in one corner of the shed. Clearly it was intended for some other purpose than firewood, but no one would notice if he prigged a couple of pieces.

He hurried into the shed, picked up two of the long rails, quickly split them in half with the ax— at least he could manage to do that much—and carried them out to the woodpile. As he reached it, Megan called that breakfast was ready.

When he entered the cabin, Josh was already at the table, and Meg was dishing out bowls of hasty pudding. She did not look up as he came in. "Please put another piece of wood on the fire. I need to heat more water to wash clothes."

He did as she bade, placing it so it would catch quickly, then lay the other three pieces beside the hearth and went to wash his hands.

While drying them, he turned back toward the fireplace just as a shower of sparks exploded across the cabin.

Josh jumped up. His injured ankle gave way beneath him and he sank down again.

Megan let out a little shriek. "What have you done?"

Stephen could not imagine. Sparks popped and crackled and shot all around them, transforming the room into an indoor fireworks display.

Megan grabbed the poker. Mindless of the sparks that were showering her clothing, she knocked the wood he had just laid on the fire to the edge of the hearth.

She tore off her apron and, folding it, dunked it in the kettle of water that always hung from a trammel attached to the lug pole across the fireplace. Then she dropped the soaking cloth over the isolated piece of wood.

It sizzled. A cloud of smoke and steam hissed upward, and the rain of sparks stopped. The acrid smell of burning cloth filled the cabin. When Megan lifted her scorched apron from the wood, the fire had been extinguished.

She turned on Stephen in a fury. "What were you trying to do? Burn down the cabin?"

"What did I do?" He was baffled.

"You put chestnut on the fire! Chestnut!"

"I do not understand." He felt like a damned fool.

"You cannot burn chestnut in a fireplace because it fills the room with sparks," Josh said in a superior tone that grated on Stephen.

"Where on earth did you find it?" Megan demanded.

"In the barn."

That seemed to upset her even more. "You mean you took our fence rails?" she cried indignantly. "Why? Because they were already split? You are even lazier than Quentin."

Her scorn flayed Stephen as painfully as Hiram Flynt's whip. "I am sorry, Megan, but I did not know."

She looked as though she would not forgive him any time soon. He supposed he could not blame her.

He glanced at the flintlock resting by the door. Now there was something that he knew how to use. He was a crack shot and he had always excelled as a hunter. It was his chance, about the only one he had as nearly as he could see, to redeem himself. He set off into the woods with a determined stride, expecting to return very shortly.

An hour later, when he still had not bagged a single animal, he was forced to admit that once again he had been overly optimistic in his assessment of himself.

Yes, he was a crack shot. But even the best marksman in the world could bring home no animal if he could not find one to shoot. He had never realized before how dependent he was on his hunting dogs to flush out game for him.

Stephen might as well have departed this morning as he had originally intended for all the use he was to Megan.

His splendid classical education at Eton and Oxford was utterly worthless in preparing him for life on this colonial frontier.

It had been the most humbling twenty-four hours of Stephen's life. He had always thought himself superior by virtue of his birth and title. But now he knew better.

He desperately wanted to prove to Megan that she had misjudged him, that he was not the bumbling incompetent she thought him. So far he had managed to demonstrate only how much he had overrated his own worth.

If Stephen was going to be of any help to Megan at all, he would have to learn how to scratch out an existence in this wilderness. And the only person he knew who could teach him was Wilhelm.

It was a bitter blow to Stephen's pride to have to go to a man he had dismissed as a slow-wit for instruction, but he was determined to prove to Megan that he could be of some value to her. It amazed him how important winning her respect was to him. So he swallowed his pride and trudged off toward Wilhelm's.

The way his luck was running today, he would most likely run into some of Flynt's two-legged dogs on the way.

Chapter 11

Meg was hanging the clothes that she had washed on a line strung between two birch trees at the side of the cabin. She looked down the slope at the road that ran along the eastern flank of the Shenandoah Valley.

Not that there was much to see, for few people traveled the road. But today a tall figure in a deerskin hunting shirt was striding purposefully northward up the road, musket in hand.

There was something terribly familiar about the proud angle at which he held his head and his arrogant stride. It took her only an instant to realize it was Stephen Wingate.

He was leaving! For a moment Meg was too stunned to think. Then she was racked by searing loss and betrayal so strong that her heart felt as though it were in a vise.

She should have known better than to trust Stephen Wingate.

Or any man.

Without so much as a fare thee well, he was heading north toward his brother in New York.

And, damn the thief, he was taking their best musket with him.

So much for his promise that he would not steal from them.

And for his promise that he would stay and help her until Josh was on his feet again.

She should have known better than to trust a man's word. Especially a man who bore the marks that Stephen Wingate did.

Meg thought of trying to run after the scoundrel and demanding her musket back, but she knew it would be futile. He was already too far away for her to hope to catch him.

When Stephen reached Wilhelm's farm, he was impressed by how neat and well tended it was. The giant was at work doing one of the chores that Stephen had come to learn—chopping wood. Wilhelm, too, used a forked tree to hold upright the length of log that he was splitting. Stephen regarded Wilhelm's large, tidy pile of cordwood with new appreciation.

The farmer assessed him for a long moment before asking, "Vhat brings you?"

"I want you to teach me to chop wood."

Wilhelm looked as incredulous, as though his visitor had confessed he did not know how to breathe. Stephen felt like the veriest ignoramus. "Will you teach me?"

Wilhelm thought about it for a moment. "Vhy you vant to learn?"

What bloody difference did it make? Still, beggars could not be uppity. Stephen, hanging on to his temper, explained about Josh's injured ankle and his own intention to stay and help Meg until the boy was healed.

"She need you for more than the few days. She need you for the harvest."

"That's a month away!" Stephen dared not remain that long. Bloody hell, he was pushing his luck staying even a few days.

Although it was clear by now that Flynt's dogs had lost Stephen's scent, he would have that two-legged dog Silas Reif and other bastards of his ilk looking for him. Reif made his living by collecting the rewards owners offered for the return of escaped slaves and indentured servants. He was said to be the best in the business. Never had Reif failed to get his man.

Stephen prayed that he would be the first.

"Even vith the boy's help, harvest vill be too much for Fräulein Drake. Stay for it, and I teach you."

"Her brother Quentin promised he would come back to help with the harvest."

The giant gave a scornful snort. "*Ach*, and you believe, too, my cow flies! You promise you stay for the harvest, I teach you many things."

Stephen was not about to make Wilhelm a promise that he feared he could not keep. "I will stay as long as I can. I can promise you no more than that."

Their eyes met and held for a long moment.

Stephen asked softly, "Is it not better that I help her for a little while than not at all?"

Wilhelm thought that over, then nodded. "Vatch how it is done." He picked up his ax and swung it, bringing the blade down squarely in the middle of the log held by the fork of the crotch. The wood promptly split in two.

"Why couldn't I do that?" Stephen exclaimed in irate frustration. "My ax buried itself in the wood."

"Vhat you cut? The elm?"

Stephen nodded.

"The elm is spongy. I show you." Wilhelm selected a length of that wood and placed it in the chopping crotch. "Vith it, you cut along the sides."

He brought the ax down five times in a pentagonal pattern around the edge of the log, separating it easily.

When he was finished, he put another length of elm in the tree crotch and handed Stephen the ax. "Now you try."

Stephen was not able to manipulate the ax with Wilhelm's precision and easy rhythm, but at least the wood was splitting.

As Stephen worked, he asked, "What did you think of Charles Galloway?"

Wilhelm's stolid face contracted in disgust. "It vas as vell for Fräulein Drake that he vas killed."

"Who was he fighting?"

"Two strangers. They vas gambling together at the ordinary. Galloway vas drunk."

"And he picked a fight?"

"*Nein*, vas the strangers. I think that vas vhy they come."

Stephen lowered the ax. "Are you saying they came here deliberately to kill him?"

The giant shrugged. "They vas never seen before. First thing they ask is about Herr Galloway."

Wilhelm's words confirmed Stephen's darkest suspicions, and now a new anxiety arose in his mind. "If they were after Galloway, do you think that Megan could be in danger?"

"They vas not seen again, but ... " Wilhelm shrugged again.

Stephen walked up the path toward the Drake cabin, well pleased with all he had learned that day. Wilhelm had even taught Stephen, as he had previously taught Josh, how to imitate the calls of wild animals when he hunted.

Stephen had felt like a damned fool walking through the woods gobbling like a turkey, but the carcass he carried was proof that Wilhelm's method worked.

Indeed he was amazed at the range of Wilhelm's knowledge. The settler might be illiterate, but he knew a hell of a lot more about the essentials of survival and farming than Stephen did.

It embarrassed Stephen now to think how he had cavalierly dismissed Wilhelm as a stupid oaf because he was illiterate. Stephen's father would not have made that mistake. Nor would his sister Rachel.

As Stephen left Wilhelm, the giant gestured toward the road that his visitor would take home. "The ordinary is a half mile north of here. You vish to go by?"

Stephen frowned in puzzlement. "Why would I want to do that? It is in the opposite direction from the Drake place."

"Notices for the runaway servants are there." Wilhelm stared out across a field where Indian corn grew in tidy rows. "Sometime the reward is large."

"What are you saying?"

Wilhelm was still studying his corn intently. "Sometimes the notices disappear."

Megan had been right about him. He was not at all slow-witted.

Stephen went by the ordinary as Wilhelm suggested and read the handbills posted on the board outside. Although there were a dozen notices for runaway servants and slaves, none was for him.

Yet.

Stephen also learned that mail was picked up

and left at the ordinary. When he asked if he could send a letter to New York, he was assured that he could, although it would take three or four weeks to reach there. A post for the north would be leaving the following day. Even better, since Stephen had no money, the letter's recipient paid the cost, not the sender.

If Megan had paper and ink, Stephen thought as he left the ordinary, he would write to his brother that night, telling him what had happened and asking him to come posthaste to help him escape Flynt. At last he would have an unimpeachable witness who could testify to his real identity.

In his letter to George, Stephen would outline in detail the route that Wilhelm had advised him to follow when he left for New York. He would ask his brother to take it to Virginia and to watch for him along the way. If Stephen was captured before he could leave here, George would learn of it from Megan.

When he reached the Drake cabin, he saw a line of drying clothes, including the scorched apron that Megan had used to douse the chestnut log. It looked ruined.

He approached the cabin door with trepidation, remembering how angry she had been at him. To his surprise, she seemed confounded to see him. Then she gave him a radiant smile.

It was not at all the reception he had expected. He wondered to what he could attribute her sudden warmth and decided that it must be the turkey he carried. He thrust it toward her. "For dinner," he said unnecessarily.

She took the bird but continued to stare at him as though she did not quite believe he was there. The warmth of her smile was generating an answering response in his body, and he turned hastily toward the door before he embarrassed them both.

He went outside, intent on remedying his failure that morning at the woodpile.

Stephen took great pleasure in splitting the recalcitrant elm log that had given him so much trouble. He wished that the Duke of Westleigh could see him now. Why the duke probably would not know one end of an ax from the other.

But he had been right in his assessment of Stephen. No one had ever dared talk to him as Westleigh had. Not even Stephen's father had been so blunt. No, his father had only looked at him with disappointed eyes. Westleigh put into words what Stephen's father had felt about his son.

And with good reason.

Stephen had thought his father old-fashioned and provincial. He had been neither, but rather a good, loving man.

Stephen's sophisticated circle of London friends had derided love, insisting that it was nothing more than a polite euphemism for lust. Yet his father and mother had loved each other, and they had been undeniably happy together.

Stephen remembered, more bitter about it now than he had been at the time, how his urbane male friends had mocked his father for being faithful to his wife when he could have had many women.

But now Stephen wondered who the real fools were.

He placed another elm log in the chopping crotch and quickly split it. His father had been caring, and his family, his people, and his land had all benefited. He had been a man of soul, the kind of man that his son now wanted to become.

Stephen was still disturbed by what Wilhelm had said about Charles Galloway's death. He strongly suspected that Meg's stepfather had been deliberately murdered, perhaps by Hiram Flynt's hirelings, and he worried that she, too, could be in danger.

He was stacking the elm lengths in neat crisscrossed rows when he heard Meg come up behind him. He turned to face her.

"I thought you had run away today," she said without preamble.

He was startled. "Why would you think that? Because I was gone for so long?"

"I saw you headed north on the road. I thought you had changed your mind about staying until Josh is back on his feet."

Her gray eyes mirrored the betrayal she had felt. Stephen remembered that Quentin had not even had the courage to face her when he ran out on her but had left behind a note.

He wanted to take her in his arms and comfort her, but he settled for touching her face gently with his fingertips. "Megan, I would not have left without telling you good-bye."

She looked so woebegone, as though she wanted to believe him but could not, that he tried to reassure her. "I promise I will never do that."

The moment the words left his mouth, he silently cursed himself for his rashness. It was a promise he might not be able to keep. If his pursuers caught him, they would drag him away, giving him no chance to tell her.

"Thank you," she said, a catch in her voice.

Trying to cheer her, he teased, "After my fiasco with the wood, you were probably delighted to think that I was departing."

"Not when you were leaving with our good musket!"

"Ah, I see. You would not have missed me." He

grinned, but he was only half teasing. "It was merely your musket you cared about."

When she did not deny it, he said, "I suppose I cannot blame you for feeling that way after the mull I made of things this morning."

Megan pushed at the wood chips on the ground with her toe. "Where were you going when I saw you on the road?"

"To have Wilhelm teach me some of the things I do not know."

She looked so surprised that Stephen chuckled. "You were right, Megan. He merely had a different education than I. And I am now willing to concede that his may have been of more value than mine."

"At least on the frontier," she said with a conciliatory smile.

"You know my father was a notable farmer, and I could have learned so much from him, had I only listened." But Stephen had no interest in such things after he had gone off to Eton, then Oxford, where his aristocratic friends had mocked rustic pursuits as the province of dull, dreary country squires, smelling of their stables.

Stephen had cared only for London entertainments.

Sorrow and guilt engulfed him like a rogue wave, and he burst out, "What a great disappointment I must have been to my father."

He slammed the ax blade into one of the log rounds and turned away, staring sightlessly at the woods that surrounded the clearing. "God, but I am so sorry and ashamed." His voice was raw with emotion. "When my father became ill, he begged me to come home from London and run Wingate Hall.

"But I refused. I thought his illness was a ploy to bring me home from the merry life in London that I loved. My father had always been so healthy and strong that I could not imagine him being sick."

Megan laid a comforting hand on his arm. "But he was."

Stephen nodded, still staring at the trees. "I should have known that my father would not lie to me. The man did not have a deceitful bone in his body. He was mortally ill."

And instead of being at his dying father's side as his life slowly drained away, Stephen had spent the time in mindless London pleasures. The contempt he felt for himself was searing.

Rachel had managed the estate for the last year of their father's life and done a remarkable job. Stephen was so proud of his exquisite sister. She and Megan Drake had much in common. Both were kind and supremely competent women. He had belatedly come to appreciate these qualities, more than beauty.

He pulled his gaze away from the trees and looked down at Megan. A wisp of hair had escaped from her cap, and he gently tucked it back with his fingers. Stephen saw her generous underlip quiver slightly at his touch. He could not resist bending his head and brushing her mouth lightly with his own.

She jerked back. "You promised."

"I promised that I would not rob you of your virtue. But surely you can spare me a harmless kiss or two."

"I am not so certain they are harmless!"

Her admission pleased Stephen. He posed a question that he once thought he had too much pride to ask. "If I had gone today, would you have missed me or only your musket?"

Her steady gray eyes faltered, and her mouth

curved pensively. "I'd have missed you," she admitted in a whisper.

"And I, you." It startled Stephen to realize how much.

Meg blinked in surprise when Stephen asked her that night whether she had pen, ink, and writing paper. "I have pen and ink, and I think Charles had paper."

She went to her late stepfather's chest, where she sorted through his belongings until she located the unused paper below the stack of documents tied with a purple ribbon. As she handed it to Stephen, she asked to whom he was writing.

"My brother George in New York. I learned today that I can post it at the ordinary."

When Stephen had finished the letter and sealed it with a bit of wax she had given him, he laid it near the edge of the trestle table. "I will take it to the ordinary in the morning."

Looking down at the letter, Meg saw that it was directed to Captain George Wingate at an address in New York. Elation surged through her. So Stephen truly did have a brother named George Wingate in New York, and he was an army captain.

Then doubt attacked her. Perhaps the man was not his brother at all, and Stephen had merely borrowed his last name. Her elation faded.

When it came to Stephen, her emotions were like a small boat caught in giant waves, lifted exhilaratingly skyward one moment and dashed into the depths of a trough the next.

Why did she vacillate so over this man?

Because his story was so unbelievable.

Yet the better she came to know him, the more it seemed to her that he must be telling her the truth.

She belatedly realized that part of her problem in accepting his story lay with her, not him. It was difficult for her to trust men. She had known too many who were not worthy of it.

And it was especially hard when the man bore the terrible marks of the whip that Stephen did. Honest, innocent men did not have such vicious scars.

Yet neither would a dangerous, brutal criminal have acted as Stephen had. Meg knew how much he wanted to flee, yet he opted to stay and help her until Josh recovered. He had put them ahead of his own safety and freedom.

If he was caught, she feared the cost to him would be very high.

And the cost if he stayed higher still to her.

Chapter 12

❧

Stephen finished milking Bess, placed the three-legged stool back against the shed wall, and picked up the milk pail. He looked down proudly at its foaming contents. He had gotten damned good at milking Bess since his first disastrous attempt nine days ago.

And thanks to Wilhelm's instruction, he was becoming proficient at a number of other skills, from carpentry to tanning that were critical for survival on the frontier.

Yesterday he had helped rescue a cow that had fallen into a ravine. He had been at Wilhelm's when the cow's owner had rushed in, seeking help. Wilhelm had dropped his own work to aid the man, and Stephen had gone along. It was good that he had, for it took all three of them to pull the animal out.

Afterward Wilhelm had explained, "Ve all help the other, for ve do not know when ve need the help in return."

Stephen carried the milk pail out of the shed into the dew-scented morning. Megan had just emerged from the little henhouse with the day's egg output in a basket and was crossing to the cabin. Stephen followed her.

132

She never ceased to amaze him with all that she did—and did so well. She worked so damned hard.

Yet it was not enough.

Wilhelm had been right when he said that she and Josh could not handle the harvest alone. There was simply too much for them to do.

If Quentin did not turn up to help her—and Stephen had no more faith than Wilhelm that he would—she and Josh would be in serious trouble.

Stephen had slept little the previous night because he had been wrestling with this problem.

And with his conscience.

By the time he arose this morning, he knew that, no matter what the cost to himself, he could not leave Megan until after the harvest.

It had been the most difficult decision he had ever made. So far he had been lucky. Flynt's human hounds had not tracked him, but the longer he stayed here, the easier he made their job. It would only be a matter of time before they found him.

He could almost feel the pothook closing around his neck. His blood ran cold. He was a damned fool to stay. But he knew for certain that he would not be able to live with himself if he deserted Megan now when she needed him.

Stephen wondered what her reaction would be when he told her he would remain through the harvest. He ruefully recalled her response when he had announced after Josh was hurt that he was not leaving. Surely by now, he had proven to her that he was not as worthless as she had thought him then.

But did she appreciate how much she needed him, especially because Josh's injured ankle did not seem to be healing as it should? Although the swelling had gone down, the boy still cried out in pain when he tried to put weight on it.

Stephen called to Megan. When she looked back at him, he beckoned to her. "Come here. I need to talk to you."

The gravity in his tone apparently alarmed her, for she set the basket of eggs on the bench by the door and hurried to him.

"What is it? About your leaving?"

He nodded.

Words rushed from her. "I understand. You dare not stay any longer. You have been very kind to tarry as long as you have. You need not worry about my brother's ankle."

"I am very worried about it. Do you think that he could have broken a bone after all?"

"No." Her gray eyes, so frank and intelligent, met his. "He is shamming."

"What?"

"He does not want you to leave."

"Why? Because he wants to get out of his chores? Bloody hell, I do not believe he is that lazy."

"No, he is not, although Quentin was a terrible example for him, and Charles even worse. Josh likes you, and I think he feels safer . . . more secure with you here."

Stephen wondered whether she shared her brother's feelings. He said wryly, "When I first arrived, Josh could hardly wait to get rid of me."

"I know, but he has changed his mind."

A wisp of honey hair had escaped her cap and trailed along her cheek. Stephen lifted it and gently tucked it behind her ear. "And what of you, Megan?" His voice was suddenly husky. "Do you like having me here?"

Her gaze fell away from his. The scarlet blush

that rose in her face was answer enough, but he wanted to hear her say it. "Do you?" he repeated.

"Yes." Her strangled voice told Stephen what it cost this proud, independent woman to admit that.

"Good, because I am going to stay and help until the harvest is in. Unless Quentin shows up first."

The look of pure happiness and relief on Megan's face filled Stephen with joy. It was reward enough for the risk he ran by remaining.

"I must tell Josh." Humor sparkled in her gray eyes. "I predict his ankle is about to undergo an amazingly quick recovery."

She started toward the cabin. Stephen watched with pleasure the unconscious sway of her hips as she walked across the clearing. He longed to see her in a gown that would show off the pretty body that he was certain was hidden beneath her shapeless dresses.

On second thought, he would love to see her in no gown at all.

Bedtime had become an escalating agony for him as he listened to her undress behind that cloth wall a few feet away.

So near and yet so far.

He hungered for her, yet he could not bring himself to try to seduce her. Not when he knew he would have to leave her. What if she became pregnant? He could not do that to her. He could not leave her, for fear she might be forced to bear his child alone in this wilderness with only Josh for company.

Megan stopped and turned toward Stephen again. The joy was gone from her gray eyes. "Aren't you afraid that you will be seized if you remain here?"

He affected unconcern. "No."

It was a lie. He was terrified that he would be, but she had too many worries already. He did not want to add to them. Instead he offered up a silent prayer that he would not be caught and prevented from helping her with the harvest.

Stephen had walked to the ordinary twice in the past week to check the board there for a handbill about him, but none had yet appeared. Nor had there been any sign that Silas Reif or any of Flynt's men had picked up Stephen's trail.

Perhaps they never would. But he knew Flynt and Reif's tenacity too well to believe that.

Megan's eyes were troubled. "But what if you are taken?"

"I am counting on my brother to come here as soon as he gets my letter." Stephen wondered how far his missive had traveled on its slow journey to New York. "George can verify my true identity." Even Hiram Flynt would not be able to successfully contest the word of a much respected British captain.

Meg said fervently, "I hope George arrives soon."

"I am certain he will. He can give me the money I need for the passage home." Without George to advance him the blunt, Stephen feared that it would be impossible for him to return to England. Although his passage would cost only a few pounds, it might as well be a thousand for all the chance he had of raising it here on the frontier.

Stephen thought with disgust of the times in London he had carelessly gambled a thousand pounds on the turn of a card. But then he had not known the value of money or how hard it could be to come by.

When he got back to England, he would be a different man.

If he got back.

Don't fail me, George. For God's sake, do not fail me. Come before Hiram Flynt's dogs do.

Chapter 13

Meg kept glancing toward the door of the cabin as she wove linsey-woolsey at her loom. Stephen and Josh were outside doing the nightly chores, and the cabin was lonely without them.

The door opened, and her brother came in followed by Stephen, who was carrying two pails of water. As Meg had predicted, Josh's ankle had undergone a rapid recovery after Stephen's announcement two weeks ago that he would stay until the harvest was in. Josh did not so much as limp now.

She was pleased with the way Stephen had taken the boy in hand to counteract the bad influence of Quentin and Charles Galloway. By both word and example, Stephen was teaching Josh to become a responsible, hard-working man.

Meg could see the results in a dozen small things, such as the woodpile. Josh no longer haphazardly tossed the lengths he cut on it but stacked them neatly as Stephen did. Stephen was gradually replacing Wilhelm as her brother's hero.

Josh said, "I wish you would play your flute tonight, Meg."

Meg sighed. "I have not the time."

"Could you not take a few minutes' break, Megan?" Stephen's rich, coaxing voice was accompanied by that irresistible smile, which never failed to melt her resolve. "Please? I love to hear you play, too."

She could not resist his entreaty.

As she got up from the loom and went over to her small leather trunk where the flute was stored, Josh told Stephen, "You should hear her play the harpsichord." The boy's face shone with pride. "Everyone says she is brilliant on it."

Meg ached for that lost instrument as a mother longs for a lost child. At Ashley Grove she had often spent hours at her beloved harpsichord, pouring out all her emotions, her joys and sorrows, her hopes and fears. But Charles had said it was too big to bring to the frontier. No doubt that was true, but he had insisted that even her violin was too big and had allowed her only her flute.

Of course Charles, ever a dandy with his own comfort foremost in his mind, had transported a chest of useless, elegant clothes and a big feather mattress for his bed.

Meg removed the case containing her flute and opened it. She slid the three wooden sections together, carefully aligning the headjoint, then warmed up with a few runs and trills before she began to play.

After performing several pieces, she told Josh and Stephen to join in and sing the next tune. As she struck up "Oats and Beans and Barley Grow," Josh immediately did so in a voice that had not yet deepened with manhood.

On the second line, Stephen chimed in. With a mischievous gleam in his eye, he jumped up and began acting out the lyrics.

"Stamps his foot and claps his hands," he sang as he stamped and clapped.

"Then turns round to view the land." Stephen whirled around, grinning with boyish enthusiasm. His rich, deep baritone sent a shiver of appreciation—and something else—through Meg.

Then his right hand came up and snatched her cap off her head. Grinning mischievously he hid it behind his back.

She broke off in midsong. "Oh, not again," she groaned, half in exasperation, half in amusement.

"Yes, again." Stephen's smile was infectious.

Her cap had become a game between them. She refused to bow to his pleas not to wear it, so he would seize it from her head when she least expected and demand a ransom for its return.

Now he held the cap high above her head. "Pay the ransom."

"What is it?" she asked, although she knew what his answer would be.

"A kiss, of course."

She gave him a chaste peck on the cheek, and he returned the cap to her.

It was a childish game, yet Meg discovered that she enjoyed such nonsense. She was amazed at how his lighthearted teasing and jesting brightened days of endless drudgery. He seemed to look for ways to make her laugh, especially when he performed "little plays"—acting out proverbs in pantomime. He was often so funny that both Meg and Josh rocked with laughter.

His company made the nights, which once had dragged for her, fly pleasurably by. Invariably he suggested some amusement for them, even if Meg's hands were busy with spinning or sewing or knitting.

Sometimes they sang rounds or he read poetry. Meg liked it best when he read one of Shakespeare's plays, adopting distinctive, fitting voices for the various key roles.

Sometimes he coaxed her into doing the women's parts while he did the men's, and they would sit very close, their heads together over the book.

Her pulse would race at his nearness. She would find herself wishing that his mouth would seek hers, not in one of those pecks on her cheek or quick, soft brushes of his lips across hers that he teasingly gave her, but in a kiss full of heat and passion like the one they'd shared by the stream.

Trying to banish her wayward thoughts, Meg brought her flute to her lips again and resumed playing.

She could no longer deny to herself that she was coming to care for her midnight stranger far more than she ought.

Once the harvest is in, he will be moving on. And then you will never see him again.

Meg's heart withered at the thought. Dear God, she could not let herself fall in love with this man. Her chin quivered, making it difficult to hold her embouchure properly, and the flute's tone went flat.

She saw Stephen's and Josh's startled expressions. Regaining control, she forced herself to finish playing the piece, then said, "I must get back to my weaving."

She began to separate the flute into sections, paying no heed to Josh's and Stephen's protests.

Meg could no longer insulate her heart from Stephen by warning herself that he must be a desperate fugitive with a terrible past. Surely, such a man would not have stayed to help her and Josh with the harvest.

Yet his story of being a wealthy English farmer reduced to his present miserable situation by an enemy who had him wrongly impressed seemed too fantastical to believe.

Especially when he had known nothing about farming when he arrived.

Stephen watched Megan return her flute to its case. He marveled at how much pleasure he found in the simple entertainment at the Drake cabin, when he had been used to the sophistication of London. Something about being with Megan gave him a peace and contentment that he had not enjoyed since he was a child at Wingate Hall.

His admiration of her grew with each passing day. She did not stop from the time she rose with the dawn until she went to bed long after dark: tending the fire, cooking, gardening, churning, combing wool or flax, spinning, weaving, sewing, mending.

It made Stephen weary just thinking about it. She reminded him so much of the tiny green and gold bird with the ruby patch on its throat that he had seen in the Tidewater. Called a hummingbird, it was never still. Its wings beat ceaselessly as it sipped the nectar from flowers with its long beak.

Yes, Megan was like the never-still hummingbird.

And not once had he heard her complain about her burden. If ever a woman had reason to do so, she did. To be yanked from the proud status and genteel life of Ashley Grove's mistress and set down in this dreadful wilderness to labor endlessly just for survival would send most women into a despairing decline. Yet she never bewailed the injustice that had been dealt her.

Josh slipped outside for a call of nature. Stephen noticed that Megan's flute case still lay open in her lap. She was watching him speculatively. "What is it?"

"Who do you think your enemy—the one who had you impressed—is?"

"I do not know. I wish I did."

"Who would benefit most by your disappearance and death?"

It was a question Stephen hated to consider. The answer was too disturbing. He got up, went to the door that Josh had left open, and stared out into the night, lit by the flashes of darting fireflies.

"Who would inherit your farm?" Meg persisted.

"My brother George, but he could not have been behind my abduction."

"Were you close?"

"Closer than most brothers until I went away to Eton." They had grown apart after that.

Megan shut her flute case and carried it to her small leather trunk. "Could George be angry at you for some reason?"

Stephen remembered the blistering letter from George that he had received in Paris during that ill-fated trip to the Continent. George had taken him roundly to task for saddling Rachel with the running of Wingate Hall:

Rachel should be making her London debut and meeting her future husband instead of being buried in Yorkshire, discharging your responsibilities.

George had underlined "your" three times. And his brother had been right, of course. As Stephen had read the letter, he had promised himself that he would make it up to Rachel by seeing that she had her belated London season the following year. But now that season, too, was already past. Was his poor sister still faithfully managing Wingate Hall while life passed her by?

"I am sorry, Rachel, so sorry," he whispered, as though the breeze wafting through the open door of this frontier cabin could carry his words across the broad ocean to the Yorkshire moors. Somehow he must find a way to make it up to her.

Megan asked gently, "Can you be certain George is not behind your abduction?"

The hell of it was, Stephen could not. But even if George wanted his elder brother dead so he could inherit his title and fortune, surely he did not hate Stephen so much that he would have wanted him to die the way his enemy did.

The cove what 'ired us wants 'im to die slow and hard, wants 'im to suffer aplenty afore 'e goes to 'is maker. If we wants our blunt, we does it 'is way.

But neither did Stephen know of any enemy who would seek such a slow and cruel death for him.

Megan placed the flute case inside her trunk. "Men often do terrible deeds when much land is at stake."

"True, but George was not interested in Wingate Hall. He was always army mad. All he cared about was getting his commission." Much to their father's disgust.

Meg closed the trunk. "Perhaps your brother has decided he wants both."

"But he cannot have—" Stephen stopped abruptly. "Bloody hell!"

"What is it?"

"I had forgotten about the agreement my father extracted from George in return for buying him a captain's commission. Under its terms, if I died without a son, George would have to resign from the army or Wingate Hall would go to Rachel."

"Could it be Rachel who is behind—"

"No!" Stephen exploded, cutting Megan off furiously. "Never Rachel!" Of that he was certain.

"What about her husband? Could he be—"

"She is not married."

"Perhaps she married since you were impressed."

Stephen knew Megan was remembering what had happened with Galloway and her mother. He recalled the letter from Anthony Denton that he had received in Paris only hours before he had left to return to England and the nemesis awaiting him at Dover.

Denton had written that he had fallen in love with Rachel—this from the man who had always mocked love—and asked for her hand in marriage. For a moment, Stephen had been pleased that his friend, whom women found irresistible, would have chosen his sister for his wife.

But then doubts surfaced. What kind of husband would such a rakehell be to Rachel? Stephen loved his sister dearly, and while Denton might make her very happy in bed, he feared he would make her very unhappy out of it.

In the long months since his impressment, Stephen had come to see his circle of idle, jaded, aristocratic friends with new clarity. It was not a happy vision.

Nor was Denton the husband Stephen wanted for his sister. He wondered uneasily whether, in his absence, Tony had pressed his suit upon her. It was said no woman could resist Tony.

Stephen hoped to hell Rachel proved that wrong.

From the fringe of trees that edged the field, Meg watched Stephen as he moved among the Indian corn that stood almost as tall as she did. He was stripped to the waist in the humid, sweltering heat, removing weeds with a hoe.

He had gained weight since his arrival. His ribs no longer stood out, and his face had lost its gauntness. Meg stared at the rippling muscles of his chest and arms, which were as brown as the wood of the walnut. The strange heat that burned deep within her when she watched him flared again.

During his weeks here, she had come to appreciate him more each day. He might not have known much about frontier farming when he had stumbled into her life, but he had learned quickly. He worked so hard without complaint that she wondered how she had ever gotten along without him.

And he was such delightful and entertaining company. Meg realized now how lonely she had been, isolated on this frontier farm, rarely seeing her neighbors. She had missed having another intelligent, sympathetic adult with whom to talk.

Stephen turned, and so did Meg's stomach as she saw his bare back. Although the open wounds had healed and the red welts had faded a little in color, his skin was still crisscrossed—and always would be—with the ugly scars of the whip.

Meg's doubt about him, which had become dormant as the weeks passed, jabbed at her again. Innocent, honest men did not bear such marks.

But, she told herself firmly, a desperate criminal would not have stayed to help her as Stephen had.

Harvest was less than a week away now, and then he would be gone.

Forever.

What would she do when he left? She could not bear to think about it, nor about how lonely she would be.

Stephen turned and began to work toward Meg

with his hoe. He was so intent on what he was doing that he did not notice her in the shadow of the trees until he was no more than twenty feet from her. He hurried toward her. A dazzling, sensual smile lit his blue violet eyes and stoked the heat within Meg into an open flame.

"What brings you here, Megan?"

"I have a favor to ask."

He leaned on the hoe, still smiling. "For you, Megan, anything."

"Actually, it is for Josh. You told me once that you read several languages. Would Latin be among them?"

"Yes. Why?"

"Would you tutor Josh in it before you leave? He is so quick at everything but Latin. It is by far his weakest subject."

"Latin is useless to him on the frontier."

Meg hung her head. "I know, but I cannot abandon hope that somehow Josh will be able to get the education he deserves. I know I am a silly dreamer, but . . ."

"We all have dreams, Megan." There was an odd poignant note in Stephen's voice. "And your dream is more unselfish and admirable than most. I will be glad to help him, but I do not have much time left."

It was the first time since Stephen had agreed to help with the harvest that he had spoken of leaving. Meg had to force her voice around the lump that swelled in her throat. "You said we all have dreams. What are yours?"

His mouth tightened. "To return to England, reclaim my birthright, and exact vengeance on the man who robbed me of it."

And Meg would never see him again.

Stephen's grimness suddenly dissolved into that

teasing smile she loved so much. He shifted the hoe to his left hand. His right hand shot up to snatch her cap from her head and hide it behind his back.

"Stop it." Her protest was weak.

He grinned. "Only when you stop hiding your glorious hair beneath this ugly cap."

"What nonsense you prattle!" But his compliment flustered and pleased Meg. Did he truly think her hair *glorious*? She tried to reach around him and grab the cap back.

He raised his arm, holding the cap above his head, beyond her reach.

She jumped up with outstretched arm but again failed to retrieve the cap from him. Her foot came down on a stone, throwing her off balance.

Stephen instantly dropped the hoe. Both his arms came around her, catching her. She looked up at him through the thick screen of her lashes. Something leaped in his eyes as he gazed into hers, and his head slowly lowered toward her.

Her heart pounded in her ears. He was going to kiss her as he had that day by the stream.

She should stop him.

But she did not.

She ached for him to kiss her like that again.

He smelled of sweat and male exertion, but it was not unpleasant, mixed as it was with his unique scent that reminded her of cinnamon and sunshine.

His lips brushed hers lightly, caressingly, back and forth. Then he nibbled gently, provocatively on her underlip, eliciting a startled murmur from her and sending excitement pounding through her.

"Oh, Megan, Megan," he breathed.

She loved that he called her Megan rather than Meg. No one had done so except her father.

His arms tightened around her, and he was kissing her hard, hungrily. She clasped her hands around his neck and kissed him back just as eagerly.

A strange little sound, half moan, half chuckle, escaped him. "Megan, what you do to me."

She wondered whether it could be anything like what he did to her.

His mouth left hers and traced her neck with erotic, sucking kisses that filled her with heat and pleasure. She never wanted him to stop.

"Meg, Meg, where are you?"

Josh's voice abruptly snapped her from the sensual spell Stephen had cast over her.

An expletive escaped his lips.

Meg felt like uttering one herself for Josh's bad timing.

Instead she unlinked her hands from Stephen's neck and reluctantly stepped away from him. Regret and frustration slid through her. "Here I am."

Josh hurried along the edge of the corn toward her. "There's going to be a cabin-raising on the day after tomorrow for the Loewys. They want to get it done before harvest starts. I told them we would come." Josh looked at Stephen. "And that you would help with the raising."

"How kind of you to volunteer me," Stephen said dryly.

Meg knew, though, that he did not mind. No matter how tired or busy Stephen was, he was always willing to help their neighbors when they needed it.

As she and her brother walked back to the cabin, Meg thought of what Josh had interrupted. Dear God, Stephen Wingate was turning her into a wanton woman.

Or a fool like her mother.

Meg clenched her hands into fists so tight that her nails bit into her palms. Meg would not make a goose of herself over a man who, in another week, she would never see again.

Chapter 14

Stephen tried in vain to ignore the tantalizing rustling behind the curtains of Megan's makeshift bedchamber, where she was changing into the clothes she would wear to the cabin raising.

What the hell was taking her so long? Was she trying to drive him out of his mind?

Stephen was shaving in front of the cracked looking glass on the wall, dressed only in buckskin breeches.

He had been so stung by Megan's blurted remark that he couldn't even shave himself that he had learned to do so. The first day or two he had looked as though he had been attacked by a crazed barber. By now, however, he was able to do a tolerably good job.

He'd do a better one, though, if that damned provocative swishing behind the curtain would stop.

The weather had turned very hot, too hot to wear the hunting shirt that Megan had made for him, and she had given him a white lawn shirt and a pair of black broadcloth breeches that had belonged to her stepfather.

The pants had to be taken in, and Megan had

wanted to fit them on Stephen as she had the buckskin pair, but he had brusquely refused. He would be damned if he would let her measure him for any more darts. The breeches could fall off him before he would subject himself to that torture again.

Instead he had insisted that she use the buckskin pair as a pattern and work from that.

"Josh, I need your help," Megan called from behind the curtains of her makeshift bedchamber. "It has been so long since I wore this gown, I forgot that it fastened up the back, and I cannot manage it."

"Your brother is outside, but I will be happy to do it for you."

"I am certain you will," she replied tartly, "but I want my brother."

"I will do it." Stephen pushed aside the curtain. Megan had her back to him and her hands were holding together the two edges of a deep blue gown. Her honey hair hung unbound about her in a burnished veil.

A tiny gasp escaped her. "You cannot come in here. I am not dressed."

If only that was true! Stephen had seen vastly more of a great many ladies' bodies than the little sliver of back that was revealed by the gap in her gown, but he knew her opinion of him would not be improved by this admission.

Her hair was such a beautiful temptation that it was all he could do to keep from burying his hands in it. His hands closed around its tantalizing softness, parting it into two sections and draping one over each of her shoulders to get it out of his way.

He began to fasten her dress with quick, skillful fingers, admiring as he did the long graceful sweep of her neck. It took him only a few seconds to close the opening. He would have liked to take longer.

No, what he would like was to remove ... He forced his mind from that thought before it had its inevitable effect on his body. He could not allow that to happen. It would be hell in these tight breeches. And all too obvious.

"I might have known you would be very good at helping a woman into—and no doubt *out* of—her clothes."

Stephen ignored Megan's waspish comment, but he could not ignore her lovely neck. As he bent his head to it, silken strands of her hair teased his face. She jumped at his kiss. As he moved his lips down the elegant curve of her neck, he felt the tremor of response coursing through her before she stepped abruptly away and whirled to face him. "Don't!"

He smiled unrepentantly. "It is my wage for my services. 'Tis cheaper than a lady's maid."

"Nay, I fear 'tis dearer." Megan turned and pushed back the curtains of her makeshift bedchamber.

This was the first time that Stephen had seen her in anything but the shapeless gowns she worked in about the farm, and his eyes widened.

He had known that she would be well formed, but he had not guessed how small, slender, and perfectly proportioned she was. The bodice of the blue gown clung to the high, pleasing curve of her bosom and was fitted to a waist that his hands could easily have spanned.

He wanted to do exactly that, but he did not wish to test her temper.

"I should like a few moments' privacy," Megan said as she went over to the looking glass.

Stephen followed her. "For that you must pay a toll."

He would have dropped another kiss on the back of her neck, but she whirled to face him. Instead he brushed her lips with a light, teasing motion, and desire twisted in him. He tried to take her in his arms, but she pushed him away.

"No, I must get ready." Her voice was shaky. "We are late."

As Stephen reluctantly moved away, he passed Galloway's trunk and thought of the documents tied with a purple ribbon inside. He was certain that Galloway and Baylis had been Flynt's tools in fraudulently acquiring Ashley Grove. He wondered again if the papers might contain any evidence to support this.

He thought of asking Meg to show them to him, then decided against it. He did not want to raise her hopes only to have her bitterly disappointed. Instead, Stephen decided, he would sneak a look at them as soon as he could be assured of being alone in the cabin for more than a few minutes.

Stephen glanced back at Meg in her pretty gown. God, but he ached to hold her slender body against his own, ached to become part of her.

But he could not do that. In a week he would be gone from here forever. Much as he lusted for her, he could not make love to her then leave, not knowing whether his babe was growing within her.

Stephen regarded the newly finished log cabin in front of him with mingled amazement and satisfaction.

He was amazed because nothing had been there this morning. He had never seen anything constructed so quickly, thanks to the dozen men who had contributed their labor.

And Stephen was satisfied because he had been one of them. It was the first time in his life that he had built even part of something with his own hands, and he was startled by the feeling of accomplishment it gave him.

He looked down at his callused hands and thought of his long hours of backbreaking physical labor on the frontier. He had willingly done it because he had been determined to prove to Megan that he was not the incompetent she had clearly thought him.

He had worked to earn her approving smile, and now he won it with increasing frequency.

As he looked at the new cabin, he recalled Megan's wish: *I would give anything for my own room, but that is a rare luxury on the frontier.*

Rare, but perhaps not impossible. He pondered how he could give it to her.

And how much he would like to share it with her.

But he had to leave as soon as the harvest was in. He was a fool to stay that long, but he had to help Megan. If only George would come. He frowned. He'd expected his brother, or at least some word from him, by now. Why hadn't he heard from him?

With the cabin raising done, a feast awaited the builders and their families on a long table set beneath the shade of twin sycamores. The table, a large slab of timber supported by sticks set in auger holes, looked to have been fashioned for the occasion.

A great variety of dishes—beef, pork, chicken, wild turkey, duck, venison, potatoes, and various vegetables brought by the workers' wives were spread along the table's length, and the delicious odors reminded Stephen how hungry he was. Megan had contributed a roasted duck that he had shot.

He had not had coffee or tea since the day he

had been seized in Dover, and he longed for the taste of them again. He looked hopefully for a pot of either drink. To his disappointment, he saw neither one.

As he turned away, a blunt, jovial settler named Hoskin inquired, "What was you lookin' for?"

"Coffee or tea."

"You'll not find none of them slops here."

"Slops!"

"Aye. Them's fit only for the quality to consume."

"Fit only for the quality?"

"Aye, only them as does no work would bother with slops that don't stick to the ribs." Contempt permeated Hoskin's voice.

In England the belief that the quality was superior was unquestioned. Stephen was startled to discover this view was not shared by the American settlers.

And who was to say they were not right?

Stephen looked around him. At the edge of the clearing Josh and some of the older boys practiced throwing one of those odd Indian axes called a tomahawk at an oak tree.

A pretty young girl about Josh's age stood in the shadow of the trees, watching him with avid interest. The lad was oblivious to her attention.

When Megan and Stephen joined the line forming for the food, he overheard Hoskin ask young Sam Tolbert, "When you and Martha gonna tie the knot?"

"As soon as a preacher comes through to do it."

"That could be months."

The prospective bridegroom grimaced. "I hope not. I have no wish, I'll tell you, to be forced to spend another winter bundling."

Puzzled, Stephen turned to Megan. "What is bundling?"

"During courtship, a couple is allowed to occupy the same bed as long as they do not undress. It is a popular custom."

Stephen thought it sounded frustrating as hell.

Almost as damned frustrating as listening to Megan undress each night behind that cloth wall.

When they had piled their plates with food, Megan led him to the table where Wilhelm and his wife Gerda were with some of their friends. Megan sat down beside Gerda, who was holding little Willy on her lap. Stephen settled himself beside Megan, casting an admiring sideways glance at her as he did.

She had piled and twisted her beautiful honey hair up into an elegant arrangement that accentuated her delicate profile and the sweep of her lovely neck.

Josh, his plate loaded with food, slid in beside Stephen although the table was so full that there was barely room for him.

A few minutes later the pretty young girl whom Stephen had noticed watching Josh so intently came shyly up to them, a plate of food in her hand.

"Josh, you promised you would eat with me," she said plaintively. "But there is no room for me."

The hurt in the girl's cornflower blue eyes told Stephen how much she had wanted Josh to keep that promise.

Josh shrugged carelessly. "I guess you'll have to find a place at another table, Rose. I want to eat with Stephen."

The girl flinched as though Josh had struck her, and her eyes were suspiciously bright as she turned away.

Stephen looked at Megan, but she was engrossed

in conversation with Gerda and had missed the exchange between her brother and the girl. "Did you promise Rose that you would eat with her, Josh?"

"Aye, but—

"A man of honor always keeps his word. Otherwise he does not give it."

Josh colored. "But she's only a girl," he said defensively. "Quentin says that girls—"

Stephen cut him off. "Quentin also deserted you and your sister, left you to fend for yourselves against overwhelming odds. Is that the example you wish to follow?"

Josh hung his head.

"Is it?" Stephen pressed.

"No," Josh admitted.

Stephen looked toward the isolated stump near the edge of the clearing where Rose had seated herself. "Then do what a gentleman would do. Go over to Rose, apologize to her, and find a place where the two of you can sit together. And next time do not make promises you do not mean to keep."

Josh left the table with his plate of food in hand and went to Rose. Stephen was too far away to hear what was said between them, but the surprise then the happiness on Rose's face brought a smile to his lips.

After the guests had finished dinner, one man brought out a fiddle and another a homemade drum, and the dancing began. It was not the stately minuets and cotillions that Stephen had been used to in London ballrooms, but exuberant jigs and reels danced with considerably more enthusiasm than skill.

Stephen led Megan out to dance. He was not surprised, given her musical talent, to find she was an excellent dancer.

Although some of the reels were unfamiliar to Stephen, he had always been quick and graceful on his feet, and he managed to fake his way through them.

He was soon caught up in the boisterous enthusiasm of the participants. Indeed, he could not remember the last time he had so much fun dancing.

After nearly an hour of vigorous dancing, Stephen was glad when the musicians took a short break.

When they resumed playing, one of the other men, a square-faced young settler, asked Megan to dance. Much to Stephen's displeasure, she accepted.

The empty space she left next to Stephen on the bench was immediately filled by a wiry, red-haired man named Ames. He had been late for the cabin raising, arriving after the log walls had been three-quarters up.

Stephen watched Megan perform the steps of a lively reel with her partner, torn between jealousy that she was with another man and admiration for the grace with which she moved.

What a remarkable woman she was. Her fiery determination and quiet courage in the face of the frontier's dangers filled him with pride. They might well have frightened off a strong man, but his Megan was undaunted.

His Megan.

It hit Stephen with the impact of a musket ball that this plain, courageous spinster had won a niche in his heart that had never before been occupied by any woman. He enjoyed a happiness and serenity with her that astonished him. He felt none of the impatience and restlessness in her company that had dogged him when he had lived in London.

The thought of leaving her and Josh here wrenched him. He would wonder each and every day whether Megan was safe and well or if the dangers and hardships of the frontier had claimed yet another victim.

Ames's boisterous voice penetrated Stephen's reverie.

"... a convicted murderer, name o' Billy Gunnell."

Stephen froze.

Ames continued, "The handbill were bein' put up when I stopped at the ordinary on the way here."

"What'd it say he looked like?" his companion asked.

"Dark, tall, skinny. Got a black bushy beard, a livid scar o'er one eye, and's wearing homespun shirt and breeches held up with a rope. Warns him's as dangerous as they comes."

Ames paused to take a gulp from the wooden tankard of liquor he was holding. "They must want him back bad. Biggest reward I hearda for a runaway servant. Enough to make me wanta go lookin' for the polecat myself."

Chapter 15

In the weak gray light of the new day, dawning overcast and drizzly, Stephen looked around to make certain no one else saw him. The muddy road was empty, and he heard no sounds from within the ordinary.

Satisfied that he was not being observed, he reached up amid the notices posted on the board and ripped down the handbill seeking the return of BILLY GUNNELL, CONVICTED MURDERER.

Stephen had lain awake most of the night, worrying about the notice. Long before dawn he had sneaked out silently and made his way slowly through the darkness to the ordinary.

He crumpled the paper but dared not throw it away. Someone might find it and wonder why it had been removed. Instead he shoved it into the ample pocket of his hunting shirt. He would burn the handbill in the fireplace of the Drake cabin when Megan was not around.

Stephen set off down the road at a jog, hoping he could slip back into bed before Megan awoke and discovered him gone.

He would be a fool to remain here any longer. The size of the reward assured that men such as Silas Reif would be combing the frontier looking for him. If Stephen did not keep running, they would find him.

But the prospect of leaving Megan forever, of returning to England alone and being separated from her by a vast sea, filled him with a cold emptiness. It was unthinkable that he would never again hear her soothing, sensual voice, never again smell her sweet scent of orange blossoms, never see her luminous smile, never feel her passionate lips against his.

In that moment he knew he had to take Megan back to England with him.

He could not leave her here, no matter what the danger to himself. When George arrived, he would have to advance Stephen the blunt for two fares instead of one—no, three fares. Megan would never go without Josh. Nor would Stephen leave him behind. He had become very fond of the boy.

Stephen would pluck both sister and brother from their life of endless, hopeless drudgery on the frontier. He would provide Megan with a life of ease and luxury in England far beyond what she could ever hope to attain here.

Of course, he would not be able to marry her.

Even if the impatient Fanny had found herself another title to wed, he still could not marry Megan. Lords of the realm chose their wives for their connections and prestigious bloodlines. It was one of the duties that went with his title. A colonial from the American frontier offered neither.

No, he could not give Megan marriage.

But would she accept that?

Certainly she would not like it. Neither did he. But it could not be helped. Stephen's mouth tightened in determination. He would have to seduce her into going with him without a wedding ring.

She wanted him. The passion with which she

kissed him assured him of that. He would make her want him even more.

Meg, dressed and ready to start the day, pushed aside the curtains of her bedchamber and stopped dead at the sight of Stephen's empty bed. Had he sneaked away, breaking his promise to stay until after the harvest. She felt a crushing pain in her heart. She heard the door open and turned.

Stephen, wearing the deerskin hunting shirt she had made for him, was slipping inside.

Relief flooded her. Whispering so she would not awaken Josh, she asked, "Where on earth have you been?"

Stephen looked dismayed to see her up. "I could not sleep, and I went for an early morning walk." He sounded breathless, as though he had been running rather than walking.

"How far did you go?"

"Up the road past Wilhelm's and back."

Meg detected an evasive note in his voice. She was assailed by the uneasy feeling that there was more to his early morning walk than he was telling her. But she could not imagine what it could be, and she let the matter drop.

After that he seemed determined to ingratiate himself with her. He insisted on weeding her vegetable garden for her. When she said she must wash clothes, he replied that it was too hot to heat the water in the cabin, which was true. Instead he built a fire in the pit in the yard and carried the water to be heated from the spring for her.

Then Stephen said he would do Josh's chores so her brother could go over to Wilhelm's to exercise his horses. Josh departed at a run before Stephen could change his mind.

While she was washing the clothes, Stephen disappeared into the cabin.

Meg hung the last of the garments on the line strung between the two birches and went back to the cabin.

As she stepped inside, she saw Stephen kneeling beside her stepfather's chest, looking unaccountably pleased with himself as he replaced clothes in it.

She stopped dead at the sight. In the weeks since his arrival, Meg had come to trust him. Now she was horrified to find him furtively going through another man's chest like a sneak thief. "What are you doing?"

He gave a guilty start and jumped up, letting the lid fall with a loud bang. He had pulled the chair Wilhelm had made for her over to the chest, and the seat still held a pile of Charles's clothing.

Meg went over to him. "What on earth are you looking for?"

Stephen plucked at his deerskin hunting shirt. "It is too hot today, and I was looking for a lighter shirt," he said easily. "You just washed the other one you gave me."

This was true, but she pointed to the garments still on the chair. "All of Charles's shirts were on top and are now sitting there. If that was what you were after, you had no need to take them all out and dig deeper."

Stephen looked flustered. "Perhaps not, but they were all of such fine quality that I hated to use them to work in. I hoped to find something older and more ragged."

She frowned. "You should have asked me before—"

"I know," he said hastily, "but you were so busy I did not want to bother you."

He flashed her that irresistible smile of his, then his hand shot up and snatched her cap from her head, distracting her. He held it above her reach.

"Give it to me," she cried.

"The price is a kiss."

Before she could protest, his mouth closed over hers gently enough at first, then it turned hot and urgent and demanding, sending liquid fire tumbling through her.

She knew that she should pull away from him, but she could not find the strength to do so. His arms felt so strong and protective and his mouth . . . his mouth drove all rational thought from her mind.

His kiss seemed different now, suffused with a determination that she did not understand, and it unnerved her.

As his lips held hers in thrall, she felt his hands unbraiding her hair, spreading it about her like a cloak. His fingers alternately combed through then smoothed it. He made her feel cherished.

You fool, harvest will be over in a few days, and he will be gone.

The door to the cabin bounced open, and Josh strode in. Meg and Stephen jumped apart as though a shot had been fired between them. Her face flaming, she turned to start dinner.

Stephen wiped the sweat from his brow and looked with satisfaction and relief at the field before him, picked clean of its corn. The harvest was in. It had been backbreaking work, but he thanked God that he had been able to keep his word to Megan to help her.

Although the harvest was over, Quentin had not come.

Nor had George.

And that was far more disturbing to Stephen. He had not expected Meg's brother to keep his promise, but he had counted on his own to come to his aid as soon as he received his letter.

And George must have received it by now. It had been more than a month since Stephen had sent it. He'd been told four weeks was the longest a letter took.

The letter could have gone astray, but Megan's question of who would benefit most from his death had caused doubt about George to fester in his mind like a deeply embedded splinter.

Stephen felt as though an unseen hand were squeezing his heart at the possibility that his brother could have been responsible for the hell into which he had plunged.

If George was his unknown enemy, Stephen should never have written him where he was. Would George contact Flynt with word of his brother's whereabouts?

Another worry gnawed at Stephen's mind. When he had gone to burn the crumpled handbill about Billy Gunnell that he had removed from the board at the ordinary, he had discovered that it was no longer in his pocket. It must have fallen out, but he had no idea where. He prayed that no one would find it.

Stephen looked up and saw Meg walking across the field toward him. The sight of her lightened his mood. So far his campaign to seduce her had been a dismal failure. About all he had convinced her to do was leave off wearing her caps. Not a very impressive performance for a man who had been noted in England for his way with women.

Hell, he had been more successful at teaching Josh Latin than at seducing the boy's sister. Stephen hoped that the surprise he had in store for

Megan tomorrow would finally soften her toward him.

As he watched her approach, he thought again how much she reminded him of the little hummingbirds he had loved to watch at Ashley Grove.

When he took her to England, he would have a jeweled brooch of that bird made for her. He had even designed it in his mind. A single huge pearl would form the bird's body. Rubies would duplicate the distinctive red patch at the throat. The bird's spread wings would be fashioned of gold set with dozens of tiny, shimmering green emeralds, and it would have a long gold beak.

It would be so fitting for Megan, given all her energy.

As Megan reached him, she said softly, "So the harvest is over."

"Yes," he said, smiling at her.

She did not return his smile. Her gray eyes were grave. "And now you will leave. You have kept your promise."

But he would not go until he could find a way to take her and Josh with him. Without George's help, Stephen had no means of paying for their passage, or even his own, to England. "Megan, I cannot go off and leave you and your brother here alone and unprotected."

"Josh and I managed perfectly well for months here without your protection, and I assure you we will again after you leave."

Stephen'd thought he'd seen joy in her eyes for an instant, but her words told him he must have been mistaken. Hurt by her ungracious reaction, he said sarcastically, "Your gratitude overwhelms me. You could not have managed the harvest without me. Nor have you spent a winter here yet."

"We will survive!"

"Will you? If I could be certain of that I would leave, but I am not."

"Go!"

"No! Bloody hell, Megan, what kind of man do you think I am?"

She gazed at him with troubled, perplexed eyes. "I wish I knew," she whispered, drawing attention to her mouth that he longed to kiss. "Will you be safe if you stay here?"

Stephen shrugged, careful to keep his face from betraying his chilling thought: *If George was his enemy, there might be no safety for him anywhere.*

Chapter 16

Meg hurried toward the Drake cabin, anxious to get home. One of their neighbors, Charles Bentley, had come for her that morning. His wife Elizabeth, who was six months pregnant, thought she might be going into premature labor and wanted Meg with her.

Although it had proven to be a false alarm, Elizabeth had clung to Meg, begging her to stay longer. Poor Elizabeth had been so insistent that Meg had complied, even though she had silently groaned at the thought of all that was going undone at home.

Meg stepped into the clearing and stopped dead as she saw the cabin. Had she walked into the wrong clearing? Since she had left that morning, a second, smaller room complete with a window opening had been added to the structure.

Stephen hurried toward her, and she exclaimed, "Where did that come from?"

He was grinning, his eyes alight with excitement, and he looked unbearably handsome. Behind him, with equally broad smiles came Josh and Wilhelm.

Stephen bowed elegantly to her, like some gallant English lord. With a sweeping gesture toward the addition, he said, "Your bedroom awaits you, my lady."

"Stephen knew how much you wanted a room of your own," Josh said. "He wanted to surprise you."

"I vould say he succeeded," Wilhelm observed.

Yes, Stephen had. Meg could not believe that at last she would have her own room.

Stephen took her arm and guided her inside the cabin. The beds in the two corners of the original cabin were still in place, but Charles's bed, the one Stephen had been using, was gone. The small window on the wall behind it had vanished, replaced by a plank door hung on leathern straps.

Stephen pushed the door open and stepped back to let Meg enter her new bedroom first.

Charles's big bed with the feather mattress was pushed against the far wall, taking up most of the space. Her leather trunk had been placed at the foot of the bed. Two clapboard shelves had been attached to the log wall and above them hung the cracked looking glass.

Finally Meg would be able to dress and conduct her toilet in private. She turned to Stephen, standing in the doorway. "It is wonderful! I am so happy."

He grinned, clearly delighted at her reaction. Their gazes met, and an invisible heat passed between them that set her pulse aracing. The sudden smoldering in his eyes told her that he had felt it, too. Her voice was not altogether steady as she asked, "However did you manage it, Stephen?"

"If the men here can raise a cabin in a day, I knew they could add a single small room. Wilhelm and I called in some of the favors that we have done for others and voilà!"

"Was Elizabeth's false labor a ruse to get me away from here today?"

"Aye," Stephen confessed.

Wilhelm appeared behind Stephen in the doorway, and Meg cried, "I love my new room! I cannot thank you enough."

Wilhelm laughed. "The joy on your face is thanks enough. I must go now."

"Can I go with Wilhelm, Meg?" Josh called. "I want to ride."

She agreed, too happy herself to deny her brother anything.

Meg went outside to see them off, then hurried back to her new room, unable to stay away from it.

She heard Stephen come in behind her. Whirling on him, she threw her arms exuberantly around his neck. "How can I ever thank you?"

He grinned and hugged her to him. Meg loved having his strong, muscled arms, so warm and protective, around her. His lips closed over hers in a long, fiery kiss. Finally he raised his mouth a fraction. The burning look he gave her through his thick black lashes sent fire coursing through her veins.

"There is one way you can thank me." His voice was husky, as though he was as shaken by their kiss as she was, and his breath was hot on her lips.

"What is it?"

His seductive smile took her breath away. "Let me share it with you."

Meg's pleasure faded into shocked indignation. She jerked away from him. "Is that why you built it for me? So you could share it with me?"

He tried to take her in his arms again, but she pushed him away.

"Megan, I built it because you wanted a room of your own so much."

"And you thought that meant I would part with my virtue to get it?"

"No, dammit, I did it because you wanted it, not because I wish to make love to you. But I long to do that, too. And you long to have me do so. Let me give you the pleasure we both want."

"I don't want it!" But she knew that she was lying. God help her, her body ached for this man's touch. She had been so certain that no man could ever have the effect on her that Stephen did.

Yet even now, despite her anger, wild, breath-taking sensations rushed through her at the thought of him sharing her bed and initiating her to the secrets of womanhood. She wanted him to be the one to do that. But honor would not allow her to give herself to a man who was not her husband.

And he was not going to marry her. Instead, if he was who he claimed to be, he would go home to England to reclaim his birthright and would vanish from her life forever.

His breath tickled her ear. "Megan, let me make love to you."

"And then you will leave!"

"Not without you."

"*What?*" She stared at his sharply etched face, hope sprouting within her like seed in fertile soil.

"I want you to come to England with me, Megan. Let me take you away from this miserable existence. I am a wealthy man there. I will give you the life you would have had, were it not for your mother's foolishness. In England you will have anything you want. You have only to ask for it."

Meg could not seem to catch her breath. Her heart was thudding. He was asking her to marry him after all. She was astonished by how quickly her objections to matrimony blew away like autumn leaves in a windstorm.

But there was more than herself to consider. "What of Josh?"

"He will come with us, of course. I will give both of you the life you deserve."

She was so elated that she felt as though her heart would burst with happiness. "So you are asking me to marry you."

Stephen's gaze wavered. He said carefully, "You will be the wife of my heart."

Meg stiffened. The euphoria that had engulfed her evaporated. He was not offering her marriage but merely a dishonorable liaison until he tired of her.

She should have known a man as handsome as Stephen Wingate would not want a wife as plain and unexciting as she. She remembered her suitors in the Tidewater, who had been so eager to marry her until they learned Ashley Grove would not be hers.

Poor Meg. A woman as plain as you can never inspire passion and faithfulness and undying love in a handsome young husband.

Her heart felt as though it had been pulverized and her pride along with it. What contempt Stephen must hold her in to make her such an insulting offer. She jerked away from him, his touch suddenly painful to her. "But not your wife in law."

The bitter hurt and humiliation etched on Megan's face made Stephen wince. Bloody hell, why did she have to be so damned perceptive? He tried to soothe her with his most seductive smile. "I assure you 'tis better to be the wife of my heart."

Although Stephen could not give Megan marriage, he would give her back far more than he took. "Once we are in England, you will live in a fine house staffed with servants. Never again will you have to cook or clean, or lift a finger. I will dress you in beautiful gowns of the finest silk and satin and in jewels that would make a duchess proud."

"And when you are tired of me?"

He doubted that would happen, but to reassure her, he said, "I will make a settlement upon you that will ensure you will live in luxury for the rest of your days."

For a moment, she only looked at him unblinkingly with those big reproachful eyes that made him feel like a cad. "Why do you *not* want to marry me?"

Why the hell does she always have to be so frank? He could not bear to tell her that she would not make a proper wife for an English lord, that aristocratic society would never accept her as his lady wife.

As he struggled to think of a diplomatic answer, she asked, "Is it because you are already married?"

"No, but . . . there are other important reasons why I cannot ask you to marry me."

"What reasons?"

Stephen continued as though she had not spoken. "But that does not mean I will not cherish you as though you were my wife, Megan. You will have a fine house, lovely clothes, and all the servants you want."

It was clear from her expression that these gifts would be far from enough to win her acquiescence. Desperately Stephen searched for something so irresistible that she could not refuse it. "I will buy you the best harpsichord in England. You will never want for anything again."

"Except marriage!" The anger and hurt were plain on her face. "What kind of woman do you think I am?"

A woman of honor and integrity. Casting about for some way to mollify her, Stephen pointed out, "But you yourself told me that you would never marry."

"Perhaps you could change my mind." Megan looked at him expectantly.

Damn it, he did not want to change her mind.

Or did he? He was stunned to realize that he would marry her if he could.

But he could not. He was an earl.

"Megan, I cannot marry you, but I promise that when I do wed, it will not affect our relationship." He meant that sincerely. His marriage would be the empty union of connections and power that was required of an English earl. With Megan he would have the happy companionship, contentment, and peace that he had found with her here in this wilderness cabin.

Megan would indeed be the wife of his heart.

"You intend to keep a mistress after you marry?" She was clearly scandalized.

Too late Stephen remembered: *I would require two things of a husband, his love and his fidelity.* Bloody hell, he was making an incredible mull of this.

He made another attempt to explain. "Megan, in England love is considered a frivolous reason for marriage, and it is the accepted thing for a husband to keep a mistress."

"Then I am very glad I do not live in England!"

Megan held herself proudly, defiantly. Stephen admired her spirit, integrity, and determination. He thought of all the lovely women in England who would have been delighted to be his mistress. But the only thing that he had admired about those eager women was their physical beauty.

He wanted Megan desperately, and he searched frantically for something short of marriage that would persuade her to accept his proposition. "Megan, if you go with me, I will give Josh the finest education money can buy."

Her eyes betrayed how much she wanted that for her brother. Stephen hastily pressed his advantage. "I am not talking about some inferior colonial university like Harvard or William and Mary. I will send him to the best English university, either Oxford or Cambridge, whichever you prefer."

Megan's face betrayed her internal struggle. She clearly yearned to have this education for her brother, and Stephen could see she was weakening. She stared down at the floor of her new bedroom, then hugged herself as though she were suddenly very cold and could not get warm.

A long moment passed before her gaze met his again, and he flinched at the sadness and disillusionment in her eyes. "So your price for helping my brother is the one thing that Charles did not take from me—my honor."

Her words froze Stephen. He felt like a damned scoundrel.

But he could not offer her marriage.

She held her head at a proud angle. "Much as I want an education for Josh, I will not sell myself for it. As for marriage, even if you offered to wed me now, I would not accept." Her quiet dignity was as great a reproach to him as her words. "I could not imagine being married to a man who thinks as you do."

Stephen was stunned by how much her words wounded him. Suddenly he felt as though it was his own honor that he must salvage. He said grimly, "Megan, if I get back to England and recover my birthright, I promise you that I will pay for Josh's education. And I will ask nothing from you in return."

She stared at him silently, her big gray eyes filled with pain and doubt. He cupped her chin in his hand and rubbed her lower lip lightly with his thumb. "Listen to me, Megan. I only want from you what you freely wish to give me. I told you before that your virtue is safe with me, if that is what you want."

"It is what I want."

He nodded in acceptance. What else could he do, even though his body ached for her? He resigned himself to another cold plunge in the stream to deflate his ardor for her.

He kissed her lightly on her lips, then left her new bedroom, shutting the door behind him. He tried to console himself with the thought that at least now she had a bedroom of her own. He would no longer have to listen to her undress each night behind that cloth no more than five feet from him.

It was no consolation.

What was he going to do about her? He could

not marry her, and he did not want to leave her here.

Hell, the whole question was moot anyhow, since he did not even have the money for his own passage to England, let alone hers and Josh's.

The pain of knowing that Stephen wanted her only as his mistress was like a musket ball through Meg's heart. Alone in her new room, she threw herself on the bed. It was the one that Stephen had been using, and his cinnamon and sunshine scent clung to the bedclothes. She buried her head in the pillow to muffle her tears and wept.

After her grief was spent, she lay on the bed, emotionally drained and devoid of energy. She heard Stephen leave the cabin and she wondered where he was going. Was he leaving for good? Perhaps it would be better if he were.

She got up and wandered listlessly into the main room of the cabin. Meg looked at the empty spot where the bed, now in her new room, had stood and noticed a crumpled ball of paper lying against the wall. Clearly it must have rolled beneath the bed and lain there unnoticed.

Puzzled by what it could be, Meg picked it up and smoothed it out. A horrified gasp escaped her lips as she saw that it was a handbill offering a large reward for Billy Gunnell, an indentured servant who had run away.

The sheet warned that Gunnell, a convicted murderer transported to Virginia in lieu of execution, was a highly dangerous and desperate man and should be approached with caution.

He was described as standing eighteen hands high with long stringy black hair; bushy, unkempt whiskers; a livid red scar on his left temple, and unusual light-blue eyes. He wore a homespun flax shirt and breeches torn off above the knees and held up with a rope.

Meg's stomach churned.

"If you are not a convict, why do you have the mark of shackles upon your arms and legs?

I was mistaken for one, a man named Billy Gunnell . . . Perhaps I resemble him.

But the handbill's description of Gunnell did not merely resemble Stephen Wingate. It described him perfectly, right down to the homespun rags he wore when he collapsed on Meg's doorstep.

She glanced down to see who was offering the reward and gasped again. HIRAM FLYNT, ASHLEY GROVE PLANTATION. She remembered Stephen's— or was it Billy's—shock when she had told him Ashley Grove had been her former home.

There are other important reasons why I cannot ask you to marry me.

Like his being a convicted murderer! The world suddenly spun around Meg as though she were in the center of a whirling top, and she put her hand out to the wall to steady herself.

"Megan, what is it?"

She jumped at the sound of Stephen's concerned voice from the cabin doorway. She turned to face him, the handbill still in her hand. Her heart accelerated at the sight of him clad only in breeches. Apparently he had gone swimming in the stream, for his hair was still wet.

He laid the towel he was carrying on the trestle table and came over to her. He tried to put his hands on her arms, but she flinched away from his touch. Wordlessly she showed him the paper in her hand.

He uttered an earthy expletive. "Where did you find it? It fell out of my pocket, and I have been looking for it for days."

"It was against the wall beneath the bed. Where did *you* get it?"

His mouth tightened. "I removed it from the board at the ordinary."

"Why? Because you are Billy Gunnell?"

"No, damn it, I am not Gunnell. I told you that before. I also told you how I was mistaken for him. I could not run the risk of having that happen again. That is why I took it down. As you can see, the description of Gunnell sounds very like me."

"Like you? It is you!"

"Megan, I swear to you I am not Billy Gunnell."

She wanted desperately to believe him.

But she could not.

Chapter 17

◯◯◯

Meg's neck and back muscles ached from hours at her spinning wheel, turning wool and flax into yarn that she would weave into linsey-woolsey.

At the trestle table Stephen was giving Josh a Latin lesson. Meg smiled, well pleased with the progress her brother was making in the subject under Stephen's tutelage.

As they finished the lesson, Josh grumbled, "I don't know why we are doing this. 'Tis a waste of time. I will never be able to go to college."

"It need not be a waste," Stephen said.

Meg stiffened, thinking that he was referring to his promise to educate Josh if she would become his mistress.

But Stephen continued, "Latin exercises and disciplines your mind as physical labor does your body."

So he did not mean what Meg thought. In the four days since he had made her that dishonorable offer, he had not alluded to the subject again. His behavior toward her had been that of a perfect gentleman. She knew the strained atmosphere between them was her fault rather than his. She was uneasy and skittish around him, while he acted as though nothing had happened. The only change in his behavior was that he seemed more solicitous of her.

Now when she arose in the morning, a basin of hot water waited at the door to her bedroom for her morning ablutions. He suggested doing what he knew would please her, such as reading *The Merchant of Venice* or acting out the "little plays" that she so enjoyed. He tried hard to make her laugh and often succeeded.

And to his credit, he still worked as hard as ever around the farm. He had begun to pull stumps from the cornfield, a difficult and arduous job that left him visibly exhausted. Despite his fatigue, he faithfully gave Josh a Latin lesson each night.

She no longer knew what to think about Stephen Wingate.

His dishonorable offer followed by her discovery of the crumpled handbill had regenerated all her old doubts about him.

He claimed he was not Billy Gunnell, only mistaken for him, but the description of the fugitive killer matched too perfectly Stephen's when he had collapsed on her doorstep. That he had gone to the trouble to take down the handbill fed her fear that he was in fact Gunnell.

Yet the better she came to know him the more difficult it was for her to believe he could be a murderer.

Meg had said nothing to Josh about the handbill. Stephen was such a good influence on her brother and the boy was so admiring of him that she did want to disillusion him by telling him that his new hero might have a dark and deadly past.

Meg twisted her neck, trying to loosen the tight muscles.

Stephen came over to her. "This is what you need." His voice was soft and caressing as he began to massage her neck and shoulders with deft hands. A jolt went through her at his touch. She told herself she should not let him do this, yet it felt so good she could not bring herself to stop him. Nor could she suppress a little sigh of pleasure. As he worked, she gradually felt her tired, strained muscles relax.

"That's wonderful." She sighed, grateful for the relief. Meg found herself wondering what it would be like to have him touch her in other places.

Intimate places that ached when he drew close to her.

Meg was filled with a yearning so strong that it startled and frightened her. This provocative man had her fighting herself as well as him. He had been right when he said she wanted him as much as he wanted her.

She had tried hard to harden her heart against him. She might still care for him, but she told herself resolutely that she wanted nothing to do with a man who saw nothing wrong in keeping both a wife and a mistress, a man who could not give her love and fidelity, a man who might well be a convicted murderer.

Meg awoke the next morning, shivering in her new bedroom. Getting up, she lifted the shutter and looked out the opening over her bed, half expecting to see frost. She did not, but the air was decidedly nippy.

It was far too early to be so cold. Was this a harbinger of a long, hard winter ahead?

She was delighted to find that Stephen had once again placed a basin of hot water outside her door. She particularly appreciated it this cold morning.

After her morning ablutions, she pulled a warm gown of yellow wool from her trunk. The cold propelled her to dress even more quickly than usual.

When she hurried into the main room of the cabin, Stephen was adding fresh wood to the fireplace. He looked up. "It has turned very cold. I must bring in more wood."

"You will need a warm cloak." Meg went over to Charles's chest, pulled from it a scarlet roquelaure and handed the garment to Stephen.

He pulled it around him, thanking her with a smile that was more warming to Meg than the fire, and went outside. She busied herself starting breakfast.

After the meal was finished, Stephen and Josh went outside. Twenty minutes later, Stephen came into the cabin alone.

"Where's Josh?"

"He wanted to go over to Wilhelm's. I told him he could."

She bridled. "You had no—"

"Megan, we need to talk." He laid his hands on her arms.

She jerked away from him. She did not want to talk to him, did not want to be alone with him. It was not that she feared he would force himself on her, but rather that she would not be able to resist his blandishments.

Not that he had offered her any since she had rejected his offer to make her his mistress.

It was herself, not him, she did not trust.

Mumbling an excuse about needing to go down

to the spring, she grabbed her green cloak from the peg by the door and rushed outside.

Behind her, Stephen called, "Running away from me?"

"No," she cried. But of course she was.

Meg hurried down the path between the myrtles and cedars and red flowering maples that led to the spring. A cold, raw wind was blowing that made her shiver despite her cloak. She told herself that she should be thankful Stephen had not asked her to marry him. What if he had and she had accepted, then bore his children only to have Stephen's—or Billy's or Earl's—past catch up with him?

She and her children would have suffered the shame of having her husband and their father revealed as a convicted murderer and dragged from them. Unfair as it was, they would have become outcasts, tainted by their father's crime. She could not inflict such shame on her own flesh and blood, no matter how much she loved a man.

Yet when she thought of the heat and yearning that Stephen's kisses generated in her, her heart ached. Dear God, she was a bigger fool than her mother.

She reached the spring, her thoughts so agitated that she paid little heed to where she stepped.

Her foot slipped on an icy patch and slid out sideways beneath her. She flailed wildly, trying to regain her balance, but she failed and fell backward.

She screamed as she tumbled into the icy water. The current, swift and frenzied down the cascade, caught her and spun her around. Her head collided with a boulder.

And blackness engulfed her.

* * *

Stephen heard Megan's scream and bolted out of the cabin into the frosty morning air, rushing down the path to the stream with the speed of a frightened deer.

He stopped by the spring, looking around wildly for her, calling her name frantically.

There was no answer. Nor did he see any sign of her.

Finally, far downstream, he caught a glimpse of something green and yellow caught in the swirling current and knew that it must be Megan's cloak and gown.

With his heart in his throat, he jumped down to the sandbar where he had first kissed her. He ran along the bank, oblivious to the frigid, biting wind and the underbrush snagging and tearing at him, in a desperate effort to catch up with that limp bundle of green and yellow being swept downstream.

Her head was not bobbing about, indicating that she was unconscious.

Or worse.

Stephen prayed fervently, desperately. *Please God, do not let her die. Help me!*

He ran as fast as he could.

But it was not fast enough.

He could not reach her, and despair even worse than what he had felt at Flynt's hands gripped him.

But he could not, would not give up. He ran on, his lungs aching, his breath coming in great gasps.

Then, just as it seemed utterly hopeless, her cloak caught on a tree snag partially submerged in the water, holding her there.

When he came abreast of the snag, he saw she

was lying face up in the water, her nose and mouth clear. The sight revived his hope, and he plunged into the swift current. It was so frigid that he gasped involuntarily.

With powerful strokes, he cut through the water to the snag. When he reached it, Megan was so white and still that for an instant he thought she was dead even though her face was not submerged. Then he saw the faint mist of her breath. "Thank God," he murmured.

Working as quickly as he could—his fingers were already stiff and clumsy from the numbing cold of the water—he freed her cloak from the snag.

Wrapping one arm around her, he swam for shore, praying she would not slip away from him.

When he reached shallow water, he scrambled up the bank with her in his arms. Shivering in his wet clothes, he stumbled along the shore. The wind slashed at him like a razor's edge. Megan was still alive, but he feared she would not be for long if he did not get those cold, waterlogged clothes off her. He had to get her back to the cabin.

"Do not die on me, Megan." He was shouting at her as though his voice could somehow penetrate her unconsciousness. "Please, do not die."

He staggered on with his heavy burden, fear and desperation giving him a strength that he had never before possessed.

By the time he reached the path between the trees to the cabin, he was gasping for breath from his exertion, but he forced himself on, praying all the while.

As he reached the cabin, his strength gave out, and he collapsed to his knees with Megan still in his arms. He pushed open the door and a blast of warm air enveloped him. He laid her on the dirt floor and scrambled in on his hands and knees after her, quickly shutting the door behind them to keep as much heat as he could from escaping.

He had not the strength to pick her up again, so he dragged her lifeless form toward the fireplace. Her wet clothing left an ugly, muddy groove in the dirt floor.

When he had her within range of the fireplace's warmth, he knelt beside her. She was blue with cold. And she was still unconscious. That puzzled him. She did not seem to have water in her lungs, for she was breathing without wheezing and coughing.

He buried his fingers in the wet mass of her hair, exploring her head gently. On the back of her skull, he discovered a lump the size of an egg. She must have struck her head on a rock when she fell and been knocked unconscious. Thank God she had plunged into the water face up and stayed that way.

Stephen tore open the drenched cloak and stared down in frustration at the yellow gown. She was shaking with cold. He had to get those soaking clothes off her immediately and warm her, but it would take too long if he tried to undress her.

He jumped up and grabbed the scalping knife. Stephen hated to destroy any garment in Megan's limited wardrobe, but he had no choice. He slit open both her gown and her chemise and peeled the soggy cloth away from her, revealing her perfectly formed body, so small and delicate and slender.

His breath caught at the sight of her high, firm, coral-tipped breasts. His gaze traveled downward to her tiny waist and the triangle of honey curls at the apex of her legs.

But he had no time for admiration. Grabbing a cloth, he dried her vigorously, then lifted her away from the wet clothes. He laid her carefully on a quilt that he had spread on Josh's bed and wrapped it around her.

Since he had installed Charles's bed in Megan's new bedroom, Stephen had been sleeping on her old one. He yanked the mattress off and put it in front of the fire, then lifted her, quilt and all, and laid her on it.

Despite the quilt she was shaking like a leaf in the wind. He had to do more to warm her. He wished to God that his sister was here. Rachel would know what to do for Megan.

He felt so damned helpless. Desperate, Stephen stripped off his own wet clothes, dried himself, then opened the quilt, and dropped down on the mattress. He covered Megan's body with his own, offering her his warmth.

He shuddered at the touch of her icy flesh against his. It was like lying down naked on a frozen pond in the dead of winter. He hugged her to him.

"Please, Megan, don't leave me," he pleaded. "I love you so."

His words, spoken aloud in the silent cabin, shocked him. But they were the truth. He did love Megan, loved her so much that he would gladly have traded his own life to save hers.

Faced with the terrible prospect of losing her to death, he realized how much he wanted this woman beside him.

Wanted her for all the rest of his days.

As his wife.

He no longer cared that she was a provincial

colonial who would not make an English earl a
proper wife. She was the only wife that he
wanted. He thought of how much he enjoyed her
company. With her he had found the peace and
contentment, the serenity and satisfaction, that
had eluded him all those years in London when
he had rushed frenetically from one pleasure to
another, restlessly searching for something—he
knew not what.

But now he had found it.

With Meg.

And it was called love.

Stephen did not give a damn whether London
society accepted her as his countess. If it would
not, then too bad. He would bloody well ignore
London and the ton. He and Megan would live at
Wingate Hall where he would see that she was
safe from the slights of society.

He thought of his sophisticated friends who
had scoffed at the idea of love between a man
and a woman. He had scoffed with them.

Now he knew how wrong they—and he—had
been.

Stephen held Megan tightly against his body,
trying to suffuse her with his own life-giving
warmth. Slowly Megan's shivering lessened and
finally stopped altogether. She moaned and
turned restlessly.

He murmured gently, soothingly in her ear,
trying to calm her as she had once calmed him in
his raging fever. He whispered to her of his love
for her, of how precious she was to him, of the
happy life they would have as they grew old together. Gradually she quieted.

And her body warmed. It was no longer like
holding a block of ice in his arms. He thought
she would be all right, but he could not be cer-

tain until she awakened. Rachel and his mother had always said that head injuries were unpredictable.

His stomach convulsed. Megan had to be all right. Nothing was as important to him as that. Not returning to England and recovering his lost birthright. Not even avenging himself on his unknown enemy.

Nothing.

He lay there clutching her to him, and he felt the rise and fall of her sweet, firm breasts against his chest grow more rhythmic.

Reassured, his own body relaxed. He was suddenly engulfed by an exhaustion more profound than had ever assailed him before in his life. He felt as though someone had pulled the plug from his reservoir of energy, and it had all drained away. This weariness combined with the warmth of the fire lulled him into sleep.

When Stephen awoke, Megan was shivering in his arms, and he heard her muttering thickly, "So cold! Warm me."

He opened his eyes. He must have been asleep for some time. The fire had burned down to embers again, and the quilt in which he had wrapped them had come open and fallen away, exposing them to the chill in the room.

"Warm me," Megan whimpered again, her eyes still closed.

Only half awake, Stephen strove to obey. He rolled over on top of her so his body again covered hers, and he wrapped her tightly in his arms. The cool air of the cabin wafted over his backside. With one hand he awkwardly grabbed a bit of the quilt on which they lay and pulled it over them.

Megan's eyes fluttered open. For a moment, they were blank and unfocused, then they settled on his face. She looked puzzled.

"Stephen?"

He was so relieved she was lucid and recognized him that he could not stop himself. He dipped his head and gave her a long, tender kiss that silently bespoke his love for her and his joy that she had survived her ordeal.

When he broke the kiss, she looked at the fireplace, then up at him in confusion. "What are we doing?"

"Bundling," he quipped.

"But, Stephen." She sounded a little groggy, as though she was not fully awake yet. "We have no clothes on."

He grinned. "Believe me, sweetheart, that is the most pleasurable way to bundle."

She seemed bemused. "Is that what you call all the women with whom you bundle?"

"Yes, since you are the only one with whom I have ever bundled." Megan looked so damned sweet and innocent that he could not resist kissing her again.

Stephen thought he heard the sound of the door opening. The wind must have caught it. Well, it could bloody well wait until he had finished giving Megan a proper kiss.

To his surprise, she returned it. The melding of their mouths became so hot and deep and exciting that his shaft hardened.

A strange man's voice boomed out. "What the hell is going on, Meg? Who is this son of a bitch on top of you?"

Stephen instantly rolled off Megan. The quilt partially wrapped around them fell away, leaving them naked.

He looked up at the intruder, a handsome man two or three years younger than himself and dressed in the finely tailored riding garb of a Tidewater gentleman. The stranger stared down at Stephen and Megan, his face a study in outrage.

Stephen belatedly noticed that a second man was standing in the shadows a few feet behind the first. Young, round-faced and bespectacled, he had the glazed look of a man who had just suffered a severe and devastating shock. Stephen's gaze did not linger on him. It was the first man who captured his full attention.

He was the one with the flintlock musket pointed at Stephen's heart.

Chapter 18

Stephen heard Megan's gasp as she frantically tugged at the quilt to hide her nakedness from the intruders. Far more concerned for her modesty than his own, he reached over to help her without taking his eyes off the young interloper who held the flintlock on him.

"Don't move an inch or you are a dead man," the stranger with the musket snapped.

Stephen froze.

"Quentin!" Megan exclaimed as she wrapped the quilt around her.

Stephen suppressed a groan. He might have known that if her damned brother showed up at all, he would pick the worst possible moment. Wearily he tried to explain, "This is not what you think. I was not—"

"I'd say there was no mistaking what you were doing, mister," Quentin interrupted. Rage radiated from his rigid body as he stared at Stephen's erect manhood. Quentin's reaction was more effective than an icy bath in deflating it.

Meg, looking beautiful with her disheveled hair tumbling about her in rich golden honey waves, asked, "What on earth are you doing here, Quentin?"

"I told you that I would be back for the harvest."

"You're more than a week late for that," Stephen snapped, his anger at the sonofabitch for abandoning Megan and Josh overwhelming his caution.

Quentin's eyes narrowed. They were hazel, not gray like his sister's. Nor did they reflect her serene calm and good humor. Instead they glittered with the look of a volatile man ruled by emotion rather than good sense. He took after his mother, Stephen surmised.

Megan's brother shoved the barrel of the flint-lock against Stephen's chest. "Who the hell are you?"

"The man who did *your* work for you here."

The hazel eyes swept furiously over Stephen's nakedness. "I can see what kind of work you do."

"This is not what you think." Stephen forced his voice to remain cool and emotionless.

"Then what the hell is it? Your lying tongue will not bedazzle me the way it clearly has my poor sister. Meg, how could you let him do this to you?"

Stephen did not give her a chance to answer. "I did not do a damned thing to her, except save her life."

"Looks to me more like you were trying to give her another one, if you take my meaning."

Stephen did, and he did not like it at all.

But it was damned hard to do much about it when he was lying flat on his back as naked as the day he was born, with the barrel of a flintlock held by a wild-eyed young hothead aimed at his heart.

"Where the hell is Galloway that he would allow—"

Stephen cut Quentin off. "Galloway has been dead for months. This farm was too much for Megan and Josh, and I have been helping them."

"Meg does not need your kind of help."

"Quentin," Megan interjected sharply, "you are wrong as usual."

Her brother's companion, a scandalized expression on his rotund face, stepped out of the shadows. Megan, apparently noticing him for the first time, gasped in shock. She jerked the quilt higher about her chin, her face reddening.

Stephen wished she would push some of the quilt his way. He felt like a nude statue on public exhibit.

Megan asked in a horrified tone, "Peter Burnaby, what are you doing here?"

Stephen's head jerked up. So this was the Reverend Burnaby, the only one of Megan's suitors who had not vanished along with Ashley Grove. She had said that he did not love her, but she had been wrong. Stephen saw on Peter's face the supreme shock and disillusionment of a man who has just discovered the woman he loves is not worthy of that love.

Peter opened his mouth to answer Megan's question, but no sound emerged, and he belatedly shut it again.

Quentin responded for him. "I told Peter that you would have come to your senses by now, Meg, and would be willing to marry him. He wanted to take you away from this beastly frontier."

Megan looked so wretched that Stephen felt jealousy shoot through him. Bloody hell, did she care so much about this moon-faced reverend? He could not stop himself from asking Peter baldly, "Do you still wish to marry her?"

Peter did not reply, but the disenchantment in his eyes was answer enough.

Quentin growled, "'Tis still a damned good thing that you came, Peter."

Megan looked at her brother blankly.

Stephen, certain he knew what Quentin meant, started to object, then shut his mouth. He had discovered in those terrifying, heart-stopping minutes after Megan had fallen into the stream just how much he loved her. He, who had not believed in love, especially not married love.

Now he knew what a fool he had been.

And he wanted to marry her. The reverend might just as well do the deed while he was here. Another minister might not be by for months.

Megan's face was a study in perplexity. "Why is it a good thing, Quentin?"

"Because Peter can marry you to this blackguard sleeping with you."

"Don't be ridiculous!" Meg's fingers explored the back of her skull. She stifled a moan as they touched a painful, swollen bump the size of a duck's egg. She was in no mood for Quentin's jests. Not when her head hurt so terribly.

"Peter will perform the ceremony as soon as you two get some clothes on. Don't look to me like there's any time to waste."

Slack jawed, she stared at her brother. Dear God, Quentin was not jesting. She could think of nothing worse than to be married to a man who did not want her except as his mistress, a man who believed infidelity was a normal and customary thing for a husband.

Especially a man who might very well be a transported murderer.

What if she wed him and bore his children, only to have his past catch up with him? Her children would be forced to watch as their father was dragged away from them and branded a dangerous criminal.

Meg would not, could not agree to a union with such a man. For the sake of her unborn children as well as herself. "*No!* I will not marry him!" She saw Stephen flinch as though she had hit him. "He is not the kind of man I want for my husband!"

Stephen's face darkened with anger. "Well, if you think that man of God is going to marry you now, he is not!"

She didn't care a fig for Peter, but that was beside the point. "So I should marry you instead? Never!"

"Meg, you must marry him," Peter burst out. "No woman who has known a man as—er, intimately as you have can do anything else."

Meg stifled an urge to strangle Peter—reverend or not. She would never be able to reason with Quentin now. Angrily she reiterated, "I will not marry him!"

"Why not?" her brother demanded.

Knowing his explosive temper, she dared not tell him her fears about the man lying beside her. She was afraid that Quentin would shoot him on the spot. Her head hurt before, but now, because of her brother, it was positively throbbing.

She looked toward Stephen, expecting him to add his protest to hers, to tell Quentin that he had no intention of marrying her either.

To her consternation, Stephen did not say a word. She supposed he could not be expected to protest much with a flintlock pointed at his heart.

So Meg spoke for him. "Nor does Stephen wish to wed me. Tell Quentin how much you do not want to do that."

Stephen never took his eyes from the musket aimed at his chest. "I don't mind marrying you," he said mildly.

"Don't mind?" Meg squeaked, her temper flaring. "Don't mind!" Why she had never been so insulted in her life. That was the most lukewarm,

unromantic acceptance of wedlock she had ever
heard. She did not want a man who did not mind
marrying her. She wanted one who yearned to do
so with his whole heart and being. She wanted a
man who loved her and would give her his fidelity.
"Well, I mind marrying you! *I mind it very much.*
And I am not going to do it!"

"I think you have the gun pointed at the wrong
half of this match, Quentin," Stephen said wryly.
"Looks like it's your sister whom you are going to
have to convince."

Quentin said sternly, "You are going to marry
him, Meg."

"I am not." Meg noticed Stephen's hand surreptitiously pulling a corner of the quilt over his torso
while Quentin's attention was focused on her. "I
will not do it!"

"You should have thought of that before you
slept with him," Quentin snapped back.

"I did not sleep with him!"

Quentin's face resembled a thundercloud about
to unleash its fury. "Are you saying he forced
you?"

"No! I'm saying that nothing happened between
us." She hesitated, suddenly uncertain. She remembered how Stephen's warm body had covered hers
when she had awakened. She turned to him, doubt
in her voice. "Nothing did happen, did it?"

His look of hot fury would have melted a frozen
river. "Bloody hell, no wonder you do not want to
marry me if that is the kind of man you think I am.
Do you honestly think I would ravage your helpless body while you were lying unconscious?"

"No," she admitted. "But what did happen? The
last thing I remember was slipping on an icy patch
by the spring."

"You fell into the stream, hit your head on a
rock, and were knocked unconscious."

So that explained the lump on the back of her head. Meg gingerly touched it again and winced.

"Fortunately, I heard you scream and ran down there." Stephen was talking directly to her, as though she were the only person in the room. "By the time I could pull you out, you were half frozen. I brought you back here, removed your wet clothes, which were turning to ice on you, and tried to warm you."

Quentin snorted, "With your own body."

"It worked! If I had not, she might not be alive now."

"So only her honor is dead."

"Your sister's virtue has suffered no damage from me, but I realize that is not the way it looks." Stephen sounded so conciliatory that Meg could scarcely believe her ears. "That is why I am willing to marry her."

She wanted to kick him. Why was he suddenly being so darned obliging? Meg knew perfectly well he did not want to marry her. Perhaps it was all an act. Yes, that must be it. He was trying to lull her brother into relaxing his guard.

She would do what she could to help. "I would prefer to continue this discussion clothed. Quentin and Peter, would you both step outside for a few minutes so we can dress?" She was confident that once Stephen had his clothes on, while Quentin and Peter were still waiting outside the cabin door, he could crawl out of the window in her new bedroom and escape on foot.

Her brother's face turned mulish. "I am not letting this bastard out of my sight, not for an instant, until he's done right by you."

Meg knew there was no arguing with Quentin when he got that stubborn look on his face. For the moment, she would appear to go along with him, but she had no intention of letting him force her and Stephen into a marriage that neither of them wanted.

Beside her, Stephen said quietly, "Go to your bedroom and dress, Megan."

Clutching the quilt around her with one hand, she pushed herself to her knees and got awkwardly to her feet.

Peter said nervously, "I must go look for my *Book of Common Prayer* in my saddlebags." He hurried outside.

As Meg closed the door of her new bedroom, she looked back at Stephen. He was sitting on the mattress, his long, well-shaped legs drawn up beneath his chin, warily watching the barrel of the flintlock her brother had trained on him.

Careless as Quentin was, she was certain that her brother's vigilance would soon relax and Stephen would be able to disarm him.

Meg was torn by conflicting emotions. Her blood flowed hot at the memory of Stephen's body pressed against hers as he tried to warm her. If she was honest with herself, she had to admit that in her heart she wanted to be his wife. But she did not want a husband who had been forced to marry her. She deserved better than that. Nor did she want a husband who could not give her love and fidelity. And Stephen could not.

Her good sense screamed at her that this man of dubious origins would bring her even greater unhappiness than Charles Galloway had brought her mother.

But she need not worry. Surely, as soon as Stephen could disarm her brother, he would flee and disappear from her life forever. She swallowed back tears at the thought. Because she wanted Stephen to see her this final time looking her nicest, Meg chose her best gown, a green silk, to wear.

"I prefer to be married in clothes," Stephen told Quentin calmly. He gestured toward a shirt and black broadcloth breeches hanging on a peg beside his bed. "Hand me those."

Quentin regarded him with scowling suspicion, clearly suspecting a trick.

"I swear I will not try to escape."

Quentin hesitated, then lowered his flintlock and reached for the clothes.

Stephen could have seized the musket and subdued Quentin in a minute, but instead he waited for the garments to be handed to him. He wanted to marry Megan. By now, he was not at all certain he would get her to wed him any other way.

So let her brother be the villain of this farce.

Although Stephen had carefully masked his feelings, he had been miffed and more hurt than he wanted to admit by her resistance to marrying him.

He put on the shirt first, taking great care to keep his back hidden from Megan's brother. He did not want Quentin to see the scars of the whip and have second thoughts about marrying his sister to Stephen.

Quentin began to pace the floor. As Stephen finished buttoning his breeches, the door of Megan's bedroom opened, and she appeared. He had never seen her look so lovely. She had done her honey hair in a particularly charming style, arranged high in front with a long sweep cascading down her back.

Her green silk gown brought out the delicate whiteness of her complexion. Stephen approved of the way the gown fit, too, accentuating her slender body and high breasts. He ached to touch them and every other part of her, to explore her with a thoroughness that would leave them both panting with desire.

And in just a few minutes, it would be his right to do so. She would be his wife.

His wife!

He had always regarded marriage as an onerous but unavoidable duty. Now he discovered that the prospect of wedding Megan thrilled him.

But it clearly did not thrill her. She looked like she was being led to the damned gallows.

As Megan walked slowly from her bedroom, she savored the frank appreciation in Stephen's eyes. She was far from pleased, though, that he was letting a golden opportunity to escape pass him by. Now was the perfect moment for him to overpower Quentin, who was watching her.

She tried to send that message to him with her eyes and a slight gesture of her hand toward Quentin. To her frustration, Stephen only smiled at her.

Where were his wits? With clenched teeth, she nodded her head slightly, but still he did not seem to understand her signals. She had never known him to be so obtuse.

"You will be married as soon as Peter can find his prayer book," Quentin said.

Trying desperately to buy more time, Meg told her brother stubbornly, "We must wait for Josh. I will not be married without him present."

"You have no choice," Quentin told her.

She glared at him furiously. "I tell you I will not—"

Stephen stepped quickly to her side. "Megan, it is better that Josh is not here. How will you explain to him why Quentin is forcing you to marry me at musket point?"

"I'll tell him the truth—that Quentin is wrong!"

The door opened, and Peter came in with his prayer book in hand.

Quentin turned to him. Once again Stephen seemed oblivious to this wonderful opportunity to disarm her brother.

Well, if he would not wrest the musket from Quentin, Meg would. She was across the room in a flash and grabbed the weapon. Caught by surprise, her brother almost lost it to her before he realized what was happening.

"Meg, what the hell are you doing?" he roared as he struggled with her for possession of the flintlock.

The gun fired with a roar and puff of powder and smoke. Its ball lodged in one of log trusses that supported the roof.

"Run," Meg yelled at Stephen. "Now the gun is empty, you have time to flee before he can reload."

Instead of rushing out of the cabin as she expected, he hurried to her and wrapped his arms tightly around her. Their imprisoning strength put an end to her struggle for the gun.

"Megan, Megan, my little spitfire, stop it." She felt his breath, warm and exciting, caress her ear, and she went very quiet. "I am not going anywhere."

"Why not?" she wailed.

"Whether you believe it or not, I am a gentleman, and a gentleman does not abandon a lady in a situation like this."

He loosened his grip on her, and Megan twisted around in his arms so she could face him. "Even if she wants him to abandon her?"

She thought she caught a fleeting glimpse of pain in his eyes, but it came and went so fast she was not certain whether she had imagined it.

"Is that what you truly want, Megan?" His voice was very sober.

No, but it is what you want. "Yes, it is what I want." She nearly choked pushing that lie past the constriction in her throat, but she managed to get it out, although far more weakly than she would have liked. That prompted her to add petulantly, "And it is what you want, too."

He skimmed her cheek lightly, tenderly with his fingertips, sending delightful shivers through her. "You fail abysmally as a mind reader, sweetheart."

Meg loved the gentle brush of his hand against her face and the huskiness of his voice. *Sweetheart.* She remembered the way his body had felt against hers as he had tried to warm her, and she could not seem to catch her breath. A torrid longing coursed through her veins.

"I promise you, Megan, that I will do everything in my power to be a good husband to you."

For a moment, she could only stare at him, stunned by his vow. *Everything in my power to be a good husband.* But what was in his power? He could not love her. By his own admission fidelity in marriage was unimportant to him.

Even if he was telling the truth and he was not Billy Gunnell, it was beyond his power to keep Hiram Flynt from dragging him back as an indentured servant. Meg knew the unscrupulous Flynt well enough to know that if he failed to find Gunnell, he would not hesitate to pretend Stephen was the missing bond servant.

No, she could not marry him. Better to have him leave now than have him taken from her after she was increasing with his child.

"Let us get this over with," Quentin said to Peter.

Planting himself in front of Meg and Stephen, Peter obediently began to read the marriage ceremony. She tried to escape, but Stephen's arm came around her and held her tightly to him.

She glared mutinously at Peter. When the time came for her to speak her vows, nothing could drag them from her lips.

When Burnaby reached that part, he looked at Stephen. "Wilt thou—" He hesitated. "I do not know your name."

"Stephen Richard Alexander Wingate," he answered so promptly that Meg's hopes rose. Perhaps that truly was his real name.

"Wilt thou, Stephen Richard Alexander Wingate, have this woman to be thy wedded wife, to live together after God's ordinance in the holy estate of matrimony? Wilt thou love her, comfort her, honor, and keep her in sickness and in health, and forsaking all others, keep thee only unto her, so long as ye both shall live?"

"I will." Stephen spoke strongly and with certainty, as if he wanted to marry Meg instead of being forced into it.

Peter turned to her, but she tried to block out the sound of his voice. She could not believe this was happening to her.

When her turn came to say, "I will," she resolutely kept her lips shut.

"Meg," Quentin warned.

She ignored him.

Stephen's hand closed over hers. "Please, Megan."

The entreaty in his rich, sensual voice was far harder to ignore, but she managed.

"Continue with the ceremony, Peter," Quentin ordered.

"No!" Meg protested, but Peter ignored her and

read on just as though she had answered him affirmatively.

When he pronounced them man and wife, Meg cried furiously, "We are not. It is not legal. I did not agree to it."

Quentin, his expression mulish, grabbed her arm, squeezing it painfully. "Of course you did, Megan. We all heard you speak your vows."

She looked expectantly at the other two men, but neither one contradicted her brother. Meg felt hot tears of anger and defeat burning in her eyes. She glared contemptuously at Peter. "What manner of parson are you that you would marry a woman against her will?"

He flinched and looked longingly toward the door, clearly eager to escape. At that moment, it opened and Josh stepped inside.

He stopped dead at the sight of its four occupants. "Quentin, you came back." He did not seem particularly pleased. Without further welcome to the brother he had not seen in months, he turned to Meg. "Why are you dressed up?"

"Our sister just married Mr. Wingate," Quentin said.

Josh's face lit with joy. "You did, Meg? Why that's capital! Now he won't be leaving." The boy was clearly far more excited about Stephen staying than Quentin returning. Then Josh's face sobered. "But it was awful sudden. Why did you not tell me what you were planning?"

Meg, her cheeks reddening, faltered at trying to explain to her young brother what had transpired.

Stephen stepped into the awkward breach. "We did not know then that the Reverend Burnaby was arriving today. After he did, we decided to have him marry us before he left. Otherwise, it might be weeks before another minister comes by. Since he has to leave immediately, we had no time to waste."

"Yes, must go immediately," Peter interjected, clearly thankful to Stephen for providing him with an excuse to escape. He hurried toward the door, as though he feared he would lose this opportunity to make his exit, and said his farewells as he went. Quentin followed his friend outside.

Meg said, "Go with Quentin, Josh."

Her brother, clearly startled by the sharpness of her tone, obeyed.

As the door shut behind the trio, Meg turned and unleashed her ire on her new husband. "I do not want to be married to you!"

Stephen looked as though she had struck him. "Why are you so upset? You sure as hell wanted me and marriage a few days ago."

"That was before I realized what manner of man you are."

His eyes narrowed. "I will tell you what manner of man I am: One who did not run away today!"

"No," she agreed, "but perhaps it would have been better for me if you had." She was his wife now, tied for life to a man who did not love her and could not give her fidelity. Her previous suitors had given her no reason to trust men, and neither did this man. Why, she did not even know what her new name was. Was she Mrs. Stephen Wingate or Mrs. Billy Gunnell or perhaps Mrs. Earl Arlington?

She was terrified of what the future held, of the heartbreak he might bring her. Tears that she could no longer hold back trickled down her cheeks.

His hands came up to capture her cheeks, and he gently brushed her tears away with his thumbs. His eyes were troubled. "Megan, why are you so unhappy about marrying me? A few days ago you would have been eager to wed me had I asked you."

"But you did not ask me! Not then, not now. I do not want a man who was forced to marry me, especially not one who believes it is perfectly acceptable for a husband to keep a mistress."

His face tightened. "Believe me, infidelity is the last thing on my mind."

"Why, because I am the only woman around?"

"Megan, I married you because I wanted to. Please, give me a chance." His remarkable blue violet eyes echoed his plea. "I will make you happy."

Oh, if only she could believe that. She desperately wanted to, but she dared not. Sadly she said, "You have no idea what would make me happy."

His eyes gleamed, and he gave her a look that made her toes curl. "In some ways, I know better than you do, my innocent." His voice, suddenly husky and enticing and full of unspoken promises, sent a tremor of excitement shuddering through her.

His mouth dipped and claimed hers in a kiss full of passion and promise.

Chapter 19

~~~~~~~~⟡⟡~~~~~~~~

Stephen felt Megan tremble in response to his kiss, and relief flooded through him. She did care for him!

Her staunch aversion to marrying him had been a bitter blow to his pride. Never had he dreamed that when he finally took a wife she would not want him. He thought of the dozens of lovely high-born women in England who had vied to be his mate.

The cynic in him suddenly surfaced. Had he not been an earl, no matter how handsome and charming he was, they would not have been clamoring to be his countess.

As he lifted his lips from hers, Megan sighed.

"What is it?" he asked in concern.

She looked wistful. "It was not exactly the kind of wedding day a girl dreams about."

Stephen was instantly conscience stricken. A woman looked upon her wedding day as the most important one of her life and wanted it celebrated accordingly. His heart ached for her and for the disappointment the day had been to her.

He would have to make it up to her somehow. Perhaps the wedding gift he intended to give her would help. He could picture in his mind's eye the hummingbird brooch that he would have made for her, but he could not afford it until they reached England.

If they reached England.

Quentin stomped into the cabin. Stephen reluctantly released Megan, silently cursing her brother for having returned far too quickly. Quentin pulled the rocking chair to the hearth and appropriated it for himself.

After he had settled himself, he looked over at his sister, standing by the trestle table, and ordered in a querulous tone, "Fix me dinner, Meg. I am starving."

Anger flashed in her eyes at her brother's rude command, but before she could respond, Stephen's arm snaked around her waist.

"Like hell she will, you lazy bastard! You are not going to order my wife around like that—especially not after all she has been through today. She suffered a blow to her head that knocked her unconscious, and she damned near drowned. Then you forced her into a marriage she did not want. Now you are ordering her to fix your dinner like she was your damned slave. You want something to eat, make it yourself or go to the ordinary."

Rage distorted Quentin's handsome face. He jumped to his feet, grabbing his flintlock. His sister gasped in horror as he raised the musket and pointed it at Stephen's chest.

"You will not talk to me like that." Quentin growled. "You will treat me with the respect I deserve."

"Any shiftless man who deserts his sister and halfling brother on this frontier as you did deserves no respect!"

Quentin's face darkened with fury. "Apologize, damn you!"

Stephen raked his new brother-in-law with contemptuous eyes. "You expect to win my respect by cowering behind a gun barrel?"

Quentin trembled with rage. The musket, still aimed at Stephen's chest, waved dangerously. "Apologize to me or say your final prayers."

"Go to hell."

Quentin's finger tightened on the trigger. A frightened shriek escaped Megan, and she threw herself in front of her new husband, shielding him with her own body.

Stephen instinctively pulled her behind him. Her spontaneous action told him far more about her feelings for him than she was willing to admit to him—or perhaps even to herself. "Do not be alarmed, Megan. The incompetent bastard never reloaded."

Quentin's face reddened at the realization Stephen was right. With a string of furious expletives, he threw the weapon to the floor and stalked out of the cabin, slamming the door so hard that the dishes on the clapboard shelves rattled.

Stephen grinned at Megan. "I think Quentin is going to dine at the ordinary."

"He has a terrible temper. I am so afraid it will get him into serious trouble."

She had good reason to worry, Stephen thought. He bent his head to kiss her again, but before he could do so, the door opened again and Josh came in. Stephen smothered a curse at this new interruption.

Josh picked up the yoke-like water carrier. "I'll bring up water."

Stephen might not have another opportunity to talk to Josh privately, and he decided he had better seize this one. "I will help you." He took the yoke from Josh and put it on his own shoulders. "I will carry this for you."

The boy followed him down the path to the stream.

As Stephen filled the buckets, he asked, "Are you happy your brother is back?"

Josh shrugged. "Quentin's almost as lazy as Galloway was."

"He will not stay here unless he does his share of the work."

Josh's eyes lit up hopefully. "You will make him?"

"I will make him."

"Good!" Josh paused, examining Stephen with a thoughtful look in his eyes. "I wish Mama could have seen you."

"Why?"

"She was always belittling Meg and telling her no man would want to marry a plain, scrawny girl like her."

Stephen was aghast. "Why in God's name would your mother tell Megan such a rotten falsehood?"

"Mama was awful to Meg, always criticizing her and everything she did." Josh looked around as though he feared someone might overhear him. "I asked Papa once why she was so nasty to Meg, and he told me Mama was jealous of her."

"Why?"

"Papa said it was 'cause Meg was so good at everything she did and 'cause she was his confidante and right hand while he ignored Mama. Nobody liked being around Mama. She always complained how sick she was." Josh's face tightened. "Then Papa had his seizure and Galloway began to court her. Suddenly she was well."

Stephen rehooked the buckets to the yoke and

hoisted them. "Was your mama awful to you, too?"

"I was luckier than Meg. Mama never paid me any heed. Meg was more my mother than she was. Quentin was the only one Mama cared about."

Stephen started up the path with his heavy burden. "Would you do me a favor, Josh, and milk Bess for me tonight? I will do your chores for you tomorrow night in exchange."

"No need," the boy said cheerfully. "I do not mind doing it for *you*."

"After you are done with your chores, instead of coming back to the cabin, why do you not go tell Wilhelm and Gerda about my marriage to your sister. I suspect they will invite you to stay for dinner and spend the night." Stephen ruffled the boy's sandy hair affectionately. "They will understand that Megan and I would like to be alone."

At least he wanted to be alone with her. He doubted she shared that desire now, but he would see that she soon did. He had felt the passion in her when he kissed her, and he intended to stoke her desire into flames that would engulf them both and consume her doubts about him. Stephen fervently hoped Quentin would remain at the ordinary for hours.

Josh gave his new brother-in-law a knowing grin. "I am so glad you married Meg." The boy's face puckered in a troubled frown. "But she does not seem very happy about marrying you."

Stephen's mouth widened in a confident grin. "Give me a little time, Josh. I intend to make her very happy about it."

Meg was sitting in her rocking chair, staring at the dancing flames in the fireplace when the door to the cabin opened. Stephen came in, carrying the water buckets.

He smiled at her, and she thought him the most handsome man she had ever seen, with the sharply etched planes of his face and his wide-set blue violet eyes beneath thick, slashing brows of midnight black. The ugly red scar over his left brow had faded to a faint white line in the weeks he had been here.

She returned his smile. "Thank you for standing up to Quentin on my behalf. I am not used to someone defending me."

His grin widened. "That is what husbands are for, love—among other things."

Meg froze at his casual use of an endearment he did not mean. She might be his wife now, but she knew full well that she was not his love. Her heart ached at the thought of being shackled to a husband who had been forced to marry her at gunpoint. "Where is Josh?"

"Milking Bess for me. Then he is going to Wilhelm's."

"Why?" Her voice quavered.

"So we may have some privacy on our wedding night." He reached down, his hands spanning her waist. He lifted her to her feet and held her in the circle of his arms. Her heart began to beat like a wild thing. Heat flared deep within her.

"Are you that unhappy to have me as your husband?" His voice was laced with pain.

Yes, she tried to tell herself—and him—but she could not force the word past the huge lump in her throat. When he held her like this, all she wanted was to stay in his arms forever.

But there were questions that she needed answered. "Why did you not run away today when I grabbed Quentin's musket?"

"Did you truly want me to run away?"

No! "Yes," she said resolutely, but her gaze dropped toward her toes so he could not read the truth in her eyes. "Why else would I have seized the gun?" To her dismay, her voice wobbled.

"Do you find me that disgusting a husband, Megan?"

No, not disgusting. Handsome, charming, thrilling. And perhaps a liar and a dangerous criminal. Even knowing that he might be a murderer, she did not find him disgusting. Surely that bespoke some unfortunate weakness in her character.

She evaded answering him by repeating her earlier question. "Why did you not flee when I gave you the chance?"

He shrugged. "Because I was wrong all those weeks ago when I told you there was nothing here worth stealing. I have now discovered there is a precious treasure here, and I do not intend to leave without it."

She looked up at him, perplexed. "What is it?" He had the oddest expression—part hurt, part tenderness, and part something else that she could not decipher.

"Can you not guess?"

She was utterly baffled. "No, I cannot."

His husky voice became a caress. "'Tis your heart."

That object promptly swelled with happiness. But surely he could not mean it. "Why would you want it? Why did you let Quentin force you into marrying me?"

"Damn it, he did not force me." Stephen's remarkable eyes darkened into fathomless blue violet pools as he brushed a wayward curl away from her face. A tremor shook her at his touch.

"I married you because I love you." Stephen said

it so softly, so gravely that it was a moment before she fully comprehended his words.

She gaped at him. *He loved her!* Her heart seemed to stop beating.

His fingertips caressed her cheek. "I did not even believe in love until I met you, Megan. You have taught me what a fool I was."

She wanted so much to believe him, but did she dare? It was hard for her to trust a man's words, especially when he professed affection for her. She thought of her suitors back in the Tidewater, who had talked eloquently of their love and admiration for her, then had vanished as soon as Ashley Grove was no longer hers. She thought of Galloway and her mother.

"You look so disbelieving." He sounded wounded. "What are you thinking?"

"Of how my stepfather lavished attention and compliments on Mama, telling her how much he loved her and how he could not live without her, when all he wanted was Ashley Grove."

Was Meg being equally gullible with Stephen? Once her stepfather had gained control of Ashley Grove, he had ignored Mama. When she had protested, he had called her an ugly, whining old bitch. Meg would never forget the look on her mother's face.

Yes, Mama had paid for her sins.

But her children had paid an even higher price.

"You insult me, Megan, to think I might be another Charles Galloway. What ulterior motive do you think I could possibly have in marrying you? Surely not this sorry farm."

"No," she admitted. She had already lost everything. She recalled what Stephen had said when he had asked her to be his mistress. "What happened to those other important reasons why you could not marry me?"

"They no longer matter to me. All I care about is that you are my wife." Stephen ran his fingertips slowly, tenderly over her face as though he were a blind man learning the contours of his beloved. His smile was so brilliant that she could not seem to breathe. "None of those reasons was as important as my need to have you beside me for the rest of my life."

She wanted to believe him so much. Dear God, she did.

His lips captured hers again in a long kiss, tender at first then escalating in heat and intensity until once again she forgot all else but the pleasure of the moment.

She closed her eyes, savoring the taste of him, savoring his cinnamon and sunshine scent. A strange contentment blossomed within her.

His tongue, warm and teasing, traced the outline of her lips. Then his mouth brushed lightly over hers, back and forth. She opened her eyes and saw that he was watching her intently through the downward sweep of his thick, black lashes.

He nibbled on her lower lip, sending an odd yearning shooting through her, before his mouth settled on hers in a fiery, demanding kiss. She found herself responding to him, her mouth as hungry as his.

Their tongues moved in an erotic mating that turned her breathing erratic. Meg hardly noticed that his hands were at the laces of her gown, loosening them then undoing her chemise.

His mouth deserted hers. She moaned in startled excitement as his lips lay a hot trail down the column of her neck, then closed over the tip of her breast, suckling her. A shudder of pure pleasure shook her. She could no longer think, only feel. She moaned again.

Stephen raised his head and smiled knowingly down at her. She felt the cool air of the room on her nipple, still wet from his mouth. She was shocked at how easily he had made her forget her doubts about him, forget everything but his kisses.

He glanced meaningfully toward her new bedroom. "I have made you my wife before God, Megan. Now let me do so in fact."

My wife. The rich huskiness of his tone ignited a strange glowing warmth deep within her that seemed to expand like a billowing cloud on a summer afternoon.

She swallowed hard and was about to assent when her doubts resurfaced stronger than ever. If she lay with him, she might become pregnant with his child. What if he turned out to be as fickle and faithless as her suitors in the Tidewater?

Her mother's words taunted her memory: *Poor Meg. A woman as plain as you can never inspire passion and faithfulness and undying love in a handsome, young husband.*

Worse, what if he was Billy Gunnell, convicted murderer and escaped indentured servant?

Meg tried to pull away from him, but he would not let her. Clearly misinterpreting the reason for her effort, he said gently, "Megan, there is no shame in this. You are my wife now."

"And I must do my wifely duty!"

"Duty?" His eyes were teasing, his smile hot and full of sensual promise. "Once I have made love to you, I promise you that you will never again look upon it as a *duty.*"

His mouth closed over hers in a passionate kiss that melted her like candle wax in a flame.

He lifted his mouth a fraction. "My dearest Megan, before this night is over, I intend to make you very, very happy that you married me."

He swept her up in his arms and carried her toward the bedroom. She recalled the stories she had heard about painful wedding nights, and she involuntarily shuddered.

Stephen looked down at her, one arched brow cocked questioningly. "What is it?"

"I am afraid."

His arms tightened around her. "I understand, my innocent, but I promise you have nothing to fear from me."

She wanted to believe him, but her brow puckered in doubt.

His own knit in reaction. "You cannot believe that I would deliberately hurt you, Megan."

No, she realized, she did not. He would not intentionally cause her pain, but some men's rods were said to be very large. Then she recalled bathing Stephen while he was ill and how puny his had been. Her fear faded.

He set her on her feet beside the bed, and his hands lightly skimmed her body. "Let me undress you, love."

She felt herself coloring hotly at the thought of him seeing her naked. Meg tightened her grip on her chemise that she was holding together. "No-o-o."

He whispered, "Do not turn shy on me now." His breath was warm and moist and exciting against her cheek. "Remember, I have already undressed you once today."

Her face grew hotter and she looked away. What had he thought then? That she was too plain? That her body was too thin and bony?

He cupped her chin with his hand and turned

her face to him. The look he gave her melted her fears and transformed her timidity into longing.

He kissed her deeply. She unconsciously released her grip on her chemise, and her arms crept around his neck.

After a moment, his hand stole beneath the thin chemise and cupped her breast. She gasped as his thumb slowly rubbed her nipple in tight little circles. She shivered with pleasure at the sensations it aroused.

She never wanted him to stop. When he did, she moaned in protest.

Still holding her mouth in thrall with his own, his hands came up to her shoulders and slid her gown and chemise down her arms. They pooled around her feet, leaving her clad only in her white silk stockings held up by lace garters, one of the few bits of finery that she had been able to salvage from her wardrobe at Ashley Grove.

He broke their kiss and stepped back to look at her. Embarrassed by her nakedness, Meg clutched her arms around her to shield herself from his eyes.

He clasped her wrists lightly in his hands and opened her arms. "Do not hide yourself from me, love," Stephen's voice was low and husky and coaxing. "You are beautiful."

She started to protest such a blatant prevarication, but then she saw his expression of rapt appreciation as he studied her. The room was cool, yet she hardly noticed, so heated was she beneath the intensity of his admiring gaze.

He ran his callused hands down her body, touching her with such gentleness, such reverence that she wanted to cry at the sweetness of it.

For the first time in her life, Meg felt beautiful. Felt worthy of a man's admiration.

He knelt at her feet and removed her stockings, his hands stroking her legs as he did so.

Stephen rose and nudged her down on the bed, then shed his shirt, baring his bronze, muscled chest to her gaze. She loved to look at him. He was as beautiful as he had just made her feel.

He turned and began to kiss her, starting at her temple and working downward while his hands stroked her thighs and her belly in a way that fed an aching need deep within her that demanded to be satisfied.

His mouth closed over her breast. His tongue, warm and wet, circled her nipple, and she moaned. She had never dreamed a man could make her feel like this.

Then his finger slipped into the triangle of curls at the top of her thighs, touching a spot so exquisitely sensitive that an astonished, elongated "Ooooo" escaped her lips.

Stephen raised his head and met her gaze, a wickedly irresistible smile illuminating his sensual face while his finger continued to perform its magic on her, bringing forth a strange flood of moisture. Her eyes widened in surprise as his finger slid within her and moved in a rhythm that made her gasp.

Her breath was coming in choppy pants, and a building excitement rippled through her.

When he withdrew his hand, she felt as though she had been deserted just as her body was poised on the knife edge of a momentous discovery.

"Don't stop!" she exclaimed in dismay.

His laugh, low and husky and pleased, sent a tremor of pleasure through her. "Like that, do we?"

"Yes," she admitted as he stood up. He turned his back and stripped his breeches off. As he turned around, she caught sight of his engorged manhood. Stunned by the size of it, she blurted, "Where did that come from?"

He looked startled as he came down on the bed beside her. "You should know. You bathed me when I was sick."

"Surely that puny thing could not—"

"Puny!" He sounded as though she had insulted him terribly.

"I am sorry, but you—it—looks so different now."

To her relief, the anger faded from his eyes, and he chuckled. "I suppose it does. 'Tis your doing that made it grow."

She blinked in surprise. "Mine?"

His laugh was deep and rich as he lay down beside her and gathered her to him. His hands moved skillfully over her body, and he whispered to her how lovely she was.

Then his mouth took her nipple while his fingers found that secret spot between her legs, tantalizing it until she moaned.

He parted her legs and braced himself above her. He lowered his head, his lips capturing hers in a deep kiss. Then she felt something large and hard pushing slowly, carefully into that secret place where his finger had been.

She felt herself stretch to accommodate it, but then it reached a barrier.

She squirmed uncomfortably. He drove into her with one quick, clean thrust, and she cried out in pain. Instantly he stilled and bathed her face with kisses while making soothing, inarticulate sounds of comfort.

After awhile, still murmuring to her, he began to move within her, slowly and rhythmically, with great care as though she were fragile crystal that might shatter.

Slowly he increased his tempo. Pain had given way to a new sensation, a building excitement, wild and fierce, and Meg found herself moving breathlessly with him in the ageless dance of love. She felt as though she were soaring higher and higher toward some elusive, magical heaven.

"Let it happen, love." His voice was low and thick and sensual.

And then she did shatter as spasm after spasm of pleasure rocked her. They seemed to ignite a similar response in his own body.

Afterward, when she could speak again, she said with wonder in her voice, "I . . . I cannot believe it."

He grinned at her, that knowing, teasing smile that turned her to liquid. "You did not find your duty so onerous after all, did you, love?"

She felt herself blushing. He laughed and drew her into his arms, holding her tightly against the strong, warm wall of his chest.

He made her feel so cherished, so protected. She thought of the response that he had coaxed from her body.

Before this night is over, I intend to make you very, very happy that you married me.

He had succeeded.

Stephen had played her body with the same virtuoso skill with which she performed on the harpsichord.

Her smile faded. One did not become a virtuoso without much, much practice. The thought froze her. Who were the women her husband had pleasured before her?

How many had there been?

How many more would there be in the future

for a husband who saw nothing wrong with having both a wife and a mistress?

Poor Meg. A woman as plain as you can never inspire passion and faithfulness and undying love in a handsome young husband.

Chapter 20

When Meg awoke the next morning, it was long after dawn. Stephen lay on his side, facing her, his arm flung possessively over her waist as though he feared she might steal away from him in his sleep.

His midnight black hair was tousled about his face. With its sharply etched contours relaxed in sleep, he looked surprisingly young and breathtakingly handsome. Only the rapidly fading scar on his left temple marred the perfection of his face.

It was long past the time to get up, but she hated to leave the bed and the warmth of his body beside her. She had never stayed abed so late since she came to the frontier.

Not that she had gotten all that much sleep. Stephen had made love to her three more times last night, each time more wondrous and ecstatic than the one before.

She smiled as she recalled the pleasure, previously beyond her imagining, to which he had initiated her. "My husband," she whispered, admiration tinged with incredulity.

Then Quentin had awakened them sometime toward dawn. He had come stumbling into the cabin, singing a ditty in a voice so slurred that his words could not be understood.

"Sounds as though he drank his dinner," Stephen had observed sleepily.

That meant Quentin would feel terrible today and would spend the day abed. Meg was not surprised that she did not hear him stirring in the other room.

She lay listening to her husband's breathing, deep and even in sleep, and thought of what they had shared in this bed.

As long as he had held her in his arms, she had been able to keep reality at bay, but now it came back to haunt her with a vengeance.

He professed to love her. Perhaps he did, at least for the moment. She thought of his masterful lovemaking and wondered again how many other women he had loved before her.

And how many more he would love in the future.

By his own admission he did not believe in marital fidelity.

And what if he was Billy Gunnell? That possibility preyed at her mind, a corrosive fear that could not be stilled. It dissolved her happiness like lye on skin.

Her mother had shown her just how blind a woman in love could be to a man's true nature, and Meg had vowed never to be so foolish. But now she wondered whether she had broken this promise to herself.

Meg remembered her husband's frantic, fevered cries when she had nursed him through his delirium. *I am Arlington. You must believe me! I tell you I am Earl . . . Arlington.*

He had been so insistent about that.

It gave her hope that he truly was not Billy Gunnell. But who then was Earl Arlington?

All her doubts and insecurities rose up again like water in a well. Her head began to throb. If only she knew what to believe. Tears trickled down her cheek. She could not stop them.

"Megan, what is it?"

She jumped at the sound of her husband's alarmed voice beside her. He propped himself on one elbow, his eyes filled with concern. His thumb tenderly brushed the tears from her cheek.

She swallowed hard at his gentleness. Surely such a man could not be a dangerous, desperate criminal. She wanted so much to believe that he was exactly what he said, a gentleman wrongly impressed.

But did she dare?

"Why are you crying?"

"I am wondering whether I am Mrs. Stephen Wingate or Mrs. Billy Gunnell."

He flinched, and his hand dropped away from her face. "Damn it, Megan. Why will you not believe me? I am not Gunnell!"

She knew her doubt was reflected in her eyes.

Stephen ran his fingers roughly through his hair in a gesture of frustration. "Do you truly think that I would lie to my own wife about that? How can I make you believe me? I have never committed a crime in my life—and certainly not murder! How can you think I am a murderer?"

Meg saw the pain in his eyes and knew she had hurt him terribly, but she had to know the truth about what she faced as his wife. "If you are not Gunnell, why did you remove the handbill seeking his return?"

"I told you why. I was mistaken for him once,

and I did not dare chance that it might happen
again."

"But what if it does happen again? What if I become pregnant and you are seized as Gunnell? Can
you promise that I will not be forced to watch the
father of my unborn child dragged off as a murderous convict who escaped his master?"

His eyes betrayed him. The sick horror and awful fear in their blue violet depths lasted for only a
second before he managed to hide it, but it was all
the answer she needed. Her heart felt as though he
had carved it with a rapier blade.

Stephen expelled his breath in a long defeated
sigh. "No, I cannot promise you." How he wished
he could. He raked his hand through his hair again.

Bloody hell, what a mess! He should have told
her the whole truth in the beginning, instead of
hiding part of it from her. The fact that he had not
been totally honest made it all the more difficult to
tell her now. She would accuse him of lying to her,
and her trust in him would be irreparably undermined. He could not chance that.

Instead he ran his hand comfortingly, caressingly
down her body, loving the soft, satiny feel of her
skin and her little shiver of response at his touch.
"Megan, I want only to make you the happiest
woman in the world."

And that was the truth.

But would he be allowed to do that? Or would
her nightmare come true? The thought of being
torn from her while she was carrying his child terrified him. He might never know what happened to
her, never see their baby, never know whether
it was a son or a daughter. Then he would truly be
cast into the deepest, darkest depths of hell.

The only way to assure his safety from Flynt was
to flee America for England. But he could not leave

Megan and Josh behind, and he had no hope of raising the blunt for three passages.

Damn it, he would have to find a way.

"You will never be safe. We will always live in fear that you will be seized."

Stephen winced at the pain and reproach in Megan's voice. "I will be very safe," he said doggedly, "once we get to England."

"England!" Megan cried in alarm. "I cannot go to England."

"You are my wife, Megan. Remember what the Bible says: 'Whither thou goest, I will go.' "

"What of Josh?"

Stephen lay a reassuring hand on her arm. "We will take him with us. I promise you that I will give him the education you want for him."

Megan's mouth set in stubborn lines. Persuading her would not be easy, and Stephen saw no point in arguing with her now when he had no idea how he would find the money. Originally he had counted on George to supply the blunt for the voyage.

But Stephen had heard nothing from his brother and no longer entertained any hope that he would. With each passing day, it looked increasingly as though George, the one who would gain most from his kidnapping and impressment, had been responsible for it.

Stephen feared his foolish letter had alerted his brother to the fact that impressment had failed to kill him. Would George notify Hiram Flynt where to find Stephen?

He should be running as fast as he could away from here. But if he fled and something happened to Megan, he would not be able to live with himself.

* * *

Quentin, clearly suffering the aftereffects of his night at the ordinary, remained in bed and declined Megan's offer of breakfast with a shudder.

Stephen said nothing, waiting until his wife had gone out to gather eggs. Then he marched over to Quentin's bed. "Get up, you lazy bastard. If you are going to stay here, you are going to earn your keep."

Quentin glared at him with bloodshot eyes. "I am sick."

"You brought it on yourself. If you want to eat today and have a bed to sleep in tonight, you are going to work for it."

"Who the hell do you think you are, telling me what to do? This is my farm."

"No, it is Megan's. Your father left it to her. And since you so kindly married her to me yesterday, I, as her husband, now control it."

Quentin opened his mouth to protest, but Stephen cut him off. "Control of a woman's property passes to her husband upon her marriage. 'Tis the law, and you know it. Now get up."

When Quentin did not obey, Stephen grabbed his arm and unceremoniously yanked him from the bed, spilling him on the floor.

Quentin yowled in protest. "What are you doing?"

"Making a man out of you—if that is possible."

Quentin's eyes narrowed with fury. "You bastard! I will not allow you to insult me."

"The truth is not an insult." If it was at all possible, Stephen would forge Quentin into a man who would not run off and abandon Meg if Hiram Flynt recaptured her husband. Stephen did not hold much hope of succeeding, but he would try. "I am going to milk Bess. When I've finished, you had better be dressed and ready to accompany me."

"And if I am not?" Quentin glared at him from the floor.

Stephen gave him a long hard stare, full of menace. "I will have no compunction about marching you outside stark naked."

Stephen led Quentin, fully clothed, toward the shed. Yesterday's cold and sharp, biting wind had given way to surprisingly warm temperatures and a soft breeze scented with evergreens. Stephen breathed deeply of nature's perfume.

The day seemed all the more beautiful to him because of the night he had spent with Megan. He smiled to himself as he remembered his bride's passion. It had surprised and delighted him. There had been nothing artful or contrived about her responses, and she had thrilled him in a way none of his clever mistresses ever had.

He rested the musket he carried against the shed. "We need to gather more wood for winter."

Quentin lunged for the flintlock that Stephen had put down, grabbed it, and pointed it at his new brother-in-law's chest. "Gather it yourself. You will not order me around."

Stephen regarded him with contempt. "You are damned good at pointing a gun at an unarmed man."

Quentin smirked. "And this time it is loaded. I saw you do it."

Their gazes met and held. Stephen kept his purposely blank, a skill that had served him well at the London gaming tables. Never taking his eyes from his opponent, he suddenly brought one hand up and seized the musket barrel, forcing it to the side.

The move caught Quentin unawares, and his finger must have tightened reflexively on the trigger. The musket fired, the ball slamming harmlessly into the branches of a flowering maple.

"Now it is unloaded," Stephen said softly. He jerked the weapon from Quentin's hand and threw it away.

He slammed his fist into his brother-in-law's face, sending him sprawling.

Quentin lay there, rubbing his jaw and staring up in shock.

"Get up," Stephen growled, "and fight like a man, you gutless bastard."

Quentin's face reddened with anger, and he staggered up. "I will kill you for calling me that."

"Not without a gun," Stephen said, delivering another facer that sent Quentin stumbling back.

Megan's brother teetered then managed to regain his balance. With a roar of fury he charged, swinging wildly. Stephen coolly dodged and parried Quentin's fists, then delivered another blow to his adversary's chin that snapped his head back.

Quentin yelped in pain then tried to charge again, with no more success than the first time.

Stephen got no pleasure from fighting such an inferior opponent and decided to put a mercifully quick end to the fray by delivering a sharp right to his breadbasket.

A whooshing sound, like air escaping a bellows, came from Quentin as he sank to the ground.

Stephen stood over the gasping man. "That is only a small taste of what I will give you if you ever point another weapon at me. Do it again, and I promise you that I will beat the hell out of you. Do you understand?"

Quentin nodded, unable to speak. When he finally recovered his breath, he said, "You could have easily disarmed me like that yesterday, and you would not have had to marry my sister."

"I wanted to marry her."

Quentin studied him suspiciously. "Why? For this farm?"

"No, because I love her."

Quentin looked so skeptical that Stephen felt his anger rising and he could not keep sarcasm from his voice. "Do you find it so difficult to conceive that a man might love your sister?"

"Well, Mama said . . ."

"Your mama was a fool!"

"No, she wasn't. If Meg had only listened to her and accepted Nathan Baylis's offer, Ashley Grove would still be ours."

"Was Baylis the judge who signed the order that made Galloway Megan and Josh's guardian?"

Quentin nodded. "Meg suspected Baylis did so as revenge on her for rejecting him."

Or perhaps Baylis entertained hopes that Galloway would arrange a marriage between his ward and the judge. "What did your father think of Baylis?"

"He had no use for him, called him a shifty-eyed lawyer who could not be trusted, but that was back before he was made a justice."

"Do you think an appointment to the bench changes a man's character?" Stephen scoffed. "Now get to work."

"I am a gentleman," Quentin whined. "I was not born to do common farm labor. You do not know what it is like to have everything that is rightfully yours snatched away from you."

Quentin's self-pity grated on Stephen. How different Megan and her brother were. "Oh, I know all too well what it is like. I lost a hell of a lot more than you did." Yes, he had: a noble title, a great inheritance, and the most precious possession of all—his freedom. "But feeling sorry for myself and sniveling about it accomplishes nothing."

"But it is not fair."

"So life dealt you a bad hand," Stephen said without sympathy. "You play it out as best you can and make the most of what you have."

After dinner that night, Stephen listened with pleasure as Megan played her flute for him and Josh. Quentin had gone off to the ordinary.

As he had departed, Stephen had warned him against getting drunk. "You will work tomorrow, no matter how you feel."

Stephen closed his eyes as Megan made the flute sing with poignant beauty. His wife was so talented, and he was very proud of her. He marveled again at the peace and contentment she brought him.

His lip curled in distaste as he remembered the restless, frenetic search for pleasure of his London days, trying—and failing—to fill the aching emptiness that gaped within him.

None of his mistresses, not even Caroline Taber, had succeeded.

But Megan had.

Stephen could hardly wait for tonight. Only concern for his bride, her body not yet used to vigorous and frequent lovemaking, had stopped him from sneaking back to the cabin for her this afternoon.

A hard knock at the door brought Megan's playing to an abrupt stop. The tranquil serenity Stephen had enjoyed as he listened to her music was shattered by the instant clutching fear that Flynt's trackers might have found him.

But it was only Wilhelm.

"What are you doing here so late?" Josh asked.

"I come to varn you of the two strangers at the ordinary, gamesters rooking all those that play vith them. Quentin is vaiting his turn."

"Dear God! He cannot resist gambling," Megan cried in alarm. "It is like a fever in him, and he cannot help himself. He will wager anything, whether it belongs to him or not." She turned to her husband. "You must stop him! Please, Stephen."

He rose reluctantly. Remembering Galloway's fate at the hands of two strangers, he could not help but wonder whether Flynt might also have sent these two. Stephen had no desire to see them, but he could not refuse his wife's fervent plea.

Silently cursing his troublesome brother-in-law, he followed Wilhelm out the door.

As the two men walked toward the ordinary, Stephen asked, "Could there be a connection between these two strangers and the ones who killed Galloway?"

"*Nein.* Men like the pair tonight are gamesters who come to the frontier after the harvest to fleece settlers."

At the ordinary, Quentin, his face bruised and swollen from his fight with Stephen, was standing beside a table where Sam Wylie and Paul Ames were playing a card game called putt with one of the strangers. The second stranger was at another table, playing with two other settlers.

Tobacco smoke drifted in a pungent haze over the rough hewn tables, and its smell, mingled with that of ale and male sweat, permeated the room, which was dimly lit by tallow candles.

Quentin's hazel eyes were fixed greedily on the pile of coin that rested in front of the stranger.

The coin held equal fascination for the other men

gathered in the room, and Stephen understood why. Those bright disks represented more than they could earn in a year of backbreaking toil on the frontier. Desperate as Stephen was for money to pay for three passages to England, he felt the lure himself.

He came up beside his brother-in-law and asked softly, "What will you stake, Quentin?"

He started, then flushed guiltily at the question.

"You bastard," Stephen hissed. "Get out of here!"

For a moment, Quentin looked as though he would defy the order. Then, seeing Stephen's hands tighten into fists, he stalked out of the ordinary.

"Where the hell is he going?" demanded one of the strangers, a wiry man with eyes no wider than slits. He clearly did not want any potential victims to escape him.

"My brother-in-law has nothing to stake."

The stranger's eyes narrowed even more at the challenging note in Stephen's voice. "Are you taking his place?"

"Maybe after I watch a few hands. I do not know the game."

"'Tis simple enough," the stranger said.

He was right. Only three cards were dealt to each player, who could make no draws or discards. Winning depended more on bluffing one's opponents into thinking one held the best cards, rather than actually holding them. Stephen had always been very good at such games. He noted that the best putt cards were the trey, followed by the deuce, then the ace.

Stephen soon perceived that when the strangers—whose names were Tildon and MacLean—dealt, their opponents rarely got good cards.

This anomaly did not go unobserved by their opponents and the other settlers. Their grumbling grew increasingly audible as they lost hand after hand.

"Damn you," Ames shouted at Tildon, "you are cheating me."

"Them's fightin' words," the slit-eyed stranger snapped. "Prove it. You'll find nothin' wrong with them cards."

The room grew deathly quiet as Ames picked them up one by one, looking for bends or marks on them, but he could find no blemish.

"I will prove it," Stephen said quietly.

He took the cards, pushed them together in a neat pile, then ran the long edge of the deck between his fingers. He suppressed a smile. It was just as he had thought. "Now I will pick out the best putt cards."

He opened the deck to a deuce of spades, then of diamonds.

Tildon twitched nervously in his seat and started to rise. Wylie shoved him down. "You ain't going nowhere."

Stephen next showed the trey of spades, then the deuce of hearts. The cards had been shaved, leaving the deuces and treys slightly wider.

Stephen looked across at Tildon. "Now I challenge you and MacLean to play me with an honest deck of cards."

Perspiration beaded on Tildon's forehead. He looked toward the door as though calculating whether he could somehow make it through the angry settlers and escape.

"Do not try it," Stephen warned softly. "You will never make it." He called to the ordinary's proprietor, "Bring a fresh deck of cards."

When the balding, pot-bellied owner complied,

Stephen ran his fingers along the edges, examined the backs, then said to Tildon and MacLean, "Shall we play?"

Stephen soon proved himself far better at bluffing than the two nervous rooks. Without the advantage of a marked deck, they were no match for him. He won back everything the others had lost to the pair, then took their initial stakes.

A resounding cheer went up from the rapt spectators when he had cleaned them out. Only then were MacLean and Tildon allowed to flee into the night.

As they ran, one of the men who had lost to them shouted, "Thieving blackguards! We ought to hang them for what they cost us."

Elation surged through Stephen as he counted the winnings piled before him. He had more than enough now to pay for three passages to England. He would be safe.

The losers, subdued and sullen, looked at Stephen. The rooks had made fools of them, cheating them of what little they and their families had worked so hard to earn.

Stephen struggled with his conscience. There was no reason why he should not keep all the money. He had not cheated the settlers, the strangers had. He had won it fairly from them.

It was his now.

But looking at the devastated faces of the losers, he knew how precious what they had lost was to them. *They will only lose it to someone else. Why should you not keep it?*

Another part of him argued: *Think of what it means to their families, think of what they will have to go without unless you give it back.*

Stephen knew how hard these men and their families had labored to earn what they lost tonight.

He knew all too well the blood and sweat that they had expended.

And he knew then that he could not keep their share of his winnings. He could not live with himself if he did.

When Stephen gave their money back to the other players, it was clear he had made himself a hero.

But what was left of his winnings would be barely enough to pay for his and Megan's passages to England. And she would not go without Josh.

Stephen must now find a way to raise the money for her young brother. Once it would have seemed like a paltry sum, hardly worth his notice.

Now it represented his life and his freedom.

Chapter 21

Two dozen wagons and carts were already parked in Wilhelm's clearing when Meg arrived with her husband and Josh for the settlers' annual after-harvest dinner. Stephen carried an iron kettle of venison stew, his wife's contribution to the dinner.

The men gathered in a knot talking, their sons practiced throwing a tomahawk at a tree at the edge of the wood, and the wives and daughters bustled around a long plank table, setting food on it.

Josh rushed off to join the other boys.

Gerda hurried up. "Vhere is Quentin?"

Meg fought back a sudden rush of tears. "He ran away this morning before we were up."

"Earliest he's ever been out of bed," Stephen said blandly.

Meg shot an accusatory look at her husband. "Quentin left a note saying that Stephen worked him too hard and he was going back to the Tidewater."

Her husband's mouth tightened. "I worked him no harder than I worked myself, Megan."

She knew that was true, but she was still so upset

that her brother had sneaked away again that she was venting some of her distress on her husband.

Stephen said wearily, "I was trying to make a man of him, but I failed."

He went over to the table and set the kettle down among the other dishes. Several of the men called to him to join them.

As Meg watched her husband of a week move toward them, she thought he looked unbearably handsome, standing so tall and straight, his raven hair shining in the sun. His features, from the wide-set eyes beneath slashing brows to the proud aristocratic nose and the sensual mouth, were perfect.

Then she thought of the tenderness and passion with which he had made love to her the past week, the joy and ecstasy that he gave her, and a warm glow enveloped her.

"Your husband is a hero since he returned to the other men vhat they lost to the two strangers at the ordinary," Gerda said as they walked toward the table. "He need not have done that."

"No," Meg agreed. Only she knew how important that money had been to him. Giving it back meant he had only enough money for two passages to England instead of three. Had he kept the money, they would all be on their way to England instead of remaining here, where he faced the daily threat of being seized.

She had urged him to go alone. She and Josh would remain behind, and he could send for them later. To her astonishment he had stubbornly insisted, "I will not leave without you, Megan."

Gerda nodded toward the table, heavily laden with dozens of dishes that bathed the afternoon air with delicious aromas. "Ve are about to eat."

After the settlers had finished devouring the feast, the men congregated near Wilhelm's corncrib with a jug of homemade liquor while the women cleared away the remains of the food before the dancing started.

A horse galloped into the clearing, drawing everyone's attention. Meg had not seen the big bay gelding before, but its rider, a burly, thick-faced man, looked vaguely familiar to her.

Instead of leaving his horse with the other guests' animals, the newcomer rode up to the men by the corncrib. Silently he surveyed them from his perch in the saddle with slow insolence.

In that moment Megan remembered who he was. Cold fear clutched at her heart.

Silas Reif!

She had seen him a few times in the Tidewater. He made his living returning runaway slaves and servants for Hiram Flynt and other plantation owners. Reif was reputed to be as mean and unscrupulous as they came. He and Flynt made a pair.

Reif's cold eyes reminded Megan of a vulture's. When they stopped on Stephen's face, her heart seemed to cease beating and fear rose like bile in her throat. An evil little smile played on Reif's mouth but did not reach those raptor's eyes that were fixed on Stephen.

Her husband looked faintly puzzled by the stranger's attention.

Reif boomed, "So we meet at last, Billy Gunnell."

A shudder ran through Meg, but by not so much as a flick of an eyelash did Stephen betray that the name meant anything to him.

"You have mistaken me for someone else." Meg was amazed at how coolly and calmly her husband spoke. She knew he had to be terrified that his worst nightmare was coming true.

He said, "My name is Stephen Wingate."

"Like hell it is," Reif growled. "I know you well enough, Billy Gunnell."

"My name is not Billy Gunnell, and I have never seen you before in my life."

Stephen betrayed absolutely nothing. Meg marveled at his composure. She could see now why he had beaten those rooking gamblers at putt.

Wilhelm stepped forward. "This man is Herr Vingate."

Reif was a big man, but he was dwarfed by the German giant. "He is not Herr Vingate. He is Billy Gunnell, one of the most notorious, nefarious murderers and rapists in the annals of English crime."

Silence descended on the clearing, and everyone's attention fixed on the two men.

Meg felt her stomach roil. The handbill had warned that Gunnell was a dangerous murderer, but it had said nothing about him being a rapist, too.

"If his crimes were committed in England, how'd he get here?" Sam Wylie demanded.

"He was transported for fourteen years."

"The English," one of the men grumbled, his voice slurred from the homemade liquor he had been imbibing, "always dumping their human garbage on us."

"I will remove this particular piece of garbage from your neighborhood," Reif said. "Gunnell here was bought as an indentured servant by a Tidewater plantation owner, Hiram Flynt. Billy escaped from his master nearly two months ago and headed this way. Mr. Flynt's dogs tracked him, but they lost his scent in the mountains east of here."

A wave of nausea swept over Meg. Dear God, it was nearly two months since Stephen had stumbled up to her cabin. She remembered him raving in his delirium about the dogs he believed were chasing him.

Reif said, "Flynt hired me to find Gunnell, and now I have."

"Like hell you have!" Stephen stood proud and defiant. "I am not Gunnell, and you know it. You do not give a damn whether you have the right man or not. Any strong young man will do as long as you can collect the reward offered for Gunnell's return."

"Aye, we know your kind," one of the men near Stephen snapped at Reif.

Another called out, "You've never seen this Gunnell, have you?"

Unease flickered in Reif's eyes, then they hardened. He gestured at Stephen. "I have now. Don't need to have seen him before. This man matches the description of Mr. Flynt's runaway, and I am returning him to his rightful owner."

Meg clenched her hand into a fist and stuffed it in her mouth to keep from screaming aloud. *Not to Hiram Flynt!* Even if Stephen was lying, even if he really was Gunnell, she could not bear the thought of him being sent back to Flynt. She knew the inhuman punishment that awful man meted out to those who escaped him.

Paul Ames interjected, "I saw a handbill awhile back describing this Gunnell bastard. As I recall, he don't sound nothing like Wingate here." He gestured toward Reif. "You got a copy of that poster, mister, you can read?"

Reif pulled a paper from his pocket and unfolded it. The crowd listened in silence as he read: "Has a livid red scar over his left eye, unkempt black hair halfway down his back, bushy black beard . . ."

Meg closed her eyes. Thank God she had cut Stephen's hair and shaved his beard before anyone saw him.

" . . . thick black brows, unusual light-blue eyes, skinny, stands about eighteen hands high." Reif broke off and pointed at Stephen. "See that scar over his left eye."

"Ain't red, though, and he ain't skinny," Ames said.

Not any longer, Meg thought. Stephen must have gained a stone or more since he'd arrived at the farm.

"What was he wearing?" someone called.

"A homespun flax shirt and breeches torn off above the knees and held up with a rope," Reif answered.

"What about shoes?"

"Barefoot."

Ames turned to Meg. "That how Wingate was dressed when he come to your farm?"

It was. Meg felt every eye upon her, including Stephen's. She saw the uncertainty and silent entreaty in his.

His freedom, his future—their future—his very life hung on her words.

But lying was wrong, and it was repugnant to her.

She wrestled with her conscience. Was it not a greater wrong to condemn a man, especially one who might be innocent, to Hiram Flynt's terrible cruelty? No one, not even Billy Gunnell, as bad as he was purported to be, deserved that. Her mouth felt as dry as a desert. She wet her lips with her tongue and prayed her voice would not come out as a croak.

"No, Stephen was wearing a deerskin hunting shirt, breeches, and moccasins." Her tone was firmer than she had expected. "He had no beard and his hair was shoulder length."

She saw the relief on her husband's face.

"She's lying!" Reif snarled.

"Meg vould never lie," Gerda cried loyally.

"Nay, she would not," another voice echoed.

If only that was true, Meg thought, feeling wretched that she had misled her friends and betrayed their trust in her. Dear God, was she sheltering—had she married—a desperate murderer and rapist?

Reif glared at Stephen. "Where do you claim to be from?"

"I *am* from Yorkshire, England."

"I'll prove you are Gunnell."

Stephen met his gaze unflinchingly. "You cannot prove I am someone I am not."

"You cannot prove you are Stephen Wingate," Reif shot back.

"Yes, I can. I have a brother, Captain George Wingate, with the British army in New York. He will vouch for my identity."

"I wager this Captain George Wingate don't exist," Reif scoffed. "You made him up because you know New York is too far away to ascertain the truth."

"But he does exist." Charles Bentley, Elizabeth's husband, stepped forward. "We came here from New York, and I knew Captain George Wingate there. He used to come into my parents' shop, and he said he was from Yorkshire." He squinted at Stephen. "This man does resemble the captain a little, too."

Reif was clearly taken aback by this, but he recovered quickly. "Why would a man whose family can afford to buy his brother a captain's commission in the British army come to America to scratch out a living on the frontier? Hell, if he came to America at all, he could afford to buy a Tidewater plantation."

Meg could see by the expressions on several faces in the crowd that this was the most effective argument Reif had yet raised against Stephen.

Reif apparently sensed it, too, for he hurried to press home his advantage. "Tell me, Gunnell or whatever the hell you call yourself, why'd you come to America?"

"My name is Stephen Wingate. I suffered a reversal of fortune in England, and I came to America to try to rebuild what I had lost."

Meg listened with a sinking heart to his calm explanation, so different from what he had told her. He made no mention of his large farm in Yorkshire, no mention of the wealth that supposedly was his in England, no mention of being seized at Dover and wrongly impressed.

"Unfortunately, after I landed in Baltimore, I was robbed on the docks and left penniless."

No mention of jumping from a frigate and swimming for his life to the Virginia shore.

Stephen continued, "I heard there was land for the taking along the frontier, so I came here for a look."

Meg would have believed him now had he not told her an entirely different story. Why, he was so persuasive, she thought in dismay, he could convince an audience that the sun rose at dusk.

Or a foolish woman that he loved her.

"This here Gunnell likes to claim he's someone else," Reif said. "When Mr. Flynt first bought him, he called himself Arlington."

Meg froze. *I am Arlington. You must believe me!* Who but Stephen would have made such a statement to Flynt? It had to have been him.

Her heart seemed to wither and die within her. Was anything her husband said the truth? She did not want to believe that he could be a nefarious rapist and murderer, but her faith in him was undermined.

Reif said, "He told Mr. Flynt that he was a rich, powerful man in England and that he would reward him well if he would pay his passage back. This man will tell any story, no matter how preposterous, to gain what he wants."

Was that what Stephen had done to her? Meg's head was spinning. So much of what Reif had said about Gunnell matched what she knew of Stephen that she feared he had to be the man the slave chaser sought.

Reif was saying, "This is a man who raped a fourteen-year-old girl in front of her family and killed her mother when she tried to protect her daughter. That is but one instance of his crimes. Others were so disgustingly cruel and depraved that I cannot describe them in the presence of ladies. Is this the kind of man you want to harbor in your midst? Not one of your wives or daughters is safe!"

Meg's stomach convulsed. Dear God, had she married a monster? Had she been that blind? The possibility devastated her.

"I tell you this man is Billy Gunnell, and I am taking him back to the Tidewater with me."

Reif would have raised the musket that lay across his saddle and pointed it at Stephen, but Wilhelm, moving with astonishing swiftness for a man of his size, jerked it from Reif's hands. "You vill take Herr Vingate nowhere."

Ames spoke up. "If this man is Flynt's runaway servant as you claim, then he's gonna have to come and pick him out from among us."

Meg saw the fear in Reif's eyes as he found himself, now unarmed, facing a group of clearly hostile men.

"I vager," Wilhelm was deliberately mocking Reif's earlier words, "this Flynt vill not be able to do that. As for you, you have vorn out your velcome."

"Best leave while you still can," Ames advised.

Reif took the advice and galloped away, shouting over his shoulder, "I will be back with Mr. Flynt. He'll not let this man escape him."

The settlers gathered around Stephen, clapping him on the back. He was grinning widely and thanking them for supporting and believing in him.

Believing in him! As Meg had so foolishly believed in him. She turned and fled around the corner of Wilhelm's cabin, seeking solitude.

When Reif had ridden up, Stephen would not have given a groat for his chances of escaping him. He had been certain that the dreaded pothook would soon be closing around his neck. But he had stood his ground.

Stephen did not delude himself that he had won more than a temporary reprieve. He knew how much Flynt hated him. The plantation owner would come very quickly to reclaim him. Stephen had to flee from here—and from the colonies—before that happened.

He had the money to pay for two passages to England. He was certain Wilhelm and Gerda, who were very fond of Josh, would agree to keep the boy temporarily until Stephen reached home and could send someone to bring the boy across the ocean. Somehow he had to persuade Megan to leave with him at once.

Stephen could not, would not go without her.

She could already be pregnant with his child. The thought that she might be forced to bear it alone as she feared, that he might never see their babe nor know what happened to her and their child, was more painful to him than any of the floggings he had endured aboard the *Sea Falcon* or at Hiram Flynt's hands.

Concealing his unhappy thoughts, Stephen forced himself to joke and laugh with the other settlers until the fiddler struck up the music and he managed to get Wilhelm into his cabin for a private talk.

When Stephen left Wilhelm twenty minutes later, the fiddler was playing a lively reel and couples were dancing to it with great enthusiasm. He looked around for his wife. Josh was with a group of boys at the edge of the wood, but he didn't see Megan anywhere.

Gerda came up to him. "Your vife went home. She is not feeling vell."

Alarmed, Stephen set off at a half run toward the Drake cabin.

He found Megan in her little room, huddled on the edge of the bed, her arms wrapped protectively about herself, staring unseeingly into space. He had never seen her look so miserable. She hardly seemed to notice him. He sat down beside her, the bed dipping beneath his added weight, and tried to take her in his arms.

"Do not touch me!" she hissed, looking at him with eyes that made him flinch. "I cannot bear to have you touch me, *Billy Gunnell*."

He recoiled from the loathing in her voice. "Damn it, Megan, I am not Billy Gunnell, and that is the truth."

Her sick, stricken expression clawed at his heart.

"Do you even know what the truth is?" Her voice cracked. "Have you ever told me the truth? Or was it all lies?"

"I have not lied to you, Megan." No, he had merely refrained from telling her the whole truth. Which, he thought guiltily, was in itself a kind of lie.

"Then you lied to the settlers and to Reif this afternoon."

Stephen had hated doing so, but it had been that or his life. No one would have believed the truth.

"Yes, Megan, I lied to them, not about who I was but about why I came to America and to the frontier. I had to lie or unjustly condemn myself to hell on earth at Hiram Flynt's hands. Would you have preferred I did that?"

She looked at him with angry, accusing eyes. "You also lied about being robbed in Baltimore."

"Believe me, I was very definitely robbed, and of a great deal more than my purse," he said bitterly. "Only the location of where it happened— Baltimore instead of Dover—was a lie."

"How can I believe you?"

"I did what I had to do this afternoon, Megan, and so did you. You lied for me, too."

"Yes, God help me, I did." The shame and the pain in her eyes tore at him. "But that was before I knew that Billy Gunnell tried to tell Flynt his name was Arlington."

His heart sank. Damn Reif for feeding her doubts anew. Stephen ran his hand distractedly through his hair.

"You were the man who told Flynt that, were you not?"

He would not lie to her. Instead he evaded. "Megan, I give you my sacred oath that I am not Billy Gunnell."

She was not to be deterred. "But you were the

man who escaped from Flynt. When you came here, you matched the description of Gunnell on the handbill. I want the truth." Her face crumpled, and tears trickled down her cheeks. "Oh, Stephen, why have you been lying to me?"

The look of pain and disillusionment she gave him razed his heart. "I did not lie to you, Megan, but I did omit part of my story."

Her hands knotted convulsively in alarm. "What part?"

Stephen pulled her into his lap, wrapping her in his arms. He took her chin in his hand and turned her face up to his so he could gaze into her troubled gray eyes.

"After I jumped from *The Sea Falcon*, I was plucked from the ocean by a ship carrying transported convicts from England to Virginia. Much of its human cargo had died from disease during the voyage. The captain, eager to make as large a profit as he could, promptly clapped me in irons and gave me the identity of one of the convicts who had died."

"Billy Gunnell?"

"Aye, Gunnell. There was no way I could prove I was not the murderer. After we landed, those of us who were not sold at the dock were handed over to soul drivers who marched a coffle of us in shackles through the countryside until we were sold." Shame at the memory permeated his voice, and he shuddered.

"I will never forget the humiliation of prospective buyers examining me as though I were an animal instead of a human being." His voice turned raw at the memory. "They poked and prodded me, even forced me to strip naked and open my mouth so they could check my teeth. Hiram Flynt bought me, and then my real hell began."

"Why did you not tell me this in the beginning?"

"Because you would not have believed me." From her look he was not certain that she did even now. "And I could not chance you would betray me to Flynt. I would rather die than be returned to him."

"I would not have sent you back to him." Unshed tears glistened in her eyes. "I know how terribly he treats his slaves and indentured servants."

Stephen held Meg tightly against him, inhaling deeply her sweet scent of orange blossoms. "It was worse for me. I had the misfortune to have Kate Dunbar take a fancy to me."

Megan's face jerked up in surprise. "Surely you do not mean Lady Katherine, the grand English lady whom Flynt married?"

A harsh crack of laughter escaped Stephen. "Believe me, Kate is no lady!"

"But she is Lord Dunbar's daughter."

"There is no Lord Dunbar."

Megan stared at him as though he were mad. "But there must be."

"I know every lord in England, and there is no Dunbar."

"But her father has a great estate in Bedfordshire called Royal Elms. Mr. Thomas, whose plantation was near ours, said he had a book on England that called Royal Elms the premier estate in all Britain."

"It is, but Royal Elms belongs to the Duke of Westleigh, the haughtiest, most freezingly condescending aristocrat in England, not to a nonexistent Lord Dunbar."

"But if he does not exist, who is Lady Katherine?"

Stephen knew a whore when he saw one, but he decided against shocking his wife. "Not a lady, I assure you. More likely she was a transported convict who was sold as an indentured servant and then escaped. I suspect that she once worked as a lady's maid in some great household, where she had learned to ape the speech and manners of her betters." But the true Kate had come out when she had brazenly tried to seduce him with a trollop's tricks.

He had done his best to discourage her interest, but in vain. He had paid for his failure with his hide. After that the jealous Flynt had made Stephen's life hell. But the cunning Kate had escaped punishment.

"Megan, listen to me. You heard what Reif said. He will be back with Flynt very shortly, and I must be gone from here before they come."

She shivered. "Where will you go?"

"To England." He sent up a silent prayer that he could convince her to go with him. "I will not be safe until I reach there. I told Wilhelm the whole story this afternoon, and he agrees that I must flee from here immediately."

Megan looked at him with desolate eyes. "Then go. Leave now, this very day."

"Not without you, Megan." He held his breath, waiting for her reply. When none came, he said, "I have the money for your passage and mine. Wilhelm and Gerda will care for Josh here until I can send for him. And I will do so as soon as we reach England. I promise."

She looked horrified. "I cannot leave my brother behind!"

"You know that Wilhelm and Gerda will take excellent care of him."

"You must go without me. Then you can send for both of us."

"And will you come, Megan?"

He saw the confusion and uncertainty in her eyes

and knew she did not know the answer to that question. Stephen was terrified that when the time came for her and Josh to embark on the long voyage across the Atlantic to join a man she did not entirely trust, she would not do it.

If she remained here, he might never see her again. He could not let that happen.

But if he stayed, he feared they both would die.

"Megan, I cannot leave you behind."

"Why not?"

Because I love you. "Because you may be in terrible danger."

She looked at him blankly. "Danger?"

"I am increasingly certain that my brother is responsible for what happened to me. I should never have written him telling him where I was." Stephen's voice choked at the pain of putting his brother's perfidy into words. "I fear Reif showed up today because George informed Flynt where he could find me."

"But why would that put me in danger?"

"You are my wife and could be pregnant with my son. He would inherit my estate instead of George. Do you think a man who would try to have his own brother killed so cruelly would show more mercy to a stranger and her unborn child when they stand between him and what he wants?"

Megan looked so green that Stephen thought for a moment she would be ill. "That is why I cannot leave you behind. You must come to England with me where we will both be safe."

Her mouth tightened stubbornly. "I cannot leave Josh."

"Megan, it is the very best thing you can do for him. I will send for him as soon as we reach London, and I will give him the best education there is—Eton, Oxford. Or Cambridge, if you prefer. It is what you want so much for him.''

Meg swallowed hard. Yes, dear God, it was.

''And this is the only hope you have of obtaining it for him.'' Stephen's voice was low and persuasive, and she felt herself wavering. ''Will you deny him his future? Surely, Megan, you love him too much for that.''

''I do, but how can I trust you to provide for him as you say you will?''

He ran his hand caressingly along her thigh. ''I swear to you, Megan, that you can.'' His hand continued to stroke her rhythmically, sending little tremors through her. ''I promise you that I will give you both a life of luxury beyond your imagining.''

She pushed his hand away, staring at him skeptically. ''Ah, yes, just as you promised Hiram Flynt you would richly reward him if he paid your passage to England.''

''Megan, listen to me—''

Tears welled up in her eyes. ''How can I believe anything you say?'' Her voice trembled. ''You promise me a life of luxury, but more likely I will live in terror of seeing you marched off to the hanging tree.''

''No. Once I am in England, I will be safe. We both will. You must believe that. Please, Megan, come with me for Josh's sake as well as ours. Wilhelm agrees with me that we must leave for England as quickly as possible before Reif can return with Flynt. I am not Billy Gunnell, but I am the man he bought.''

''Surely you have legal redress. A justice would surely—''

He cut her off. ''Just as a justice refused Galloway's petition to make himself your guardian?''

Sarcasm permeated Stephen's voice. "No, Megan, I will never be safe from Flynt while I am in America."

She knew he was right, but the thought of abandoning what little she had and leaving her brother behind, even temporarily, to follow this man across the sea terrified her. She gave voice to her worst fear. "But what if you are Billy Gunnell?" What would happen to her and Josh then?

"Damn it, I am not! Megan, Megan, how can I convince you to trust me?" He hugged her to him.

Despite her doubts, she found herself curling into him, accepting the warmth and comfort and protection that his body offered her.

His hand resumed stroking her leg from ankle to calf. She loved the feel of his callused fingers, so warm and gentle, and she made no protest. His hand moved higher beneath her skirt, caressing her thigh, and the pace of her breathing shortened.

"Don't," she said, halfheartedly trying to push his hand away and failing.

His other arm tightened around her. "Please come to England with me."

"I am afraid."

"Take a chance, Megan. Where is the courageous woman who braved the dangers of the frontier to try to preserve a pitiful inheritance for her brother? Why will you not do this when it will make both Josh's and your future so much brighter?"

Stephen's eyes pleaded with her. His hand still stroked her lovingly. "Where is the brave woman who took in a disreputable stranger when he collapsed on her doorstep and saved his life? Why will you not do something now that may be necessary to save both our lives?"

"Because I am afraid to trust you," she blurted.

The pain that shadowed his face told her how badly she had wounded him.

"Megan, do you truly think a man who has stayed here to help you at great danger to himself, a man who treats you as I treat you, can be a raping, murdering polecat like Billy Gunnell?"

No!

But what if he is lying to me as he lied to the settlers this afternoon?

She would not know for certain until she reached England. Only there would she find the truth about him.

Yes, she had to take the chance and go with him. There was no other way. Swallowing hard, she said in a quavering voice, "I will go with you."

His face brightened with joy. He kissed her exuberantly, then reassured her, "You will not regret it."

If only Meg could be certain of that.

Chapter 22

❦

Meg stepped from the quay where their ship, *The Raleigh,* had docked in front of the London customs house. For the first time in seven weeks, she felt solid ground beneath her feet. To her dismay, even it seemed to move. She swayed, disoriented.

Her husband's strong arm came instantly round her waist, and he steadied her against his muscular body, warm and reassuring. "Careful, love. It took you six weeks to get your sea legs; you will not lose them in a minute."

It had been a dreadful voyage across the Atlantic, slow and punctuated by wild storms that had blown them off course and made almost everyone aboard the ship seasick. Only Stephen and a handful of the crew had escaped the mal de mer. Meg had not.

There had been moments during the stormy voyage when she had been convinced that the ship was about to sink, and she was very glad Josh was not with her to share that fate. Yet she had wondered in terror what would happen to her brother if she did die. The hardest thing she had ever done in her life was to leave him with Wilhelm in Virginia.

She had nearly despaired of seeing land again

when at last England had been sighted through the gray Atlantic mist. She had been jubilant.

But today, as the rushing tide carried their vessel up the Thames, the great water highway to London, her happiness faded into dismay as the city came into view. A thick black pall of coal smoke hung over it like a funeral shroud, obscuring all but the buildings nearest the river.

The day, cold, gray, and drizzly, had already depressed her spirits, and they sagged even lower as she saw the dreary, disparate clutter of buildings crowded together along the Thames, without a single tree or other splash of nature's green to relieve the bleak monotony of man's haphazard handiwork. She had gaped in amazement at the ramshackle collection of buildings on London Bridge, which spanned the river.

Now as she left the quay with Stephen, the mingled odors of smoke, unwashed bodies, rotting fish, garbage, and dung clawed at her nostrils and again sent her stomach into revolt.

Ahead of her, much of the imposing customs house was hidden from view by small wooden sheds. Stephen explained that incoming cargos were stored inside them until the merchants had cleared the goods with excise officials in the main building.

All around her, noise and confusion reigned as hundreds of people swarmed about, shouting and jostling each other. She looked back toward *The Raleigh* and could not pick it out in the stark forest of sail-less masts formed by the many ships at the quays.

London was the most dismal city Meg had ever seen. Not that she had seen that many cities. She was instantly homesick for the clean fresh air, the serene quiet, and the beautiful natural vistas and forests of Virginia. The thought that both her homeland and Josh now lay beyond the sea made her want to weep in despair.

An even more painful thought haunted her. What if Stephen was not what he claimed to be? She had swallowed her doubts and accompanied him, but now the moment of truth was at hand, and apprehension clutched at her.

Perversely her nervousness made her feel guilty, for he had been so kind and solicitous to her during the voyage—holding her head when she was ill, massaging her back, and hugging her to him when she feared the ship was sinking.

"You look so white, love," he said now, his arm still around her. "Are you feeling poorly?"

Her legs were wobbly, and she nodded. He led her to a bench, where she sat down gratefully.

"Wait for me here."

She did as Stephen bade. When he returned a quarter of an hour later, he shepherded her to a hackney coach he had procured. Although its interior smelled of mildew and the leather seats were old and cracked, she was grateful to be out of the swirling crowds and the damp cold.

When the coachman heard their destination, he gave Stephen a doubting look and asked whether he was certain he had it right.

"Of course I have it right," her husband snapped. "Why would you think I do not?"

The man gave him a calculating look. "Ain't dressed like ye belong in that neighborhood." He turned and climbed up on the box.

As the coach creaked forward, Meg asked, "Where are we going?"

"To my London house."

It quickly became clear from her husband's exuberance as they passed sights familiar to him that he loved this awful city and was overjoyed to be back. Meg could not share his enthusiasm. Instead she wearily leaned her head back and closed her eyes to the city. If only she could as easily close her ears to its raucous noise and her nostrils to its evil stench.

Stephen's excitement at returning to London faded as he watched his wife, who rested her head wearily against the cracked leather of the hackney. She looked so pale and thin and wan. The ocean voyage had been far harder on her than he had foreseen. She had been very brave, though, never complaining about her misery, but its manifestations had been too obvious to conceal.

Well, he would make it up to her. In a few minutes they would be at his elegant London house. When he had left for the Continent, he had ordered it kept open with a skeleton staff of well-trained servants to await his return.

He took Megan's hand and squeezed it reassuringly. "Once we reach my home, I will have you tucked up in the most comfortable feather bed you have ever slept in, and I will have Cook make something that will tempt your appetite."

His wife would be very surprised indeed when she saw the opulence of his house. It would help the dreadful voyage to England seem worth it to her.

And it would finally put to rest her doubts about him.

He smiled in anticipation of Megan's astonishment and delight when she discovered just how high and how well she had married. Her elevated status as his wife was the one secret that he had continued to keep from her until he could reclaim his birthright. It would have done no good to tell her earlier. She would not have believed him, and it would only have sharpened her doubts about him.

But now she would see how badly she had misjudged him.

Megan's eyes fluttered open. "How long will we have to stay in London?"

"At least a fortnight."

Megan's face fell. Clearly the city that Stephen loved did not appeal to her. He sought some way to mollify her. "I want to order a proper wardrobe for you while we are here." In his experience nothing soothed a woman's ruffled feelings as effectively as expensive new gowns or a handsome piece of jewelry.

That reminded him of the very first thing he wanted to do, even today if he could manage it. He intended to visit the master jeweler who in the past had executed Stephen's designs for him. He would commission the jeweler to make the hummingbird pin that he had designed and meant to give to Megan as her belated wedding present.

When the hackney came to a jarring stop in front of his impressive house of portland stone, he was pleased to see Megan's eyes widen in surprise.

"What is this?" she asked.

"My London house. I told you I was a rich man, love. Wait here until I let my servants know we have arrived. They will be stunned enough just to see me. I must give them a moment to adjust to my return before I present them with their new mistress."

As Stephen started up the steps, he realized that the windows were shuttered and the house looked closed up. He banged the knocker loudly over and over, but no one responded.

He was dumbfounded. On whose order had the

house been shut? What had happened to the well-trained servants whom he had expected to welcome his return? Who had taken it upon himself to dismiss them?

Stephen stifled an expletive. He did not even have a key to let himself into the house. He had never needed one before. A porter had always been there to open the door for him.

What the hell was he to do now? His wife looked to be on the verge of collapse, and he wanted to get her into bed as quickly as possible before he went in search of answers to the many questions that plagued him. Fear gnawed at the pit of his stomach. Perhaps it would not be as easy as he had thought to recover what was his.

As he went back to the hackney, the driver asked, "Where now?"

Stephen looked at him blankly.

"If it be a room you're lookin' for, me knows a woman who lets 'em reasonable like. Me can take you there."

Stephen nodded. He needed to conserve his tiny hoard of coin until he succeeded in replenishing it. As he climbed back into the coach, Megan gave him an inquiring look.

"The house has been closed up," he said tersely. The sudden apprehension and doubt on her face were as painful to him as a spoken reproach. "I will take a room where you can rest while I set out in search of some answers."

Stephen had to swallow his disappointment when the hackney driver deposited them at a grimy brick building with a linen draper's shop on the ground floor and rooms to let above.

He was even more dismayed when he saw their shabby room, sparsely furnished with only a lumpy mattress on a narrow bed, a battered clothespress, and a washstand with a cracked and chipped pitcher and basin. The unappetizing smell of overcooked cabbage permeated both the room and the hall.

It was such a far cry from the room in which Stephen had expected his wife to spend her first night in London that he wanted to pound the thin, soiled wall in frustration.

Although Megan said nothing, she looked as disappointed as he felt about the room. He had promised her luxury if only she would come with him to England, and instead he had given her this.

"Do not even bother to unpack," he told her. "We will not spend the night here, but I need a place for you to rest while I go see Walter Norbury, my London agent, about obtaining funds and having my house reopened. Then I will have the blunt to take us to a better place."

He went downstairs and set off in a hackney to visit Norbury.

When the vehicle deposited him at his destination, Stephen was so eager to see his agent and bring an end to his two-year nightmare that he had to fight the urge to run into the man's suite. Surely once Norbury saw him, Stephen would have his birthright restored to him and his pockets full of money.

In the outer chamber, a thin, supercilious young clerk, whom Stephen had never seen before, looked up from a ledger in which he was entering figures. He gave the visitor a long, silent perusal, making Stephen acutely conscious of his worn, unstylish clothes. From the scornful curl of the clerk's lip, he clearly found the caller wanting.

Stephen, his pride stung, said coldly, "The Earl of Arlington to see Walter Norbury."

The clerk made a rude noise, then laughed derisively. "If you be the Earl o' Arlington, me be the king o' England. You no more be the earl than me. Me knows the captain."

The captain! So George had assumed Stephen's title. To do that, George had to have managed to have his elder brother declared dead. How could he have done that when Stephen had not been missing the required seven years? Certainly he could not have done it without Walter Norbury's compliance—and perhaps even his connivance.

Bloody hell, whom all had George bribed to help him in his plan to rid himself of his brother and seize his estate? The implications shocked Stephen. No longer certain who might have been involved in his kidnapping, he did not know whom he dared trust.

He could not make a mistake in this regard. Megan's life as well as his own depended on it.

He could think of only one person he could trust for certain. Rachel. His sister would never betray him.

It occurred to him that George must have returned to England if this clerk knew him. "Where is the captain now?"

"Back in America with 'is Majesty's army."

Where, no doubt, he had contacted Hiram Flynt after receiving Stephen's letter, determined to eliminate the inconvenient brother who had not died as easily as George had expected.

"And what of the captain's elder brother?" *Me. The real earl!*

"Disappeared, 'e did, while on a journey to the Continent. Heard they fished 'is body out o' the sea."

Stephen froze. Had some bloated, nameless corpse been passed off as him? Did that stranger's body now lie in the family mausoleum at Wingate

Hall beside his parents? And where was Rachel? "Is the earl's sister at Wingate Hall?"

The clerk shrugged. "Far as me knows."

"I want to see Norbury."

The clerk sniffed in contempt. " 'E don't see the likes o' you."

"Oh, yes, he does," Stephen growled, pushing through the gate in the railing and heading for the door to Norbury's office.

The man jumped up from his stool and planted himself in Stephen's path. " 'Im's not in there."

"As if I would believe you," Stephen snapped. He pushed the man out of his path and rushed into Norbury's office, only to discover the clerk had spoken the truth. The room was empty.

He turned on the clerk. "Where the hell is he?" Stephen's enraged face apparently persuaded the man to answer the question. " 'Im's in the country, awaiting on 'is grace, the Duke o' Westleigh." The clerk paused, clearly expecting Stephen to be as awed by the duke's name as he was. "Don't expect 'im back afore a week."

Stephen was stunned. "So Norbury works for Westleigh now, does he?"

The clerk's chest puffed out proudly as though the association enhanced his own status in the world. "Aye, 'e does."

Feeling defeated and betrayed, Stephen left Norbury's office and stepped back into the street. He had thought he would be safe once he stepped on English soil again, but now he realized that if Norbury and others were involved in the plot against him, he would be in danger here as well.

What the hell was he to do now? Stephen had counted on Norbury to identify him instantly as the missing earl and restore him to his wealth.

He stiffened as an appalling thought gripped

him. If his enemies succeeded in doing away with him, his wife would be left alone, friendless and penniless, in a strange land hostile to those without connections or wealth.

Once I am in England I will be safe. We both will. You must believe that. Please, Megan, come with me.

Bloody hell, how could he even look her in the eye?

And to whom could he turn for help? He thought immediately of Anthony Denton. His old friend Tony would surely help him.

Stephen jumped into a hackney, giving the driver the address of Denton's rooms on a fashionable street off Piccadilly.

But when he reached them, he discovered that Tony no longer lived there.

"Where is he?" he asked the landlord.

"Rusticating in the country where his creditors cannot find him," the man said bitterly. "Sneaked away in the night, owing me half a year's rent, he did."

Although Denton lived an expensive life, Stephen had no inkling that he was in financial trouble. "Do you have any idea where in the country he might be?"

"Heard he was up north somewhere trying to persuade a rich heiress to marry him. He'll run through her fortune soon enough, just as he did his own."

Bloody hell, Stephen hoped the woman was not Rachel. She deserved so much better than Denton. Her brother cursed himself for going off to the Continent and leaving her alone and unprotected. How could he have been so damned irresponsible?

Perhaps, he thought guiltily, he deserved what had happened to him on that ill-fated journey.

After leaving the landlord, Stephen stood in the

street, trying to think to whom else he could apply
for help. Unfortunately, at this season of the year,
all of his friends would be at their country estates,
not in London.

And whom did he dare trust? What he needed
was an incorruptible man of absolute integrity and
sterling reputation who would vouch that Stephen
was who he said he was.

Only one man came immediately to mind, the
Duke of Westleigh. Much as Stephen disliked the
duke's freezing hauteur, no one would ever dis-
pute his word. But given his undisguised contempt
for Stephen, would he even bestir himself to help?
*More likely he would laugh in my face, and tell me I
richly deserve my current fate. And perhaps I do, but
Megan does not.*

Stephen started to hail another hackney, then
stopped himself. His meager supply of coin was
dwindling rapidly, and he must conserve it. He
had not foreseen the possibility that once in London he would not be able to draw immediately on
his own funds. Now he did not know when he
would be able to do so.

How different his homecoming was from what
he had imagined. He set off, walking rapidly
through the damp gloom. The cold pierced him,
and he wished he had a warmer coat. He was dismayed by how gray the city looked and how
shabby some of its buildings were.

The raucous shouts of street vendors, the curses
of coachmen, and the clang of wheels on cobble-
stones assaulted his ears painfully. His nose wrinkled in distaste at the stench of horse droppings,
coal smoke, and rancid odors that drifted from
food stalls.

He had not noticed before how crowded the city
was. Its residents were far ruder than he remem-

bered. People constantly jostled and pushed him as he walked. He could not recall that happening before.

A bewigged man whose rich clothes proclaimed him an aristocrat walked toward him. The crowds parted, carefully making way for him. Stephen realized then that it was not the city that had changed, but himself. No one paid him any heed now that he no longer wore the elegant garb of an aristocrat.

He was just another nobody.

In the past, he had rarely walked in London but had ridden in his handsome equipage protected from the rabble.

Walking along the same streets now, with their refuse-filled gutters, gave him an entirely different view of London. It was no longer the bright city of amusements and welcoming mansions he had remembered, but mean and noisy and rank. No wonder Meg had looked so appalled.

Suddenly Stephen was eager to leave London behind, to escape to the country and to breathe again the clean air of Wingate Hall.

And to see his sister. To find out from her the truth of what had been done to him.

Rachel would tell him all that had transpired in his absence. Perhaps she might even know who else was involved in George's plot against him.

Another possibility occurred to him, so horrifying that he gasped involuntarily. Rachel would have done everything in her power to stop such a conspiracy against him. If she had, what price had she paid?

The thought sent cold chills through him. Bloody hell, he had to get to Wingate Hall as quickly as possible.

Stephen broke into a run.

Chapter 23

Meg was lying on the lumpy bed, her eyes closed to block out the dingy room that was such a far cry from the luxury her husband had promised her. If only her ears could as easily block out the raucous yells and the noisy clatter of London traffic on the street below.

She missed Josh dreadfully. She should never have let Stephen talk her into going with him and leaving her brother behind. She felt so guilty about deserting him, although he had been willing enough to remain in Virginia with Wilhelm and Gerda for a little while.

But would it only be a little while? She shivered. Would she ever see her brother again?

She heard the door creak, and her eyes fluttered open. Stephen slipped in quietly, shutting the door softly behind him. She looked at him with hope that died at the sight of his bleak face. It told her that whatever he had discovered while he was gone had not been good. "What did you learn?"

When he did not immediately answer, she asked, "Are we leaving here now?" Her mouth felt parched.

"Not until morning, when we will catch the early stage for Yorkshire and Wingate Hall."

She frowned, confused. "But you said we would be in London at least a fortnight."

"I know, but the situation turns out to be vastly more complicated than I anticipated. It may not be as easy to reclaim my inheritance as I thought."

Meg's stomach convulsed and fear gripped her. Stephen had reassured her that once they reached England, he would be safe and able to reclaim the property and wealth that were rightfully his.

She thought of how he had promised to send his old tutor to bring Josh to England as soon as they landed. So far she had seen no sign of servants or of the wealth he boasted of possessing. The house to which he had taken her today had been most impressive, but had it ever been his? Her mouth was suddenly as dry as dust. "What did your agent say?"

Had there ever been an agent? Her tenuous trust in him was slipping away like sand into the sea.

"Norbury is out of town, but it appears he may have been involved in the plot against me. The only person I dare trust now is Rachel. That is why we are going to Yorkshire tomorrow. I have to see her." His mouth hardened into tight lines. "Please, Megan, do not look at me like that."

"I cannot help it." She thought of Josh, separated from her by the wild Atlantic. "You promised you would send someone for my brother as soon as we landed."

"And I will as soon as I possibly can."

She felt a tear drop on her cheek. "Will I ever see him again?"

"Of course you will." Stephen tried to gather her in his arms, but she pulled away from him. She no longer knew what to believe. She had gone against her better judgment and agreed to accompany him. More and more it looked as if she had been an even bigger fool than her mother had been over Charles Galloway.

To Meg's relief the stagecoach at last left behind the congestion and confusion, the stench and the din of London, and rattled through leafless woods and across rolling hills on the Great North Road toward Yorkshire.

What she could not leave behind was the chatter of the other passenger in the stagecoach, a hugely fat woman who talked incessantly.

Beleaguered as Meg was by doubts about her husband and his veracity, she still missed his company. He had taken an outside seat on the stage when he had learned it was cheaper than one inside with his wife. The day was gray and cold, and she worried about him exposed to the elements, but she had seen the careful way he had counted out the money for the tickets and knew he had nearly exhausted their meager funds.

Her arrival in England had been so different from what he had promised her. Why had she believed him?

She made a halfhearted attempt to listen to the fat woman, who sat on the seat opposite her chattering away. She had introduced herself as Mrs. Hockley.

Her only interest seemed to be gossip about "the quality," as she called the English aristocracy. She clearly, although wrongly, assumed that her trapped listener was equally fascinated by the salacious details of the scandals she related with such relish.

Meg gathered that most of Mrs. Hockley's extensive knowledge came from her sister, who worked as a seamstress for a French modiste called Madame d'Artemis. Apparently Madame was very popular with fashionable ladies, and the sister had much opportunity to overhear their gossip.

And to faithfully relay it all to her sister.

Meg listened with growing disgust to Mrs. Hockley's stories about the outrageous excesses, shocking marital infidelities, and illicit romantic intrigues of England's lords and ladies. They might be highborn, but their morals were very low indeed. Meg could not help wondering aloud, "Is any aristocrat in the land faithful to his or her spouse?"

Mrs. Hockley, oblivious to the sarcasm, merely shrugged carelessly. " 'Tis the way with the quality—both male and female. They prefer others' spouses to their own, and no one thinks anything of it."

Well, Meg did, and she wanted nothing to do with such people. She was very glad that her husband was not a noble, for she had no wish to associate with them. She better understood now, however, Stephen's calm assumption that a man would keep a mistress after his marriage. Clearly it was, as he had said, the accepted thing. But that made it no less repugnant or immoral to her.

As Mrs. Hockley babbled on, Meg thought of Stephen's comments about Kate Dunbar. "Do you know anything about a Lord Dunbar?"

"Nay, never heard o' a lord by that name. Where does he hail from?"

"His estate is called Royal Elms."

"Nay, you have it wrong. Royal Elms belongs to the Duke of Westleigh."

So Stephen had been right about that.

"They say Westleigh's duchess is the greatest beauty in the land, but my sister thinks that cannot be. She's never seen the duchess, but she says she cannot imagine that any woman could be more beautiful than Lady Caroline Taber, Sir John Taber's wife and the late Lord Arlington's mistress. What a man his lordship was—so handsome and charming. My sister says all the ladies loved him, but he dallied only with the most beautiful. He used to bring all his mistresses to Madame to dress."

"*All* his mistresses!" Meg was so scandalized by a man having an assortment of mistresses that she could think of nothing else.

"My sister says he had wonderful taste. Knew precisely what would most flatter a woman, whether it be clothes or jewels, and he was very generous. A good many women other than Lady Taber wept when he died, including his betrothed, Fanny Stoddard."

Meg thought waspishly that she would not have wept for such a faithless man who would betroth himself to one woman while keeping another man's wife as his mistress. She said sarcastically, "His late lordship clearly was a busy man among the ladies."

Stephen had the stage drop him and Megan off at a crossroads tavern that was popular with Wingate Hall's tenants and laborers in the hope of gleaning some advance warning of what he would find when he reached his home.

He helped his wife down from the conveyance with a sigh of relief. Bloody hell, but it had galled him to be forced to take Megan to Wingate Hall in a common stage. As it was, though, he had barely had enough blunt for two fares to Yorkshire, and one of them a cheaper outside seat at that.

The trip had cost more than he had expected. Now he did not have enough money left to buy his wife dinner at this tavern or to hire a horse from its stable to ride to Wingate Hall. He would have to walk to his home, and it would be a very long hike.

Stephen had never before journeyed by public conveyance or been forced to dine and sleep in wayside inns, and he devoutly hoped he would never have to do so again. Always before he had traveled in one of his elegant equipages, stopping at the great country homes of his friends for shelter. Once again he had not appreciated what he had until he lost it.

Megan looked over the peaceful vale where a half dozen stone cottages were scattered about. "What a pretty valley. How far are we now from your farm?"

"You are on it. This entire valley is part of Wingate Hall's holdings."

Her expression told him she was skeptical that the land belonged to him.

The stage lumbered noisily forward, leaving them standing by the roadside in front of the tavern.

Stephen suggested, "Why do you not walk about a bit and explore your new home while I stop in the tavern to see what I can learn?"

She shrugged. "It will feel good to stretch my legs, but please don't be long."

"I will not," he assured her.

She turned and headed down the road toward the cottages. During the trip north, Stephen had felt her faith in him bleeding away as though from a slow wound.

Hell, he could not blame her. What he had been able to give her so far had been so different from what he had promised her back in Virginia. He knew she was frightened, but to her credit she had not reproached him with words.

Only with her bleak eyes.

Stephen watched her stroll down the road for a moment before he went into the tavern. It was poorly lit, with only two narrow windows set high in the wall. Most of its illumination came from a blazing log in the fireplace. The air in the badly ventilated room was heavy with the smell of smoke and hops.

Four men were gathered at one of the rough plank tables, talking and laughing over tankards of ale. Careful to keep his back to the fire so his face would be obscured, Stephen joined the men. He had no coin to waste on ale, but they were so engrossed in their conversation that they did not seem to notice he was empty-handed.

Stephen recognized none of the men, but from the looks of their rough clothing and weather-beaten faces, he was certain they were farmers.

He was embarrassed to realize that although they undoubtedly were his tenants, he could not identify a single one of them. His father would have known them and every member of their families by name, as well as any problems they might have.

Two of the quartet looked to be in their thirties. They were big men with steel gray eyes as hard as their faces. The resemblance between them was so strong that Stephen figured they were brothers. The other two men were smaller and a little older.

"Are you Wingate Hall tenants?" Stephen asked them.

"Aye," the bigger of the brothers answered.

Stephen was careful to speak colloquially. That and his worn clothing would keep them from guessing his identity. "What kind o' place be it for tenants?"

" 'Tis a fine place now the Duke o' Westleigh's took it o'er," the larger brother said.

Stephen was certain he could not have heard right.

"Sam's right," the smaller brother agreed. "Damned lucky we are to have the duke."

Stephen was nonplussed. How in hell could Westleigh have bought Wingate Hall?

Easily, Stephen realized with gut-wrenching pain. The estate was not entailed. If he had been declared dead and George had inherited it, he could not be stopped from selling it. It had to have been George; Rachel would have died before she sold a single acre of Wingate Hall. "I thought the Earl o' Arlington owned it?"

Sam gave a contemptuous snort. "Went running off to the Continent, he did, and got himself killed, leaving that greedy Wingate bitch in charge."

Stephen was stunned into speechlessness at hearing his sister called a bitch. Everyone at Wingate Hall had loved Rachel. What on earth could have changed that?

"Aye, she nearly destroyed us all," Sam's brother said. "And the estate, too. She bled it and us alive. I'll tell you, the duke and duchess, they've had their hands full, they have, undoing all the damage she done."

Stephen was surprised to hear that Westleigh had finally married. He'd thought the condescending duke would never find a woman he thought good enough to be his wife. What surprised him even more was the real affection the tenants seemed to have for the duke.

"We're well rid o' Arlington," Sam said with a sneer. "He cared naught for his estate, couldn't even be bothered to visit it. That one cared only for his London pleasures. The duke's comin' be the best thing that happened to the people hereabouts since Gentleman Jack."

"Gentleman Jack?" Stephen asked.

Sam's brother took a gulp of ale. "The highwayman who kept us from starving while that Wingate bitch was milkin' us o' everything we could raise."

Stephen would love to see the haughty Westleigh's reaction to the assessment that he was the next best thing to a highwayman. "How did the duke acquire Wingate Hall?"

"From Arlington's younger brother. Him's an army man and weren't interested in running it, thanks be to God."

How could Stephen's solicitor have let that happen? He knew about the secret agreement that if George did not resign his commission to run Wingate Hall himself, ownership would pass to Rachel.

And how could Rachel have changed so much? The woman Sam described bore no resemblance to his sweet, caring sister. In a voice trembling with emotion, Stephen asked, "Where is the Wingate woman now?"

"In hell where she belongs," Sam growled.

"Surely you jest!" Stephen yelped in shock.

"Not me. Where else would the bitch be, I ask you, when she died by her own hand?" Sam retorted. "I tell you, there was not a single soul to mourn that one."

Stephen was so stunned that he was paralyzed mentally and physically.

Wingate Hall sold to Stephen's old nemesis, the Duke of Westleigh.

Rachel dead, an unmourned suicide.

Had George somehow managed to turn the tenants against Rachel, driving her to such despair that she had taken her own life?

If Stephen had been declared legally dead and Westleigh had bought Wingate Hall in good faith, it was unlikely that Stephen could ever get it back.

And he had no one to blame but himself. He had lost the estate that had been home to generations of Wingates because of his own carelessness. He had been too damned feckless to come home and assume the responsibilities of his inheritance.

"You all right?" Sam's voice seemed to come from a great distance away.

Hell, no, Stephen was not all right. He would never be all right again.

He staggered up from the chair and out the door. He fled blindly from the inn yard and up the hill away from the vale. He ran until he collapsed in a panting heap at the foot of a rowan tree standing like a lonely sentinel at the top of the hill.

The full desperateness of his situation hit him. Everything was gone. Rachel, his home, his inheritance. He had nothing, barely enough to buy his wife a stale crust of bread for their dinner.

He had dragged her here, first to London, then to Yorkshire. He had overridden Megan's doubts and convinced her to accompany him, promising a far better life for both her and Josh than she could ever hope for in America.

A better life! Christ, what a joke! He did not even have the wherewithal to provide a roof over their heads that night.

He cared much more about what happened to her than what happened to him.

He had to think of something.

Or he could not face his wife again.

Would this nightmare never end?

As Megan wandered across the vale, she thought that at least she now knew Wingate Hall existed. But was Stephen truly its owner? He must be, she told herself. Why else would he bring her here?

Still, she was uneasy. If it was not his home, they

were in terrible trouble, for she knew they had no money left. She had seen how carefully her husband had doled out his coin for food and lodging during the journey and the very real concern on his face as he had paid for their breakfast that morning. She was certain he did not have enough for another night's lodging or even dinner.

What if Wingate Hall was not Stephen's? What if it had all been lies? She fought off the fear that clawed at her, telling herself firmly that the estate had to be his. Surely he would not have made the expensive journey with her all the way here, using the last of their money, if it was not. Only a madman would have done that.

As she walked past the stone cottages, she was impressed by how neat and well maintained they were. When she reached the cottage farthest from the inn, she saw a magnificent chestnut stallion tied to a post beside a frisky bay mare.

Beyond the horses, a path led into a beech wood. She continued on, intent on exploring it. Not until she was on the far side of the cottage did she see the man leaning against the trunk of a leafless oak tree.

Dressed in buckskin breeches and a russet riding coat, he was talking with great animation to the baby that he held in his arms. Although Meg was too far away to make out his words, the tender, vibrant timbre of his voice assured her that he spoke lovingly.

She was so touched by the sight that she stopped to watch the pair. The man must have felt her gaze on him for he looked up. Seeing her, he boosted the baby to his shoulder and headed toward her.

Tall and muscular, he was one of the handsomest men Meg had ever seen. His face was strong, with a broad forehead, aristocratic nose, prominent cheekbones, a mouth that looked as though it smiled often, and a jutting jaw. The slanting rays of the setting sun on his blond hair seemed to turn it golden.

He greeted her with a friendly smile. "Are you visiting someone here? You do not live on the Wingate estate."

That surprised Meg into asking, "Surely you do not know everyone who lives on this estate?"

"But I do." The baby, its little fists flailing, was twisting in his arms, trying to see the new voice that it heard. He shifted the infant from his shoulder and cuddled it protectively against his broad chest. "I am its steward."

"And you live in this pretty little cottage?"

"No, I am waiting for my wife. She is an herbal healer, and the man who does live here is ill. She is treating him."

"Is this your baby?"

He looked down at the child with such love and pride that Meg's heart caught. "Yes, this is my son Stephen. He is named for his uncle."

"My husband is named Stephen." Meg smiled a little wistfully. If they were to have a son, would her husband look at their baby as this man gazed at his?

He asked, "What is your name?"

"Meg."

"I am Jerome. You are from the American colonies, are you not?"

"How did you know?"

"I have a good ear for accents. What brought you to the mother country?"

"My husband is English. He wanted to come home."

Little Stephen, apparently unhappy at losing his father's attention to Meg, gave a little wail of protest, and Jerome began to talk to him. Within a minute of regaining his papa's attention, he was laughing and gurgling again.

The last of the sun's orange rim sank below the treeless moor to the west, and Meg said, "I had better get back to the tavern and my husband."

But when she reached the building, Stephen was not there, and no one she asked knew where he had gone.

She stood outside the tavern and looked toward the vale for her husband. She did not see him, but Jerome, his son in his arms, was mounted now on that magnificent chestnut stallion. She presumed the woman on the mare beside him was his wife. As Meg watched, the couple rode off down the path that led into the woods.

She watched them for a moment before turning in the opposite direction. At the top of the hill where a rowan tree stood, she noticed a huddled figure at its foot. She headed in that direction.

She was halfway to the tree when the figure rose awkwardly to his feet, and she saw that it was Stephen. He shuffled toward her as though he were an old man whose body was racked by pain.

As the gap closed between them and Meg could see his features more clearly, her heart sank. He had the look of a man who had suffered devastating shock and grief and was still stunned.

She hurried up to him. "Dear God, Stephen, what is it?"

"Rachel is dead." His voice sounded as hollow as an empty sepulcher. "Wingate Hall has been sold to the Duke of Westleigh. It is no longer mine."

For a moment, bitter doubt gripped Meg. Had Stephen ever owned it? Then she instantly felt contrite. Looking at him she could not doubt that he had sustained a shattering shock.

Meg threw her arms around him and hugged him. He grasped her hard to him, accepting the silent comfort that her arms and her body offered him as he struggled to regain control of his emotions.

He was shaking his head back and forth as though to deny the tragedy. "I cannot believe Rachel is dead."

"How did it happen?"

"They say she killed herself, but I cannot believe that."

"What will we do?" Meg shivered. The temperature was dropping, and it promised to be a cold night.

"There is a boarded-up lodge in a remote section of the estate not far from here. We will have to walk there. We can use it tonight."

"And what of tomorrow?"

And all the tomorrows after that?

He shook his head again. "I will try to talk to Westleigh. Perhaps he will help me."

But Stephen's tone told Meg he had little hope of that. "You do not think he will?"

"No, he made his scorn for me scathingly clear. No doubt it will please him greatly to have me grovel before him, then to dismiss me with that freezing hauteur of his, telling me I richly deserve my fate." Stephen's expression was as bleak as his tone. "And perhaps I do, but you do not."

He started walking. "Come, this is the way to the lodge." He led her past the cottages, then turned up the path through the beech wood that Meg had seen Jerome and his wife take earlier.

The day had vanished, but fortunately the night was clear. Thousands of stars glittered in the celestial canopy, and the bright moon was only a sliver short of being full.

It was also cold. Meg shivered in her cloak and wished she had a warmer one. As she followed her husband down the moonlit path, she tried to choke down the terror that clutched at her. What would happen to them now? Would she ever see Josh again? The question was like a knife through her heart.

As though sensing her devastating thoughts, Stephen suddenly turned to her and hugged her to him. She saw tears glistening on his cheeks. "Megan, love, somehow I will find a way for Josh to join us and to make this all up to you. I do not know how yet, but I swear I will."

And she knew he meant it. Her moment of doubt passed. This was the man who had stayed to help her on the frontier despite great danger to himself, the man who had given back part of his winnings that he urgently needed for himself to the other settlers.

And she knew he would do everything in his power to keep his promise to her. She smiled up at him.

"Oh, Megan," he groaned. He kissed her then, fervently, desperately. They clung to each other in the moonlight as though they were the last two creatures in the universe.

Later, after they had resumed walking, Meg asked, "What was this abandoned lodge used for?"

"My grandfather built it for his own purposes."

"And what were those?"

"You will not like the answer."

"Tell me."

"He housed his mistresses in it when he was in residence at Wingate Hall."

Stephen was right. Meg did not like the answer.

It reminded her how lightly her husband and other Englishmen regarded marriage vows. How could she blame Stephen for feeling as he did about marital fidelity when infidelity was the accepted behavior? His own grandfather had flagrantly indulged in it.

Her face in the moonlight must have betrayed her reaction because Stephen reached for her hand and squeezed it. "Have no fear that I will use it for that purpose. My father ordered it boarded up, and I intend to keep it that way."

"Why did he have it closed?"

"He had no need for it. He loved only my mother." Stephen smiled at her, his hold on her hand tightening. "As I love only you, Megan."

Despite the desperateness of their plight, her heart suddenly lightened.

Meg judged they had been walking for more than a half hour and were deep in a mixed wood of oak, sycamore, and English elm when Stephen said, "The lodge is just ahead of us."

They stepped into a small clearing. Directly before them was a substantial structure of gray slate. They were facing the side of it, and Meg saw a smaller building, apparently a stable, behind the larger.

She blinked as she realized that the building was not boarded up as Stephen had said. Instead smoke curled from its chimney, and light beckoned through its windows, one of which was partially open.

She heard Stephen's sharp expletive then his exclamation, "What the hell?"

Chapter 24

~ᴄᴏ~ᴏↄ~

Stephen stared in disbelief at the lodge. He had assumed it was still closed up. His father, who had hated the insult the structure had been to Stephen's grandmother, had never allowed it to be used again during his lifetime.

After his father's death, Stephen had done nothing to countermand that, and he could not believe Rachel would have either. That left only Wingate Hall's new owner. "Westleigh must have ordered the lodge opened."

Stephen was baffled by whom the duke would have assigned to live there. It was too grand for estate workers, yet too distant and isolated for the duke's guests.

In the moonlight, Megan's face was drawn with fatigue and hunger. She did not look as though she could walk another step. Yet the night was growing colder by the moment, and they must have shelter.

Stephen said, "I—I do not know what we will do now." It hurt to have to admit that. "Perhaps whoever is staying in the lodge can be persuaded to give us a little food and shelter for the night." He touched Megan's arm. "Stay here while I talk to the occupants. Do not go near the lodge until I call you. I want you out of harm's way should the inhabitants take exception to unexpected late visitors.''

It galled Stephen to be reduced to begging at a door that he had once owned and that should still be his. But he would do anything, no matter how humiliating, for Megan. He had been robbed of his birthright and left destitute with no way to care for her. Bloody hell, she deserved so much better than this. He thought of his promises to her that he had unwittingly broken, and anger gushed within him like a spring.

He left Megan at the edge of the wood and moved toward the lodge. As he neared it, the silence of the night was broken by sounds drifting through the partially opened window, the unmistakable noises of a couple in the throes of climaxing passion.

Then a familiar voice, deep and rich and husky with satisfaction, drifted to him on the breeze. ''My sweet temptation, what you do to me.''

Westleigh's voice.

Damn him! He was using the lodge for the same purpose that Stephen's grandfather had—to entertain his whores!

Stephen's fury, fed by thoughts of all that had been stolen from him, of the terrible brutality he had suffered, of the duke's freezing contempt for him, and of his fears for his wife, suddenly exploded.

''Goddamn you, Westleigh,'' he shouted.

Scarcely knowing what he was doing, Stephen, still yelling curses at the duke, bounded toward the door. Finding it unlocked, he threw it open with such force that it crashed against the wall with a resounding bang.

He stormed inside and promptly slammed into

a small pier table that held a lighted taper in a silver candlestick. He managed to grab the candlestick before the table overturned with a loud crash.

Stephen stood in a hallway with open doors to his left and right. A trail of discarded clothing, both male and female, led to the closed door at the end of the hall. Stephen could not imagine the icy, controlled Westleigh in such a wildly impatient passion, but clearly he had been.

Stephen righted the pier table and replaced the candle. A lantern on a trestle table in the room to his right revealed a kitchen, but the room on his left was too dark to decipher.

The door at the end of the hall was thrown open with as much force as Stephen had attacked the front entrance.

The Duke of Westleigh, naked as the day he was born, rushed into the hall. He wielded an ugly iron poker that he must have grabbed from the fireplace, clearly intent on subduing the noisy intruder who had interrupted his assignation.

The duke advanced on him menacingly with the poker.

Stephen took an involuntary step backward. Westleigh was the only man he knew who, even naked, could look so damned formidable.

And, Stephen belatedly remembered, the duke owned Wingate Hall now. There was nothing Stephen could do but brazen out this farce he had started.

Westleigh was eyeing him with unnerving intensity. "Who the hell are you?"

Suddenly the duke's eyes widened, and his hand holding the poker fell to his side. "Arlington?" His voice was tentative, uncertain, no more than a shocked whisper.

Stephen refused to confirm or deny it. "What do you think?"

"Hellsfire, Arlington, it is you!"

At last someone recognized him. What irony that it should be a man who had so little use for him.

"Thank God, Arlington, that you are back at last."

The duke sounded overjoyed. Stephen was nonplussed that Westleigh of all people should seem so delighted.

"I have never been so glad to see anyone, but why the hell did you burst in here like this? I thought you were a madman." The duke bent over to snatch up the pair of breeches, clearly his, that had been discarded on the hall floor.

Stephen said honestly, "I was enraged that you were bedding your whore here."

The duke's eyes suddenly turned murderous. "Damn you, the only woman I sleep with here or anywhere else is my duchess." He looked toward the door he had come through and called, "My love, you cannot guess who is here."

Stephen was more concerned with Wingate Hall than Westleigh's odd choice of places to bed his wife. "I do not know what deal you struck with my brother, but I am determined to buy this estate back from you." Westleigh, who was famous for his financial astuteness, would no doubt demand a huge sum.

The duke's head shot up in surprise. "Why would you want it?" His eyes were suddenly piercing. "You could not even be bothered to visit here before you disappeared."

"What you say is true, but that was then. I deserved the tongue-lashing you gave me. I was a damned fool."

The duke's eyebrows raised quizzically. "Are you claiming to be a changed man, Arlington?"

"Yes, although undoubtedly you will not believe that."

A woman with a quilt wrapped around her rushed through the door at the end of the hall.

"*Stephen!*" she cried joyously. In the instant before she propelled herself at him, he caught sight of a face he had thought he would never see again. It was shining with such happiness that his heart turned over.

Clutching the quilt to her with one hand, she wrapped her other arm around him, laughing and crying simultaneously. "Stephen! It is you. I knew you were not dead! I knew it!"

"Rachel!" Dazed, he hugged his sister to him, trying to reassure himself by the solid warmth of her body that she truly was alive. When finally he accepted that she was, his tears mingled with hers. He had thought he would never hold her like this again. They clung to each for a long time, their embrace silently reaffirming their enduring love for each other.

At last Stephen drew back a little, looking first at his sister in his arms, then at Jerome, who had pulled on his breeches and was buttoning them. Stephen frowned as the obvious belatedly dawned upon him. "Why are you here, Rachel?"

The duke answered for her. "Because she is my duchess."

Stephen's arms dropped away from her in shock. "Is that true, Rachel?"

Her smile grew even more brilliant. "Wish me happy, big brother."

From the look of her, she needed no wishes from him to make it so. She was already very happy. For a moment, Stephen was dumbfounded. He had never even considered the possibility that his dear little sister might marry of all men, the Duke of Westleigh. But now that Stephen learned she had, he decided, rather to his own surprise, that he was well pleased with the match.

His approval had nothing to do with either the duke's title or fortune. He had only to see the way Westleigh looked at Rachel to know that he loved her. Stephen was certain that unlike Anthony Denton, the duke would make her an excellent husband, caring and responsible.

"I am delighted, Rachel." Stephen hugged her exuberantly to him again. "I was so worried that while I was gone you might have succumbed to Anthony Denton's lures and married him."

That comment drew Stephen penetrating scrutiny from Rachel's husband. "But Denton was one of your closest friends."

"That does not mean I do not know what kind of husband the rakehell would have made Rachel. What I care about most is my sister's happiness."

"The truth is I never liked Denton," she said. "I felt as Papa did, that he was a bad influence on you."

Stephen smiled lovingly at her. "You always were wiser than I, little sister."

Westleigh watched him with a bemused expression. "Perhaps you are a changed man after all, Arlington."

Looking at the duke, Stephen thought he was not the only man in this hall who had changed, but he said with a smile, "Indeed I am. What I suffered the past two years taught me what is important. It will not be easy, but I hope to become the kind of master of Wingate Hall that my father was."

The duke broke into a wide grin. "Then I am delighted to hand Wingate Hall back to you."

Stephen gaped at him. "Are you saying you are *giving* the estate back to me?"

"I do not own it, Arlington. You do."

"*What?*"

Meg waited anxiously at the edge of the wood where Stephen had left her. After he had stormed around to the front of the lodge, she had heard a loud crash, as though a piece of furniture had fallen to the floor, followed by the angry voices of a strange man and her husband inside the cottage.

Now, though, she heard nothing. No shot had been fired. Nor was there any sound indicating a fierce struggle. Despite her husband's warning not to go near the lodge, she had to know what was happening. She hurried to the lodge door and found it standing open.

Inside her husband was hugging the loveliest woman she had ever seen in her life. The exquisite creature had waves of ebony hair, huge eyes, a perfect nose, and a lovely smiling mouth framed by two charming dimples.

Jealousy ballooned in Meg. Belatedly she noticed Jerome, the man she had met earlier that day. Now clad only in breeches, he was smiling broadly as he watched her husband and the woman embracing.

Then he saw Meg standing in the door. For a second he looked puzzled, then comprehension seemed to dawn in his eyes, and he moved past Stephen and the woman to Meg.

"The little American." He gestured toward her husband. "Is this the Stephen to whom you are married?"

Meg nodded in confirmation.

The beauty broke away from Stephen and stared

at Meg with a shocked, incredulous expression. "This is your wife, Stephen?"

Jerome asked Meg, "Why did you not tell me that you were Arlington's wife?"

Arlington's wife. Meg stared at Jerome blankly. What on earth was he talking about?

Stephen stepped to Meg's side and took her cold hand in his warm one. "You have met my wife?"

"Aye, I met Lady Arlington by Tom Sanders's cottage this afternoon."

"Why do you call me Lady Arlington?"

"Because you are the Earl of Arlington's countess," Jerome answered.

You must believe me. I tell you I am Earl . . . Arlington.

Stephen squeezed her hand. "Why did you not tell me you had met the Duke of Westleigh this afternoon?"

The friendly, charming Jerome bore no resemblance to the freezingly condescending duke whom Stephen had described. "But you told me you were Wingate Hall's steward." An accusatory note crept into Meg's voice.

"So I was, until your husband's return." Jerome put his arm possessively around the beauty. "And this is Rachel, my duchess and your husband's sister."

Meg's relief at discovering the woman's identity was so intense that she felt faint. Still, she could not help but think how ugly and ungainly she must look beside such an exquisite creature.

The duke gave his wife an adoring look, then told Stephen, "Now that you are here to claim Wingate Hall, perhaps I can convince my duchess to go home at last to Royal Elms."

Meg was too dazed by the stunning revelations of the past few minutes to absorb them. Wingate

Hall did belong to Stephen after all, and he was an earl, and she, a countess. His sister who supposedly had killed herself was very much alive. "But Stephen told me Rachel was—"

Her husband interjected, "I was told wrong."

Meg felt as though she were in a dream. She stared at her new sister-in-law. Rachel returned the inspection, surprise and something else—was it disapproval?—in her expression. Who could blame the gorgeous Rachel if she thought Meg an unworthy countess for her brother?

"Stephen," Rachel's voice was troubled, "what of Fanny?"

Meg's heart constricted. Who was Fanny?

Her husband's mouth tightened. "Bloody hell, do not tell me we are still supposed to be betrothed. I was certain that the ambitious, impatient Fanny would have found another suitable title and fortune to marry by now."

Jerome interjected, "She has—in fact, she has been betrothed since last summer—but she has not yet married the unfortunate man."

"Who is he?"

"Lord Felix Overend."

Stephen burst out laughing.

Meg stared at her husband, astonished that he could find his betrothed forsaking him for another man so funny. But then the English nobility had very different ideas about marriage and the sanctity of its vows than she did.

"That mincing fop Felix!" Stephen exclaimed. " 'Tis a match made in heaven."

Jerome grinned. "In hell, you mean. They deserve each other. Frankly I would not have blamed you for disappearing to escape marriage to that harridan. I think I would have."

"Clearly you discerned the real Fanny beneath

that simpering facade. I wish I had before I offered for her." A hint of a smile tugged at the corners of Stephen's mouth. "Speaking of marriage, I never thought you would condescend to ask any woman to marry you."

Rachel's musical laugh rang out. "Oh, he did not ask me."

"Yes, I did—eventually," her husband protested.

The silent communion that passed between the spouses was so full of love that Stephen was delighted for his sister. She and Jerome clearly enjoyed the same kind of rare union as his mother and father.

The kind of union that he hoped he and Megan would have.

Rachel picked up the candlestick. "Let us go into the drawing room." She led the way into that small, cozy room and gestured for Megan to sit on a sofa. When she complied, Stephen sat down beside her and took her hand in his.

He quirked an inquisitive eyebrow. "What I do not understand, Jerome, is why you would bring my sister here to make love to her."

The duke and his duchess exchanged a look so hot and blatantly sensual that Stephen was startled.

"This place has special significance to us," Jerome said. "Your sister abducted me and brought me to this lodge, and here she had her wicked way with me."

"I do not believe that!" Stephen said flatly. "I know my sister."

Rachel laughed again. "Not when I am in love."

Her husband laughed, too. "Yes, it is amazing what Rachel in love will do. I bless the day that I came to Yorkshire."

"I heard in the tavern that a highwayman named

Gentleman Jack got you to come here." Stephen could not resist adding with a gleam in his eye, "The tavern patrons considered you the next best thing to that rogue."

Jerome laughed. "Gentleman Jack is as dear to their hearts as he is to mine."

Mischief sparkled in Rachel's violet eyes. "Gentleman Jack was a modern-day Robin Hood."

"Was? Is he dead?"

"Retired," Jerome said firmly.

A baby's wail, high and distressed, came from the room at the end of the hall. Rachel disappeared into the chamber and reappeared a moment later with a chubby baby, blinking sleepily, in her arms.

She smiled at her brother. "Meet your nephew and namesake, Stephen Morgan Parnell."

He stared in surprise at the yawning infant, who showed no interest in his uncle. "My little sister, a mama?" Stephen felt the sting of tears at the back of his eyes. "I have missed so much."

Rachel smiled. "But you are home now. That is all that matters."

Stephen looked at Megan. She was watching the baby with a dreamy look in her eyes, and he knew she was thinking of what it would be like to hold her own child.

Their child.

Stephen was amazed at how much he wanted that, too.

Little Stephen caught sight of his father and reached out his fat little arms to him. As Jerome took him from his mama, the baby gurgled happily.

Stephen told his sister, "I am honored that you named the next Duke of Westleigh after me, but I am amazed that your husband would have permitted it, knowing what he thought of me."

Jerome's mouth turned up in a wry smile. "I am becoming more reconciled to it by the moment."

"Is it true that I still owe Wingate Hall?"

"Certainly it is. I have only been its steward until your return. Your London agent, Walter Norbury, is here and can give you an accounting tomorrow." Jerome smiled. "He will be overjoyed to see you."

"I need no accounting." Stephen knew that his estate could not have been in more capable and honest hands than the duke's. "I thought you owned Wingate Hall. I thought I had been declared dead—"

"Not likely!" Jerome said. "Neither Rachel nor George would have allowed that. They were both so certain that you were still alive."

"*George*, too?" Bloody hell, could it be that his terrible suspicions about his brother were wrong?

"Certainly," Rachel interjected. "Both George and I never gave up hope that you were alive. We loved you too much to accept your death until we had irrefutable proof."

Could it possibly be that George had not been his enemy after all? Suddenly so agitated he could no longer sit still, Stephen jumped up and began to pace.

"But I wrote George a letter in New York, begging him to help me." There was a raw edge to Stephen's voice. "I got no answer from him." Silas Reif had come instead.

"George has been on a mission to Canada," Rachel said. "We had a letter from him only yesterday. He wrote he was finally about to return to New York after a two-month absence. Your letter must have arrived while he was gone."

So George was not his enemy after all! A wave of relief washed over Stephen that the brother he loved had not been responsible for what had happened to him. So intense was his emotion, he felt as though his legs might collapse beneath him.

Jerome asked quietly, "You still do not know what happened to you, do you, Arlington?"

"I know that an enemy had me impressed. I thought it must have . . ." Stephen's voice trailed away, unable to put into words the terrible injustice he had done his brother with his suspicions.

" . . . been George," Jerome finished for him.

Rachel gasped in shock, but Jerome said, "I am not surprised. At first, I, too, mistakenly believed that he was behind your seizure at Dover."

"George would never have done—"

Jerome hastily cut his wife off. "I realized that, too, once I met him."

Stephen's mind teemed with questions. "And this afternoon at the tavern, I was told that Rachel was dead."

His sister said, "You must have misunderstood."

"But the men there were complaining that I had gone off to the Continent, leaving you in charge. They said you subsequently killed yourself."

"They were not talking about Rachel," Jerome said. "They were talking about Sophia Wingate."

"Sophia Wingate?" Stephen was so stunned that he collapsed on the sofa beside Megan. His voice rose incredulously. "Uncle Alfred's wife?"

Jerome nodded.

"But I would never have left that slut in charge of anything." Why, the mere thought of it revolted Stephen. "Alfred proved what a blithering idiot he was by marrying her."

Jerome said, "It was Sophia who had you seized and impressed aboard *The Sea Falcon*."

"What?" Not in his wildest dreams would Stephen have guessed that woman was behind his kidnapping. "Bloody hell, why would she do that?"

"To gain control of Wingate Hall."

"But that was impossible."

"You are wrong," Jerome said. "She did exactly that. She forged your name to a document that removed Wingate Hall from Rachel's management and placed it under Alfred's. The document also named Alfred as Rachel's guardian. Since poor Alfred was dough in Sophia's hands, she controlled the estate and damned near ruined it."

The cove what 'ired us wants 'im to die slow and hard, wants 'im to suffer aplenty afore 'e goes to 'is maker. Stephen frowned. "But the ruffians who sold me to the press gang said a man had hired them."

"Sophia's brother did the actual hiring on her orders."

"Bloody hell, I knew that she hated me because I tried to stop Alfred from marrying her, but that hardly merited doing what she did to me."

"Of course not, but she was mad." Jerome gave a little shudder. "And diabolically clever. It took me a long time to discover just how clever."

"My God, my God!" Stephen could scarcely believe what he was hearing. Megan took his hand, and he squeezed hers hard, as if doing so could help him better grasp the stunning news. "And when she learned that you were about to expose her, she killed herself?"

"No, she died by her own hand, but it was not suicide." Rachel's voice wobbled. "When Jerome confronted her with the evidence, she tried to kill him with a dagger dipped in poison. He was struggling with her when she accidentally scratched herself with the poisoned tip."

Stephen was so stupefied by these revelations that he was speechless. So the hell that he had been through had been Sophia Wingate's doing! And he had thought it was George's. Stephen was painfully conscious of how terribly he had insulted his poor brother.

He thought of his dreams of retribution on his enemy that had driven him on when it would have been so much easier to have curled up and died. "What kept me going through the worst of my ordeal was my determination to get back here to England and punish the bastard who had me impressed."

Jerome asked, "How do you feel about being too late to do that?"

Stephen thought for a moment, then said slowly, "Disappointed that I cannot inflict my own revenge for what I have been through. Yet I am vastly relieved to discover that the brother I love was not responsible. I feel terrible for having slandered him."

He fell silent again, staring at his infant nephew, asleep in Jerome's arms. Stephen yearned for the day when he would hold his own son, his and Megan's, like that. He thought with joy of the family they would raise at Wingate Hall, and the horrors of the past receded.

For too long, Stephen had accepted his pleasure-mad friends' beliefs of what would bring him happiness. Now he knew how wrong they had been. Each man had to discover for himself what would make him happy. No one could make that decision for another.

Nor did life lie in the past, in regrets and in seeking retribution for wrongs done, but rather in enjoying the present to the fullest and in striving to make the future what he wanted it to be.

And that was what Stephen intended to do now.

He smiled and said with absolute honesty, "I am thankful that Sophia is dead and can cause us no more harm. Now I simply want to put it all behind me."

Chapter 25

Meg had never seen Stephen so ebullient.
It was much later that same night, and
they were ensconced in the earl's elegant bedchamber at Wingate Hall.

The previous two hours had passed in a blur to
the weary Meg. First, Jerome had left the lodge for
the hall. He had returned a short time later accompanied by a groom named Ferris, who seemed
more friend than servant to the duke, and two
horses to transport Meg and Stephen.

When they reached the hall, a late supper that
Jerome had ordered was waiting for the hungry
travelers. Meg was famished when she sat down to
the table, but her appetite faded as she observed
the footmen who served them. The dismayed, disapproving glances they cast in her direction told
her they were disappointed by their new mistress.

She could not blame them. Their own livery was
considerably more elegant than her shabby traveling clothes, and she must look especially plain beside her husband's breathtakingly beautiful sister.

After they ate, Stephen led Meg up to the earl's
private apartment.

Now with his shirt open at the neck and his
sleeves rolled up, he moved around the bedcham-

ber, touching familiar objects affectionately as though to reassure himself that he was at long last home.

He grinned at his wife. "What do you think of your new home, love?"

Meg looked around her at the finely crafted French furniture and the elegant cut-velvet hangings on the bed and windows. Her gaze stopped at a large portrait on the wall of a woman, not as beautiful as Rachel, but lovely nonetheless. Meg wondered with a pang who the woman was that her likeness hung on the wall of Stephen's bedchamber.

Turning to him, Meg saw that he was eagerly awaiting her judgment. She could not help smiling at his excitement and enthusiasm. He was clearly as proud of his home as she had once been of Ashley Grove, and with good reason. "Wingate Hall is most impressive."

Indeed it was.

What Meg liked best about it was that, despite its age—one section dated back to Tudor times—and sprawling size, it had a comfortable, homey atmosphere, and she told Stephen that.

He was obviously pleased. "That was my mother's doing. My father used to say that she made it into a home. You would have liked her. You remind me a great deal of her." He nodded toward the portrait that had caught Meg's eye. "That is my mother."

Relief coursed through Meg at learning that the portrait was of her husband's late mother. But she could not fathom how that lovely woman could possibly remind him of his plain wife.

"My father loved that painting of her. After she died, he had it hung there so he could see it when he awakened each morning."

Meg looked around the elegant bedchamber again. Stephen had told her that he was a very wealthy man, but she had not truly believed him. She had thought at best he was exaggerating both the size of his fortune and his position in society, but now she realized that instead of hyperbole, he had been guilty of understatement. "Why did you not tell me what Earl Arlington meant?"

"I wanted to surprise you."

The gleam in her husband's eyes told Meg how excited and delighted he thought she must be to discover that she was a countess. But after the tales she had heard about England's ignoble nobility and their casual attitude toward their marriage vows, she had no desire to be part of it.

In England, love is considered a frivolous reason for marriage, and it is the accepted thing for a husband to keep a mistress.

Well, love was not frivolous to her but the *only* reason to marry.

And, God help her, she did love Stephen Wingate, even though she understood now why he could not return her love nor give her the fidelity she must have from a husband.

Her heart seemed to sink through her feet. What was she to do now?

"Besides," her husband was saying, "I was afraid that you would think I was trying to hoodwink you if I told you I was a lord of the realm. Would you have?"

"Most likely," she admitted. If she doubted that he was Stephen Wingate, well-to-do farmer, even less would she have believed that he was an earl.

Stephen came up to Meg, and his hands settled gently on her arms. "Jerome kindly offered to dispatch one of his ships to Virginia immediately to bring Josh to England so you can be reunited more quickly with him. I will have my old tutor Reynolds sail aboard the vessel. You could not ask for a better guardian for your brother. Reynolds can work with him during the voyage to prepare him for Eton. Be assured I will give your brother the education that I promised him."

Meg, delighted that she would see Josh much sooner than she expected, threw her arms around her husband and hugged him exuberantly. "Thank you, Stephen, oh, thank you! I miss Josh so much."

Her husband smiled at her. "I know you do. When the ship is due to reach London, you and I will go there to greet Josh when he lands."

Stephen's head dipped, and he kissed first her temples, then the tip of her nose, and finally her mouth. She felt her body responding, as it always did, to him.

His arms encircled her, pulling her against him, and she trembled involuntarily as she felt the hard length of him against her. His kiss deepened, roughened, grew more urgent, and she felt her own yearning spiraling up within her. His mouth left hers to drop kisses down the curve of her neck.

She moaned, and he raised his head, smiling down at her. "Well, love, have you finally accepted once and for all that I am not Billy Gunnell and that I did not lie to you about the kind of life you would enjoy once we reached England?"

"Forgive me for doubting you. Had I truly thought you were Gunnell, I would not have crossed the Atlantic with you."

"I know that." His hands gripped hers for a moment, then he began to loosen the laces of her gown. He exposed one coral crest, and his tongue made lazy circles around it while his hand toyed with her other nipple, sending fire and need shooting through her.

He pushed her garments away, sending them tumbling about her feet, then picked her up. He lifted her over the discarded clothes and carried her to the great tester bed with its ornately carved posts and canopy. Pulling back the covers, he laid her on it.

He bent his head so it was only a fraction above hers and whispered in a voice husky and rich with sensual promise, "Now let me make love to you in your new home with nothing between us but the truth."

While Meg might have lingering doubts about the future of their marriage, her body knew no such limitations. She was as eager as he was, and her own hands reached up to unbutton his shirt. He groaned aloud, disposing of the buttons of his breeches as she worked on his shirt.

When they were naked in the bed together, he set about leisurely pleasuring her. Once again he proved to her that he knew her body better than she did.

By the time he took her, she was writhing with need in his arms, and she welcomed him with a passion that matched his own. They soared together into a dazzling mutual explosion that left them stunned and panting.

When their bodies separated, he immediately gathered her to him in his arms and whispered, his breath hot and exciting against her ear, "You will never regret coming to England with me, Lady Arlington."

Lady Arlington. Dear God! Meg's exhausted mind belatedly made a connection it had failed to make before. *No woman could be more beautiful than Lady Caroline Taber, Sir John Taber's wife and the late Lord Arlington's mistress. My sister says all the ladies loved*

*him, but he dallied only with the most beautiful. He used
to bring all his mistresses to madame to dress.*

Meg's stomach roiled as though she were back
on the stormy, wind-tossed sea. Dear God in
heaven, she was married to that handsome, charming, and utterly faithless lord, a man who loved
only for the moment. What little hope she had that
she had wed a man who could cherish her and be
faithful died within her.

Stephen stroked her body lovingly. His handsome face, with its sharply etched planes and midnight black brows, was alight with happiness and
relief. "At last my nightmare is ended."

But Meg feared hers was only beginning, married as she was to a man who had been forced to
wed her, no matter how good a face he had tried
to put on it, a man for whom marital fidelity was
a foreign concept.

He would never even comprehend that she
would happily trade all his wealth and the impressive title he had bestowed on her for his lasting
love and fidelity.

"Will you go to London for the season, Stephen?" Jerome inquired the following afternoon.
He asked the question lightly, but Stephen knew
the duke rarely made casual inquiries.

"No, I will not take Megan there." Stephen was
seated, facing his brother-in-law across a small tulipwood table in the library at Wingate Hall. "I fear
she will not be accepted by society, and I will not
let anyone or anything hurt her."

He was determined to protect her from people
like Lord Oldfield and his wife, the two most
poisonous gossips in all London. As far as Stephen
was concerned, the venomous pair deserved each

other. But he would not let their malicious tongues—nor anyone else's—wound Megan.

Jerome frowned. "You must at least introduce your wife to society. If you do not, it will feed ugly rumors about her and your marriage."

"I will not take her to London."

"No, you need not take her there. Instead Rachel and I will hold a ball in Megan's honor at Royal Elms." Jerome rose and went to a pier table that held a full brandy decanter and several glasses. "Would you like a brandy?"

Stephen nodded, and Jerome poured the rich umber liquid into two glasses. "We will invite only the cream of society." A mischievous gleam shone in Jerome's cyan eyes. "People like Lord and Lady Oldfield will be gnashing their teeth over being omitted."

"Indeed they will." Stephen could not help grinning at the thought.

"So will your former betrothed Fanny Stoddard. Believe me, everyone will be vying for an invitation."

Stephen knew Jerome was right. Invitations to the duke's great estate were always much prized. Megan would be introduced to the ton in grand style with the full support of her husband and the formidable Duke of Westleigh arrayed behind her.

During the ball, Stephen would make certain that everyone there saw how much he loved her, and that should go a long way toward quieting the unkind rumors that would inevitably swirl around her.

Then they could retire quietly to Wingate Hall and eschew society. In truth, he looked forward to that prospect.

Jerome handed Stephen one of the brandies. "Will you miss London?"

Stephen swirled the brandy in his glass. "You will be amused. What I dreamed of while I was in America was not London but Wingate Hall."

Jerome smiled at him. "So you are your father's son after all."

"Aye." Stephen felt a lump swelling in his throat. "If only he had lived long enough for me to discover that." He pretended to take a sip of brandy while he recovered his composure.

When he succeeded, he said, "I am deeply indebted to you and my sister for repairing the damage Sophia did to the estate. The people here love you and Rachel. They are not particularly happy to see me return from the dead. I could see it in their faces when we rode out today."

"If you manage the estate wisely, and I think you will, they will come 'round quick enough."

"You have more faith in me than you used to."

"With good reason. You are not the same man you were before you disappeared. That man would not have survived your ordeal." Jerome stared thoughtfully at the contents of the glass in his hand. "Tell me about your wife. She has the manners and bearing of a lady of quality."

Stephen smiled proudly. "Yes, she has an innate dignity, does she not? She was once the mistress of a plantation every bit as fine as some of the great country houses here in England."

"What happened to it?"

"Her father left it to her, but a bastard by the name of Hiram Flynt swindled her out of it with the assistance of a dishonest justice."

"Hiram Flynt," Jerome echoed. "Why does that sound so familiar to me?"

"I cannot conceive, unless I mentioned that he is the Virginia planter who bought me as an indentured servant."

"How did he cheat Megan of her plantation?"

"When her father died, Flynt ordered a fortune hunter named Charles Galloway, who was deeply in debt to him, to court and wed the widow so he could have himself appointed Megan's guardian."

"Thus giving him control of the plantation?"

Stephen nodded. "Documents I found in Galloway's trunk show that both he and the justice who signed the guardianship papers, a man named Baylis, were in Flynt's pay."

"Where is Galloway now?"

"Killed in a tavern fight."

"Convenient," Jerome remarked dryly.

"Yes, is it not? Will you help me recover Megan's estate from Flynt?"

"Only tell me what I can do."

"Megan tried to appeal the guardianship, but the General Court in Virginia denied her a hearing. The only avenue left is to the king in council here. I have brought all the documents I found in Galloway's trunk to England with me. Would you use your power to see that she gets a hearing?"

"Certainly." Jerome stared thoughtfully at his brandy glass for another moment, then set it down abruptly on the table. "Now I remember why Flynt's name is familiar."

The duke hurried to a tulipwood writing table and sorted through a stack of letters. He extracted one and unfolded it. "I received this a few weeks ago in a packet of letters forwarded to me from Royal Elms. It was addressed to a Lord Dunbar there. Since there is no such lord, I took the liberty of opening it. It was from a Hiram Flynt, who seems to be under the mistaken impression this nonexistent Lord Dunbar is his father-in-law."

Stephen burst out laughing. He could not help it.

Jerome looked puzzled. "I fail to see the humor."

Nor would Hiram Flynt when he learned the truth about the wife of whom he was so proud. The lying Kate would be lucky if her husband, given his explosive temper, did not kill her. "Flynt married a woman who passed herself off as Lady Katherine Dunbar, the mythical lord's daughter."

"Do you have any idea who she truly is?"

"I suspect a whore who was transported as an indentured servant and subsequently escaped her master."

"Flynt's letter says he and his wife are about to embark for England, and they plan to come to Royal Elms so he can meet his father-in-law." A devilish gleam shone in Jerome's eyes. "I think, Stephen, that I will arrange a most memorable reception for Hiram Flynt at Royal Elms."

In a small withdrawing room off the long gallery at Wingate Hall, Meg watched Stephen intently examine the clothes dolls, sketches, and fabric samples of the modiste he had summoned.

Her husband was devoting a disconcerting amount of time and attention to the gown she would wear to the ball that Rachel and Jerome planned at Royal Oaks to introduce her to society. Stephen was clearly determined that his wife would not be too great an embarrassment to him.

Immediately after Jerome had announced that he and Rachel would hold the fete in Meg's honor, Stephen had sent to York for the modiste, reputedly the most fashionable dressmaker in the entire north of England.

"I would prefer to send to London for Madame d'Artemis, but there is not time," he had told Meg. "The ball is too soon."

He used to bring all his mistresses to madame to dress . . .

Meg swallowed hard at the unhappy thought that she was far from the first woman to whose dress he had devoted so much time and attention.

Her mother had told her daughter so often she was plain and scrawny, that Meg had never found any joy in selecting fashions, knowing she could not do them justice the way other women with more voluptuous figures did. Yet Meg was fascinated and excited by the modiste's display of rich silks, velvets, and satins in a brilliant palette of colors.

Never in Virginia had Meg seen such intricately draped and pleated designs, elaborate and richly ornamented with fine lace, embroidery, ribbons, ruching, and ruffling. They were ball gowns fit for a queen.

Meg would have been delighted with any one of them, but none met Stephen's approval. She watched in dismay as he impatiently discarded one design after another.

Finally he turned over one of the sketches and began to draw on the back of it. He worked silently for several minutes while Meg enviously examined some of the clothes dolls that he had rejected. She particularly yearned for a bright blue satin confection, draped and swagged over a wide white satin petticoat and trimmed with row after row of lace ruffles.

Stephen finished his sketch and handed it to the modiste. "This is what I want."

She took it and frowned. "But, my lord—"

"It is what I want," he repeated firmly.

Her lips pursed in disapproval. "But, my lord, at least reconsider the neckline. It should be square. No one wears—"

He cut her off. "This is the way I want it."

Meg stole a look at his sketch and swallowed her disappointment when she saw the simple, unornamented, unswagged gown with the V neck that he proposed. Even its petticoat was not nearly as wide as those in the samples.

A plain gown for a plain wife. He clearly did not wish to waste his money on a hopeless cause. The modiste's face told Meg that she was equally dismayed by his choice.

"Now for the material." Stephen picked up the swatches of cloth. He tossed aside the rich satins and velvets in favor of a subdued deep green silk that looked positively drab among the vivid colors of the other samples. For her stomacher and petticoat, he selected cream silk.

"My wife also needs other clothes," he said briskly and proceeded to choose a generous number of other garments for her. Meg's pleasure in this, however, was severely dampened by his inevitable selection of the simplest designs the modiste offered.

Meg thought of Rachel's beautiful gowns, so much more elaborate than what Stephen was choosing for her, and felt a pang of envy. Surely it could not be because he wanted to keep the cost down, for he had already given her an enormous sum of what he called "pin money" for her incidental expenses.

Rachel came into the withdrawing room, and her brother showed her the designs he had picked for his wife. She frowned as she looked over his choices. "But, Stephen, she will need more elaborate gowns than these for the London season."

"I am not taking her to London for the season."

Rachel looked startled. "You are not? But you never miss one."

His mouth tightened, and he said curtly, "The gowns I have selected will do very well for her in Yorkshire."

Meg looked from Rachel's astonished expression to her husband's displeased one. *Why does he not want to take me to London? Is he embarrassed to be seen with his colonial wife that he was forced to marry?*

A lump swelled in Meg's throat, and she feared she could not hold back her tears. She turned and headed blindly for the door.

Behind her, Rachel said, "Still, Stephen, the ball gown you selected for Megan is not—"

He interrupted her, saying irritably, "I know what will best become my wife."

As she reached the hall, he called, "Megan, wait for me."

She stopped and turned. He hurried to her and took her arm. "You will look lovely at the ball, Megan."

But she knew he was wrong.

Two days later, Meg and her husband stood on the steps of Wingate Hall, waving farewell to Rachel, Jerome, and little Stephen. The Westleighs were going home to prepare for the ball in Megan's honor.

As the coach started up, Rachel cried through the window, "Good-bye. We will see you at Royal Elms in less than three weeks."

The departing coach picked up speed. "I hate for them to leave!" Meg burst out. She would miss the duke and duchess, especially at night, when the two couples acted out little plays, indulged in lively conversation, or sang together while Jerome accompanied them on his guitar.

These nights offered Meg a welcome respite from

the doubts and fears that haunted her about her marriage.

Jerome had been so kind, friendly, and solicitous of Meg that she had been unable to understand how Stephen could have called him the most freezingly condescending aristocrat in all Europe.

Meg was still a little awed by the gorgeous duchess and frightened at the prospect of succeeding her as mistress of Wingate Hall. Everyone loved Rachel, and with good reason, Meg had concluded. It would not be easy for any woman to fill that role after her. And especially not for a colonial nobody, whom even the servants looked down upon. Their expressions when she addressed them betrayed their true sentiments about her.

"I will miss Jerome and Rachel terribly," she confessed to Stephen. "Now I must try to fill Rachel's very large footprints as mistress of Wingate Hall."

"Just as I must fill Jerome's and my father's as its master. Are you not excited by the challenge?"

No, she was not. She was daunted and frightened, but she would meet it. Her mouth tightened in determination. Let the servants look askance at her. She would run Wingate Hall with the skill that had made her father so proud of her when she had managed Ashley Grove. It would not be easy, but she would do it.

She might not be the wife that Stephen would have chosen. She was not a woman to permanently capture the heart of a charming rake like him, but he would find no fault with her performance as the mistress of his household.

Meg would show Stephen that she was not a total failure as a wife.

Chapter 26

$\sim\!\!\sim\!\!\infty\!\!\sim\!\!\sim$

Meg reluctantly made her way to the drawing room to greet her unwanted callers, a Lord and Lady Oldfield.

She wished Stephen was here with her instead of out somewhere on the estate. She had no notion whether the Oldfields were close friends of her husband's as they had told the butler, or merely more of the curious who had come to scrutinize her.

Word of Lord Arlington's return with his American wife had spread with amazing rapidity and drawn a surprising number of aristocratic callers who came to look her over and find fault. They made her feel as though she were a freak with two heads or three arms.

A wave of loneliness and desolation washed over her. She was friendless in this new land, where everyone looked down upon her, and she felt as though she had no real purpose.

After Rachel's departure nearly a fortnight ago, Meg had resolutely taken over the management of the household. But she had quickly discovered that running a great house in England was not the same as a plantation mansion in Virginia.

For one thing, she had so many more servants

here, and they were far better trained. They did not require the instruction and supervision that had taken so much of her time at Ashley Grove. Wingate Hall ran so smoothly that she often felt superfluous.

Stephen was so busy with the estate that she scarcely saw him, except at night. He had been so enthusiastic since he had come home, bristling with energy, embracing control of his land, eager to learn everything he could about it. He exuded an unconscious air of authority. No one would doubt he was the master of a great estate.

With a wife who was not his match.

A woman's shrill voice, presumably Lady Oldfield's, drifted from the drawing room. "What can Arlington have been thinking of to marry some poor colonial without breeding or family connections?"

The words froze Meg. She stood outside the drawing room, unable to force her feet forward.

"They say she is not even pretty," a contemptuous male voice said.

"Only consider what it does to the Wingates' bloodlines. Society will never accept her, no matter how many balls the Duke and Duchess of Westleigh give at Royal Elms in her honor."

"The duchess is trying to put the best face possible on this disaster! Why would Arlington tie himself to such an unacceptable creature when he has always had any woman he wanted?"

"Poor Lady Caroline Taber is positively distraught over his marriage," the shrill female voice said. "Not that she should worry. If his countess is as unattractive as they say, Arlington is certain to turn to Caroline again very shortly."

My sister says she cannot imagine that any woman could be more beautiful than Lady Caroline Taber.

Meg felt as though an icy north wind was blowing across her heart. It was intolerable to her to be married to a man who did not want her, a man who would ignore her while he lavished his attentions on his beautiful mistresses.

Especially, Meg thought with a gulp, when she loved her husband as much as she loved Stephen. She had tried so hard to protect her heart from him, but she had failed miserably.

Poor Meg. A woman as plain as you can never inspire passion and faithfulness and undying love in a handsome young husband.

The shrill voice, as grating to Meg's ears as the screech of fingernails on metal, said, "I should like to have seen the rage Fanny Stoddard, Arlington's former betrothed, flew into when she learned he had returned to England married to someone else."

"What complaint can she have when she wasted no time becoming betrothed to Lord Felix Overend after Arlington disappeared."

"But it was Arlington whom she wanted. I hear she is heartbroken."

A servant stepped into the hall. Embarrassed to be seen hovering outside the drawing room, Meg shook off the paralysis that gripped her and forced her rubbery legs to carry her to face her critical guests.

The man, short and portly, rose and bowed. "Lord Oldfield at your service, Lady Arlington, and this is my wife." He nodded toward his companion, who had remained seated. She was a thin woman, but more attractive than Meg would have suspected from her voice.

Her ladyship looked Meg over with cold eyes, clearly disposed to find fault. When she finished, it was obvious from her expression that she saw nothing in her perusal of Meg to change her mind about the new countess's fitness to be Arlington's wife.

"Please be seated," Meg said, taking an armchair opposite her visitors. "Do you live near here? You must forgive me, but I do not yet know the names of all my new neighbors."

Oldfield said hastily, "We arrived late last night from London."

Meg noticed he had not answered her question about whether they were neighbors, but she said politely, "How kind of you to call upon me so quickly upon your arrival in Yorkshire."

"We heard you are leaving for Royal Elms on the morrow," Oldfield said. "We could not let you depart before we had a chance to welcome you to England. Your husband is such an old and dear friend of ours."

That surprised Meg. They did not seem like a couple Stephen would particularly like.

"We are so sorry that we shall not be able to attend the ball the duke and duchess are giving in your honor, but our schedule is so full, it is all but impossible for us to do so." Lady Oldfield gave Meg a sly look. "Although, of course, if you were to expressly request us to come, we should do everything in our power to be there. We would not want to seem *unwelcoming* to you."

"You do not seem that at all. I would not dream of inconveniencing you by asking you to come to the ball."

From the sour look on Lady Oldfield's face, this was not the response she had wanted. Seeking to turn the conversation away from the ball she dreaded, Meg asked, "How far is your home from here?"

"Some distance," Lady Oldfield said sharply. "We spend most of our time in London. I look forward to seeing you there for the season. I shall be happy to take you under my wing."

"How kind of you, but my husband has decided that we shall not go to London for the season."

"Not go!" Oldfield exclaimed. "Surely you cannot have that right. Your husband loves London. He would never miss a season. Mark my words, you will be going."

"Of course you will," his wife chimed in.

"I must say London has been a duller place since your husband disappeared, especially for the ladies." Malice glinted in Oldfield's eyes. "Tales of his escapades among the petticoat company used to keep us much entertained. We look forward to having him back."

"Especially since that wicked charmer Anthony Denton is hiding from his creditors in Northumberland. He and your husband were great friends, you know." Lady Oldfield smirked. "Let me tell you about your naughty, naughty husband."

After spending much of the day meeting with tenants, Stephen strode into Wingate Hall. As he started toward the stairs, he heard the harpsichord, its music full of tumult and passion, of haunting loneliness and sorrow. He had no doubt who was at the keyboard.

He wished he understood why his wife was so unhappy. Instead of being delighted at how well she had married and the luxury that Stephen could give her, Megan seemed to be growing increasingly distressed.

And increasingly distant from him. An invisible wall was rising between them, and he was at a loss to understand why.

At first he had been so content to be home at Wingate Hall with the woman he loved, to know

that his enemy was dead and could never trouble
him again, to have Megan safe and his estate restored to him, he had failed to grasp immediately
that she did not share his joy.

Of course, she missed Josh, but Stephen had already sent his old tutor to America for the boy.

Despite her unhappiness, though, she was proving to be the excellent mistress of Wingate Hall that
he had known she would be. He was proud of the
way she had taken over the running of the household after Rachel's departure. It could have been
no easier for her to take on this task than it had
been for him to take back control of his estate from
the much-respected Jerome.

He had seen the dubious way the servants had
looked at her when she first began to give them
orders. Snobbery was endemic among the servants
in a great house. They basked in the reflected status
of their master and mistress. Wingate Hall's servants had looked askance at having a much-loved
duchess replaced by a colonial who in their narrow,
provincial eyes lacked birth and breeding.

But Megan, with her energy, innate kindness,
and no-nonsense ways, had already begun to win
their respect. Yes, Stephen was damned proud of
her.

It was time they talked about what was making
her so unhappy. He slipped into the music room,
noiselessly closed the door, and turned the key in
the lock so they would not be disturbed.

Megan, lost in her playing, did not seem to notice her husband's entry.

"Such sad music, love."

She started, and the music ended with jarring
abruptness as her hands fell away from the keyboard. He sat down on the bench beside her, her
sweet scent of orange blossoms enveloping him.

Megan slid away from him, but he put his arm around her and pulled her to him. He felt her stiffen in his embrace.

His jaw tightened in dismay. What caused this reaction to him? Did the occupants of the coach he had seen pulling away from Wingate Hall as he had ridden up to the stable have anything to do with it? "I saw a coach leaving as I arrived. Who were your callers?"

"Your dear friends, Lord and Lady Oldfield."

"Bloody hell, what were they doing here?" There was no one he less wanted Megan exposed to than the malicious Oldfields. It was to spare her from people like them that he had decided against taking her to London.

"I believe they are neighbors."

"*Neighbors!* Is that what they said?"

She frowned. "I don't know they actually said it, but they intimated."

"Well, they are not. Their home is in Dorset, the other end of the damned country. What the hell were they doing here?"

"They said they wanted to welcome me to England."

Megan did not need their kind of welcome!

"They are not able to attend the ball for me at Royal Elms, but if I wished to expressly invite them, they will try to go."

"Try! They would break their damn necks to get there. They are not going to the ball because they were deliberately not asked. Jerome would not allow that pair to set foot in Royal Elms. They obviously came here hoping to extract an invitation from you. I hope you did not give it to them."

"No." She dropped her gaze, and her gray eyes were hidden from him by her lowered lids and the burnished sweep of her thick lashes. "They said Fanny Stoddard is heartbroken over our marriage."

"Believe me, Fanny has no heart to break!"

Megan looked shocked. "How can you say that about the woman you wanted to marry?"

Stephen had not wanted to marry Fanny. He had wanted to forge an alliance with Lord Stoddard and his vast political power. But telling Megan why he had made Fanny an offer would hardly raise him in his wife's esteem.

"If Fanny is suffering any emotion at all, it is thwarted ambition. She wanted to be the wife of a rich earl from a prestigious family. She still prefers that to being the wife of a younger son, even though he is as rich as Lord Felix."

Megan was staring at Stephen as though he had just sprouted a second head. "Why did you ask her to marry you?"

"I told you once that for a man of my position in England, love has nothing to do with his selection of a bride." But that was before he met Megan.

"Especially when a musket is pointed at his heart."

"Bloody hell, Megan, that is not the reason I married you. I did so because I *wanted* to. I did not want to marry Fanny." But he could see from his wife's expression that she believed him even less now than she had earlier.

"Lord Oldfield cannot understand why you married me when you have always had any woman you wanted."

Stephen was so dumbfounded that he blurted, "Bloody hell, surely he did not say that to you! I will kill him!"

"No, I merely overheard him, but his wife regaled me with tales of your naughty past."

Stephen flinched at the pain in Megan's eyes. He

could imagine some of the stories that vicious harpy had told Meg. Clearly his wife had not been regaled but shocked. *Damn the Oldfields!* He did not blame Megan for being appalled at the man he used to be. He was appalled himself.

"I will not deny what I was, Megan—a callow, selfish, irresponsible fool. But that was the past." And the beautiful women he had bedded then had been no better than he. Had he not been the rich and handsome young Earl of Arlington, they would have taken no notice of him.

But Megan, so different from those women that she hardly seemed of the same species, would not understand that they had been as faithless and pleasure-hungry as he was.

"Listen to me, Megan. I know you are shocked by my past. But I was a stranger to love then. I did not even believe in it. I thought it a pathetic illusion of hopeless romantics. Now I know better. You taught me, Megan."

Yes, she had. She might not possess the physical beauty of his former mistresses, but she had a beauty of spirit and character that filled him with a contentment and a happiness that he now knew were far more important.

He took her chin in his hand and turned her face toward him. His mouth settled on hers in a long kiss, full of tenderness and passion. He felt her stiff opposition to him melt gradually away with ago-nizing slowness.

But at last she was returning his kiss fervently.

He continued to hold her mouth captive while his hands removed the pins from her hair, letting it tumble down in honey waves. He spread it about her like a cloak and beneath its cover began to sur-reptitiously unfasten her stomacher and bodice, then her skirts. As he worked, her silken hair, moving and shifting like a drifting cloud, caressed his hands.

He slid her gown and shift down her shoulders and caught the sweet weight of her breast in his palm. His mouth, still covering hers, smothered her gasp. She made a halfhearted effort to push him away, but his thumb began circling her nipple while his lips made a slow, nibbling journey down the lovely curve of her neck.

With a lingering sigh, her resistance turned to complaisance.

His mouth replaced his thumb on the rosy peak, and she arched in pleasure. As he suckled her, his hand dipped beneath her skirt and caressed her thigh.

Little whimpers escaped her, firing Stephen's own desire. He yearned to take her instantly, and he had to fight his own body to continue his slow seduction of her.

She was leaning back now against his arm. If it had not been there, she would have tumbled backward off the bench, so lost was she in the pleasure he was giving her.

God, but he loved the way her body twisted and writhed beneath his tongue and his hands. Her woman's core was already wet and welcoming. There was no coyness about her. Her response was as open and direct as Megan herself.

Such a passionate creature, he thought admiringly. He would not have traded the woman in his arms for any ten of his beautiful former mistresses.

Stephen glanced over at the settee and dismissed it as too short and uncomfortable. He rose from the harpsichord bench, pulling her with him. He set her on her feet only long enough to slide her bodice and shift from her shoulders and let them join her skirts around her ankles. Then he lowered her to the carpet in front of the fireplace.

"What . . . are you . . . doing?" she stammered.

The flames cast a rosy glow over her body and made the luxurious waves of her hair shimmer. He stared down at her admiringly while he shed his own clothes. "I should think it is obvious."

For a moment Meg was so enthralled by the sight of his strong, powerful body revealed in the firelight that she was paralyzed.

Then a scandalized gasp of protest escaped her lips, and she grabbed frantically for her garments, determined to cover herself before an unsuspecting servant walked into the room.

He dropped beside her on the carpet and swept her into his arms, catching her wrists behind her back and pulling her against him.

She tried to wrench them free. "A servant will come in!"

"I locked the door."

Her eyes widened, her thoughts transparent.

"No, I did not lock it because I intended this. I wanted to talk to you in private."

"Then let us talk."

He gave her a wicked grin, full of sensual promise. "I find this an even better method of communicating."

"'Tis the middle of the day."

Stephen's seductive grin merely widened. How could any woman resist it? Meg wondered. Still, she tried. "'Tis wrong."

"Nay," he whispered, his breath moist and hot and exciting against her cheek. "You are my wife. What we do is sanctioned by God. 'Let no man put asunder, what I have joined together.'" He lifted his head slightly and winked at her.

"You are blasphemous!"

"Nay, God intended that a man make love to his wife." Stephen's lips closed over hers, stopping further protests.

He was infinitely patient with her, his mouth and his hands lavishing her with attention until she was begging him to take her. When at last he slid into her slick depths, she arched up to meet him. He began to move within her, slowly first, then more vigorously.

She climaxed before him, racked by spasms and soft cries, and he came only a moment behind her. When he was spent, he gathered her into his arms and, still joined with her, held her hard against him.

Megan's eyes opened with a start. She was uncertain how long she had napped. How could she have possibly fallen asleep like this, lying in her husband's arms naked before the fire in the music room?

Dear God, she was becoming as wanton as some of the ladies whose scandals the Oldfields had related to her. Her hands clenched involuntarily as she recalled those unwelcome guests. They had told her more about her husband than she wanted to know. Indeed, it was difficult for her to reconcile the feckless, pleasure-seeking, amoral man they had described with the Stephen she knew.

When the Oldfields had exhausted their stories of Stephen, their conversation had turned to the latest London scandals involving marital infidelity. Once again Meg had been shocked and appalled by the casualness with which the English aristocracy regarded their wedding vows. Apparently not a single lord in England was faithful to his wife. Except perhaps for Jerome. Oldfield had made a snide comment about how besotted the duke was by his wife.

And why should he not be? She was the most beautiful woman Meg had ever seen.

But Stephen had not married a beautiful wife. And Meg could not hope that he would be faithful to her.

Meg belatedly realized that her torso was covered. Raising her head slightly, she saw her husband's riding coat was draped over her. He must have done that after she had fallen asleep.

She turned her head and looked at his sinfully handsome face, so close beside her own. His eyes were closed, his expression relaxed and happy. She had never dreamed a man could make her feel the way he did when he made love to her. No wonder he had been so easily able to bed whatever woman he wanted.

Her heart contracted painfully at the thought of him pleasuring other women as he did her. It was unbearable to think of him going to another woman's bed, yet she would have to learn to bear it.

A man used to his pick of the most beautiful women in the land would not long be content with such an unattractive wife as Meg. Indeed, she had nothing, not beauty, high birth, nor fortune to bring to this marriage he had been forced into by her brother.

Meg tried to slip away from her husband's arms, but he tightened his grasp around her. His eyes fluttered open. "Do not go away. We have not talked yet."

"What have we to talk about?"

"I want you to tell me why you are unhappy, Megan. What troubles you?"

"My future."

He stared at her, his blue violet eyes perplexed. "What do you mean? Your future is assured."

"Is it?"

"Of course, you are my wife and the Countess of Arlington."

A wife you do not want. She felt as though her chest were one great, aching bruise. "I am alone, a stranger in a strange land."

"Bloody hell, Megan, you are not alone. You have me. You have Rachel and Jerome. Soon you will have Josh."

"But what will happen to me if you . . . " She feared her voice would betray her, and she finished the question silently . . . *when you tire of me?*

"If I should die? You will be a rich woman. I have already had the papers drawn up. I have settled a fortune on you."

What she wanted him to settle upon her was his undying love and fidelity, but her pride would not let her tell him that. Although he said he loved her, she had no illusions that such a man would be faithful to her for long.

Chapter 27

~~~⚬☉☉⚬~~~

Meg hardly noticed the elegantly landscaped grounds of Royal Elms, with carefully planned vistas to delight the eye from every vantage point. She was far too engrossed in staring at the massive stone palace rising like some magnificent classical temple on the hill in front of their coach. Twin cupolas flanked the great pediment of its central block and long, rusticated pavilions extended on each side.

Astonished by its size and beauty, Meg mumbled, "It is very . . . very . . . " Her voice faded as she was unable to think of a word that would adequately describe the mansion. "No wonder it is called the premier estate in all England."

She tried to squelch the nervousness she felt about the fete that would be held tonight for her in this magnificent house. They had been scheduled to arrive at Royal Elms the previous day, but a drunken stagecoach driver south of York had swerved unexpectedly and hooked a wheel with Stephen's traveling coach, damaging its front axle. It had taken a day for repairs.

Their coach slowed as it rounded the circular driveway in front of the great house's entrance. Another equipage ahead of theirs had discharged its passengers, a distinguished looking gentleman and his lady, and was moving on.

The couple had ascended to the pillared portico by the time Stephen's coach stopped. The woman halted there and turned to look out at the prospect, undoubtedly breathtaking, that the hilltop afforded. Meg could not stop herself from gawking at her. Except for Rachel, the woman on the portico was the loveliest creature Meg had ever seen, and she felt positively ugly in comparison.

Each feature of the woman's bewitching oval face, framed by rich auburn hair, was perfectly sculpted. Her elegant brows arched above large eyes the color of rich chocolate. Her nose was aristocratic. Her mouth was ripe and sensual. So was her body. Tall, she was clad in an elegant gown that enhanced the tempting curves of her full bosom and her minuscule waist. It was the kind of body that men dreamed of.

A smothered sound, rather like a strangled expletive, escaped from her husband, seated beside her. She glanced toward him and saw that he, too, was gaping at the woman, an arrested expression on his face. He looked stunned, as though he could not believe his eyes.

Meg tried to tell herself that any man not yet in the grave would notice such a great beauty, but the indecipherable look in her husband's eyes ate at her heart. The woman and her companion disappeared inside Royal Elms, but Stephen continued to sit motionless, as though the sight of her had turned him to stone.

Meg swallowed hard, jealousy chewing at her. She reflected bitterly that she, plain thing that she was, had never had that effect on her husband. Nor would she ever have it on any man. "Who is that woman? Do you know?"

It was a moment before her question seemed to register with Stephen. He nodded. "Lady Caroline Taber."

His words were like a searing brand across Meg's heart.

Stephen's mistress!

Much agitated, Stephen followed Jerome into his library and shut the door hard behind them. "What in bloody hell is Caroline Taber doing here?"

Jerome turned to face his irate guest. "Attending the ball in your wife's honor."

"Why the devil did you invite her? You know what we used to be."

"Aye, and I did not invite her. Your sister, who knows nothing of your past relationship with her, did. Taber is an old friend of mine. When the wily Caroline complained to Rachel that their failure to receive an invitation to the ball must have been an oversight, she thought that indeed was the case and extended one. By the time I learned of it, it was too late to do anything about it."

Stephen was alarmed and apprehensive about his volatile former mistress attending Megan's ball. "Damn, tonight is neither the time nor the place for me to have to deal with Caro. It should be done in private." And done very carefully. "I hope to hell she does not create a scene that will embarrass Megan."

Jerome looked appalled. "Hellsfire, surely she would not?"

"Oh, she is quite capable of it."

"Perhaps seeing you with a wife you love will discourage her."

"What do you think?" Stephen asked bleakly.

Jerome frowned. "That Caroline is too convinced of her own charms to see the obvious."

The duke went over to his desk and removed a black velvet jeweler's case from the top drawer. "This arrived yesterday for you from Duncan Richter, the jeweler."

"Ah, my belated wedding present to Megan, a brooch that I designed and had made. I want her to wear it to the ball." Stephen took the case from Jerome, opened it, and smiled. Richter had executed the jeweled hummingbird precisely as Stephen had wanted.

Jerome settled himself in an armchair and gestured to Stephen to do the same. "Did Rachel tell you about the letter she received yesterday from George?"

"Yes." It had been written in haste to tell her Stephen's letter had been in the mail that had accumulated for George in New York while he was in Canada, and that he was departing immediately for Virginia to help his brother.

George's letter had been dated the day after Stephen and Megan had sailed for England.

"I have another bit of news for you," Jerome said. "The king, or more accurately the committee of the Privy Council set up to deal with such matters, has agreed to hear Megan's appeal. We will argue that Ashley Grove was taken from her by fraud and that it should be restored to her."

Stephen sighed in relief and gratitude. "Thank you, Jerome."

"As Megan's husband, you must appear for her at the hearing in London. I will go with you."

"What are our chances of winning?"

Jerome shrugged noncommittally.

Stephen's spirits sank. "I would appreciate it if you did not tell Megan about the appeal. I cannot bear to build up her hopes, then have her disappointed."

"How will you explain your journey to London to her?"

"I will tell her I must go on business, which is the truth. If she knows the real reason, and the case goes against us, she will be devastated."

Jerome nodded. "The protective husband."

"Yes," he admitted.

"I must warn you that sometimes protecting one's wife from sorrow can have unforeseen and unfortunate consequences. I myself learned that the hard way."

"I will not have Megan disappointed," Stephen said firmly. "When will the appeal hearing be held?"

"In three days, but fortunately it does not begin until that afternoon. We will have to leave at dawn that morning and travel by horseback."

"Why can we not leave the previous day?"

"I am expecting Hiram Flynt then, and we will both want to be here for that."

"Did 'Lord Dunbar' get another letter from him?"

"No, I hired Neville Griffin, the agent who ferreted out the truth about your seizure and impressment at Dover. He had a talk with the bogus Lady Katherine when she and Flynt landed in London. Her background, by the way, is what you thought it was. Her sentence was commuted to transportation on the condition she never return to England."

"And now that she has, she will be imprisoned to serve her original sentence?"

"That is what should happen, but Griffin and I worked out an agreement: her freedom in exchange for some fascinating evidence she has against her husband and for her cooperation in getting him to Royal Elms." Jerome gave Stephen a sly smile. "I do not think you will want to miss the reception I have in store for him."

Meg listened in amazement as Stephen instructed Jane, Rachel's maid, in minute detail on the hairstyle and makeup he wished his wife to wear for the ball in her honor.

He looked unbearably handsome in coat and breeches of blue figured silk. The garments had been tailored to perfection, accentuating the muscular breadth of his chest and the slimness of his hips. Beneath his coat, she saw a matching waistcoat. His cravat was of Mechlin lace.

Meg stared in helpless admiration at his noble face, wondering how any woman could resist those remarkable blue violet eyes beneath slashing black brows.

From what she had heard about him before his impressment, perhaps no woman had.

As Jane did her hair, he continued to hover, making certain that the maid followed his instructions to the letter, piling the honey waves high on Meg's head in an intricate style with the back left long and flowing.

When it came time for cosmetics, Meg quickly discovered that Stephen knew more about what was in those mysterious pots the maid had brought with her than his wife did.

"A bit more of that beneath her eyes," he said, pointing to one of them. After the maid complied, he pointed to the rosy contents of another pot. "Some of that on her cheeks."

His knowledge about a lady's toilet seemed to be inexhaustible. Meg's already depressed spirits fell even further as she thought about how he had come by all his expertise. How many other women at the ball tonight, besides Lady Caroline, had been his mistress? Meg cringed inwardly at the thought of how poorly she would look on Stephen's arm in comparison to that beauty.

When he was finally satisfied with the maid's work, he said, "Now for her gown."

Jane helped Meg into it. The gown was still a disappointment to her. Why had Stephen chosen it for her? It was so simple, and she knew from the elaborate designs the modiste had shown them that she would be the most plainly dressed woman at the ball.

Stephen went to the bedside table and opened a drawer.

"Does Madame wish to see herself in the long looking glass in the dressing room?" Jane asked.

Madame did not. "No, that will be all, Jane." The maid was clearly surprised by Meg's answer. But even with all the work Jane had done on her, Meg knew she would look plain and drab beside her sinfully handsome husband in the Royal Elms ballroom. Meg feared that if she saw her image in the glass, she would not have the courage to appear in a ballroom crowded with beautiful women like Lady Caroline.

Meg's stomach roiled at the ordeal ahead of her. She dreaded it more than she had ever dreaded anything in her life. Pulling stumps to clear a field would have been more to her liking.

As the door closed after the departing maid, Stephen came over to Meg, carrying a small black velvet box. His smile was dazzling. "You look lovely."

The way he said it would have made Meg think she was beautiful, had she not known better. No wonder he had so many ladies eager to bed him.

He handed her the box. "This is for you. It is my wedding present to you—or one of them. I hope to have another for you next week," he added mysteriously.

Meg opened the case and gave a cry of surprised pleasure at the sight of the most unusual brooch she had ever beheld lying on a bed of white satin.

It was fashioned in the shape of a hummingbird similar to the ones that she had enjoyed watching at Ashley Grove. A single large pearl formed the body. Its spread wings were fashioned of gold set with dozens of little green emeralds. As she looked at it, the gold and the green shimmered as those birds had. It was the most exquisite piece of jewelry she had ever seen.

"Oh, Stephen, it is beautiful. Where did you get it?"

"I designed it and had it made for you."

Her heart did an odd little dance at his answer. No one had ever given her such a lovely and distinctive gift.

"It is how I think of you, my little hummingbird. I wanted a gift worthy of you, one that is as special as you are, love."

The way he said it, the softness in his voice and his eyes, almost made her believe that she truly was his love instead of the wife he had been forced to marry. Then Meg thought of Lady Caroline, and a lump that seemed the size of a boulder rose in her throat.

"I want you to wear it tonight." He pinned it at the base of her gown's V-neck. When he was satisfied with its placement, he smiled. "Come, it is time to go down."

As he led her toward the door, she accidentally caught a glimpse of her face in a gilt-framed wall mirror. She could scarcely believe it was she.

Whatever was in those mysterious pots, the contents had worked some kind of magic on her face.

Her eyes looked larger and brighter. Her high cheekbones and the delicate structure of her face were accentuated. Eager as she was to find fault with herself, she had to admit that she had never looked so well.

In the great ballroom of Royal Elms, crystal chandeliers and wall sconces glittered in the candlelight. Meg trembled with nervousness. Her legs shook so badly that she feared they would fail her. The fact that she was flanked by Rachel, Jerome, Stephen, and Jerome's brother, Lord Morgan Parnell, helped only a little.

Sumptuously clothed people, talking noisily, filled the beautiful room, with its intricately designed plasterwork ceiling and long windows. When Meg and her escorts had appeared on the steps leading into the ballroom, all conversation died instantly and every eye turned to stare at her. She looked down into the sea of faces and saw only critical scrutiny and hostility.

Her stomach convulsed as all those disapproving eyes measured the new Countess of Arlington and found her wanting.

Stephen, apparently sensing her fear, tightened his grip on her arm. On the opposite side of her Jerome took her other arm in his and gave it a comforting squeeze.

An overwhelming urge to flee engulfed her, but she forced herself to stifle it, thanks to the support of the four persons with her.

Then came the introductions. Meg looked in dismay at all the strangers lining up to be presented to her. Sensing her unease, Stephen smiled at her. "Pretend that you are back at Ashley Grove, greeting your visitors."

"But I knew everyone there."

"You will soon know everyone here, too."

Whether she wanted to or not.

Nevertheless, Stephen's suggestion helped, and her years of making visitors comfortable at Ashley Grove came to her rescue. She had always been good at drawing people out, and now, thanks to her husband's conversational clues as he introduced her, she found herself able to say at least a few words to each person.

She was startled by the way the beauties in the crowd fawned over Stephen. Each time one came up to him, Meg wondered unhappily whether the woman had been yet another one of his mistresses.

As she had feared, her gown was simpler by far than the bright satin, velvet, and brocade ones worn by the other women guests. She wondered again why Stephen had insisted upon this design for her.

After the receiving line ended, Stephen was drawn away by a distinguished looking man whose name Meg could not remember, leaving her with his sister.

Rachel looked even more gorgeous than usual in an elaborately swagged violet satin gown that brought out the color of her remarkable eyes, so like Stephen's.

A very pretty woman of perhaps thirty, whose name Meg remembered was Lady Ellerton, approached them. "That is the most beautiful brooch I have ever seen, Lady Arlington."

Meg was surprised that the woman would even notice, for she wore an ornate diamond and ruby necklace with matching earrings that looked as though they should have been part of the crown jewels.

"Where did you get such a unique piece? In America?"

"No, here. My husband designed it and had it made for me."

"Did he?" The woman's expression was suddenly wistful. "How lucky you are."

Meg had the feeling that she was talking about more than the brooch.

"I am quite envious," Lady Ellerton said as she moved on.

When she was out of earshot, Meg turned to Rachel. "Her necklace must be worth far more than my brooch."

"But her husband did not design—or even choose—the pieces for her. They are only part of the Ellerton family jewels, which go to each marchioness. The jewelry is hers for as long as her husband lives, and then it will be passed down to her son's wife. Knowing how Ellerton ignores his lady, I suspect that he has never once bought her a piece of jewelry or even thought of doing so. He is too busy buying it for his convenients."

Meg swallowed hard. Would that soon be her fate, too? Would Stephen ignore her while he devoted himself to his mistresses?

An unforgettable face appeared in the doorway. Meg asked Rachel, "Is that Lady Caroline Taber?"

"Yes, she is a great beauty, is she not?" Rachel answered casually, as though it was the most natural thing in the world for Stephen's mistress to be attending a ball honoring his new wife. How lightly infidelity was treated by the English ton.

Caroline avoided her hostess and Meg. Instead she went to a circle of men who welcomed her effusively.

Meg felt the sting of tears at the back of her eyes. How could she ever hope to compete with such a woman for her husband's affections?

Stephen returned to his wife's side. His brilliant smile razed her heart. "It is time we danced."

For the next two hours, he scarcely left her side, dancing time after time with her. She was deeply grateful that he had not mortified her by granting her one dance and then abandoning her as most of the other husbands, except for Jerome, had done to their wives.

Finally Jerome's brother, Lord Morgan, managed to pry Meg away from Stephen.

As he led her to the dance floor, he inquired, "Are you having a good time?"

"Yes, of course." Better than she had anticipated, she realized in surprise. She certainly could not complain that Stephen was neglecting her.

She glanced toward where they had left her husband and saw that he was already surrounded by four beautiful women. Jealousy streaked through her.

Stephen hardly noticed the four women trying so hard to capture his interest. He slid away from them as quickly as he could manage without being rude and went to a quiet corner where he could watch his wife as she danced with Lord Morgan.

Jerome joined him, and he, too, eyed Megan as she danced with his brother. "Your wife is lovely tonight."

"Yes," Stephen agreed. She had needed only a flattering gown and hairstyle and a subtle application of cosmetics to enhance her natural prettiness.

"I own that when I first saw her gown tonight, I was as dubious as Rachel about it," Jerome said. "It is so plain and subdued next to the other women's, but I should have known, given your reputation, that you would choose what would most flatter her."

"Megan is too small and delicate for that frippery."

"You are right. She stands out beautifully."

Yes, she did. The simplicity of her gown, with only the spectacular hummingbird brooch nestled at the gown's neckline, set her apart from the other overdressed women like a perfect jewel amid gaudy paste. Stephen suspected more than a few ladies would soon be wearing similar gowns.

"That deep green color flatters her, too," Jerome noted.

It did, accentuating Megan's lovely complexion and bringing out the green flecks in her gray eyes, as her husband had known it would. "I am very proud of her."

"You should be. I know how nervous she was tonight and what an ordeal it must have been for her to face a ballroom full of critical strangers, but she carried it off with the grace and dignity of a queen."

"Yes, she did," Stephen agreed.

"Between that and your obvious love for her, I am certain much of the speculation about your marriage has been laid to rest."

It was what Stephen had intended. He had broken society's unwritten rule that a husband did not dance attendance on his wife at such an affair. He had lavished attention on Megan in order to show the haut ton that he loved her and that he intended to be a faithful husband to her.

The music ended, and Stephen left Jerome to reclaim his wife from Lord Morgan before anyone else stepped in. But he was stopped by the Duke of Carlyle, who was intent on hearing about Stephen's adventures in Virginia.

By the time he managed to escape the tenacious duke, he could no longer see Megan. He hurried up to Lord Morgan. "Where is my wife?"

"In the ladies' retiring room."

Stephen was headed in that direction when Lady Caroline Taber, whom he had been assiduously avoiding all night, stepped directly into his path.

When Meg came back into the ballroom from the retiring room, she looked around for Stephen. She saw him only a few feet away, deep in a private conversation with Lady Caroline.

Meg was so close to them that she heard him say, "This is not the time or place, Caro. I will be in London three days from now, and I will see you then privately."

Meg was dumbfounded. He had said nothing to her about going to London in three days. In fact, he had told her during their journey to Bedfordshire that they would spend a few days at Royal Elms before returning to Wingate Hall. He had not mentioned any change in these plans to her.

Did he intend to leave her here or send her back to Yorkshire while he went to London to be with his mistress?

"I will call on you then, Caro."

"It would be better if I came to you at Arlington House. We will have more privacy there." The smoldering, seductive look that Caroline gave Stephen left no doubt as to why she wanted more privacy.

Meg could not bear to hear another word. She and her husband had not even been back in England a month, and already his infidelity was starting.

Poor Meg. A woman as plain as you can never inspire

passion and faithfulness and undying love in a hand-some young husband.

Her heart felt as though it had been ground into dust. Stephen would never be hers again.

In that moment Meg knew that if he went to London to be with his mistress, she could not remain in England. She refused to live in a parody of a marriage with a husband who had been forced to marry her and preferred his mistresses.

She asked only two things of her husband, his love and his fidelity, and it was clear to her now that he could give her neither for long. She would go home to Virginia where she intended to support herself as a music teacher. It would not be easy, but it would be better than the misery of a marriage to a husband who could not give her what she required.

Meg turned to flee the ballroom and in her blind haste ran into Lord Morgan.

He instinctively caught her, steadying her with his hands. When he saw her face, his brow wrinkled in concern. "What is it?"

"Nothing," she croaked in a voice that betrayed what a lie her reply was.

He did not challenge her but looked beyond her. His eyes widened, and she knew he saw her husband with his mistress. His grasp on her tightened. "Come, my lady. Give me the honor of dancing with you again."

"Please, I do not want to dance."

"Nonsense," he said, taking her arm firmly and leading her toward the dance floor. He whispered, "It is not wise, my lady, to leave a ballroom as precipitously as you were about to. It gives idle tongues too much to speculate about."

She knew he was right, and she was grateful to him for trying to help her. The orchestra began to play a minuet, and she stifled a groan. She did not think she could force her leaden feet to perform those intricate graceful steps. "Please, you must excuse me, I am not up to dancing."

"Why not?"

Meg glanced involuntarily toward her husband and his mistress. They were still talking. Stephen's head tilted down so it was very close to the lady's. Meg fought back her tears.

"Do not let Lady Caroline worry you."

"Not worry me!" Meg looked at Lord Morgan as though he were mad. "She is very beautiful. I am very plain."

"You sell yourself short."

"False flattery will not make me feel better," she said tartly.

His quizzical look reminded her of his brother. "Lady Arlington, beauty is in the eye of the beholder. I doubt very much that your husband appreciates Lady Caroline's nearly as much as you do."

Before she could ask Morgan to explain, he swept her into the intricate steps of the minuet.

Stephen, acutely conscious of all the curious eyes that were surreptitiously watching him with his former mistress, wanted desperately to get away from Caroline.

He looked down at her pouting face. He recognized the wild look in her eye. She was on the edge of a tantrum, and he wondered whether he would succeed in averting it.

He knew why she was in a rage. He had ignored her—and every other woman present tonight—to lavish attention on his wife. Any other woman would have accepted the message he had sent, but not Caroline. Jerome had been right. She was too convinced of her own charms to see the obvious.

Stephen was determined to avoid a scene here, and that meant postponing her congé until they were in London. He did not care for himself whether Caro unleashed her fury on him now for everyone to see, but it would shock and humiliate Meg. Not for the world would he allow that to happen.

His wife was already disgusted enough at the man he had been. He hated to think how much further such a scene would sink him in her estimation.

Caro said, "I will call on you at Arlington House."

"You cannot call on me there because it is shut up." Thank God it was, and he had this excuse to rebuff her. "I will be staying with the duke at Westleigh House."

"You cannot stay there! He is a great friend of Taber's, and he will not condone your—"

Stephen did not intend to give Jerome anything to condone. He interrupted her. "*I* will call on *you*."

He was not looking forward to that meeting. At the very least Caro could rail and scream at him when he told her their affair was over. She liked to throw things when she was angry. Perhaps, he thought wryly, he ought to warn her husband to have all the porcelain locked up before Stephen called.

Once Caro's unpredictable temper had helped Stephen stave off boredom. Now he wondered why he had ever put up with it.

Or her.

Remembering Caro's scenes made him appreciate all the more his wife and the peaceful contentment that she had brought to his life.

Caro said petulantly, "I know you would never have married such an unattractive little mouse unless you were forced into it."

Stephen did not know which made him angrier, Caro calling his wife unattractive or saying he had been forced to marry her.

He said through gritted teeth, "I was forced into nothing. You should know me better than that, Caro."

"Of course you were," Caro said airily. "Dance with me."

He would not do that. It would only give the gossips more fodder, which was what Caro wanted. Jerome was passing a few feet away, and Stephen caught his eye, hoping the duke would understand the silent message he was sending him.

Apparently he did, for he came over. "Lady Taber, you must allow me the honor of dancing with you. I know you will excuse us, Arlington."

The duke rarely danced, and it was considered a coup for the recipient of this attention. Clearly it was not an invitation that Caroline would turn down.

As she and Jerome whirled away, Stephen mentally thanked his sister for having had the good sense to marry Jerome. Stephen could not have wished for a more astute, reliable brother-in-law.

He looked around the room, intending to reclaim his wife, but she was dancing again with Lord Morgan.

He noted with pleasure that the women who had fawned over him at the beginning of the ball left him alone now. Several men had commented to him on his obvious love match.

Unfortunately his message had been understood by everyone but Caro.

Chapter 28

The following day, Stephen stood just inside the door of a small anteroom, positioned so he could unobtrusively view the great marble hall of Royal Elms. With him were Megan, Lord Morgan, Neville Griffin, a middle-aged matron, and two local constables whom Griffin had brought with him in anticipation of Hiram Flynt's arrival.

He cast a worried glance at his wife. Since the ball, she had been so quiet and subdued. All his efforts to find out what was troubling her had failed.

The knocker sounded, and the butler opened the door. Stephen saw Hiram Flynt's broad face, heavily scarred by smallpox.

A rush of hatred and rage poured through Stephen. He thought of the whippings he had suffered at Flynt's hands; he thought, too, of the torture the brutal bastard had inflicted on undeserving servants and slaves.

Stephen longed to kill him with his bare hands. It was all he could do to let the scenario Jerome had devised for Flynt's comeuppance play itself out.

A heavyset, thick-chested man, Flynt pushed aggressively past the servant, as though he feared the man might deny him entry. His left hand was locked around the wrist of his wife, Kate, a statuesque woman with flame red hair.

"Where is your master?" Flynt snarled at the butler. "This is a poor welcome for a daughter he has not seen in months and the new son-in-law he has never met. I would have thought he would have been on the portico, awaiting our arrival."

Charming to the end, Stephen thought caustically.

Jerome, resplendent in an elegant *habit à la française* in burgundy velvet trimmed with gold braid and buttons, appeared at the top of the grand marble staircase. Never had Stephen seen the duke look so imposing.

"I am the master here," Jerome thundered. "Who are you that you dare burst into my home like this?"

He started slowly down the long marble staircase, exuding a hauteur so icy that even Flynt was clearly chilled by it. He stammered, "I am your son-in-law, the husband of your daughter here."

Jerome fixed him with a contemptuous stare. Flynt involuntarily took a step back, releasing his grip on Kate's arm. She backed quickly away from him.

"Liar!" Jerome thundered again. "I have no daughter. And if you had an eye in your head you would see that this woman is my age."

Flynt's bravado was deserting him. "Lord . . . Lord Dunbar?"

"I am the Duke of Westleigh. Royal Elms has belonged to my family for three hundred years. I do not know what criminal extortion you are attempting with this crude scene, but at the very least you will answer to the law for criminal trespass."

Flynt was sweating now. "But Lord Dunbar . . . "

"There is no Lord Dunbar." It was Jerome at his haughtiest and most intimidating.

"There must be."

From the anteroom, Stephen could see the large beads of sweat collecting on Flynt's forehead.

Jerome looked at the intruder as though he were a loathsome insect unworthy of his notice. "You dare to question the Duke of Westleigh?"

Flynt whirled and started toward Kate, huddled against the marble wall. "You lying bitch!" He raised his arm to hit her.

"If you lay a hand on her," the duke's frigid voice froze Flynt's arm, "I will have you whipped at the cart tail."

"You . . . you would not dare." But Flynt's voice held no conviction.

Jerome came slowly down the stairs, exuding uninhibited scorn. "I will wield the whip myself."

"But . . . but I am an important man, a rich landowner in the Virginia colony. My name is Hiram Flynt."

"Not quite," Stephen said, stepping into the hall. "Your name is Thaddeus Hiram Flynn, wanted for crimes in seven shires, ranging from murder to robbery."

"And infamous for your inhuman treatment of your victims," Lord Morgan said, stepping up beside Stephen. "Before you vanished eleven years ago, you gave highwaymen a bad name."

Stephen wondered why Lord Morgan should sound so incensed by that.

Flynt's eyes bulged as he belatedly recognized Stephen. "You! What are you doing here!" He turned toward the duke. "This man has been telling you lies about me. He is an indentured servant who escaped from me. He—"

The duke cut him off. "He is the Earl of Arlington and my brother-in-law. Do you dare to claim otherwise? Now you commit criminal slander along with your other offenses."

Flynt, his face the color of chalk, was sweating profusely now.

Stephen nodded to the matron, still in the anteroom, to come into the hall. He pointed to Flynt. "Mrs. Waite, is this the man who killed your mother?"

"The very same." The woman's eyes filled with tears at the memory. "And for no reason but she was crippled with the rheumatism and could not move fast enough to suit him."

Flynt lunged for the woman, his hands grabbing for her throat, but Stephen was too quick for him. As the woman screeched in fright, he drove a hard fist into Flynt's midsection. The air left the swine's body with a loud swoosh and he staggered backward.

As Flynt recovered his balance, Stephen's fist caught him beneath the chin, snapping his head back. It felt so good. Stephen had longed to do this so many times when Flynt had stood over him, whip in hand, and he had been helpless to retaliate.

His fist came up again and smashed Flynt in the nose. There was a sharp crack, and Flynt yowled in pain.

Jerome nodded to the two constables. "Take this man away."

"Clap him in irons immediately and keep him well guarded," Neville Griffin warned them. "Remember how he escaped from the Stafford gaol."

Griffin had learned from Kate that Flynt had escaped from that gaol eleven years earlier and seemingly vanished from the face of the earth. Flynt—or Flynn—had taken his stolen loot and fled to

America, where he had used it to buy a plantation in Virginia.

Stephen watched with intense satisfaction as Flynt was led away, blood streaming from his broken nose. He had his revenge on the cruel bastard. All that remained now was to regain Ashley Grove for Megan.

Once he had done that, he and his wife could put the past behind them and begin to build their future.

Kate came over to Stephen. "Is it true, then? You are Lord Arlington?"

He nodded. "You do not seem unhappy to see your husband jailed."

"I hope when next I see the scum, he is dangling from the hanging tree."

"Such wifely devotion," Stephen remarked wryly.

"He deserves none. I'm covered with his marks." She pushed up one long sleeve of her gown, exposing ugly bruises, some fresh, some yellowed with age, along her arm.

Stephen winced at the sight. So Kate had not escaped her husband's ire. "No wonder you are so anxious to embrace widowhood."

"He only married me because he had grandiose dreams of coming back to England as a swell."

"Neville Griffin says we have you to thank for exposing Flynn's criminal past here in England."

"He kept copies of handbills offering rewards for his capture hidden in a secret compartment in his desk. I think he was proud that so much money was put up for him." Kate's eyes gleamed maliciously. "When I found them I thought I might find a use for them here, and I brought them with me."

Now she turned to Griffin with distrustful eyes.

"Do you mean to keep your word to protect me from him and give me my freedom?"

"Your husband will not trouble you again, and you are free now. I am about to leave for London. Do you wish to accompany me?"

"Aye." Kate accepted Griffin's arm and swished out of Royal Elms with all the grace of the lady she pretended to be.

That night, after Stephen and Megan were in bed, he finally told her that he would be leaving for London at dawn. He had held off telling her as long as possible, because he could not divulge his purpose until he knew the outcome of the hearing. He would not have her hopes crushed should the appeal fail.

"Why did you not tell me sooner that you were going?" There was a peculiar catch in Megan's voice that Stephen did not understand.

"I was preoccupied with Hiram Flynt's arrival."

"When will you be back?"

He did not know how long the hearing would last. "I am not certain. I should not be gone more than a few days."

"Why are you going?"

"Important business." He hoped she would not ask what kind, but of course she did. He said evasively, "It is too complicated to discuss when I am as tired as I am tonight."

"I see."

He disliked the angry edge to her voice. To his surprise, she did not question him further, only rolled to the far side of the bed and turned her back to him.

He disliked that even more.

Stephen scooted over and tried to take her in his

arms, but as he turned her to him, she pushed him away. "Leave me alone."

Dismayed and mystified by her response, he demanded, "What the devil is the matter?"

"It's too complicated to discuss when you are as tired as you are tonight." She hurled his words back at him in a tone thick with sarcasm.

He attempted again to take her in his arms, but she struggled against him and he let her go. She promptly turned her back to him again.

"Megan, I promise I will tell you all about my business in London when I return." He had not intended to mention the appeal to her if it failed, but now, after promising her, he would have to do so. He prayed the appeal would succeed.

"Tell me now!"

"Not tonight." He caressed her arm lovingly with his hand and felt her stiffen beneath it.

"Don't touch me!"

"Sweetheart, please let me hold you while I can," he begged.

Her rigidity dissolved. She rolled over and went into his arms. "Yes, while you can," she breathed softly. Suddenly she was hugging him as fiercely as if it was the last night that they would ever have together.

It pleased Stephen that she was clearly as unhappy as he was over the prospect of being separated, even for a few days.

Her mouth sought his in a long, deep kiss. His own passion fired, dissolving his exhaustion, and he could think of nothing but burying himself in her sweet, hot depths. He ran his hand caressingly down her body to her woman's place and discovered that her body was as ready for him as his was for her.

He plunged into her, and she arched up to meet

him, then moved in unison with him, her movements as eager and vigorous as his, sending them spiraling higher and higher toward a fiery, all-consuming sun that knew no night.

Stephen could not remember such a magnificent climax. His innocent, passionate wife had taken him to a place he had never been before. He gathered her tightly against him. *I have everything I want.*

Hugging his wife and his happiness to him, he fell instantly into a deep, dreamless sleep.

Chapter 29

∽◦◦◦◦∽

Meg pretended to be asleep when Stephen rose an hour before dawn the following morning and dressed for his journey to London.

He did not know it, but they had said their final farewell the previous night.

She had hoped it would not come to this. When he had said nothing yesterday about London, she thought he must have changed his mind about meeting Lady Caroline. Meg had been devastated to learn last night after they were in bed that he still intended to go.

She would not stay with a husband who could not give her the only two things she wanted from marriage. As soon as Stephen departed, she, too, would go to London, where she would board a ship that would take her home to Virginia.

Meg had lain awake all night, wrestling with the question of what she should do about Josh. Stephen had promised to give her brother the education in England that she longed for him to have. Without it, what hope would her brother have?

Her heart, already broken by her husband's conduct, shattered into even smaller pieces at the thought that Josh would board Jerome's ship for

England while she was crossing the Atlantic to America.

Somewhere on that broad, wild ocean they would pass without knowing it. When he arrived in London, only Stephen would be there to greet him.

Meg did not want that, but Josh must have the education he would receive here.

It was his future.

And she could not rob him of that. She loved him too much.

Her husband liked Josh, and she was confident that he would honor his promise to send him to Eton and then to Oxford or Cambridge. But to make absolutely certain of that, she would leave Stephen a note telling him that if he did so, she would gladly give whatever testimony he needed to win an annulment of their marriage. Then he would be free to marry whomever he wished.

For a man as rich as Stephen, Josh's education would be a small price to pay for his freedom.

Meg forced herself to lie very still as Stephen moved about the room. She prayed he would leave speedily. Instead she heard his footsteps approach her. His lips gently brushed her forehead. Their soft caress undid her, and her eyes fluttered opened.

"I did not mean to wake you." His breath tickled her cheek. "I will be back as soon as I can, love."

Tears of farewell clogged her throat. "Good-bye, Stephen."

Her stricken voice clearly startled him. "You make it sound as though you will not see me again. I promise you I will return as soon as I possibly can, and we will go home to Wingate Hall."

Where you will ignore me as your grandfather ignored

your grandmother. But Meg would not let Stephen do that to her.

She would not return to Wingate Hall.

Stephen brushed her cheek gently with his fingertips. "Go back to sleep."

How could Meg do that when she had not slept at all?

After the door closed behind her husband, the tears she had been suppressing ran down her cheeks. She forced herself to get up and dress.

Then she wrote her farewell letter to her husband. After signing her name, she added a lengthy postscript:

I have one more favor to ask. When Josh's ship arrives in London, please meet him as we had planned to do together. I can't bear for him to arrive without someone he knows to greet him. Tell him, please, how much I love him. I will miss him dreadfully, but the education you will give him is far more important.

Meg left the letter on the bedside table. Stephen would find it when he returned. Then she slipped quietly out of the bedchamber and headed for the stables.

After considering how to get to London, she had decided that the best way was to follow her husband's example and ride on horseback.

She would go to the duke's stable and announce she wanted an early morning ride. Once she was mounted she would head straight for London. She hoped that Jerome would forgive her for taking one of his horses.

When she reached London, she would go immediately to the Thames and sail on the very first ship to America. She did not think that Stephen would make any attempt to stop her, but if he did, it would be better if she was gone as quickly as possible.

She blanched at the thought of making that terrible voyage across the Atlantic again—and alone this time—but there was no help for it.

Meg dared not take a portmanteau with her, for it would arouse suspicion. Instead she had put on as many layers of clothes as she could manage beneath her riding habit, then donned a shapeless brown cloak to hide her increased girth. She had compressed a few other necessities into a small bundle.

Thank God her husband had been so generous with what he called her pin money. She had plenty to finance her trip to America and more than enough to tide her over until she could support herself.

At the stables she asked the boy there to saddle a horse for her. "One with stamina, please, for I am in the mood for a hard ride."

That clearly surprised him, but he obediently disappeared inside.

At least a quarter of an hour dragged by. Meg fidgeted impatiently. Although the morning was cold, she was too warm beneath all her layers of clothing, which made her move clumsily, rather like an old lady. At last the boy returned, accompanied by a stocky man whom she recognized as Ferris, the duke's groom who had brought horses to the lodge for them on the night they had reached Stephen's estate. Now Ferris was leading a handsome chestnut and a bay gelding with a sidesaddle.

"Your mount, my lady," he said politely, nodding at the gelding. He had an unnervingly intelligent pair of gray eyes that seemed to read her mind. Meg did not like the odd look in his eyes as he examined her bulky figure and the small bundle she carried.

He led the gelding to the mounting block and helped her into the saddle. All the clothing she wore restricted her movements, and she had never felt so awkward in her life.

As she rode out of the stable yard, she heard another horse behind her. Turning, she saw Ferris had mounted the chestnut and was following her.

She whirled on him angrily. "What are you doing?"

"I am accompanying you, my lady."

"I do not wish you to accompany me. The duke may require your services later in the day."

"His Grace has gone to London with your husband."

She had not known Jerome intended to go with Stephen. "Then you may have the day off," she said graciously. "I am going to ride alone."

"I am sorry, my lady, but the duke would have my head if I permitted you to ride alone over countryside that is strange to you."

This was a complication she had not foreseen. She silently debated what to do. Better, she decided, to get as far away from the stables as she could before confessing the truth about her ride. He was, after all, a servant. He would not dare try to force her back to Royal Elms, and perhaps she might even be able to bribe him to keep her secret.

"Very well, but I ride where I wish," she told him sharply. "If you must accompany me, I insist you not hinder me. I intend to ride hard."

"So I surmised, my lady."

His tone was so dry that she looked at him suspiciously. He was not like any servant she had met before, and he did not sound like one either. His diction was as good as that of the fine lords and ladies who had attended the ball in her honor.

"Have you been with the duke long, Ferris?"

"A very long time, my lady."

No matter what pace Meg set, Ferris's mount remained a half length back of her own. If he noticed that they had left behind not only Royal Elms but Bedfordshire as well, he gave no indication of it. At midmorning, when she slowed her lathered bay to a walk, her companion rode up beside her.

"It is too far to London without changing mounts, my lady. There is a posting house ahead that the duke uses."

Meg stared at him in speechless surprise.

"I must insist we change horses there. His Grace is most particular about how his animals are treated."

"Why . . . why would you think I would be going to London?"

He raised his eyebrows. "Why would I think you would be going anywhere else on this road?"

The man was as intelligent as she had suspected. "You will not stop me!" she warned him fiercely.

"I do not intend to try." He paused. "But I do intend to keep you safe."

She stared at him. "Why are you doing this?"

He looked at her oddly. She had the feeling that he was remembering another time and another woman. "I like adventurous women, my lady." He smiled at her. "So does His Grace."

Darkness was settling on London as Stephen left the Tabers' mansion in Berkeley Square. A light drizzle was falling, and he was glad that he had come in Jerome's town chariot. As he started toward the equipage, he touched the bruise on his left cheek and winced.

When he had told Caro their affair was over, she was incredulous. After he finally convinced her that he was not joking, she acted every bit as badly as he had feared she would.

Damn woman must keep half the porcelain factories in Europe in business.

Fortunately her aim was almost as bad as her temper.

It was too late to ride back to Royal Elms tonight, and he would have to stay in London until morning. Strange how little that appealed to him. Once he had not been able to tear himself away from the city, but now its pleasures no longer held any appeal for him. All he wanted was to return to Bedfordshire and the happiness that he found in his wife's arms.

He could not wait to tell her that Ashley Grove again belonged to her. After a surprisingly short hearing and deliberations, the Privy Council committee had set aside Justice Baylis's guardianship order, ruled that Hiram Flynt had obtained Ashley Grove by fraud, and ordered it restored to Megan.

Stephen was about to climb into the chariot when he heard the clatter of galloping hooves. He glanced toward the noise and saw Jerome and his brother reining to a stop behind the equipage. Even before he saw their expressions, Stephen knew that something must be terribly wrong for Lord Morgan, whom Jerome had left in charge of Royal Elms, to come to London.

Stephen's first thought was Megan, and fear gripped his heart. "What is it?" His voice came out hoarse and alarmed.

Morgan handed him a note. In the fading light, Stephen made out that it was addressed to him in Megan's handwriting. "Your wife left this for you."

Stephen broke the seal and scanned its contents.

He looked up at Jerome and Morgan in stunned disbelief. "She says that by the time I read this she will be on her way back to Virginia."

"Not quite, but she is already aboard a ship that sails on the night tide."

Stephen felt as though he had been poleaxed. "She is here in London? How did she get here?"

"The same way we did, on horseback," Jerome said as he dismounted. "She went directly to the Thames."

Terror for her safety ripped at Stephen's gut. "Bloody hell, has she no idea how dangerous it is for a woman to go there alone?"

"She is not alone. Ferris is following her. He will watch over her until the ship sails, which will be very shortly." Jerome handed him the reins of his mount. "You have no time to lose. Take my horse. Morgan will go with you, and I will follow in my chariot. I pray you will reach the ship in time."

Meg stood at the rail on the deck of the merchant brigantine, watching the sailors scamper among the rigging as they prepared to weigh anchor. Their shouts filled the air. In a few minutes, she would leave England forever.

She would never see her husband again.

Not that he would care. No doubt he would be delighted to shed the wife he had been forced to marry.

Despite her efforts to hold back her tears, they ran down her cheeks in a waterfall of pain and grief as she thought of the husband she loved so much.

Too much to tie him to a woman he did not want.

It was her gift to him—his freedom.

Her hand slipped over her heart, and she felt the

hummingbird brooch pinned to her shift beneath several layers of clothing. She should have left it behind, but she had not been able to force herself to do so. It would be her treasure to cherish through the long, lonely years ahead.

The officers were barking orders with greater urgency now. The guttural curses of the sailors, rushing about on the deck, grew more fierce. Then they were raising the gangplank.

It was too late now for Meg to leave the ship. Her tears fell faster, but she told herself firmly that what she was doing was the best thing for everyone.

Is it? What about yourself?

She swiped at her tears and squeezed her eyes shut as though that would somehow also shut out her doubts.

The shouts of the sailors took on a new tenor. She heard the gangplank clang and the thudding feet of a sailor running in her direction, but she was too miserable to pay any heed to the commotion. She kept her eyes tightly closed, fighting to hold back another deluge of tears.

Suddenly rough hands grabbed her arms and jerked her around. Meg's eyes flew open.

Stephen!

Looking angrier than she had ever seen him.

She shrank back, trying to pull away from him.

"Damn it, Megan, come with me."

"No!"

Cursing vehemently, he grabbed her and swung her up in his arms. By the time she recovered from her shock and could react, one of his arms had imprisoned her own while the other had her legs locked together.

"Put me down," she cried, but she might as well have been talking to the Thames. He stalked down the gangplank with her in his arms, past gaping sailors and Lord Morgan Parnell. What on earth was he doing here?

Stephen carried her along the quay. As he reached its end, a chariot stopped abruptly in front of them. The door opened and Jerome jumped out. He grinned. "I see you were in time."

"Barely," Stephen growled, clearly still in a fury.

"Put me down," Meg cried again.

He dumped her inside the chariot and climbed in after her. "Drive, I do not care where," he shouted at the coachman, then slammed the door.

The equipage rolled forward.

Stephen turned to her, anger fairly steaming from him. "Bloody hell, Megan, the least a husband deserves is to have his wife tell him to his face that she is deserting him, instead of leaving him a note he would not find until she was on the high seas." Stephen pulled her letter from his pocket. "I expected better of you. This was a trick worthy of your damned brother Quentin."

She stared at the note. "How did you get that?"

"Ferris got word to Rachel that he thought you were running away. She discovered the note in our bedchamber and had Morgan bring it to me."

"But how did you know I was aboard that ship?"

"Ferris again. He sent a message of your whereabouts to Jerome at his London house. Thank God, the man had the good sense to insist on accompanying you on your ride. I can see why Jerome is so fond of him. Why the hell did you run away like this?"

"I want to go home."

"Your home is at Wingate Hall with me."

"But it is not! I don't belong there. I never will. Virginia is my home, and I want to live there."

He sighed. "Is that truly what you want?"

"Yes." It was a lie. What she wanted was to be with Stephen, wherever he was, but she had to be firm for both their sakes.

"Very well, then *we* will live in Virginia."

She gaped at him in shock. "But what of Wingate Hall?"

"Much as I love it, I will give it and everything else I own away before I will be separated from you."

She saw from the determination in his blue violet eyes and the stubborn set of his jaw that he meant it. "But I am not the proper wife for an English lord. You know that, and so do I."

"I know nothing of the sort!"

"Yes, you do. You hate being shackled to an unsuitable, ill-bred colonial like me."

"Your breeding is above reproach, and you are the *only* suitable wife for me."

How could he expect her to believe such a lie? "If I am so suitable, why did you tell Rachel you would not take me with you to London for the season?"

"I can hardly take you with me when I am not going myself."

"And why are you not?"

"I am tired of London. I prefer the company of my wife at Wingate Hall."

"Where the plain, drab creature will not embarrass you in front of your aristocratic friends?"

"How can you even think that I feel that way?" Stephen exploded in anger. "Have you any idea how proud I was of you at the ball?"

"If you were so proud of me, why did you choose that plain gown?" She could not keep the hurt from her voice.

"You did not like it?" Stephen sounded stricken.

"But it was perfect for you. You are much too tiny to wear elaborate styles. They would be disastrous on you. You needed a simpler gown that would set you apart from all those other overdressed women, and that is what it did."

His explanation stunned Meg, and it was a moment before she managed to stammer, "I notice you did not ask me to come with you to London today."

"Because I came here to—"

She interrupted, suddenly hurt and furious. "I know why you came. To resume your affair with Lady Caroline Taber."

"Damn it, Megan, that is not the reason I came to London."

She made no attempt to hide her pain and incredulity. "I love you too much to—"

"Do you know, Megan, this is the first time you have ever told me that you loved me?"

"But you know I do." How could any woman not? "I would never have come to England with you otherwise."

"Megan, Megan, do you not think that I need the words, too?" His voice cracked with emotion. "Have you any idea how much I have longed to hear them?"

"No," she admitted. "It never occurred to me that you might need them."

"Well, I do."

"But you were forced to marry me."

His jaw clenched. "I was not forced to marry you. How many times do I have to tell you that I wanted to do so? It was you who was forced to wed me. Hell, the way you were acting toward me, I thought it might be the only damn way I would get you to marry me."

He ran his hands though his hair in frustration.

"I love you, Megan. How can I make you believe that? I have tried to tell you, and you will not believe me. I have tried over and over to show you. But, damn it, nothing seems to work. I do not know what else I can do to convince you."

She wanted to believe him, wanted it so much, but then she remembered why he had come to London.

"You started to say you loved me too much to— what?"

"To share you with your mistresses."

"Megan, I have no mistresses. They are in my past. I told you Caro is not the reason I came to London today."

"You saw her today. Do not deny it! I heard you arranging it at the ball."

Meg saw comprehension dawn on his face. "So that is what this is all about! Yes, I agreed to call on her because I had to be in London today anyway. I preferred to tell her in private, not in a ballroom with two hundred other people, including my wife, that our affair was over. Caro has a violent temper."

"And you did not know what to expect?"

He touched his cheek. "Oh, I knew what to expect," he said ruefully, "and unfortunately I was right. I could have sent her a note ending our relationship, but I believe a man should have the courtesy and courage to do so face-to-face."

"As I should have had the courtesy and courage to tell you I was leaving." Meg's heart had seemed to take soaring flight at his avowal that he had broken off his affair with Lady Caroline, but still she had to ask, "Why did you end it?"

She had never seen Stephen look so exasperated. "The answer is as obvious as why I am in this chariot with you. I ended it because I am married to you, because I know how important fidelity is to you."

But not to you. "I am not certain any lord or lady in England knows what the word means."

"Believe me, this lord does. Just as my father did. I intend to be as faithful to you as he was to my mother."

She frowned, torn between bright hope and black doubt.

"It was on your behalf, Megan, not Caro's, that both Jerome and I came to London. We appealed the Virginia court's ruling on Galloway's guardianship of you to the king in council. The committee that heard the appeal ruled today that Flynt obtained Ashley Grove through fraud and ordered it restored to you. I told you that I hoped to have another wedding present for you within a week, and now you have it."

For a moment, Meg could only stare stupefied at him. It was all too much for her to assimilate. Ashley Grove, hers again. Stephen had ended his affair with his beautiful mistress. He wanted Meg so much that he would live in Virginia with her if she wished. But she knew how much he loved Wingate Hall and, in truth, all she desired was to be with him now that she knew he truly did love her.

Stephen looked disappointed. "I was anticipating a more, er, demonstrative reaction."

And she gave it to him then, throwing her arms around him, hugging him hard to her and kissing him fiercely. He returned her kiss with equal fervor, making her feel loved and cherished—and very happy.

When at last their mouths separated a fraction, he breathed, "Now that is more what I had in mind."

"Oh, Stephen, I want to live *with you* at Wingate Hall."

He gave her a searching look. "Are you certain?"

"Yes! Oh, yes."

His face lit with happiness. "And we will both be on hand, my love, to greet Josh when he arrives."

Stephen's hand came up to cup her breast, and his head jerked back in surprise. "I can hardly find you beneath all those clothes. How many layers do you have on?"

"Too many. I did not dare take a portmanteau, so I wore as much as I could."

He suddenly looked anguished. "Megan, how could you leave me?"

"I thought you would be happy to be rid of me."

"You are the only woman I want in my life, the only woman I have ever loved." He brushed her face gently with his fingertips. "If you would have trusted your little brother and his future to me, could you not have trusted me with your heart?"

"I—I was afraid you would break it."

He touched her cheek gently. "My love, why would I break my most precious possession? Can you not see that I am no longer the man I was when I was seized at Dover? My tribulations taught me what is important to me, and you taught me what love is. I intend to be the kind of man that you want as a husband. I will be worthy of your love, Megan."

Her happy heart fluttered like a hummingbird as she fathomed how deeply Stephen cared for her.

Still, she made one final attempt to bring him to his senses. "You will be happier without me."

He hugged her to him. "*You* are my happiness, love."

She nestled in the warmth of his strong, hard

body, the last of her doubts slowly, surely ebbing away on the consuming tide of his love for her. She smiled up at him.

"And you are mine."

Here's an advance peek at
MIDNIGHT BANDIT,
Marlene Suson's captivating,
steamy sequel to *Midnight Lord*,
coming soon from
Avon Books.

England, 1743

"**S**tand and deliver!"

The cry of the lone highwayman rang out in the clear, moonlit night. The slow-moving coach on which the bandit's brace of pistols was trained clattered to a halt.

Lady Daniela Winslow was proud of how deep and firm her voice sounded. This was her sixth highway robbery since she had begun posing as "Gentleman Jack," the legendary knight of the road. By now, she played the role with the bravado it required.

It had not been so the first time, though. Then she had been so nervous that she had scarcely been able to get the words out of a mouth as dry as sunbaked earth. Her heart had thudded so loudly that she had feared her victim, a despicable cur notorious for his ill treatment of his wife, children, and servants, could hear its thunderous beat.

Fortunately, he had been even more frightened than she. Once she had told him she was Gentleman Jack, he had all but thrown his fat bag of coin at her.

It had been much the same with her other victims. The use of Gentleman Jack's name had reduced them to instant, docile compliance. No one suspected that Daniela was not the notorious highwayman. Nor even of his sex.

Gentleman Jack, a latter-day Robin Hood who robbed the rich to help the poor, had mysteriously vanished without a trace three years ago. Daniela decided to resurrect him for her own purpose.

It helped that she was exceedingly tall for a woman—a trifle under six feet. To facilitate her masquerade, she had read every account that she could find of Gentleman Jack, then faithfully duplicated his costume, dressing all in black down to her mask, hat, and gloves.

The coach of her latest victim was drawn by four spirited blacks. Its polished ebony finish and silver trim shone in the moonlight. The coachman's box was richly caparisoned, and the crest upon the door proclaimed its owner was not merely wealthy but titled, too.

Yes, he must be a plump pigeon indeed. She thought of all the good she could do with what she plucked tonight.

The coach most likely was carrying its occupants to Greenmont for her brother Basil's ball. She hoped they were friends of Basil's because she heartily disliked each and every one of them and had no compunction about robbing them. Her conviciton that they deserved to have their purses lightened eased her conscience.

Daniela aimed one of her pistols at the coachman on the box. "Reach for the sky."

In her previous robberies, the terrified coachmen had obeyed her with alacrity. To her surprise, this one, a short, stocky man of about thirty, did not seem in the least apprehensive. Indeed, as he slowly obeyed her command to raise his arms, she thought she saw a smile tugging at one corner of his mouth in the moonlight.

He looked as though he were pleased to see her. Daniela wondered whether he hated his master so much that he was delighted to see him robbed.

Belatedly it occured to her that two other things were odd about this coach, and a prickling of alarm danced along her nerves. First, it was traveling at a very slow speed on such a bright night. Second, it had no outriders and only a lone coachman on the box.

Fighting down growing trepidation, Daniela kept one pistol trained on the coachman while she rapped sharply on the equipage's window with the other. "Open up."

The coach door swung out, revealing its sole occupant, a man of imposing size and elegant attire. He carelessly lounged on the seat, his hands thrust into the pocket of his cloak.

Daniela's mouth beneath her mask dropped open at the sight of him. Not that she recognized him. She knew she had never seen him before. She would have remembered that magnificent face, broad at the forehead, tapering to a granite chin. Penetrating, deep set eyes without a hint of fear in them met her challengingly.

Most unnerving of all, though, was the wicked grin on his sensual mouth.

She had a pistol aimed at his heart, for God's sake, and he had the impudence to grin at her.

Affecting her deepest growl, she ordered, "Reach for the sky or ye'll be afeeling the bite o' me barking irons." She had read that had been a favorite command of Gentleman Jack during his robberies.

To her consternation, the man on the seat only laughed. "At least you have that much right." He had a deep, lazy voice that matched his relaxed posture.

His nonchalance was both maddening and disconcerting. Why was he not taking her seriously? Determined to bring him to heel, she demanded, "Your money or your life."

"Neither, I think," he said calmly, still sprawled upon the seat.

Daniela was nonplussed by his imperturbability. Blast it, didn't the fool know enough to be frightened?

Except he did not look like a fool. He looked like the most fascinating, divinely handsome man she had ever seen. Even the way his thick russet-colored hair curled about his face pleased her. Daniela had thought herself immune to men, but excitement stirred within her.

Fighting to keep her voice deep and stern despite her growing nervousness, she warned, "Hand over your money and valuables or I will shoot you."

He studied her with unhurried thoroughness. After a long silence, he shrugged negligently. "Then shoot."

Blast it, what was she to do now? The thought of shooting any man, and especially one who was unarmed, made Daniela's stomach convulse. She could not possibly do such a thing.

But neither could she let him know that.

She struggled to keep her pistols steady. "Do not trifle with me," she said in as curt a voice as she could muster in the face of his infuriating calm. "I am Gentleman Jack."

The name had brought her other victims instantly into line. She expected it to do the same with him.

Instead his smile vanished. "Like hell you are!"

The certainty in his voice so nonplussed her that she forgot her deep, carefully rehearsed voice. "What do you mean?"

His piercing eyes suddenly narrowed speculatively. "I mean you are not Gentleman Jack."

How the devil did he know that? Desperate to recover control of the situation, Daniela said, "You are wrong." Her words came out in a high, feminine squeak.

"Hell and damnation," the stranger said in clear disgust, "not only are you not Gentleman Jack, you are not even a man."

That unnerved Daniela so completely that she could only stare at him aghast. Dazed, she unconsciously let her grip on the pistols sag.

Suddenly, before she knew what happened, he sprang from the coach, grabbed her wrists, jerked her from the saddle, and forced the weapons from her hands.

She had never seen a man move so quickly.

"Pick up her guns, Ferris," he told the coachman, who was scrambling down from the box.

As Ferris retrieved them, the shock that had paralyzed Daniela turned to fear, and she began to fight her captor. She was a strong woman, but she was no match for him.

He pinned her against the side of his coach, holding her there with his big body. Both her wrists were imprisoned in one of his powerful hands.

Daniela was so tall that she either looked down upon or stood eye to eye with most men, but not this one. She had to tilt her head back to look into his chiseled face. In the moonlight, his glittering eyes were as hard as blue diamonds.

Terror washed over Daniela. She had been captured in the act of highway robbery, a hanging offense. She felt the sinister shadow of the gallows fall over her, and shuddered at the shame she would bring upon herself and her family.

But most devastating of all was the thought of

the people who so desperately needed her help and how she had failed them.

Daniela fought to stop the trembling of her mouth. She could not, would not cry. She would not let this man see her weakness. She would meet her fate with courage and dingity.

He asked, "What is your name?"

She glared defiantly at him, determined to cling to the fiction that she was a man. "Dan . . . Daniel Roberts." It was almost true—except for two a's and a surname. She had been named Daniela Roberta Winslow after her father's two brothers.

"Liar." His free hand grabbed a handful of her long, flame-red hair and held it in front of her face.

To her chagrin, she realized that during their struggle the black hat she had worn low over her forehead had been knocked off. Her maddening hair, unruly as always, had escaped its restraints and tumbled down about her shoulders.

Her captor's grim gaze locked with hers, and a sudden, inexplicable heat quite unlike anything she had ever experienced shot through her. Something about the way his eyes widened made her wonder whether he felt a similar sensation.

She was suddenly conscious of the hard strength of his body imprisoning her against the side of the coach. His grin returned, more wicked and teasing than before, accelerating her pulse.

His mouth dipped toward hers.